THE SLEEP OF EMPIRES

THE SLEEP OF EMPIRES

PART ONE OF THE BOOK OF THE NULL

DAVID ANNANDALE

Published 2025 by Pyr®

The Sleep of Empires. Copyright © 2025 by David Annandale. All rights reserved. No part of this publication may be reproduced, stored in a retrieval system, or transmitted in any form or by any means, digital, electronic, mechanical, photocopying, recording, or otherwise, or conveyed via the Internet or a website without prior written permission of the publisher, except in the case of brief quotations embodied in critical articles and reviews.

Cover illustration © Shutterstock / EyeOfSauron / Timmed
Cover design by Ashley Calvano and Paula Guran
Cover design © Start Science Fiction

Inquiries should be addressed to
Start Science Fiction
221 River Street, 9th Floor
Hoboken, New Jersey 07030
Phone: 212-431-5455
www.pyrsf.com

10 9 8 7 6 5 4 3 2 1

ISBN 978-1-64506-113-7 (pbk.)
ISBN 978-1-64506-127-4 (ebook)

Printed in the United States of America

*For Margaux, with all love and gratitude for
the greatest adventure I could ever know.*

CHAPTER 1

They were the last line of defense. Beyond them lay the road to the ruin of empires. If they failed to stop what was coming, if they failed to stop *who* was coming, the way would lie open. The terrible slide to war would begin. They held the fates of great powers in their hands. Only they did not know this. No one did.

Not even the gods.

What Horwun Linkmere knew was that he was cold. He crouched in the trees by the side of the Korvas Road, caught in the middle of a spring squall. The wind sharpened its claws as it blew over the Ghaunt River to Horwun's right. The rain fell in sheets, and gusts sent it slashing across his face. It dug its fingers into his clothes, working its way through the leather to grasp him in a clammy, icy fist. Instead of sheltering him, the leaves above poured streams onto his neck, tracing cold trails down his spine. The soles of his boots were cracked, and his feet swollen and numb.

Horwun knew he was cold. He knew that he would give his take from the last year for a roof and a fire. He knew that the day was well on its way to being a lost one. More than anything he wanted to stand up and walk away.

Only he couldn't. The loss of face he would suffer would be lethal. Delner, hungry to lead, would push Horwun out given half a chance. A lack of prey on the roads today was forgivable, as long as Horwun maintained discipline, keeping the gang in place until it became clear there would be no travelers.

The hunting in the Ghaunthook region was generally easy, but not always reliable. The village lay close enough to Northope to have a steady flow of trade. It was small enough that the flow often took the form of a trickle of individual traders and farmers who decided they couldn't wait

1

THE SLEEP OF EMPIRES

for the greater security of the once-a-month caravan. The trickle interested Horwun and the other carrion birds along the Korvas Road. Northope's patrols did not reach as far as Ghaunthook, and the village barely had the resources to protect the boundaries of the settlement proper. Easy prey, as long as there was prey to be had.

None so far today. Horwun shivered. He leaned over his folded arms, clutching himself more tightly. He gained no warmth. All he felt was the sodden leather. One more hour, he told himself. One more hour to twilight. There would be no travelers then. He could lift the ambush with no loss of authority.

Though he still watched the road, he no longer gave it his attention. He thought longingly of the cave his band had claimed in the hills to the southeast. Its floor would be dry. Its mouth was wide enough to accommodate a fire. His eyes glazed over, the hour stretching ahead as if it were a century.

He almost didn't see them. Two figures emerged from the curtains of rain. They jolted him to awareness, and he breathed a silent prayer of thanks that Delner did not appear to have spotted them. Their silhouettes were indistinct in the gray. Horwun judged them both to be men, one of average height and slim build, the other very tall, imposing even from a distance of a hundred yards. *Watch him*, Horwun thought. Still, just two. Easy for the five of them to take.

He mimicked the caw of a crow, alerting the band. He looked across the road to the deepening shadows beneath the trees on that side. A bush waved three times against the wind, Delner signaling readiness. Horwun rocked back and forth on the balls of his feet, easing the cramps in his legs. He drew his sword.

He was about to engage in the most important struggle of his life.

He did not know this. But neither did the gods.

Latanna Forgrym thought about rebirth. She wondered if it were possible. She knew what Alisteyr Huesland would say, when he arrived, if she asked

DAVID ANNANDALE

him. He would say tell her that rebirth was what he had come to offer. He would be very poetic, very well spoken. Very sweet.

He would also be very wrong. She was contemplating something far more crucial than a romantic metaphor, no matter how profoundly Alisteyr felt its reality. Perhaps she was thinking in the wrong terms. Maybe she had the wrong word. She needed something stronger than *rebirth*. Perhaps *re-creation*. A new arrival out of the void, an identity unsullied by the strangling weeds of family history.

She shifted from one foot to the other, then leaned against the tree. The oak was massive, so thick that its trunk straddled the boundary of the Forgrym and Huesland properties. Above her, mossy, moldering linen lay stretched over wooden planks that had been assembled into a crude platform between two forking branches. The construction was clumsy, the work of the children she and Alisteyr had been well over a decade ago. She doubted the platform would support their weight now, but it did keep the rain off her. She appreciated the symbolic value of meeting here. The spot had always been theirs. It represented the possible end to the conflict between their families.

Latanna gazed at the surrounding woods, thinking that the long survival of the platform spoke to more than hope for the future. It was also a sign of decay, of just how pathetic the Forgryms and Hueslands had become, and how risible their war. Since the properties met here, where were the patrols? Why was it so wild? Why had the subterfuge of children gone undiscovered?

Sad, all of it. Useless. Again, she felt the need for a new creation. The longing went deeper than her heart. It lived in her bones. She felt her family name shaping her identity with as much force as if it were her body itself. If she dug back far enough into history, there was pride to be had in the utterance of *Forgrym*. But encrustations of corruption, vainglory, and futility formed her inheritance from more recent generations. There was no scraping it clean, not when her father kept adding to the grime. The only true cleansing would be annihilation.

THE SLEEP OF EMPIRES

But the purity of the void was denied to her. She could not create from nothing. So, she would work with the possible. She would end the decay. She would put a stop to a war that had been drained of meaning a century ago. That much, she could do.

Latanna heard Alisteyr crashing through the underbrush. The paths through this region of the woods were overgrown. She and Alisteyr were the only humans to pass this way at all. She wondered if that would change, should they reach their goal.

Goal. Is that what you want to call it? Don't use that word when you're talking to Alisteyr.

No. She would not. That would be cruel.

She took a step away from the trunk and straightened her cloak. As Alisteyr reached the shelter of the oak, the steady patter of the rain became a hammering. It had begun to hail. Large stones snapped twigs as they fell through the tree cover and bounced on the ground.

"You had a near escape," Latanna said.

Alisteyr laughed. "I did." Then his face turned anxious. "Am I late? Have I kept you waiting?"

"I was early. It's nice being away from the house."

Alisteyr nodded, solemn now. "I know." His eyes, the blue of fresh spring skies, gazed at her with an adoration she did not believe she deserved. It was also one that she could not return in the way *he* deserved, though she was trying her best.

"Let's talk about getting you away from that house forever," Alisteyr said. He dropped to one knee and took her hand.

"You really don't have to do it this way," she began. After all, she had been the one to first broach the subject.

"Yes, I do. I want to." He was the one with the passion. "Latanna Forgrym," he said, taking her left hand in both of his, "I call upon Ártimára to witness my words to you. As this tree has been the sanctuary for our friendship since our childhood, so would I have my love be the same for you."

4

DAVID ANNANDALE

Latanna controlled a wince, and felt awful for having had to do so. Poetry had never been Alisteyr's strong suit, and his analogy was as labored as it was over-rehearsed. Yet that wasn't what pained Latanna. What hurt was Alisteyr's sincerity, the commitment of his entire being to truth of his words. Latanna's response was a poor answer to what Alisteyr offered.

"I ask, then," Alisteyr continued, "that you stoop to my level and bless my hand with yours in marriage."

Latanna looked down at the man before her. His brown hair was so fine, it had barely been slicked down by the rain. His features were elegant to the verge of being delicate, as if the beauty of his ancestors were encountering the faded state of his family's power. Latanna's father, Marsen Forgrym, fought a war he could not afford. The Hueslands fought a defensive battle empty of hope and interest. Alisteyr's family had no greater goal than survival. He, though, hoped for more. He had energy and fire, and in this moment, he was dedicating them to her.

She did love him. She always had. What troubled her was the degree and the kind of love. It was not what she saw before her. She was too conscious of the soundness of the idea of their marriage. An end to the Forgrym-Huesland feud would benefit both families, and Ghaunthook itself. The war had damaged the village. Perhaps the stability of a peace might lead to a rebirth of Ghaunthook's fortunes.

These were all good things. She was very much aware of them, and wanted to bring them about. Marriage was a transaction, and she would be engaging in a fine one here.

She was far too rational.

She stared at her friend. She smiled at him. And then, her heart contracting with an awful terror of hurting him, she said, "Yes, Alisteyr Huesland, I would be your wife."

It was not until much later that she realized that she had invoked no gods.

* * *

5

THE SLEEP OF EMPIRES

No lanterns illuminated the library of the University of Árkiriye. Pilta ne Akwatse ran between the stacks by feel alone. He had a small lamp concealed within his robes. He would need it to find the book, but he didn't light it yet. He didn't dare. When he had told the human trader that he feared nothing in the library's darkness, he hadn't been speaking the full truth. He didn't fear the dark, but he did fear what light might summon. He feared the librarian. Skiriye ne Sincatse's commitment to perfection extended to the absolute observance of edicts. Pilta's mere presence at this hour was a monstrous contravention of the rules. He tried not to contemplate what would happen if someone caught him with the book.

The fear exhilarated him.

He was a shadow and a wind. He was silence itself. When he reached the door to the crypt, he imagined even the dust had been undisturbed by his passing. He crouched before the door and felt for its lock.

"How will you get in?" the trader had asked.

Pilta had smirked. "No door can bar an elf. Not even our own. Perfection in all things, human. Remember that. And my gift is the perfection of lock picking."

Another lie. He was, though, a very good thief. He had stolen the key from Skiriye's desk. Now he placed it in the lock and turned. The door opened without a creak.

He descended the steps, into unknown territory, and took the risk of lighting his tiny lantern. A marble staircase spiraled down, just as the trader had told him. The human had also said exactly where he would find the book. Pilta shook his head, astonished that the woman had known so much. As he descended, he wondered just how long and how expensive the trader's quest for information had been. Who had been suborned to provide information that could only have come from the most forbidden of catalogs? Or had a human spy somehow managed to peer into those pages? Every now and then, such fools were caught and executed in view of the human quarter.

It occurred to Pilta that he should have negotiated a higher fee. The deeper he went into the dark, the more the enormity of what he was doing sank in. He still had time to back out. Even if he was caught, he had done no worse than trespass. He hadn't yet crossed the line into theft.

The coin kept him going. Whatever he should have demanded, he would soon have enough to cover his tuition and lodging for the next term. He had had a lean summer. Hunger bored him, and he looked forward to leaving it behind.

Pilta reached the bottom of the stairs. He breathed in air drier than on the upper floors of the library, dry as bleached bone, dry as frozen time. Lanterns hung from the low vaults of the ceiling, the light watchful yet still. The aura of disuse surrounded him.

It took an effort to take the first steps away from the stairs. In the realm of dead knowledge, there should be no movement. There were thousands of books here, all of them unwanted, dangerous, heretical. Yet the Most Perfect Council would never permit their destruction. What had been created must not be destroyed. Suppressed, buried, and forgotten, but not destroyed.

Did even the Council really know what lay here? Pilta hoped not. Perhaps his theft would never be discovered.

He went right, walking past stone bookcases, counting. At the eleventh, he turned down the row. The book waited near the end of the row, on the bottom shelf. Pilta crouched and held his lamp close to the spines. The volume was very old, the human had said. It would probably be the oldest one there, and it would be quite thick. He saw a likely candidate, the black hide of its binding cracked and graying. He put the lantern down and pulled the book out. Still crouched, he opened the book. He didn't recognize the language. It wasn't elvish, nor any of the human tongues that he knew. Strange runes marched across the pages like the claw marks of night. Looking at them made him feel cold inside. Something opened in his chest. Guilt and terror circled it, but the thing itself was empty. A dark absence spread through his blood.

THE SLEEP OF EMPIRES

He slammed the book closed. The dull slap broke the crypt's thick silence like a thunderclap. Pilta held his breath. The silence returned. He rose, tucking the book under his arm. The chill of what it held inside leeched through the binding and through the thin weave of his tunic.

He hurried back to the staircase and up the spiral. At first he thought the book was making his arm grow numb. Then he realized that the deeper cold came from within, from the cry of his soul, wounded from an encounter with something ancient beyond naming, but familiar, too. The thing that lurked in the pages wanted to make itself known. If he wanted to hold fast to his self and his world, Pilta had to clutch the salvation of ignorance with all his strength.

He wanted the book out of his possession. He thought about returning it to its shelf, but he had come too far up the stairs. He had an impulse to pour his lantern's oil over the book and set it alight. He tried to push the terror away. Another couple of minutes, and he would deliver the book to the trader, and the task would be done.

He reached the door and pressed his ear against it. His breath caught. Someone was moving around in the library. A few moments later, he recognized the iambic rhythm of the librarian's limp. There were other footsteps, too. Skiriye had not come alone. Pilta's mouth dried. The inevitability of capture loomed before him.

Put it back, an inner voice pleaded. *Put it back. Take the punishment that comes from trespass. You can survive that.*

Yes, he could. But it would not be pleasant, and he would be expelled. The payment for the theft was now necessary for his continued survival. He was in too far.

He hesitated on the edge of panic, one bad option after another skittering through his mind. An idea presented itself. It made him tremble, because to act on it would be to throw himself into the jaws of the librarian's harsh mercy. He forced himself to accept that he would be caught no matter what. Then he opened the door and rushed to his chosen doom.

DAVID ANNANDALE

* * *

The travelers stopped walking, surrounded. They were being sensible, Horwun thought. He circled the duo while the rest of the thieves waited for his signal. He savored his favorite moment: the prey at bay, nowhere to run, nothing to do but wait for his judgement. He felt the corner of his mouth twitch in amusement and disgust. Once in a while, he entertained himself by indulging in a pretense of kindness, sparing the prey's life. Crippling it, true, but sparing it all the same.

These two, though. There was no question of that game here. He would kill them, and be glad of it. As he thought of their blood on the ground, he experienced a strange sort of joy. It felt like *relief.* And he knew it to be holy. He was not a man who expected much of the gods. His prayers even to the trickster Parserin were perfunctory when he remembered them at all. But he would sleep tonight with the knowledge of having done a great thing. The certainty of approaching the finest moment of his existence puzzled him, but he thrilled at its blessing.

The two travelers were male. The smaller of the two was a kaul. Surprising to see one this far west of Korvas. Perhaps an escaped slave. Like his companion, he wore leathers. His features were typical of the race: wiry, hairless, pocked skin the color of bad bone and stretched too tightly over the skeleton. An upturned nose that was almost absent. Thin lips that pulled back over teeth a bit longer and sharper than a human's. Eyes so deeply sunken into the shadows of their sockets that they were little more than glinting darkness. A creature of walking death. The kaul looked around, eyeing the men, then settled its gaze on Horwun. There was no change in his expression, nor in his steady, monotonous whisper to his companion.

"Calm . . . calm . . . calm . . . calm . . ." the kaul said.

The other figure was male. Horwun couldn't decide on the race. He thought he saw traces of elf in the face, though the eyes were even more deeply recessed than the kaul's, and the frame far too massive for any elf,

THE SLEEP OF EMPIRES

or human, for that matter. The skin tone, gray as the end of all dreams, did not speak of any human culture. Horwun wondered if the traveler was diseased.

"Calm . . . calm . . . calm . . ." the kaul murmured. His companion stayed motionless as stone.

The rain turned to hail. The kaul winced. So did Horwun. The blows on his hood were solid. The kaul's friend did not react at all.

The kaul said to Horwun, "Let us pass."

"No," Horwun replied. His revulsion peaked. He didn't even care if the travelers carried any money. He just wanted to see them dead. He lunged with his sword at the big male. In his peripheral vision, he saw Delner and the others rush in.

"Strike," the kaul said.

Horwun wondered why his blow missed, and why his balance felt wrong. Then he saw his arm in the road, his blood mixing with mud and rain. Something huge blurred, he blinked, and the male's sword had gutted him.

He fell. The hail battered his face, but he didn't feel it as the terminal ice spread over his body. Gray stained the world, the gray of spreading nothing, the gray of the traveler's flesh. Horwun heard the *snap* and *chunk* of bone and meat parting, and the spitting hiss of opened veins as his men went down.

He had not wept since childhood. He did now, in the last moments before the victory of the ice. He wept because he had an intimation of a great secret, one that even the gods did not know.

He wept for his terrible failure.

CHAPTER 2

The merchants were skeptical. They looked around the empty courtyard, then back at Garwynn Avennic.

"Transformative," said the first. His name was Yehan, and he had the hard look of a native to Korvas: distrustful of anything meant to impress him, reluctant to believe in the possibility of good fortune. Korvas was the capital of Wiramzin, and its wealthiest city, but the fractured political realities of Wiramzin made the presumption of any long-term good fortune a dubious one.

"Tall order," said the other, Rellis. He sounded no less doubtful, but he grinned, ready to be entertained. Like Garwynn, he had the dark skin of a Kamastian, and a newcomer from that empire, to judge by his accent. His stance was relaxed, his humor easy. Garwynn wondered how long he had been living in Korvas. He was dressed well, his woolen jacket and leather boots suited to the cooler climate of Wiramzin. They were in fine shape, but not new. Their colors were brighter than Yehan's, though the patterning was local. Not a recent arrival, Garwynn decided, curious to know what had led Rellis to move to Korvas. Garwynn could think of plenty of reasons to relocate to prosperous, politically stable Kamastia. A move the other way was always a bit harder to explain. He had never properly understood why his grandparents had journeyed north. Trade was a possibility in Rellis' case, he supposed. Garwynn chose to believe a love match had brought Rellis to the city. He seemed to be someone who had chosen, rather than been compelled, to come to Korvas, and was not unhappy in his decision.

Garwynn felt lucky Rellis was the senior partner of the firm. He looked open to taking a risk for the sheer joy of it. Yehan seemed cautious to the point of rigidity.

THE SLEEP OF EMPIRES

They stood in the courtyard before the merchants' leather goods warehouse. The most recent caravan had passed through the day before, and it would be the best part of a week before the space filled with horses and carts again. Now, with a faint drizzle starting, it was a blankness of gray stone. A dull space, but more than big enough for what Garwynn proposed.

"Transformative," Yehan said again, somehow turning the word into an imprecation. He was middle-aged, like Rellis, but his face was more worn, the skin around his eyes wrinkled into a permanent scowl. "What are you planning to do? We use this courtyard. I don't want it turned into a lake of fire or a swamp."

Are you being deliberately stupid? Garwynn kept his smile respectful. "By transformative, I mean the experience of wonder that will await your guests." *How powerful do you think my magic is, anyway?* "After the performance, the courtyard will be exactly as you see it now."

"With the addition of a happy audience, I hope," said Rellis, still grinning.

"Exactly," Garwynn said, grateful. "An audience that will spread the word of the generosity of your firm far and wide."

Yehan still looked skeptical, but there was more interest there now. "There are other spectacles we could arrange," he said to Rellis.

"Not at this price," Garwynn put in. "And for only one performer."

"Asking twice what any acrobat would charge."

"Maybe, but you would never hire just one acrobat, would you?"

"No," Yehan admitted. "But magic . . ." He made a face. "With acrobats, there is no risk."

Garwynn bit his tongue. If Yehan was not conscious of the absurdity of what he had just said, pointing it out would do no good. Besides, he knew what Yehan meant. The risks that came with a juggler or acrobat performance were known, containable, rarely given much thought. With magic, the range of things that could go wrong was much wider, the probabilities of mishap greater. Even then, the chances of harm befalling the audience were minute. It was far more likely that Garwynn would be unable

DAVID ANNANDALE

to make anything happen at all. *I will, though. I can do this. I'm good enough now.*

Good enough for the petty miracles he would perform.

"What risks?" Rellis said to Yehan. "Do you think he's going to make the earth swallow our guests?"

"No," said Yehan.

"So what's the worst that can happen? Our young friend stands up and makes a fool of himself." He winked at Garwynn to show he thought that eventuality was unlikely.

Garwynn's mouth went dry at the thought. He struggled to hold his smile of engaging confidence in place.

"Even if it goes wrong in some way," Rellis continued, "that's still entertainment to be had."

"If you say so," Yehan said.

Garwynn's pulse beat stronger. The scales were tipping in his favor. "That's right," he said. "One way or another, you have my word your guests will be pleased by the spectacle."

"Your word?" Yehan's look was sharp.

"Or I forfeit my payment," said Garwynn.

"Well then," said Rellis, all smiles, "I am satisfied."

Yehan hesitated long enough to make a point, then nodded.

Garwynn bowed to them both. "You will be pleased," he promised.

He left the courtyard and plunged back into the main street. The foot traffic was heavy, as ever. He moved nimbly through the crowd, slipping only once on the muddy cobblestones. The smoke-blackened stone façades of Korvas dripped from the recent rain, and the sky threatened more. Garwynn glanced up and picked up his pace.

As he headed back toward his quarters, a small room in a boarding house in the warren-like center of Korvas, he felt a mix of triumph and terror. A success with Yehan and Rellis would open many doors for him. This was the first time he had managed to interest patrons with their sorts of connections. If all went well, he had ensured himself several weeks of

13

THE SLEEP OF EMPIRES

work for the two merchants, and the possibility of much more to come. He could almost imagine making a living now.

Is this why you left Ghaunthook for Korvas? an unwelcome voice asked.

No, it was not. It was a long, long way from the destiny he had once dreamed would be his.

Destiny, he thought. *There's a word I should know better than to take seriously.*

Back in Ghaunthook, he and Alisteyr had, as children, imagined stories together of the feats they would accomplish as adults. Alisteyr had never really put those stories away. He still dreamed of becoming the hero of a saga. Garwynn had believed he knew better, that his dreams didn't soar as high and as far beyond possibility. He had tried to internalize that lesson when he had come to the understanding that Alisteyr did not feel about him the same way that he did about Alisteyr.

But had he really been more realistic? He had come to Korvas, after all. He had come here in the belief, half hidden from himself, that he might become something.

He knew much more now. The hardest lessons had been outside the university. He had put the dreams away. This would do for now.

For now? the voice asked, cynical.

For now, he told himself. He allowed himself that much hope.

Pilta walked down the central aisle of the library. He tried to keep his mind off what was coming by enumerating the long list of his fortunes. He had performed a fine dance last night. Bad luck that he had made a mistake at some point and the guards had become alert to the presence of an intruder. But good luck that he had locked the door to the vaults behind him without being caught. And good luck that Skiriye had joined in the search for the trespasser. So, she had not been in her office, and Pilta had made it there to return the key to the desk. Most importantly, he had sequestered the stolen book in the stacks. Bottom row of the third aisle from Skiriye's office, ten feet in from the main passage. Closer to Skiriye than Pilta would have

14

DAVID ANNANDALE

liked, but a fair chance, he hoped, that no one would stumble upon it there. He didn't like trusting that element to luck, but there had been no choice. He had known he was going to be caught. And so, he had been, less than a minute after he had hidden the book.

There was cause to be thankful here too. There had been time to reach an aisle relevant to his courses. There had been time to find a volume on Árkiriye's architectural history. There had been time for him to work on a suitably fearful and contrite face.

Looking frightened had taken very little effort.

He had been found by a guard. That too, was lucky.

So much good fortune, he told himself. He should not be greedy, and mourn that his luck had ended now.

When he passed the aisle where he had concealed the book, he did not look to the side. *Well done*, he thought. One more victory. Then he reached the door to the librarian's office, and the victories came to an end.

Pilta knocked. He pulled the door open when the cold voice told him to enter.

"Close the door," said Skiriye ne Sincatsë.

Pilta obeyed, then stood in silence, his head bowed.

"Look at me."

Pilta obeyed again, even more reluctantly than he had been to set foot into the chamber. He met Skiriye's eyes only for a moment. Then he had to break the gaze. That had been enough to feel the scouring judgement of those eyes.

She knows. She has to know. There was nothing her gaze could not rip from his soul. *Passomo preserve me.* He wanted to weep. *She found where I hid the book.* His knees trembled. But he did not look down. The last gossamer thread of his hope depended on obeying her absolutely.

The librarian stood behind her desk, rigor personified. Her robes were black, threaded with gold and red. The lines were runes, entwining prayers to Passomo and Sánmaya, a simultaneous, somber propitiation of the creator and of the giver of law. Skiriye was tall, and so thin she seemed a giant.

15

THE SLEEP OF EMPIRES

Her hair, drawn back in a white, braided cone, accentuated the severity of her face's long planes and hard angles.

The office mirrored its occupant's devotion to perfection. The small stacks of books on the desk, nestled at either end of the oak surface, were symmetrical in height. A sheaf of vellum sat in the mathematical center of the desk. Shelves lined the walls, the dark spines of the books interrupted at regular intervals by devotional icons. Behind the desk, a bronze rack held two objects. One was Skiriye's ebony cane. The other was a thing that Pilta could not look at or his legs would fail him.

"Explain yourself," Skiriye said. Her voice was quiet as the turning of pages, cutting as a rapier.

"I am falling behind in my studies," Pilta said. That much was true. "I was hoping to catch up." *Keep your answers simple.* Skiriye had no patience for long speeches, and the more he spoke, the more likely he would be to trip himself up.

"So, you trespassed in order to do more reading?"

"Yes, First Librarian."

"You are unable to complete your work in the periods allotted. Is this what I am to understand?"

Pilta saw where this was going. He tried to swallow past the cold stone that had formed in his throat. "I . . ." He didn't know how to finish the sentence. He tried again. "I wanted . . ." That was no better. He had no good answer to Skiriye's question. He stopped trying to respond. What was coming could not be stopped. He had known this since last night when he had made his decision. Anything he said now was pointless. Better to accept his fate and get it over with than delay it by a few wasted breaths. He fell silent.

Skiriye waited to see if he would try again. When he did not, she said, "I see. I am correct, then."

Pilta lowered his eyes, then caught himself and looked up again. He made a concerted effort not to wince.

16

DAVID ANNANDALE

"Failure is a form of imperfection," Skiriye said. "One of the most basic. While true perfection is beyond us all, not to strive for that ideal is an unforgivable dereliction. I will not permit such shame to taint this library. Do you understand, or is your imperfection so abject I will have to explain myself further?"

"I understand, First Librarian," said Pilta.

"Good. Your tutors will deal with you as they see fit. My care is exclusively for the crime of trespass and what it represents." She turned to the rack at her side. Now Pilta could not look away. Skiriye grasped her cane with her left hand, and the handle of her whip with her right. The lash was about twice the length of Pilta's arm. It was made of fine, intricately braided leather. Barbed jewels stood out along its length. It was a work of exquisite artisanship, the product of studied, patient attention to cruelty. It had its own perfection.

Pilta had seen the results of the whip's touch. So had all who studied in the library for any length of time. Skiriye purged imperfection with zeal.

"Come with me," she said.

Pilta followed her out the side door of her office. A staircase led off the corridor beyond, and she took it. Her stride was long and swift, even with her limp. The theory across the University of Árkiriye, barely voiced above a whisper, held that her infirmity drove her to the extremities with which she punished others' flaws. She was a curiosity, inspiring as much gossip as she did fear. In the elvish empire of Beresta, visible disability was rare. Actual deformities were forbidden, the infants killed immediately, their families then paying ruinous restitution tithes to the temples of Passomo. The word on Skiriye was that she had lost her right foot to an accident in early childhood. The stories about the supposed nature of the mishap were legion. Pilta had heard too many to trust any. But if she had been the victim of another's carelessness, another's imperfection, then he could imagine that as a reason for her cruelty.

Not that this understanding did him any good today.

17

THE SLEEP OF EMPIRES

His mouth dried as he followed her up the spiral staircase. He had to rush to keep up. He would only make what was coming worse by lagging behind and inviting her greater wrath.

At the top of the stairs, Skiriye opened a door and stepped out onto a narrow marble span. There were no guard rails, and there was barely room for a single person to walk. From the ground floor, the span resembled a gleaming thread. It extended into space to the center of the library, a short distance beneath the dome. Pilta did not look up. The dome's fresco, a representation of the gods creating Eloran, offered no source of inspiration now. It was oppressive, the exultation of power while he was at his most helpless. He kept his eyes on the cage suspended beside the end of the span. It was an artifact as lovingly crafted as Skiriye's whip, as beautiful, and as savage. It was a dodecahedron of interlocking bronze rods. The joins were seamless, as if the construct had been formed by crystalline growth. The doors were invisible until Skiriye opened them, folding them back to either side. The entrance took up a third of the cage's height and width.

The span widened into a platform here. Skiriye stood to one side. Without turning around, she waited for Pilta. He walked past her and stepped into the cage. The base was a bronze mirror. Manacles hung before him. Without being told, he placed his wrists in them. The weight of his arms triggered a mechanism and they grasped him, their hold as seamless as the rest of the bronze lattice. Gears clanked, and the chains, linked to the cage's supporting cable, rose, lifting his arms above his head, and pulling him into the air. Two other manacles clicked shut around his ankles. They must have been attached by Skiriye, but it seemed as if the machinery of the cage itself had reached out to take him. The chains pulled his legs apart and back until he hung at an angle, spread-eagled, staring down at the mirror. It reflected the fresco and his position within the center of the design. The gods surrounded the cage, and Sánmaya, she of the law, pointed directly at him. There was no forgiveness in her gaze. In a few moments, his blood would fall onto the image below, the blood he would have to clean later, and still there would be no forgiveness.

18

DAVID ANNANDALE

Pilta heard Skiriye take up her position behind him. He gritted his teeth. He reminded himself that he was going to live.

After the second lash, the thought was no longer a comfort.

Latanna waited until the following morning before she spoke to her father. She hadn't wanted to deal with Alisteyr's proposal and the subsequent confrontation with Marsen on the same day. She could have. She felt strong enough. But there was no point in piling up the ordeals. So she avoided Marsen for the rest of the day and the evening. It was not difficult. They were the only two family members in Forgrym Hall. She had barely seen him for the entire week.

In the late morning, she walked down the manor house's staircase, past the worn tapestries, her footsteps echoing in the dank air. The house was always cold. Marsen could no longer afford to keep fires burning in more than a couple of rooms at once. Though the rain from the last few days had finally let up, its touch still reached deep into the walls. Latanna's clothes felt clammy. She was used to it. She was used to all kinds of cold. She could have entertained the thought that her marriage to Alisteyr would create the possibility of future warmth in the house of Forgrym. She did not grant herself that luxury.

She was acting for a better future. That was not the same as hoping for one.

At the foot of the staircase, she paused, listening to the sullen echoes of life in the house. She heard the distant clatter of the servants in the kitchen, preparing the midday meal. Then, after a moment, the scrape of a chair against a stone floor to her right. She walked down the hall and entered the chapel.

The eight-sided chamber was as cold as the rest of the house, and darker. The tapestries here were in better condition, though, and Marsen had managed to hang on to most of the icons. He sat in an iron chair before the altar to Tetriwu. Constructed of wrought iron with gold filigree, the altar was a squat cone whose peak became the crossed spear, sword, and

19

THE SLEEP OF EMPIRES

axe of the war god. Marsen's head nodded slowly as he performed his obeisances. His outstretched right hand traced a path through the air, pointing to the angles of the weapons in turn, ending with the tip of the spear, then starting again. It was an observance of triumphalist violence, and a prayer for his own petty victories.

Every time Latanna set foot in the chapel, her contempt flared, and she had to struggle to conceal it. She did not always succeed. Today, she made a special effort to hide what she thought of her father's devotions. The Forgryms had been exclusively faithful to Tetriwu for generations. *This is where you have brought us, war-creator,* Latanna thought. *To petty, ruinous, pointless conflict.*

She stood quietly in the doorway. Marsen started, suddenly aware of her presence. He stood up from the iron chair. Its arms were edged, sharp enough to cause pain but not draw blood. He turned to face her, a big man, hard in the eyes and limbs, running soft in the belly. He wrapped a hand built for crushing bones around the back of the chair. "You have a good reason for interrupting me, I suppose."

"I think you know what it is."

Marsen's eyes narrowed. "I heard rumors. I didn't want to believe you would betray your family so completely."

"Father, theatrics don't suit you. They don't serve your purpose either."

Marsen folded his arms. "Tell me, then. Straight out. Say the words."

She shrugged. If there was to be a formality to the moment, so be it. "Alisteyr Huesland has asked for my hand in marriage. I have accepted."

Marsen's lips twitched. He, too, had a deep well of contempt.

Oh, you are my father, Latanna thought. *And I am your daughter. May the gods protect all who know us.* They resembled each other in their instinct for strategy, and in their features. She wore her hair longer than he did, but it was the same deep black, and she had his pale green eyes. She had inherited his strong facial features. She hoped hers had not yet begun to harden into his cruelty.

"I'm surprised the Huesland whelp found the courage to propose," said Marsen.

"I may have given him the idea."

"No doubt." Marsen shook his head. "You speak as if either of you has the power to make that decision."

Good. They were moving past the perfunctory display of outrage, heading toward the practical state of affairs. That was the field on which Latanna wished to do battle with her father. That was where she had gathered her army. "True," she said. She and Alisteyr were the property of their parents. "We don't have that power."

"You think the Hueslands will give their consent?"

"I do."

The smile was definite now, and as hard as the eyes. "You think I will?"

"If you listen to your self-interest. That isn't something you're always good at. I hope you will be in this instance."

The smile vanished for a moment, then it returned, now more vicious. "Elgin Hawkesmoore is on his way here from Korvas," Marsen said.

"I know."

"We have almost concluded our negotiations. Once they are successful, he will propose to you."

"I know that too. Why do you think I made sure Alisteyr made his proposal first?"

"That's irrelevant. I do not give my consent."

Latanna smiled now, making Marsen's grin vanish. Did he really think he could intimidate her? And was he that disappointed that he could not? "I really think you should reconsider," she said.

"Why?"

"If you try to impose Elgin Hawkesmoor on me, I will fight you. You know I will. It will be war, father, and it will be ugly. And if, for the sake of argument, you should carry the day in the end, what does that get you? Elgin is the youngest son. How much influence do you imagine you will

THE SLEEP OF EMPIRES

gain with the Hawkesmoores? Their interest in the match is to extend their reach from Korvas. Once you give consent, you will have nothing else of value to offer them. You will have no leverage. You will be at their beck and call. Is that what you are hoping for? To be their serf?"

"Go on."

His expression had become neutral. She couldn't tell if she had convinced him. He had not dismissed her reasoning out of hand, though. He was listening.

"My alternative gives you much more."

"Instead of an alliance with the most powerful family in Korvas, I forge a bond with our sworn enemies. Where is the advantage?"

"Isn't it obvious? The feud is draining us, Father. How much longer can you afford it? I doubt the Hawkesmoors will have the patience to fund the petty squabbles of Ghaunthook. You'll be their serf in short order. If, though, you agree to my marriage with Alisteyr, the drain stops. Your holdings are still larger than the Hueslands'. You will be the most powerful party in that alliance. Think what Forgrym influence will become in Ghaunthook." She despised making the case in these terms. She could think of few things that would make a positive difference for the village more than the total elimination of Forgrym power. She would have to make do with an end to the active harm of the feud. If this was the argument that would win her the day, she would use it.

Marsen looked thoughtful. Latanna hoped his pragmatism would speak to his pride more than his fury.

He cocked his head. "And what are you getting out of this?"

She thought before answering. Marsen did not believe she loved Alisteyr. If she tried to tell him she did, she would undermine her cause. She would also sound like she was trying to convince herself. She chose a truth Marsen would believe. "I will gain freedom from life under the Hawkesmoores," she said.

Marsen laughed. "I wonder if you really hate wealth as much as you think you do."

DAVID ANNANDALE

"Their wealth is not what I hate."

Her father snorted. "Those are not the words of a woman who claims to lecture me on the realities of the world."

"Perhaps not," Latanna said. "That doesn't mean my arguments are wrong."

That neutral expression again. The hard man thinking, calculating, examining two very different forms of victory, deciding which was the real one. "We will speak again," Marsen said at last.

Latanna nodded, her face as neutral as Marsen's, and left the chapel. She wanted to smile, but she suppressed the urge. She kept it tamped down when she walked out of Forgrym Hall and headed down the road through her father's land toward the center of Ghaunthook. She needed to walk, to breathe, to let the actions she had taken settle in her soul. She did not trust her impulse to smile. She did not know if she had won yet, and even if Marsen wound up conceding, it felt like hubris to declare triumph when she still felt so many doubts. She was venturing further and further out onto thin ice. She could hear it crack, and the distant bank she hoped to reach might be a mirage.

Some of the servants in the fields waved to her as she passed. She returned their greetings. *We are all in bondage to my father*, she thought. *Mine is more luxurious, and perhaps I have scope to act for us all.*

The arrogance of the thought made her blush.

The road wound through many fields that lay fallow, and others being reclaimed by the forest. Everywhere she looked, she saw the physical evidence of Forgrym decay. She had dreams of remaking the land. The task would not be for the glory of the family name, or so she hoped. She wondered about her motivations now. She was very conscious of the foul blood that ran in her veins. If she bested her father in the power game, was she breaking away from her inheritance or embracing it?

Though the rain had stopped, the day was overcast and dark, the morning feeling like late afternoon. Beyond the Forgrym land, the forest grew thick and pressed in on the road before giving way to a sodden plain

23

THE SLEEP OF EMPIRES

in the approaches to the village center of Ghaunthook. As Latanna reached the plain, she heard someone crying out. The voice rose and fell, babbling nonsense. Syllables of agony, wonder, and desperate, uncomprehending anger poured out of a raw throat. Midway between Latanna and the first of the houses, a man staggered back and forth across the road. His hands clawed at the air. She drew nearer, and his howls turned into a keening. The sound was mindless, bereft of anything except pain.

There were two other people on the road, a bit past the madman. One was short and slight, the other very tall. They appeared to have been heading to the town, but had turned around. They approached the man. The short figure leaned its head toward the tall one, and then the other seized the screamer. Latanna broke into a run, then saw, as she drew near, that this was not an attack. The pair, a kaul and a tall male of indeterminate race, were restraining the man, holding his arms behind his back and keeping him from harming himself. He had already clawed more than the air. His cheeks hung in flaps, and one eye was missing. Telltale yellow tears ran down his face.

"Hold . . . hold . . . hold . . ." the kaul said to his companion, his voice a steady rasp, calming yet sibilant. Then he placed his hand lightly against his friend's left arm and turned to Latanna. He nodded shortly. "Cloudblossom," he said.

"Yes," said Latanna. She recognized the man now. His name was Veschel. He had worked on the Huesland farms once, but had fallen deeper and deeper into the cloudblossom abyss during the last few months. She had seen him, ragged, begging for coins outside the Laughing Chimera. He stank of the drug. Its smoke clung to his clothes and skin. She breathed through her mouth, and even then, the sharp, rotting, sweet tang reached into her head. The edges of her vision rippled, very slightly, with the stale, faded echoes of another person's hallucinations.

Veschel was not the only cloudblossom slave she had seen recently. There were more and more in Ghaunthook, living wraiths lingering at the fringes of village life, ignored, pitied, or despised by the people around them. The final madness of the drug was violent. By that point, the sufferers could no longer tolerate any other human presences around them, and they fled to die in the woods. Those that did not became threats to others, and the watch had to kill them.

"Hold," the kaul told his friend. Veschel moaned, his thick, yellow tears streaming. To Latanna, the kaul said, "You know him, my lady?"

"I do."

"His end is near."

"I know. He is beyond help."

The kaul nodded. "But not beyond mercy."

Latanna looked at the other stranger. She had seen frightening strength in the cloudblossom victims as they entered their final hours, but the big man (if he was a man) showed no strain as he held Veschel in place. He watched the kaul with absolute concentration, as if his friend were the only solid reality in a world of mist.

The fact of a kaul being the one giving orders in any circumstance at all was something that Latanna already knew would be a source of wonder for her in the hours ahead. What mattered now, though, was what the kaul had suggested.

"He won't suffer?" she asked.

"He will cease to suffer," said the kaul.

Nothing lay in Veschel's future except execution by the watch or the slower, howling starvation in the woods. The kaul had spoken of mercy. That would be a gift for Veschel, even if he didn't know it. She nodded.

"Do you wish to turn away?"

"No." If she could do nothing for Veschel except bear witness to his end, then she would do that for him.

"Very well." The kaul turned back to his friend. He withdrew his hand from the other's arm. "Without pain," the kaul said.

The other broke Veschel's neck so quickly that Latanna wasn't sure how he had done it. He had Veschel pinned, and then his arms were around the addict's neck and against the back of his head. The movement had the grace

THE SLEEP OF EMPIRES

of bird flight, and the suddenness of lightning. There was a click like two stones striking each other, and Veschel's wail cut short. He slumped, quiet, his head hanging at an angle.

"Wait . . . wait . . . wait . . ." the kaul said. He touched the other's arm again. "Does he have family?" the kaul asked Latanna.

"No."

"A place of burial?"

"He would be put on a collective pyre."

The kaul frowned. "There is no cemetery?"

"There are two, but not that we can use. The new one is not open to the victims of cloudblossom. There is a fear that they will taint the land. The old one cannot be used at all."

The kaul seemed about to ask another question, then changed his mind. "We will bury him in the forest, then," he said.

"That will be well."

"Carry," the kaul said, and his friend lifted Veschel over his shoulder. "My lady," the kaul said, and they began to walk up the road in the direction of the woods.

"Who are you?" Latanna asked.

The kaul paused. "I am Kanstuhn," he said. "I call him Memory. Perhaps that is cruel, but it serves well enough."

"My name is Latanna Forgrym," she said. "I will answer for you, if the need arises."

The kaul smiled, death amused by Latanna's offer. "That need never has, but your kindness will be remembered." He bowed this time. The gesture was sincere, and somehow Latanna had never felt so honored. "You have our thanks," Kanstuhn said.

Latanna watched them go. They turned off the road once they reached the forest. She could make them out for only a few moments more, a small figure and a large one, pallor and mystery, before the gloom swallowed them, and she was alone once more.

26

CHAPTER 3

The last stretch of the road was the hardest one. With the Marsen house growing larger in Alisteyr's sight, he felt painfully conscious of walking where no Huesland had set foot in generations. None that had lived to record the act, at least. He caught himself before he looked around for an ambush. If Marsen wanted him dead, there was nothing he could do. He was on Forgrym land, unarmed, and what he knew about fighting came from the lais he read. He had tried his hand at writing a few, and he kept his descriptions of combat to a minimum. Those moments always rang false to him, even though they figured large in his imagination before he put words on parchment.

He knew his limitations, though he despised them.

If I'm going to die, let it be with head held high.

He flushed, embarrassed by the thought. It belonged to daydreams and stories.

This is no legend. I am no hero.

Though he truly wished he could be.

Alisteyr reached the covered porch. He eyed the door and gathered the courage to knock. He told himself that having made it this far was a good sign. He drew on his last conversation with Latanna for the rest of the strength he needed. They had met at the market in the center of Ghaunthook, two days after his proposal, and she had delivered what was good, if terrifying, news.

"I don't think he's going to try to kill you," Latanna had said. "But you don't have to agree to go to the house. I could push him to pick neutral ground."

"Would that make much of a difference if he *does* plan to kill me?"

"If he thought he could get away with it, he would have done it long ago. He can't be that brazen. There are still consequences."

THE SLEEP OF EMPIRES

That was true. The feud had exhausted the Hueslands, and his parents had little desire in pursuing it beyond holding the line against Marsen. But he could guess what would happen if an assassin cut him down in Ghaunthook. They would see both houses burn to avenge him.

"I'd feel better if you weren't actually *in* the house, though," Latanna said.

"No. I'll go."

You knew there would be tests, he reminded himself now. *You* hoped *there would be.* And that was true. He wanted to prove himself worthy of Latanna. Now came the first test. It wasn't on a scale that belonged in a lai. Not yet. But it was a start.

He raised his hand, but the door opened before he could knock. The man who stood behind it did not look like a servant. His name was Seck, and Latanna had warned Alisteyr about him. Alisteyr had been braced, but not braced enough for the reality. Seck was a bit shorter than Alisteyr, and almost twice as broad. His clothes were the rough leathers of a sell-sword, and the scars on his forearms and face had not come from domestic service. One nasty slice had healed badly into a knotty ridge running from his left eye to the right of his chin. It turned his nose, mouth, and beard into mismatched halves, broken along the angry pink fracture. He looked at Alisteyr with a contemptuous eye. The left half of his mouth twitched. He bowed and gestured for Alisteyr to enter. The actions were the mocking imitation of servitude. "Welcome," he said. His voice was a hoarse rasp, barely containing a laugh.

"Thank you," said Alisteyr, reasonably sure that he spoke without a tremor. He played along with the man's act. *You're pretending to be a servant, and you want me to see through the act and be afraid. Fine. I'll pretend I believe you really are a servant.* He thought he performed well. He walked past Marsen's hired man. A doorway on his right opened into the hall.

Marsen stood before the fireplace in the center of the room, his expression hard, his eyes coldly amused. He said nothing when Alisteyr entered.

28

DAVID ANNANDALE

The silence became uncomfortable. Alisteyr's shoulder muscles tensed. He wondered how much it would hurt when the blade pierced his back.

None did.

Marsen went another minute without speaking. Alisteyr caught himself shifting his weight from foot to foot. He resented the game, but he could see no way out of it. He had no choice but let Marsen show who had the power here. Alisteyr was a supplicant. He had no bargaining power.

"So," Marsen said at last, "we both know what you want. We should talk about what I want."

Alisteyr pressed his lips together. The insult to himself and to Latanna stung. Instinct, honor, and love demanded a response. An inner voice that sounded a lot like Latanna said, *Don't take the bait. Don't give him an excuse to throw you out.* When he was sure he wouldn't do anything stupid, Alisteyr said, "What do you want?"

Marsen grinned. Instead of answering the question, he changed the subject. He waggled a finger at Alisteyr. "Proving yourself," he said. "That's what you're doing."

Marsen waited. Alisteyr tried to find an answer that didn't make him look like a fool. He couldn't.

Marsen pushed him. "Isn't it?"

Now Alisteyr had no choice. "Yes," he said, ashamed at how ridiculous the truth sounded, and furious at himself for feeling the shame. His face burned.

"So here you are, come to confront the dragon in his den."

"That's not . . ." Alisteyr sputtered. He did not know how to finish.

"Yes?" Marsen asked. He waited again, his grin growing broader all the time. "What? You don't think I'm a dragon? You think I'm weak?"

"I do not."

Still that grin. "No. I don't think you do." He shrugged. "You made a gesture by coming here. A nice one. Very brave. It wouldn't have meant anything if you thought I was weak. Am I right?"

THE SLEEP OF EMPIRES

No answer was free of humiliation. Alisteyr said nothing. He flushed again. Even his silence felt like a performance. Marsen was peeling open his layers of self-delusion, eviscerating him by words alone.

"I think I'm right," Marsen said. He nodded. "Rather impressive. And your love healing the rift between the families, that's quite good too. Except that wasn't your idea, was it?" He waved a hand. "No matter. The point is you believe in the idea now, and you're willing to die for it."

"I would die for your daughter," Alisteyr said. He didn't care how theatrical those words sounded. They were the truth.

"I believe you," said Marsen. "I do. At least, I believe your sincerity. But this *is* my daughter we're discussing." He stopped smiling. His expression became hard. "Sincerity isn't good enough. Not nearly good enough."

"What would be?" Alisteyr asked.

"I'm glad you asked," said Marsen.

The human was waiting for Pilta in a narrow lane running between the back walls of an offertory chapel to Passomo and a line of residences reserved for students of the university. The only illumination came from both ends of the alley, where it joined the main avenues. In the gloom, the ivory-white marble of Árkiriye's architecture had faded to the gray of bone. Pilta had expected the trader to be wrapped in a dark cloak, a figure of shadows, or as close to one as a human could manage. Instead, she wore her market clothes, her face uncovered. She was middle-aged by human standards, her features weathered and polished a leathery brown by years of travel in the sun and wind. She stood under an arch of the chapel's rear colonnade. There were no services at this time of night, and the location was secluded. Even so, if she was caught, not just outside the human quarter, but leaning against a pillar, a human desecrating holy ground, she would be lucky if she got away with nothing worse than having her hands cut off.

She straightened as Pilta hobbled close, and, to his relief, stepped away from the narrow, fluted column. He had no illusions about what he was doing. He was stealing from one of the great repositories of elvish

DAVID ANNANDALE

culture for gold, and at the command of a human. The crime went far beyond blasphemy. Even so, he didn't like seeing the human in contact with a building sacred to Passomo.

"What happened to you?" the woman asked, watching Pilta's limp.

"Nothing that wasn't expected," he said. "All part of the plan."

She raised an eyebrow. "I hope this was worth it, then," she said, producing a coin purse. Despite the expression of concern, she didn't offer to increase the payment.

Pilta debated playing up his injuries. It wouldn't be hard. The pain was genuine. And he hadn't given her the book yet.

But the thought of holding onto the book for even another few moments repulsed him. He wanted it gone from his possession. He didn't want to know its secrets. The agreed price seemed more than fair now. If the woman had asked Pilta to pay *her* to take the book off his hands, he didn't think he would object.

Pilta pulled the book out from inside his tunic. He had wrapped it in linen. The woman handed him the purse and took the book. Pilta waited while she removed the cloth. She opened the book, rifled quickly through the pages. She winced, but nodded, satisfied. She folded the linen around the book again in a hurry and put it in the felt bag she carried. "Our business is concluded," she said.

"Yes," Pilta said, relieved. He pocketed the gold and watched the merchant head off to the right, in the direction of the human quarter. He didn't see how she could avoid being spotted by the watch.

What do you care? he asked himself. *You're done. You have what you needed.*

He should leave the alley and return to his residence. There were only a few hours before he would have to face his tutors again, and he needed what sleep he could get. His back was a cross-hatching of agony.

He should go. He really should.

But he was curious. Not about what was in the book. No. But why would anyone want it? And how did the woman think she was going to reach the human quarter?

THE SLEEP OF EMPIRES

He knew better. He really did.

He followed her anyway.

When she stepped out of the alley and onto the avenue, the merchant's gait changed. It went from a stride to short, rapid steps, a panicked trot. Her head hunched down into her shoulders. Pilta stopped at the intersection, keeping a careful distance between them. He became just one of the idly curious on the promenade. People turned to look at a sight that was unusual without being unheard of. Humans were forbidden from leaving their market quarter, but Parkäre Avenue was only a few minutes away from the demarcation line. There were some elves who engaged in transactions that could not take place in the market. The nature of those transactions was unspoken, but hardly unknown. The perfect citizens of Árkiriye turned their eyes away. If the acts were not acknowledged, they did not exist. The woman had adopted the guise of anxiety. If Pilta had happened to see her now for the first time, he would have assumed she was rushing back to the human quarter, conscious to the point of terror of her transgression, and in that consciousness diverting the gaze of all she passed. It suited them to refuse awareness of her presence. Convention made her invisible.

Turn around, Pilta told himself.

He kept following.

The human quarter squatted at the edge of Árkiriye, hovels and market stalls a collection of shame next to the soaring architecture of the city, whose towers had the elegance of gossamer, yet a strength that withstood millennia of elements without blemish.

The market was still lively. The stalls had closed hours ago, but the preparations were in full swing for the dawn departure of the large caravans heading for Wiramzin. There were plenty of elves here, merchants willing to get their hands dirty and travel with humans for the sake of their trade. Twice, Pilta almost lost track of the woman as she made her way through the crowd. He moved closer. His clothes were shabby enough for him to blend in with the other elves. No one here was from the elite of Árkiriye's society.

32

DAVID ANNANDALE

The woman joined a crowd of humans gathered around the lead wagons of a caravan. In the glow of the lanterns, he saw her greeted casually by the other itinerant merchants. She was known here.

I can go now. He knew how the woman planned to leave the city. He knew where she was heading.

Only he didn't, not really. And he didn't know why, or what she wanted with the book.

He didn't need to know. All he had to do was turn around and walk out of the market.

"Passenger or merchant?"

Pilta managed not to jump. He turned to his right. One of the elves in the caravan was looking at him.

Neither, he thought, but he said, "Passenger."

"You shouldn't have agreed," Latanna said.

"What choice did I have?" Alisteyr sounded more aggrieved by her reaction than by her father's demand.

They were sitting at a corner table in the Laughing Chimera. Latanna had her back to the wall and a good view of the tavern. She and Alisteyr had been here for hours. She would keep them here for as long as she had to. It was after dusk, and the crowd was still growing. Pipe smoke gathered under the oak ceiling beams. Lanterns and the fireplace cast a warm, flickering, orange light over the room. The tavern's namesake snarled above the bar. It was a wooden sculpture of the front half of the beast. Its forelegs extended, claws out, it seemed to leap from the wall. The artist had been skilled, but eccentric. The lion and goat heads gaped, but the eyes were so comically wide that the monster looked amused instead of fierce.

"You had the choice of not committing suicide," she told Alisteyr.

"He gave us his consent! What would you have liked me to do? Turn him down?"

Latanna sighed. "You're letting hope get in the way of reality." *And not for the first time.* "He wants you out of the way. His consent was a means to

33

THE SLEEP OF EMPIRES

an end, and that end is your death. Can't you see how this will work? The last of the Hueslands dies of his own foolishness, and Marsen Forgrym, blameless, doesn't have to lift a finger."

"He's given his word," said Alisteyr. "He'll have to honor it."

He's not listening. She hadn't really expected him to. Even so, she tried again. "He won't have to honor it because you'll be dead."

Alisteyr put his hand on hers. She felt the tremor of excitement in his touch. Marsen's consent, even contingent, granted them the license to be together openly. By tomorrow morning, Ghaunthook would be consumed by a single piece of gossip.

"I'm not going to die," Alisteyr said, his eyes shining.

By all the gods, he really believes that. Of course, he did. Whatever else she thought of her father, she had to admit that Marsen knew what he was doing. He had given Alisteyr a quest. A quest with her hand in marriage at the end. From Latanna's perspective, the gambit was so transparently manipulative, it was laughable. But Alisteyr could only see the narrative of his dreams.

She didn't say, *You're condemning us both.* Beaming with heroic pride, Alisteyr would not be able to hear her.

Alisteyr stretched. "Should we go?"

"Not yet."

"Why not?"

"We're waiting for someone."

Kanstuhn and Memory walked in not long after. It had not been a huge gamble to hope they would. The life of Ghaunthook flowed through the Laughing Chimera. If the pair were still in the village, they would show up sooner or later. She was relieved to see they were still around.

People made room for them as they entered. No one wanted to associate with a kaul. And no one, clearly, wished to give offense, either. Latanna guessed a hard lesson had been taught by Memory. Recently, she thought. The pair could not have been in Ghaunthook long. She would have heard of them, otherwise.

34

DAVID ANNANDALE

Alisteyr was staring. "A *kaul* . . ." he began.

"Yes," she said. "Be civil." She gestured to Kanstuhn.

The kaul nodded to her and led Memory over, murmuring the whole time. "Sit," he said when they arrived at the table. "Calm, calm, calm." He placed two tankards down.

Alisteyr stared back and forth at the pair, his mouth hanging open in surprise.

"You are sell-swords, I hope," Latanna said.

The kaul smiled. "When called upon, my lady. Do you call upon us?"

"I do."

"Latanna," said Alisteyr, "what are you doing?"

"Did you plan on going alone?" She looked at him steadily. Miraculously, he did not object. Perhaps the surprise of sharing his table with a kaul had jolted him into actually *listening*.

"Calm, calm, calm," the kaul murmured. "How do you come to call upon us?" he asked Latanna.

"Alisteyr will explain." If she could not convince him to abandon the quest, then he should take the lead in describing it. Though his idealism frustrated her, she did not begrudge Alisteyr his ability to dream.

Was her dream of peace between the families any more realistic? The means were, she had thought. *Why did father do this to Alisteyr? Because of you. This is his response to your proposal. This is his countermove.*

Maybe Kanstuhn and Memory could be her block against Marsen's offensive.

She caught herself thinking in strategic terms. *This is not a game. Alisteyr is ready to die for you.* Her heart twisted in pain.

"Latanna's father wants me to prove myself worthy of her hand," Alisteyr said. "So, he has set me a task. I am to retrieve a tiara that belonged to one of the great Forgryms of the past."

"Calm, calm, calm," said Kanstuhn. "The tiara is where?"

"Still worn by its owner. Elisava Forgrym is interred in the family vault, in the old village cemetery."

THE SLEEP OF EMPIRES

"Why does this village have two?"

"Because of the sins of our families," said Alisteyr. "Both were once greater than they are now. At the height of their powers, and of their feud, they called upon powers they should not have."

Latanna felt a squirm of shame. She cursed ancestors dead for more than a century.

"Calm, calm, calm," Kanstuhn said. "They made war on each other with magic?" he asked, his voice dropping to a rasping whisper.

Alisteyr nodded. Latanna tried to picture the arrogance and the power necessary to engage in such madness. Magic was so rare, and so uncontrollable. The Forgryms and the Hueslands had been able to summon it. They had not been able to control it.

"The struggle ended in disaster for both families," said Alisteyr. "And for Ghaunthook. Both houses have been in decline ever since. They are shadows of what they once were. Many people died. And the cemetery cannot be used any longer."

Latanna snorted. She couldn't let the understatement pass. "Tell them why," she said.

"It is unclean," Kanstuhn guessed.

"It is," said Alisteyr.

"It's dangerous during the day," Latanna said. "At night it's lethal. And that's at the surface. No one has been foolish enough to descend into a vault."

While they spoke, Kanstuhn kept one hand on Memory's arm. The touch of the kaul kept him placid. He drank his ale slowly, regarding the tankard with surprise every few moments.

"The dangers do not reach into the village?" Kanstuhn asked.

"The things that walk there are held close to their graves," Alisteyr said.

The kaul nodded. The answer pleased him. "That is well. That is well. Limits are always well. They speak of weakness. One must know of weaknesses."

"Including one's own," said Latanna.

36

"Especially one's own," Kanstuhn agreed. He met her gaze, and both of them glanced at Alisteyr at the same time. He didn't notice.

"Do you know yours?" Latanna asked.

"I try to. I know some. There are others that will, I am sure, be revealed to me in time. I try to eschew arrogance."

"What about your friend's?"

Kanstuhn smiled. "His great weakness is clear to all. What is less clear, even to me, is if there are any others."

"How long have you been companions?"

"Years, for me. Always, for him." The smile became sad.

"You have his measure, then."

"Hardly. But enough for some purposes." He patted Alisteyr's shoulder with a skeletal hand. Alisteyr paled, but suppressed his shudder. "We will see your betrothed safely through his test." He spoke respectfully, but Latanna thought she heard a faint undertone of entertainment.

Alisteyr's eyes widened in surprise at the ease of the agreement, and also, Latanna thought, with relief. "We haven't discussed payment," he said. "My family is not rich anymore, and Latanna's father . . ."

"What you will offer will be enough," said Kanstuhn. The look he gave Latanna was a somber one. It had the strength of a vow.

CHAPTER 4

Elgin Hawkesmoore wore the dust of the road like a mark of power. He hadn't changed from his traveling coat before joining Marsen in the chapel. He leaned against the iron chair, casually slapping some dirt from his trousers. Marsen winced at the sacrilege. Elgin didn't appear to notice. He looked bored, and when he was bored, his brow wrinkled in a petulant frown.

Elgin was taller than Marsen, and thin. He wore his blond hair long. His narrow features, tyrannically symmetrical, took pride in the absolute certainty of their beauty.

"You agreed to their marriage," Elgin repeated. He slapped at dust once more, the clap of leather on leather bordering on a threat.

"Under an impossible condition," said Marsen. "This changes nothing. The young Huesland is going to march happily off to his death, and my daughter's betrothal to you will be announced at your next visit."

"I don't think Father is going to be pleased." Elgin spoke as if Marsen had said nothing.

"He should be pleased! With no heir, the Hueslands will be a spent force at last."

Elgin snorted. "You mean you aren't?" Before Marsen could answer, he continued. "The Huesland snot might live."

Marsen shook his head. "He won't."

"But if he did. Then what? What is your word worth?"

"It binds like iron. But they won't marry. I won't break my word, but I'll strangle him myself if I have to."

Elgin shrugged and walked away from the chair. "As long as you do what is necessary. I won't have my interests hurt."

"They won't be. You have my word."

38

DAVID ANNANDALE

"Your word," Elgin sneered. He shook his head and left the chapel. A few moments later, Marsen heard him mounting the stairs toward his guest chambers.

Marsen unclenched his fist. Blood welled in the gouges his nails had made in his palm. Latanna's earlier words came back to him. *You will be at their beck and call. Is that what you are hoping for? To be their serf?* He had just experienced the reality of his future treatment by the Hawkesmoores.

But you knew, he reminded himself. *You always knew.* It was the price to be paid for victory over the Hueslands and at least a partial restoration of the Forgryms. There were always masters to be served. He had chosen his, and the alliance with them would make him the master of Ghaunthook, even if the Hawkesmoores never set foot here again.

Elgin would, though. *His interests.* Marsen understood. The youngest son had to look outside his family to secure his fortune. If his eldest brother was heir to the throne of the family's empire, Elgin's duty was to establish new colonies of wealth. He had one here in Ghaunthook. Marsen wondered if Elgin had told his father what he had done. He wondered if Elgin kept a safe distance from the source of his wealth. He had his doubts. He wasn't sure a safe distance was possible.

Stay alive until the wedding, you arrogant bastard, Marsen thought. Then Elgin could do as he pleased with himself.

Latanna returned from town at midday. She had gone looking for Alisteyr and his bodyguards. There had been no sign of them. She hoped that was a good omen. She hoped that meant they were making their foray into the old cemetery in broad daylight. Now, as the house came into view, she saw an ill omen for herself. There were Hawkesmoore men loitering outside. Their livery of red and silver shone in the sun, a bright, sparkling insult to her hopes.

Latanna turned off the road before any of them noticed her. She cut across the fields, into the woods beyond them, and made her way toward the rear of the house. She came as close as she dared without leaving the

THE SLEEP OF EMPIRES

shelter of the forest, turned to an oak she had come to know through long practice, and climbed in the branches. Hidden by the leaves, she rested her back against the trunk and settled herself down to wait. She felt no shame in hiding in the tree as if she were still seven years old. She would feel shame in being stupid, and walking into the house at this moment would have been stupid. From early childhood, she had learned when it was in her best interest to avoid her father's sight. The tactics she had learned then were just as useful in adulthood.

Perhaps even more useful, because the stakes were higher.

From where she sat, she could see the house through a filter of branches and leaves, and had a patchy view of the stables. She thought about her next move. So Elgin Hawkesmoore had arrived in time for her father to play his murderous little game with Alisteyr. The way Marsen expected events to unfold was obvious. Latanna wondered what he would make of Kanstuhn and Memory. Though she was hardly less worried than she had been about Alisteyr's ability to get himself killed, she smiled, picturing Marsen sputtering in a helpless mixture of frustration and wrath. It was Kanstuhn, she decided, who would most enrage her father. She had *asked* for help from a *kaul*. She didn't think there were words to encompass the humiliation that represented for Marsen.

She was beginning to think in terms of spending the night in the oak when she heard shouted orders in the courtyard. Elgin had emerged from the house and was calling for his horse. Latanna crawled forward on the branch, her skirt dangling on either side of it, until she had a better view. The younger Hawkesmoore and his men rode away from the hall, but not, as she would have expected, toward the center of Ghaunthook. They took a path that entered the forest and swung east. It had once been a road, but was badly overgrown now, with only the occasional patch of gravel remaining. No one had had a good reason to take that route for many years.

What you're thinking of doing is not a good idea, Latanna told herself. *If Alisteyr proposed it, you would be livid.*

True. Then again, Alisteyr wouldn't be careful. She would be.

40

DAVID ANNANDALE

She waited until the sound of the horses had almost faded away. Then she dropped down from the tree and followed.

The path curved around the southern end of Ghaunthook, eventually intersecting with the Korvas Road. It kept going, heading deeper into rarely frequented woods, until it reached a stone bridge across the Ghaunt. The bridge was not just disused. It was shunned. There had been no repairs made in a century, but its initial construction had been solid. It was sound enough for someone to cross the river. There was no reason for anyone to do so here. The path on the other side led nowhere, except past the old cemetery, and onward to the blasted shell of Forgrym Castle.

Latanna listened to the hollow sound of hooves on stone. She shook her head, angry with herself, and kept following. The sun, still high in the sky, gave her the courage to keep going. She would not, she told herself, have let her curiosity drag her this far at night. She wondered if Elgin and his men were stupid enough to take this route then. She rather hoped they were, and would again soon.

For now, though, her need to know more pulled her along. Anything she could learn about Elgin might be something she could use against him.

Once she was sure the horsemen were far enough ahead of her, she crossed the bridge, keeping to the middle of the span. There were big gaps in the sides where stones had fallen into the steady current of the Ghaunt. On the eastern bank, the path wound uphill. On the left was the forest. To the right, the wall of the old cemetery. The sun beat steadily against the brickwork. It was a hot day, unseasonal for the fall, but the wall was cold. It rejected the warmth of the sun. It breathed against Latanna's arms, and the cold sank fangs into her skin. She kept her eyes focused on the path, grateful that the wall was too high to see over, and hurried as fast as she could through the patches of shadow where the trees reached over the path, grasping for the wall and what it kept on the other side.

Don't do this, Alisteyr, she thought. The protection of Kanstuhn and Memory seemed paltry now. *We'll think of another solution. Don't let my father kill you. For the sake of all the gods, don't die for me.*

41

THE SLEEP OF EMPIRES

Somewhere up ahead, a man laughed. The sound jolted her from her thoughts. Her hate of the Hawkesmoores, and what they meant for her future, rushed needed warmth through her veins. She hurried forward, and soon the path left the cemetery behind.

The ground continued to rise. The forest thinned, until at last the terrain became barren. Latanna paused at the edge of the woods, looking up the stony rise to Forgrym Castle. Elgin and his men had gone inside the ruined walls. Latanna waited several minutes, scanning the ramparts for a guard. She saw no one. Boisterous laughter came from inside the castle. There were no guards, then, because either Elgin did not believe anyone was following, or did not care if they were.

Latanna hesitated a few moments more, conscious of the risk. *If this goes wrong, I'm going to be very upset about my own stupidity.*

In the end, her hate for Elgin and his arrogance won out. *You don't care if anyone knows what you're doing, you bastard? Maybe you should.* She left the cover of trees and ran up the slope, making for a point on the wall a dozen yards from the gate. She crouched low, beside a gaping hole in the ruins. She waited for her breath to slow, and her heart to stop hammering, so she could hear if anyone was approaching. When no one did, she slowly straightened, then looked around the edge of the hole.

Forgrym Castle had been completely gutted on the night the two families fell. Only the shell of the outer walls remained of the fortress. They were blackened and slowly rotting, their outlines softened by storm and wind. The shell was cracked in numerous places, and the gates were rusting fragments. The walls were no barrier to anything anymore. Beyond the wall, virtually no trace of the buildings remained. There were mounds where rubble had been covered over with dirt, and with what grew in the former grounds.

Inside the walls, the land was as rich as the terrain outside was empty. Latanna stared. On the low hill that once had been the keep, fists to his waist, Elgin turned back and forth, his coat swaying, the lord of all he surveyed.

He surveyed an immense crop of cloudblossom.

DAVID ANNANDALE

The stems, knee-high to a man, swayed back and forth, though there was barely any breeze. The flowers, which gave the plant its name, were huge, round, and white. They looked insubstantial as fog, too delicate to retain their shape, and were beautiful in a mocking, sickly sense. Latanna instinctively held her breath. The blooms looked as if they were ready to float into the air and spread into white, choking tendrils. Rationally, she knew they would not. The blooms had to be compressed, treated until they were a tight wad soaked in its combustible oils. Elgin and his men walked through the midst of the crop, unconcerned, though she noted that they all wore gloves, and were being careful not to handle the plants.

The stems leaned in closely when the men passed, brushing the blossoms against trousers. A few of the men kept trying to jerk away from the touch of the flowers, but there was nowhere for them to go. The cloudblossom formed an unbroken carpet of menacing white from wall to wall of the castle's shell.

Elgin showed no anxiety around the blossoms. His posture was that of a man delighted. Latanna thought he should be. She had never heard of a crop so huge. The poison of cloudblossom was extremely concentrated. The product of just two plants, spread over time, would have been enough to enslave and kill the likes of poor Veschel. An immense fortune surrounded Elgin. The youngest of the Hawkesmoores had established his own source of wealth.

"So?" Elgin shouted, laughing. "So, Dawun? What do you say now?"

"I'm surprised," said a man walking along the base of Elgin's hill. It was hard for Latanna to tell his age from this distance, but he seemed a bit older than the other men-at-arms. "I didn't think it would spread this fast. What did you do?"

"Nothing!" Elgin clapped his hands. "Nothing! I just saw what there was to see, that's all. I saw how fast the plants were growing in this earth. Give them time, I thought. That's all they need. And now look!"

Dawun did. "Incredible," he said. He sounded uneasy. "But why do they do so well here?"

43

THE SLEEP OF EMPIRES

"Isn't it obvious?" said Elgin. "The ground is tainted. Perhaps not as badly as the cemetery, but enough."

The other men stopped celebrating now. Their initial enthusiasm for the obvious riches of the plantation faded at Elgin's words.

"Should we be here?" one of the men asked.

"Are you planning on taking up the cloud?" said Elgin.

The man shuddered. "No."

"Then you can be here." He started down the slope. "I've spent a night here. I live still."

There was some laughter. It sounded forced.

"All right," said Elgin. "We'll leave." He bent toward one of the plants, studying it. "What do you say, Dawun? Another week to maturity? A month at the most?"

"I would think so, yes."

"Get used to being here, then," Elgin told the others. "There will be work to do. Workers to oversee."

Latanna withdrew before they mounted their horses. She hurried back down the hill, into the trees, and along the path. Though the cold of the cemetery reached for her again when she passed its wall, she barely noticed the chill this time. Her thoughts roiled with hate.

Stop him, stop him, stop him. The words pounded through her mind with the beat of her footsteps.

Stop him, stop him, stop him.

For the first time in her life, she began to consider what the best tactic would be to have a man killed.

Alisteyr arrived at the old cemetery with Kanstuhn and Memory in late afternoon. The sun cast shadows at a sharp angle, and its light became brittle as soon as they passed through the gate. Alisteyr paused on the other side of the wall. He looked up at the weakened sun, and the reality of what he was undertaking finally began to sink in.

DAVID ANNANDALE

"Should we be doing this now?" he asked Kanstuhn. "It wouldn't be better in the morning?" It had taken him more hours than he would have liked to prepare, and he knew he looked like a child playing a game next to the other two. His sword had come down through the generations of Hueslands. Though the last person to use it had been his grandfather, he and his father had taken good care of it. It was polished, it was sharp, and it felt heavy in its scabbard. When he had flourished the sword before strapping it to his side, it had felt like someone else's weapon. The leathers he had donned for armor looked silly next to Memory's. They were oiled, ancient, more ornamental than practical. They belonged on a wall, not in the field.

"Watch, watch, watch," Kanstuhn was saying to Memory. To Alisteyr he said, "Where we are going, it is always night." He shrugged at the waning afternoon. "This will suffice to get us there."

"Good," said Alisteyr. "That's good." He had no intention of backing down. But he really did not want to die. As long as Kanstuhn was satisfied with how things were going, he would take courage from that.

He looked ahead at the expanse of the cemetery before them. *This is what you've always wanted*, he thought. *Marsen and his games don't matter. You're going to prove who you are to yourself and to Latanna.*

They had entered the gate in the middle of the southern wall. To Alisteyr's left and right, and on the slope ahead, the graveyard spread out. Monuments, gravestones, and vaults crowded in on each other. The stones leaned drunkenly, many half-sunken into the soft earth. The instability of the ground had toppled monuments. Obelisks lay on the crushed roofs of vaults, and broken statues had rolled down the hill. Dismembered arms pointed at nothing.

"A large cemetery for a small village," said Kanstuhn.

"Ghaunthook is old," Alisteyr told him. "And it's smaller than it used to be." He grimaced. "The war between our two *great* families saw to that."

Kanstuhn nodded. "May I see the map?"

THE SLEEP OF EMPIRES

Alisteyr hesitated for a moment, feeling he should be the one to lead the way forward. Then he reminded himself once more that he did not want to die. From inside his coat he produced the rough map Marsen had sketched for him.

"Watch, watch, watch," Kanstuhn murmured to Memory. He examined the map, then looked out at the cemetery. He smiled thinly. "Marsen Forgrym does not want your task to be an easy one," he said.

"I'm sure he doesn't. What is it? Do you think he lied?"

"Lied? No. I don't think so. Your families were the greatest in Ghaunthook, yes?"

They still are, Alisteyr almost said. He flushed with shame at the impulse. It was that misplaced pride that kept wars going long after the battlefield had been destroyed. "Yes," he said.

"Then their tombs will be grand. Hard to hide." Kanstuhn held the map out and pointed upslope and to the left. "Do you see where there appear to be many vaults close together?"

Alisteyr nodded. He could just make out what looked like a cluster of peaked roofs surmounted by the crossed weapons of Tetriwu.

"I will say that is a single tomb," Kanstuhn went on. "It is in the right location." He slapped the map. "The path Forgrym has drawn is not direct. He would have you take many paths on the way there. They invite confusion."

Alisteyr looked at the drawing and tried to compare the winding route on it with the reality of the cemetery. Had he been here alone, he would have been immediately reduced to guesswork about the turns he was supposed to take. "Can you follow this route?"

"I can. Do you wish me to? Do you trust the guidance of Marsen Forgrym?"

Alisteyr snorted. "I trust his enmity. Nothing else."

Kanstuhn gave him back the map. "Then we will be more direct, yes?"

"Yes."

DAVID ANNANDALE

They moved deeper into the graveyard. The light became even more brittle, until it seemed like it should snap at any moment and plunge the land into night. The air grew colder. A breeze, clammy as a dead man's hand, pressed against Alisteyr's face. He walked on a path of broken cobbles, thick with moss. In the corners of his eyes, he kept seeing movement, the tombstones leaning forward to fall against him. Wherever he looked directly, though, they were motionless. And there were other things flickering at the edges of his vision.

"Do you see . . ." he began.

"I do," said Kanstuhn. "They do not attack."

"So there is no danger?"

"Not yet."

"Oh." Alisteyr felt his face drop.

Kanstuhn saw, and added, "Be reassured." He nodded at Memory. "He is vigilant."

Alisteyr realized that Kanstuhn had stopped whispering to Memory to watch. The huge sell-sword was alert, his head moving back and forth slowly as he scanned the cemetery, his blade in hand. It disturbed Alisteyr to consider that the threat was so omnipresent, so continuous, that Memory did not need to be told what to do. But he had no doubt, looking at the sell-sword's stony focus, that nothing could take them by surprise.

Marsen's sketch had called for Alisteyr to take a long detour to the right before moving further upslope. Kanstuhn led them on a zigzagging diagonal route toward the Forgrym monuments. He took short paths left and forward, sticking where possible to the wider avenues between the tombs, but plunging down the narrower ones if they offered the chance of reducing the length of the journey. The vaults grew taller and pressed in closer. Their doorways were gaping maws, and Alisteyr realized that they were the source of the cemetery's wind. It emerged from behind the locked grates and the dark archways. It rose from beneath the ground, a faint whisper from each individual tomb, merging into a vast choir. The wind held back its full

47

THE SLEEP OF EMPIRES

force, waiting for the proper moment to become a scream. For now, it contented itself with swirling around Alisteyr, wrapping him in the cold and damp, whispering threats and promises that he could not quite understand.

Kanstuhn must have noticed the frightened concentration on his face. "You must not listen," the kaul said.

"I don't want to."

"Then do not. If you listen, you might understand. That will be harmful."

"Then I won't." He tried to distract himself by humming under his breath. No tune would come, but the effort to make any noise at all took his focus away from the whispers. Still they did not leave him alone, and the deeper into the cemetery they went, the more insistent the wind's voice became.

It took less than half an hour to make the winding journey to the Forgrym tombs. Alisteyr looked for the sun. It was only just visible over the high roofs of the vaults. He would soon lose sight of it, and surely, then, there would be nothing to keep the daylight from cracking like thin ice.

With an effort, he forced himself to examine the mausoleum.

What had appeared, from a distance, to be many vaults close together were clusters of spires on the roof of the mausoleum. The building was huge, more than a hundred yards long on each side. Where so many of the other monuments were tilting to one side or another, the mausoleum's walls rose perfectly straight, though the structure had sunk into the earth. All but one of the steps leading to the entrance had been swallowed by mud and moss. The masonry was cracked and stained. The Forgrym coat of arms surmounted the doorway, three pikes in the center of a field. The carving had been eroded to the point that it was just three vague scratches in emptiness. At some point in the past, someone had surrounded the mausoleum with a massive chain, as if trying to imprison a dangerous animal.

Kanstuhn examined the padlock before the door. It was as large as Alisteyr's head.

DAVID ANNANDALE

"Can you unlock it?" Alisteyr asked.

"Likely. The better question is whether we should wish to. This chain has a purpose." Kanstuhn sniffed the air. "This is a bad place. But it may grow worse if we remove the chain. What walks these grounds is contained by the walls, yes?"

Alisteyr nodded. "As far as I know." At the very least, the cemetery's contamination did not reach Ghaunthook itself. He would not be able to live with himself if, by his actions, he brought harm to the town. And he would not be able to face Latanna's eyes. "Is there another way in?"

Kanstuhn examined the southward façade of the mausoleum. He pointed at the stained glass windows, almost all of them broken. The chain did not cover the apertures, and they looked just large enough for Memory to pass through. "There," he said. "We can enter and leave without breaking a barrier."

The kaul moved to the nearest window and scrabbled up the wall like a lizard, grabbing handholds Alisteyr could barely see, and propelling himself upward after resting his feet on the chain. He crouched in the window, peering inside. He nodded, apparently satisfied. He looked back at Memory, said, "Come," and jumped down into the tomb. Memory followed. Alisteyr was startled by the grace of the huge mercenary. Where Kanstuhn had moved in quick jerks, Memory seemed to flow up the wall, the pack of supplies he carried weightless. He disappeared inside. There was a murmur from Kanstuhn, and Memory returned to the window, holding out an arm for Alisteyr.

Alisteyr stepped forward, his throat dry. *Here we go*, he thought as he took Memory's hand. *Now we are committed. Now we cannot go back.*

The wind whispered, *Ever.*

Memory lifted him up and over the sill.

Alisteyr found himself inside a chapel to Tetriwu. It was large enough to have held several score mourners, and Alisteyr pictured the pomp of internments as they must have been at the height of the families' power. He wondered if the Huesland vaults were as grand, then pushed the thought

49

THE SLEEP OF EMPIRES

aside. He didn't care. The grandeur that had been was responsible for the horror this cemetery had become.

Massive candles, coated in dust, perched on iron candelabra on the periphery of the chapel. Kanstuhn took one, lit it with the flint he produced from the pouch hanging from his belt. He walked around the hall, lighting the other candles. When he was done, the shadows seemed even darker for having been pushed back to the corners.

Kanstuhn handed the candle to Alisteyr. "You will keep this," he said. "Bring light wherever you can. Where there are torches or candles, do not ignore them."

"I understand," said Alisteyr. *This, at least, I can do.* He turned around, taking in the temple and its stone pews. "Where do we go?" He saw no other door except the exit.

Kanstuhn brought him and Memory to the western end of the chapel. He pointed to the base of a marble slab that Alisteyr had taken to be the altar. There were depressions in the floor along the edge of the slab, and an arc of scratches leading away from the southwest corner of the stone. "Our door," said the kaul. "Push," he said to Memory, pointing to the slab.

Memory put his shoulder against it. The slab ground back with a harsh scrape of stone against stone, though its movement was smooth. It revealed a staircase descending into darkness.

"What you seek will be down below," Kanstuhn said.

Somehow, the statement of the obvious did not strike Alisteyr as superfluous. It felt more like a ritual. "Yes," he said nodding. "What we seek always is, isn't it?"

The kaul smiled his death's head smile. "It is the way of things," he said, and started down the stairs.

CHAPTER 5

Skiriye ne Sincatsë did not see the first few reports of Pilta's absences. Those were filed by his tutors, and had no bearing on her duties as librarian. She noticed, in passing, that he was not present in the book stacks, and saw this as a further failing on his part, another way in which he fell criminally short of perfection. Had he been serious about redemption, he would not have let his wounds interfere with his research. He would have been here, shouldering the responsibilities of injury and duty. Skiriye had a lifetime of experience with both. She had no time for such weaknesses as Pilta's, and she dismissed him from her thoughts.

But the reports of absenteeism accumulated. They reached the critical number to trigger a disciplinary report, and when it arrived on Skiriye's desk, it held her attention.

"Librarian Sincatsë?" Paruwa ne Ek asked. "You seem troubled."

Skiriye looked up at her assistant, then back down at the report. "Pilta ne Akwatse has not attended lectures since receiving his punishment," Skiriye said.

"Malingering?" Paruwa asked, spitting the word.

"I think that is unlikely." Pilta would have incurred a far greater punishment. The cumulative penalty for missing all of his classes would have been lethal in his weakened state.

"What does he think he's doing? He's only making things worse for himself."

He would be, Skiriye thought, *if he were here*. She stared at the list of absences, and felt a stirring of alarm. Pilta was impoverished. It would have to be more than pain that kept him away from the university. For the likes of him, there would have to be a profit motive. And if that motive was enough to make him vanish altogether, then the profit would have to be a

THE SLEEP OF EMPIRES

considerable one. It would have to outweigh, at least in appearances, his prospects if he continued his studies.

"He said he was here to do more reading," she muttered. Then, her eyes widening, the alarm becoming full-blown, she said, "No. No. *I* said that was why he trespassed. He just didn't contradict me." She thought back to her interview with Pilta, seeing now that he had never actually said why he had been in the library in the middle of the night. He had let her come to her own conclusions. He hadn't even had to lie. She had done it for him. He had told her nothing but verifiable truth. Indifferent student that he was, his skills in deception had their own ring of perfection.

So what was he doing? How might he profit from being in the library when he should not?

Skiriye's alarm became anger. She would have whipped Pilta to death if he had been before her. Because he was not, she turned her anger on herself. She should have known. She should have seen through him.

"Librarian?" Paruwa asked again, his voice cracking as he saw Skiriye's growing fury.

"I want an inventory of our holdings," Skiriye said. "A complete one."

Paruwa blinked. "Of course, Librarian. By what date do you hope to complete—"

"Within three days."

Paruwa's jaw sagged open.

"I will dictate a letter that you will take to the chairs of every discipline in the university. I will need the labor of all students until the task is completed." There were thousands upon thousands of volumes on the shelves. It would take an army to inventory them in three days. So she would commandeer that army. "I suspect a theft," she said.

"Could he have been that foolish?"

"He was anything but foolish. We have suspected nothing until now and he has been gone for a week. I want him found," she said, doubting very much that this desire would be met. "And I want to know what he stole." That goal, at least, she could enforce.

52

DAVID ANNANDALE

Paruwa took her letter, and the University of Árkiriye went to war. The students arrived in massed ranks in the library, and each was given a section of the shelves to verify. The legions swarmed over the stacks, and Skiriye walked among them, her cane tapping her impatience against the floor, reminding the students of her presence. Pilta had caused her wrath, but he was not here. They did not wish to suffer in his stead.

They completed the inventory in two and a half days.

There were no books missing.

As evening fell on the third day, Skiriye and Paruwa lingered in her office, going over the compiled records, searching for what had been overlooked, and finding nothing.

"He must have stolen something," said Paruwa. "We found him in the library."

Skiriye froze. She saw the second level of Pilta's deception. "He let us find him," she said.

"I don't understand."

"He let us find him where we did so we would not look elsewhere."

The blood drained from Paruwa's face. "By the hand of Passomo, he wouldn't have dared."

"You don't think so? Having dared this much? And what would have been worth the risks?" Now that she saw clearly, none of the books in the open shelves would have been a sufficient prize. He could have sold them for a fine profit, but not one to justify gambling with his life.

But below, in the crypt . . .

Skiriye opened the drawer of her desk. The key was where it had always been. She wracked her brain, trying to think if Pilta could have taken it, and replaced it, that night. After a moment she stood, snatching up the key. How Pilta might have accomplished a theft didn't matter. What did was what he had stolen.

"Wait for my return," Skiriye told Paruwa, and left the office.

As she made her way to the crypt, she thought ahead to her inevitable interrogation at the hands of the Most Perfect Council. They would ask

53

THE SLEEP OF EMPIRES

about the key. They would ask about safeguards. Access to the crypt was not forbidden to scholars, she could argue. It was merely controlled. Until today, the idea that someone would find it worth their lives to risk stealing one of those books would have been preposterous. Such a thief would have to be desperate and stupid.

Evidently, Pilta was both.

And her defenses were imperfect. That her procedures were known to, and unquestioned by, the other authorities in the university was not an excuse. What remained for her to do was to learn what she could that might repair the damage.

She did not allow herself the illusory hope that nothing had been stolen. She had no time for illusions. She had never had. The capacity for illusion had been taken from her at birth along with her foot.

She knew the stories the students told about her accident. The tales flourished, with new ones sprouting every year. The uncertainty suited her. It kept the rumors far from the truth, and since her parents had both died in the last border war with Wiramzin, more than two centuries ago, she was the only person who knew the truth.

The foot had not been lost in an accident. Her father had cut it off with his sword.

She had been born with the foot deformed, and her parents had decided she would be spared. Pride had driven the choice, not mercy or love, and it was one that she understood completely. Had she been able, she would have urged her parents to the same action. Her mother had a seat on the Most Perfect Council, which would have been jeopardized if it had become known that she had given birth to an imperfect child. The family's name would have been sullied, forever diminished no matter how generous their restitution tithes to Passomo, no matter how many perfect children might follow. Her parents preserved their names with the amputation. They took no chances, and had no further children. They kept her wound hidden during her infancy, and then created the story of an accident once she began to walk. She did not know how they had contrived to

DAVID ANNANDALE

make the story so vague yet so convincing, but she admired the perfection of the achievement.

Her task now would be to preserve the honor of the family name by doing what she could to correct her error.

Skiriye unlocked the door to the crypt and descended the stairs. The task she faced was immense. She would not sleep until it was complete.

She could not send an army of students into the crypt. The full records of the holdings were for the librarian's eyes only, and those records had their limits. There were many books here that no one had read since they had been written, and many that no one *could* read. There was no quick way to find what had gone missing. But every day that passed compounded her error, so she began with a visual inspection.

The shelves were crowded. No books were permitted to leave the crypt. If she saw a gap between books, that was where she would focus her attention. She began to walk, slowly, between the stacks, running her gaze up and down their heights, not taking a step until she was satisfied she had missed nothing within the reach of her arms.

Hours passed. Her eyes burned and her head throbbed with the effort. Several times she had to stop and rest until her vision cleared. Shortly before dawn, she saw a gap that was not at the end of a shelf.

Skiriye crouched. She ran a finger back and forth across the empty space. *What did you take, you wretch?* The stone shelf was cold to her touch, too cold. The thought seized her that she felt the lingering power of the absent book. She snatched her hand away, her concern mounting. She was less worried now about the impact of the theft on the library than on the world outside. No book was consigned to the crypt without good reason.

Skiriye returned to her office. She found Paruwa slumped over in his chair where he had been all night. She had forgotten him, but he had obeyed her command to wait. He jerked awake when she entered and stood, eyes blinking away sleep. "Did you find anything, Librarian?" he asked.

"I did. Leave me for now, but return in an hour. I will have messages for you to deliver."

THE SLEEP OF EMPIRES

"To the university council?"

"And to the Most Perfect Council."

Paruwa did his best to hide his fear as he stumbled out of the office.

Skiriye unlocked a large drawer in her desk and removed the heavy volume it contained. She leafed through the pages, running her hands down the columns until she found the entry for the position where the stolen book had been. She frowned. There was no title, no description, no provenance. There was only the record to acknowledge that the book existed. Many of the other entries said little about the books beyond their titles and their provenance. Anyone seeking a particular book would already have to know something about its nature and what it contained. But at least there were titles. Skiriye stared at the entry, seeing another absence, as if the book's disappearance had wiped its memory from the catalogue too.

The less recorded about a book, the more of a threat the work must be. The knowledge of what it contained must be extremely restricted. Skiriye could conceive of the possibility that *no one* knew what was written in its pages. She did not like to imagine something so dangerous, a book whose ideas were so terrible they must never be known, but whose power somehow also prevented their destruction.

The risk of having such a book out in the world was monstrous, and she would have to bear the responsibility for its escape.

Skiriye tapped the entry's page absently, thinking through the paths open to her. There were ways in which the worse the threat was, the greater her opportunity for action. She reconsidered her initial approach. She would do more than sound the alarm.

When Paruwa returned, she knew what she needed to do.

"What messages do you wish me to send, Librarian?" he asked.

"There will be a report for the university," Skiriye said. "That can wait. Write first to the Most Perfect Council. I would request an audience."

The book should not have been consigned to the library's crypt. It should have been secured absolutely, or destroyed. She could use these facts

DAVID ANNANDALE

to pry loose more, and from there expand her range of possible actions. She would attack before she needed to defend.

They descended the stairs into the depths of the mausoleum. Alisteyr lit every torch he saw and took one to carry. The act felt both trivial and reassuring. Taking care of light while he trusted others to do the fighting didn't feel like the behavior of a hero of myth. It did, though, feel like a way to stay alive.

Kanstuhn and Memory descended with their blades drawn. Kanstuhn's step was so light, he barely seemed to touch the stairs. Memory also walked without sound, moving with surprising grace.

At the bottom of the staircase, they found themselves in a long vault. Floor-to-ceiling alcoves contained the stone coffins of the Forgryms, the names of the dead engraved over each alcove. Archways ahead and on the right and left opened into more chambers. The air was dank, and the walls glistened in the torchlight. When Alisteyr breathed in, it seemed like gossamer worms reached into his lungs. The taste of wet ashes coated his tongue. He ran his eyes over the names, hoping that Elisava might be here, and the search would be done quickly.

She was not.

Kanstuhn glanced quickly into each of the other chambers. "Empty, empty," he said to Memory. He paused at the far one. The glow from the central vault showed scorch marks around the doorway. "Risk."

Alisteyr was about to ask why they didn't search for Elisava's tomb in the other vaults first. Maybe they wouldn't have to deal with the third. He thought better of it when he saw the concentration on Kanstuhn's face. The kaul was concerned first with survival, and guarding against possible danger. The search would come after.

They entered the damaged vault. It showed the scars of an explosion. Fire had blackened the walls, and the alcoves had collapsed onto one another. Shattered coffins spilled bone fragments onto the floor, which had buckled

THE SLEEP OF EMPIRES

upward from the blast. Some of the engraved names were still visible, but only just.

The floor had heaved upward most violently at the base of the left-hand wall. The rubble rose like a wave, and on the other side of its crest, a shaft dropped into darkness. A slumped alcove hung over the edge of the abyss like a severed upper jaw. The inscription had been largely obliterated by the explosion, but Alisteyr could just make out the beginning of the name he was seeking. Elisava's coffin was gone. The bottom of the alcove had collapsed into the shaft.

"Do you think Marsen Forgrym knew?" Kanstuhn asked.

"No," said Alisteyr. "I can't imagine he's been here. No one comes to the cemetery. It's too dangerous." *That's why he sent me here. He expects me to die.* The reality of the cemetery had stripped away his illusions of heroism, leaving him with the cold truth of Latanna's logic. He was so grateful for Kanstuhn and Memory's company that he felt ill.

They examined the shaft. It descended further than the light of the torch could reach.

"Rope," Kanstuhn said to Memory. "Rope, rope, rope."

Memory obeyed, pulling a length out of his pack and making it fast around a jagged stone at the lip of the drop. He tossed the other end down the shaft. Alisteyr listened for the impact, but heard nothing.

"It isn't long enough," he said.

"Perhaps not," said Kanstuhn. He took another torch from Memory's pack, lit it, and dropped it into the dark.

The torch fell for a long time. Alisteyr's knees weakened with terror. At last came the thunk and echo of an impact. Alisteyr stared at the tiny, distant glow. He could not tell how far away the bottom was from the end of the rope. "Isn't there another way?" he asked.

"No," said Kanstuhn, and Alisteyr felt a new surge of gratitude, because the kaul was calm and not contemptuous. "You did not expect this to be simple."

"No." Alisteyr managed a smile. "But I did hope."

58

DAVID ANNANDALE

Kanstuhn smiled back, briefly, then turned to Memory. "Descend," he said, and once Memory was on his way, Kanstuhn followed.

"Is the rope strong enough?" Alisteyr worried.

"Yes. You follow too," Kanstuhn said.

Alisteyr shuddered, but the thought of being left alone in the crypt was worse than the anxiety of the fall. He took the rope, swallowed the fear that it would slip through his sweaty palms, and began a slow, clumsy, swaying climb down.

He could not stop thinking about falling. The rope jerked with the movements of Kanstuhn and Memory as if it were trying to throw him off. Alisteyr gripped it like death and climbed down one agonized hand-width at a time.

There was a crash of a heavy weight onto stone, and the rope began to swing more freely.

"What is it?" Alisteyr shouted. "What happened?"

"All is well," Kanstuhn called. "Memory is down. Keep coming."

Down? Alisteyr thought. *How far did he have to drop to make a sound like that?* He didn't look. He stared at the dark stone before him, black as hard night. He kept going. Gradually, he began to make out details in the stone. He had descended into the glow of torches once more.

The rope jerked again. There was another sound of a body landing, but softer this time. "All is well," Kanstuhn said again before Alisteyr could ask. "Pay attention. Look down. You are almost there."

Alisteyr tried to swallow the broken glass in his throat. He looked down. He could see the bottom now. Kanstuhn and Memory were standing there, waiting for him. The rope stopped about ten feet above Memory's head.

Alisteyr's eyes bulged. He clenched the rope tighter. "I can't . . ." he rasped. *How did Memory survive that fall unhurt?*

"Come to the end and let yourself drop," said Kanstuhn. "Memory will catch you."

"I don't . . . I don't know . . . I . . ." Words tangled and died.

THE SLEEP OF EMPIRES

"He caught me. I am well. You will be well. All is well."

Kanstuhn spoke to Alisteyr with the same calming cadence and repetition he used with Memory. Alisteyr let the rhythms embrace him. He looked away from the ground, descended a few more handwidths, looked back down and up again, then kept going until his feet were a few inches above the end of the rope. He swayed gently back and forth above the floor, a pendulum weight.

Too far. Too far.

"Let go now," said Kanstuhn.

"I can't."

"Can't? All you need do is nothing. Let the rope go."

Alisteyr stared at the wall ahead of him one more time, and opened his hands. The moment of his fall was a sickening eternity. Then something grabbed him, hard, arresting his fall, bringing him to a stop with a sharp jerk. Memory put him down.

Alisteyr kept his footing. He held on to that much dignity, thanks to Memory. *I didn't scream*, he thought. *There's that too.*

Kanstuhn walked in slow, careful circles with the torch, studying the space. They were in a square chamber of modest size, with a doorway in the south wall. The explosion appeared to have originated from a mound of rubble in the center of the room. Alisteyr searched the rubble for the body of Elisava and the tiara. He found nothing but pieces of the shattered coffin. "Where is she?" he said.

"Taken, perhaps," said Kanstuhn.

"By whom?"

The kaul shrugged.

"It doesn't seem possible," said Alisteyr.

"Many things don't," Kanstuhn said, implying he had seen a fair number of impossibilities in his time.

"Perhaps the explosion destroyed the body."

"Let us hope not."

DAVID ANNANDALE

Memory prowled the periphery of the room, blade unsheathed, face blank but eyes alert. Kanstuhn did not need to remind him to be wary. It was as if a sense of danger was imposing itself upon him, moment by moment.

Kanstuhn pointed to the walls. Their brickwork was fine, smaller than in the vault above. "The construction is different," he said. "This is not part of the same structure."

Memory stopped at the doorway. He froze, a faint quiver running down his frame.

Kanstuhn approached him. "Threat?" the kaul asked.

Memory stepped through the doorway, into the hall beyond. He walked like a wolf about to strike.

Following Kanstuhn's example, Alisteyr drew his sword too and approached the doorway. He felt like a child at play, a hindrance to Memory and Kanstuhn. He should not have come. He should have paid the sellswords and left them to it.

Memory cocked his head. "What . . . ?" Alisteyr began, but Kanstuhn held up a hand. Alisteyr listened. He heard a faint, rhythmic scuffling and tapping. He looked a question at Kanstuhn, who shook his head.

They moved down the hall, and now Alisteyr realized where they were. The walls were modest brickwork, plaster still clinging in patches. On his right, a wood-framed window looked out onto solid rock. "This is a house," he whispered.

Kanstuhn nodded.

It made no sense, yet Alisteyr knew he was right. The chapel they had left behind was small, a modest chamber for an unexceptional home.

Unexceptional other than the fact that it was buried more than fifty feet beneath a cemetery.

The rhythmic sound came from a chamber that opened off the far end of the hall. As they drew closer, Alisteyr made out a whispered, keening rasp, the sound of the last notes of despair before death, endlessly drawn out. Madness and grief entwined, and now that he heard the dusty cry, it

THE SLEEP OF EMPIRES

reached into his heart, filling him with a mournful terror. He did not want to see what grieved, but it pulled him forward, as distant yet as certain as death.

He didn't realize he was walking faster until Kanstuhn grabbed him, holding him back. But the kaul was struggling against the undertow of the wail too. It grew louder as they drew nearer, and then both of them were stumbling past Memory to the entrance of the chamber.

The space looked as if it had once been a small temple. The floor was circular, and the walls curved up to form a perfect hemisphere of a dome. In the center of the room was an altar, also circular. Around it, the wailing skeleton of Elisava Forgrym spun.

Only a few dry, moldering strips of flesh still clung to her bones. Her grave clothes were a dress, a wedding gown as gray and tattered as the remaining flesh. It flowed like billowing veils around her as she danced. On her head was the tiara of gold and silver. It flashed so brilliantly in the torchlight, it seemed to be the true source of light in the chamber.

Elisava's whirling dance took her around and around the altar, arms outstretched, skull tilted back and jaws wide in ecstatic grief. She gave voice to pain that rose and fell and twisted into a song more dreadful than a scream. The song repulsed. It made Alisteyr's flesh crawl, yet it held him fast in its grip. It commanded all who heard it to join in the mourning.

Alisteyr staggered into the room, dragged in by the whirlpool current of the wail. The skeleton's head snapped upright and the corpse spun toward him. Fingernails, long as claws, sliced into his armor. The leather rotted instantly, crumbling away to leave his chest exposed. He tried to raise his sword to protect himself, but his arm wouldn't move. The wail held him still.

Beside him, Kanstuhn trembled, as transfixed as he was.

Elisava turned again, the steps of her dance rapid and complex. Her hand came around, reaching for his flesh.

62

DAVID ANNANDALE

Memory stormed past him and hurled himself into the skeleton. The impact knocked Elisava back against the altar. Her keening turned into a shriek of anger. She flipped up onto the altar with a spider's speed and grace. She slashed at Memory with both hands, the strikes a blur of motion. His leathers rotted, and the corpse's nails cut through his skin. The line of a wound appeared, but no blood, and his flesh did not decompose.

With the rhythm of the wail disrupted, Alisteyr felt his will returning to him. His arms remained locked to his side, but he could shuffle his feet slightly, and he inched his way back toward the doorway.

The skeleton seized Memory, lifted the huge sell-sword into the air, and threw him across the chamber. He hit the rear wall hard enough to snap a man's spine. Memory just grunted in anger and got to his feet.

Elisava flew through the air at him, a screaming bird of prey. She clawed at him again. She dragged her nails down his face, once again leaving lines where the flesh was cut, but no other sign of a wound. He swung at the skull with his blade. The sword connected, but did no damage. The skeleton grabbed Memory and threw him again. Elisava leapt, gown flowing behind as if in a strong wind, and landed on Memory before he could rise.

The dead thing screamed and screamed and screamed, shredding his armor and slashing madly at flesh that refused to rot. Memory grappled with it. The skeleton ignored his blows, pursuing the attack with furious purpose.

Memory shot a hand up and grabbed the tiara. There was a sharp crack as he yanked at it. A blue-white flash filled the chamber. Alisteyr saw nothing but a dazzling pulse for several moments. Behind the light, he heard Memory cry out, and the skeleton's shriek hit a frenzied pitch of terror.

The light faded. Memory held the tiara, fragments of skull clinging to its base.

Elisava was frozen in mid attack. Her wail faded to a brittle whine. Memory brought his massive fist against the bones, and now they shattered

63

THE SLEEP OF EMPIRES

like glass. The monster collapsed in a heap of shards. The tattered gown floated gently to the ground, falling over the remains like a spider web.

Alisteyr blinked. He took a deep breath. His limbs tingled as he regained control of them. Kanstuhn gasped, and moved toward his friend.

Memory stood up, his gaze held by the tiara in his hand.

"Calm . . . calm . . . calm . . ." Kanstuhn began.

Then Memory spoke.

"How long has this waited for me?" he asked.

CHAPTER 6

All right, so far, Garwynn thought. *Nothing bad, nothing missed. The people are entertained.* On the stage that had been erected against the warehouse wall, he threw his head back and spread his arms wide to welcome the fireworks burst above the courtyard. Sparks trailed down, greeted by applause and some excited laughter.

See? All will be good.

Oh, really? You're sure?

He wasn't. His palms were slicked with sweat. His mouth went dry as the moment of truth came.

He had performed no true magic yet, only sleight of hand. He was good at it, and he sold it well enough for the audience. But sleight of hand was not magic. The difference between the two was obvious, even to those who had never witnessed the real thing. The moment of transformation was never seen. The miracles were all lies.

Yehan and Rellis stood with their families and guests of honor close to the stage. Yehan was frowning. Rellis looked amused, but Garwynn doubted he would be any more willing to pay up than his partner if Garwynn did not perform as promised. It was time to be transformative. It was time for real magic.

I can do this.

He had learned so much of what was not possible. With that knowledge had also come insight into what *could* be done. It was little enough, but it was real, and that would make all the difference.

If he managed to reach even that high.

"From the gods come everything," he intoned, projecting his voice to the far walls of the courtyard. "The gods gave us the world. They give us rain." He cupped his hands as if to catch the last of the falling sparks. "And from the rain comes growth. Yet how often does it seem that creation arises

65

THE SLEEP OF EMPIRES

from nothing?" He had rehearsed the speech often enough that the words came automatically, and he had to work to speak them as if this were the first time. But the question at the end suddenly felt fresh, imbued with meaning he did not understand. In the time it took him to draw a breath and gather his strength, he wondered if he should stop now.

Yehan was waiting for him to fail.

So Garwynn didn't stop. He focused on his cupped hands. He whispered too softly for the spectators to hear, but they would see his lips move, and think he was casting a spell. The syllables he uttered were not words, though. They were tools, fragments of shaped sound that focused his concentration. The words were a dowsing rod, pointing his mind toward the rare seams of magic that still coursed through the suffocating mundanity of the world.

He tapped into the ancient strength, and creation arose from nothing.

Light blossomed just above his cupped hands. It began as the red of sunrise, and brightened into a gold so bright it turned the courtyard into day. The ball of light spun. Eddies gathered, grew stronger, and became defined. The sphere took on form. Petals peeled away from the center. A stem descended to Garwynn's palms. The flower stretched in a delicacy of exhilaration.

Yehan's eyes had gone wide. The wonder of the audience washed over Garwynn. The flower turned before him, the gold now becoming less dazzling so that the details of the creation became more visible. It was not the perfect blossom of his imagination, the flower before which all others would fade. Every wrinkle and fold of the petals were clear to him. The flower was smaller than his fist, though, and the finer details would be lost on even the nearest spectators. He wanted the blossom larger. He had never managed anything greater than what was before him now, and even then, not at every attempt. But oh, if only it would grow.

Then it did.

The petals unfurled with a sudden access of hunger and the blossom expanded. Now it was as big as his head. Then as wide as his arms could

DAVID ANNANDALE

stretch. And still it grew. The stem twisted and lengthened, turning into a vine as thick as his arm. There was a serpentine flow to its swaying movements that Garwynn didn't like. He had not imagined them. The flower was gathering a reality to itself that was beyond his control. The golden head, immense now, covered the central half of the courtyard. It nodded forward and back, left and right, a knowing bow to the people dwarfed beneath it.

Garwynn heard the shouts of awe from the crowd. He could not enjoy them. The flower had slipped its bonds. There was power in the night that he had never imagined, and he feared it.

Stop, he thought. He stepped back, dropping his hands. *Stop*. He cut himself free from the wellspring of magic and became once more entirely present in the moment. For the space of two shuddering breaths, the flower continued to grow, blazing day across entire blocks of Korvas. Then, with a sigh of fading light, it bowed once more and vanished.

His extremities going numb, Garwynn managed to advance to the front of the stage and echo the flower's bow. The muscles of his face were suddenly unfamiliar, but they obeyed his commands and he smiled. He kept up the performance of an artist humbly triumphant with the perfection of his own work through the rapturous applause. He held the smile when Yehan and Rellis came up to him.

"That," said Yehan, "was astonishing. You were modest in your promises." He clapped Garwynn hard on the back. "You're going to make a fortune!"

Rellis looked more serious. He congratulated Garwynn too, and thanked him, but he kept glancing around as if expecting the flower to return, unbidden and unwelcome. "That," he said, "was indeed transformative." He tried to laugh. "I don't think I am the same man that rose this morning."

I know I'm not, Garwynn thought.

"I had not heard," Rellis said, "that a display on that scale was even possible."

THE SLEEP OF EMPIRES

"It depends on circumstances," Garwynn lied. He shrugged, hoping modesty covered his anxiety. "You were an appreciative audience. That's always the key to a good performance."

"Once we've spread the word, you're going to have plenty of appreciative audiences," Yehan promised.

Garwynn was no longer sure he wanted them.

Memory's voice was deep and rough, as if it were shaped at once by great strength and great age. It made Alisteyr think of an echo from within a bottomless well. It sounded like night.

Alisteyr and Kanstuhn stared at Memory. When Kanstuhn finally spoke, his voice shook. "You can talk."

"I can." Memory frowned, absently turning the tiara over and over. "Is that unusual?"

"You couldn't before now. Do you know where you are?"

Memory looked around. "No."

"Do you remember anything?"

Memory shook his head.

"Do you remember what you said about the tiara a few moments ago?"

"Yes. That it has been waiting for me."

Kanstuhn laughed. It was a strange laugh, the laugh of a soul whose world has shifted suddenly and irrevocably, and, giddy with shock, embraces the change. "You may not remember anything before this chamber, but you are forming memories now." He hesitated. "Do you know me?"

"Not your name, no," said Memory. "I know you are my friend, though."

"My name is Kanstuhn. This human is Alesteyr Huesland. Has your name returned to you?"

Memory grimaced. "No."

"Perhaps it will. I have been calling you Memory, and will still, if that does not offend."

68

The gray sell-sword chuckled. "Irony," he said. "I know what that is well enough. It seems to me that I have an intimate acquaintance with it, though I can't tell you why that is. 'Memory' I will be, then, for now. So. Why are we in this place?"

"We are here in answer to this human's need," said Kanstuhn. "You hold the object we have come to find."

Memory looked down at the tiara. He frowned again, looking both troubled and curious.

"Why did you say it has been waiting for you?" Alisteyr asked.

"I don't know. I can recall the words, but not the impulse that prompted them."

"May that be the last of the past to be lost to you," said Kanstuhn. He turned to Alisteyr. "With your permission, I would be curious to examine the tiara."

"So would I," Alisteyr said, picking up the torch he had dropped while gripped by the skeleton's wail.

They gathered with Memory at the altar. The sell-sword took the torch and held it over the stone, illuminating the tiara as Kanstuhn looked at it closely, running his fingers over the detail of the carvings. It was beautiful, Alisteyr thought. The exquisite craftwork marked it as clearly more valuable than anything he had ever seen in Ghaunthook. At the same time, he felt little desire to touch it himself. It was a cold thing. He expected the metal to freeze his fingers.

The band and the crown were made from gold and silver so completely entwined that they seemed to be a single element, the reflections of light shifting between the two colors depending on the angle as Kanstuhn turned it slowly around. Another material, of a black more profound than obsidian, wove itself around the entire shape in a thread so fine that it was almost invisible. At the center of the crown was a perfectly round jewel, blood red. Its depths seized the eye and did not let go. Alisteyr felt that it was staring back at him.

THE SLEEP OF EMPIRES

"This is very old," said Kanstuhn. "I am no jeweler, but I have a passing knowledge of things that are valuable. A needed skill in our profession. I have never seen anything like this. If it has always been in the Forgrym family, then it has been there for a very long time."

"Is it safe?" That was the question that concerned Alisteyr.

"That seems doubtful, doesn't it?"

Alisteyr and Kanstuhn looked from the tiara to the dust that had been the howling corpse.

"What *was* that?" Alisteyr whispered.

"I have not encountered its like, either," said Kanstuhn. "You asked if this relic is safe. What we witnessed strongly suggests a connection between it and the creature Memory destroyed. There is power in this thing. That alone makes it dangerous."

"And I'm supposed to turn it over to Marsen Forgrym."

"A man not to be trusted with power, from what you and his daughter say."

"I wouldn't trust him with anything."

"Yet your vow binds you to delivering the relic into his hands."

"Fulfilling your vow doesn't mean the relic *stays* in his hands," Memory put in.

Kanstuhn nodded. "An important consideration." He looked at the tiara a bit longer, then offered it to Alisteyr.

Alisteyr took a step back, hands raised. "I . . . I'd rather not." The thought of touching the tiara made his skin crawl. The idea of taking it into his possession was more than he could bear.

"Understood," said Kanstuhn. He handed the tiara to Memory, who slipped it into his pack. "It is a thing of unease. As is this buried house. There is age here, of a kind that I do not understand." He looked around. "The temple of this house too," he said, and shook his head.

Alisteyr looked around at the walls, taking in their details now that the threat to his life had passed. Every surface in the temple had been carved with runes to Tetriwu. The runes were crude, the work of vandals, not arti-

70

sans, and clearly more recent than the construction of the temple. There were faint traces of older, finer carvings underneath the war god's marks. Not enough remained to tell what they were. The altar had been defaced in the same way. Alisteyr thought he could make out the faint suggestion of a circle under the violence of the chipped stone.

A thought struck him. He asked Memory to show him the tiara again. "I want another look at the jewel," he said.

With Memory holding the tiara, and Kanstuhn the torch, Alisteyr stared at the jewel. "It's engraved," he said. The marks were so fine his first glance had missed them.

Kanstuhn looked too. He jerked, startled. "Not engraved," he said. "That is filigree."

The same deep black filament that coiled through the rest of the tiara was here too. It went around the circumference of the jewel, forming a circle that had two minute breaks, one in the upper right quadrant of the ring, the other in the lower left. Now that he saw the breaks, Alisteyr's eye connected them in an invisible diagonal line cutting across the jewel. The line was a present absence, a defining yet nonexistent flaw in the jewel's face.

"Does the symbol mean anything to you?" he asked Kanstuhn.

"No."

Memory stared fixedly at the jewel. He seemed on the verge of saying something.

"You recognize it?" said Kanstuhn.

"I'm not sure. I feel I should."

"Mysteries compounded," said the kaul. "I had never imagined we would find ties to your identity in Ghaunthook."

"Ties we can't fathom," Memory said, frustrated.

"Not yet," Kanstuhn added.

It was full night when they emerged from the mausoleum. Kanstuhn led the way swiftly from the cemetery. A strong breeze slithered over the tombs,

THE SLEEP OF EMPIRES

carrying the whispers of the vaults. The voices were angry. They snarled in Alisteyr's ears. They hovered at the back of his neck. His skin prickled in the constant anticipation of the touch of a claw.

But Memory walked behind him, and the sound of his footsteps gave Alisteyr courage. He did not have to look over his shoulder, fearful of spectral faces. The sell-sword was calm, his stride sure.

Alisteyr did look back once, all the same. Memory smiled at him. In the light of the torch, his flesh was the same bleached gray as the tombs, and etched with shadow. He was a thing of the grave, but had Alisteyr under his protection. "I hear them too," Memory said. "The dead are angry because they cannot have their prey."

"I hope you're right."

The voices dropped away suddenly when they passed through the gate once more, and had the wall between them and the cemetery. Alisteyr breathed easily for the first time in hours. He finally relaxed when he saw lanterns glowing in the windows of Ghaunthook.

It was late, but not too late for the Laughing Chimera. Alisteyr couldn't face the prospect of sleep, and Kanstuhn and Memory were fully intent on saluting their success with ale.

"You know that you like the taste?" Alisteyr asked Memory.

"I do. As I know speech, and how to wield a sword."

Latanna was waiting for them at the tavern, sitting at the same corner table where the four had met before. Alisteyr's heart leapt when he saw the relief on Latanna's face.

"How long have you been here?" Alisteyr asked as they sat down.

"All evening." She grasped his arm. "I can't believe you're still alive, you glorious fool." She turned to Kanstuhn. "Thank you," she said. Then she looked puzzled. She had noticed that Kanstuhn was not placating Memory.

"It has been an eventful night," Memory said to her.

Her eyes widened. "So I see," she said after a moment.

"A successful one too," Alisteyr told her.

72

DAVID ANNANDALE

"You have the tiara? My father will be apoplectic." She grinned. "May I see it?"

Memory produced it from his pack. He leaned forward, shielding the view of the relic from the rest of the tavern, and the other three followed his example.

"Beautiful," said Latanna. She was staring at it oddly, like someone trying to recall a dream hovering at the edge of remembrance.

"Wait," said Alisteyr when she began to reach for it. "It's dangerous." He told her about the thing that had been wearing it.

She hesitated. "Do you feel any ill effects from touching it?" she asked Memory.

"None."

"I touched it also, and am unharmed," said Kanstuhn. "Nevertheless, I do not trust it. Nor should you."

"All the same," said Latanna, "either Alisteyr or I will have to handle it in order to return it to my father. As much as I would like to see the look on his face if the two of you accompanied me into his house, his anger at such a liberty might undo what I've managed to accomplish so far."

Alisteyr tried to summon the nerve to reach for the tiara. This was his quest. It was his duty to present the prize to Marsen Forgrym. Before he could force his hand to move, Latanna had taken the tiara from Memory.

She looked wary, and then she smiled broadly. "No flames. No rotting flesh. I don't feel the need to kill any of you."

"Don't joke," said Alisteyr. "If you had seen what Elisava had become. . . ."

"I'm sorry," she said. "I really feel nothing wrong." She traced the contours of the design. "It feels like I've found something I'd lost."

Alisteyr's throat dried. "I think that is something that should have stayed lost."

"Yet you found it, because we need it." She passed it back to Memory. "Will you keep this safe until I have to give it to my father?" To Alisteyr, she said, "Better?"

73

THE SLEEP OF EMPIRES

The fact that she had given the relic to Memory so casually unknotted some of the tension in his shoulders. "Yes," he said.

Turning to Kanstuhn, Latanna asked, "Are you planning to move on right away?"

"No," Memory answered. His response was so sudden and emphatic that it startled all of them. Himself too, Alisteyr thought.

"I'm glad," said Latanna.

"There is another task you would ask of us?" said Kanstuhn.

"Yes." She lowered her voice. "It concerns cloudblossom."

The kaul looked grim. "We will be interested," he promised.

"Good. First, though, we should pay a visit to my father."

"It's not too late?" Alisteyr asked. He had imagined confronting Marsen again during the day. He wasn't sure he could face more than one monster in a single night.

"Oh, he'll be up," Latanna said. Her eagerness was ferocious. The hard look in her eyes reminded Alisteyr of her father.

Marsen did not disappoint. Latanna had never seen him look stricken.

They were in the main hall. Marsen had taken his place by the fireplace, his position of power, when she had entered with Alisteyr. When, without ceremony, she handed him the tiara, his expression froze. She thought she might even have seen a crack of fear looking out at her from those hated eyes.

He held the tiara as if it might bite him, then placed it on the mantel with a show of studied indifference. Already, Latanna could tell he was calculating again, working out how to turn the new state of affairs to his advantage. His loss of assurance had been brief. It had been real, though, and she had witnessed it.

"Well?" said Latanna.

"You are to be congratulated," Marsen said to Alisteyr, every syllable dragged out in chains.

74

DAVID ANNANDALE

"That's generous of you, Father," said Latanna. "Now, Alisteyr did as you asked. He proved himself worthy, following rules that the two of you seem to find rational. Alisteyr has fulfilled his side of the bargain. Your turn. You gave your word. You will bless our marriage."

Marsen glared at her in silence for a long time. She stared back, her gaze even, her calm stronger than his rage.

In the end, Marsen said nothing. He gave a nod. It was short, so brusque that Alisteyr winced.

"Thank you, Father," Latanna said. "Alisteyr, would you mind waiting for me outside?" Kanstuhn and Memory were there, on the road before the porch. With them, Alisteyr would be safe from a sudden outburst of wrath from her father. If Marsen grabbed a sword and ran Alisteyr through, he could still say that he had given his consent and kept his word.

Alisteyr bowed to Marsen. He looked as if he was trying to find the right words to bid his future father-in-law a good night. Then, realizing the futility of the effort, he left.

"Thank you," Latanna said again. "I know what you thought was going to happen tonight. You were wrong, as you can see. Alisteyr is still alive. I hope you'll consider the possibility that you were wrong to prefer marrying me off to Elgin Hawkesmoore."

"I'm considering quite a few things."

"I imagine you are. Do please be careful in that regard."

"Did you just threaten me?" Marsen snarled.

"If I did, it was in response to your threat. If you did no such thing, then it was simply an expression of concern." *Gods preserve me, I'm sounding more and more like him.* On the walk to the house from the tavern, instead of expanding on her hint about cloudblossom, she had asked Kanstuhn and Memory to remain in Ghaunthook at least until she and Alisteyr were wed. They had agreed, and now, at last, she had a counter to Marsen's capacity for violence. *Try sending one of your brutes after Alisteyr. See what happens.*

75

THE SLEEP OF EMPIRES

Latanna crossed the room and picked the tiara off the mantle. If Marsen was going to treat it so carelessly, she would take it into her care. Marsen took half a step back from her. He was trying not to look uncomfortable, but his gaze kept straying to the relic.

She didn't understand the distaste he and Alisteyr showed for the tiara. Kanstuhn was wary of it, but didn't try to avoid touching it. When she held the tiara, she felt nothing unpleasant. It was a beautiful jewel, unlike any she had seen in the Forgrym treasuries, and she liked it.

"It doesn't surprise me that you're disappointed to see Alisteyr alive," she said. "What does surprise me is that you don't seem pleased to recover a family possession this valuable."

Marsen visibly wrestled with how to answer her. He looked concerned, which was a disturbing novelty in her father. "It wasn't in our possession long," he said. "It was a gift to Elisava from Rosan Felgard."

"Felgard!" Latanna was impressed. The Felgards ruled Northope, the fortress that protected Ghaunthook and its neighboring towns, and watched over the region's border with Beresta. "Another match with political prospects."

Marsen shrugged. "Another younger son. I assume the tiara was from his family's treasury." He shrugged again. "There was no marriage. Elisava died as the ceremony began."

"Died how?"

"From no visible cause," Marsen said significantly.

"Poison, then."

"So the family has always assumed."

"And Rosan Felgard?"

"Killed by bandits on his return journey to Northope."

"How convenient."

Another shrug. Then Marsen pointed at the tiara. "Elisava was wearing that when she died. Its associations are unpleasant."

Is he telling me to be careful? Does he want me to get rid of the tiara? "Then it needs new associations." She chuckled. "Dying didn't stop Elisava from

76

dancing. Being buried didn't keep her jewel from surfacing. I will be wed in this."

Marsen turned pale. "I think you should not."

Alisteyr would no doubt agree with you. What a strange omen that is. Yet there was no danger to her in the relic. She ran her finger over the vortices of its patterns, and felt its welcome. It would not harm her.

She was going to say so to Marsen. Before she could speak, she heard shouting from outside.

The horsemen arrived shortly after Alisteyr stepped out of the house. They rode up the drive, their leader out front, the others grouped tightly behind him.

"Who is this that is calling?" Kanstuhn asked.

"Elgin Hawkesmoore and friends," said Alisteyr.

"Your rival."

"Yes."

"You have met?"

"I haven't had that bad luck before now, no. I recognized the livery."

"They are powers in Korvas," Kanstuhn told Memory. "A Hawkesmoore in Ghaunthook." He shook his head, his smile ironic. "How impressive. What an honor for the village."

Kanstuhn and Memory positioned themselves side by side, just ahead of Alisteyr, shielding him. Elgin and his five escorts stopped a few yards away.

"What do we have here?" said Elgin. He grinned.

Alisteyr flinched inwardly. He knew that kind of grin too well. It was the grin of the bully. The grin of a man, and it was almost always a man, who saw the world as existing for his convenience, and would fly into a rage whenever it failed to conform to his expectations. The grin of a man who was not only convinced of his superiority to everyone else, but took for granted that they acknowledged his superiority too.

Alisteyr hated Elgin on sight. He hated the fact that he was frightened of the man even more.

THE SLEEP OF EMPIRES

"I see a weakling who fancies he can claim my bride," said Elgin. "I see a kaul, who must have escaped his master." When he turned to Memory, there was only the smallest hint of uncertainty in his face when he regarded the tall sell-sword. His guards had their hands on the hilts of their blades, though, and he had the confidence that came with numbers. "But what are you, gray one?" he said. "Not human, nor elf, nor kaul. Tell me, because I'm curious. What kind of obscene bastard are you?"

Memory said nothing. He cocked his head slightly, studying Elgin as if he were an interesting insect. Alisteyr became more and more frightened about what might happen.

"You are addressed by a Hawkesmoore," said one of the guards. "Better answer, or you'll wish you had." He was a big man, broad in shoulder and face. His nose looked like it had been broken more than once, and the tip of his left ear had been cut off. He had the air of someone who relished violence, and who had found his calling in life by serving a master who encouraged his worst instincts.

"Maybe he can't speak, Dawun," said another of the men, a wiry sort with a face like a rotten lemon. "I think he's the idiot we've been hearing about."

Elgin smiled again, his lips thin with contempt. "Is Netsch right?" he asked Memory. "You can't speak?"

"I can speak," said Memory. "I was just studying you. I'm going to remember you. That's a new thing for me." His voice went cold. "You seem worth remembering."

"Well, you don't," said Elgin. He turned to Alisteyr. "You, Huesland. Make yourself useful. Let the Forgryms know that Latanna's intended is here."

The guards dismounted, though Elgin remained mounted.

"See to my horse, kaul," said Netsch.

Kanstuhn sniffed. "I think not."

There was a moment of silence. Netsch took a step forward, grip tightening on his sword. "You dare?" he said.

78

DAVID ANNANDALE

"More than would please you," said Kanstuhn. "Less than would please me at this moment. But I have come to help this man your master insults, not to make his life more difficult."

Netsch spat at Kanstuhn's feet.

Memory moved with a casual grace, as if there were no more effort or import in his actions than the opening of a door or the shooing of a fly. He grabbed Netsch by the neck and threw him to the ground, grinding his face in his own spit. Netsch writhed under his grip, but might as well have been pinned by a tree.

Elgin and the rest of his guards drew their swords. "Release him!" Elgin shouted, pointing at Memory with his blade.

Kanstuhn's sword had appeared in his hand. He looked from one guard to the other, as if trying to choose between an embarrassment of riches.

Memory looked up at Elgin, utterly unconcerned. "No," he said. "Not until your rat apologizes to my friend."

The demand that a human bow before a kaul was a slap across all their faces. Elgin turned purple with anger. His men snarled threats.

"Enough!" Latanna's voice cut through the night. "You are all guests on my father's land. If you have any shred of honor, you will remember yourselves."

Marsen appeared behind her. Father and daughter were both furious, their hate directed at different parties.

Alisteyr wished himself far away.

Kanstuhn sheathed his blade and bowed to Latanna. "Your pardon, lady. You correctly recall us to our manners."

Memory straightened, lifting Netsch like a sack of turnips, then giving him a shove that sent him stumbling against his horse's flank.

After a long moment, Elgin said, "Out of respect for my future bride, I will let the matter pass. This once." He sheathed his sword. Slowly. His bodyguards did the same. Netsch rubbed dirt from his scraped face. He glared at Kanstuhn and Memory.

79

THE SLEEP OF EMPIRES

"I'm sure your bride-to-be would thank you for your magnanimity," said Latanna. "Though I do not know who this person might be."

"Haven't we had enough of games?" Elgin asked, expecting the world to right itself and obey him again.

"We have," said Latanna. "They're over. Ask my father."

Marsen winced. He turned back inside the house. Elgin leapt off his horse and followed him inside, his guards trailing uncertainly after him.

Latanna took Alisteyr's arm. "I think we should see your parents tonight also. Unless the hour is too late."

It took a bit for Alisteyr to get his tongue working again. He managed to speak without a tremor. "They won't mind being woken. Not at all."

He started walking down the road with Latanna. Kanstuhn and Memory followed.

"Do you think Elgin will send his men after us?" Alisteyr asked.

"I'm going to hope my father will convince him that it would serve no purpose," said Latanna.

"It would entertain us if they did come," said Kanstuhn.

Alisteyr shuddered.

CHAPTER 7

In the morning, Kanstuhn and Memory walked slowly around the Huesland farmhouse, examining it with an eye to defense.

"They really do need our help, don't they?" Kanstuhn said.

The house had not weathered time and conflict as well as Forgrym Hall. Even in the dark, the Hall's decline in fortunes had been visible, but the home of Marsen's rivals was more humble, and more battered. Kanstuhn saw little to suggest the Hueslands had once been powerful. When the original homes of the two families had been destroyed, the Hueslands had built their new abode without the thought of recapturing past glories. The farmhouse was larger than a number of the others that Kanstuhn and Memory had passed in the Ghaunthook region, though not by much. It bore the wounds of past fires and storm damage. Patchwork repairs on its walls and roof did their best to hold decay at bay. They were only partially successful.

The cultivated lands around the house were shrinking. The forest gnawed at their ragged edges. Some fields had not seen crops for years. The farm made Kanstuhn think of a mangy dog.

He could not fault the welcome of the Hueslands, though. Rasmus and Elda appeared genuinely grateful to him and Memory for saving Alisteyr's life. They could not hide the anxiety they felt in his presence, and Memory's indeterminate race did not sit easily with them, either. They swallowed their fears, though, and took the sell-swords into their home.

Decay spread its tendrils through the interior of the farmhouse as well. Water stains marked the walls. The rugs were worn, and the framed paintings in the main hall so darkened by smoke that their subjects were almost indiscernible. The house had a library, though, which impressed Kanstuhn with the size of its collection. The books, held in floor-to-ceiling shelves,

THE SLEEP OF EMPIRES

were better cared-for than almost anything else in the house. All three members of the family seemed proud of that room, and that was where Kanstuhn, Memory, and Latanna had been brought and given wine to toast Alisteyr's announcement.

Elda had embraced Latanna with tears in her eyes. "You are giving us peace," she had said. "We will be in your debt forever."

Latanna had looked very uncomfortable.

She knows what she is doing, Kanstuhn thought. *She acts out of principle, yet guilt assails her. Interesting.*

He and Memory finished their tour of the exterior. They started down the poor dirt track that led from the house, running west through the forest to the road that marked a firm boundary between the Huesland and Forgrym lands.

"We can't defend that house from attack," said Memory.

"Agreed. We cannot permit a siege."

"A defense built on an attack, then, if the need arises."

"Agreed again." If Hawkesmoore and his men came for Alisteyr, Kanstuhn and Memory would meet them outside the house. Last night had been useful in gaining some measure of the enemy. But there would be more to learn. They would not be as easy to dispose of as the bandits he and Memory had encountered outside Ghaunthook. Then again, the way he and Memory would fight had changed. They were both capable of independent action now. "So that is something else that exists in your store of knowledge," he said. "You made a sound evaluation of our defensive position. I wonder what else you know of warfare."

Memory thought for a long moment before answering. "Quite a bit, I think. I have just been asking questions of myself, and finding I know the answers."

"A bit of your past returning, perhaps."

"Perhaps. If it is, it comes with no sense of identity. I know things in the way a book knows them. Where there should be a self, there is only void."

DAVID ANNANDALE

"Yet you have a self. There might not have been before. But you made decisions last night. You choose to hold Elgin Hawkesmoore in contempt." Kanstuhn chuckled. "There are many who would say you demonstrated a moral sense."

Memory didn't laugh. "If I did, I don't remember what shaped it. Was it you?"

"You give me too much credit."

"I doubt that. Will you tell me where we met?"

"In Appiran. Three years ago."

"Appiran," said Memory, testing the syllables.

"Does the name mean anything to you?"

"No. Where is it?"

"To the west. It is a disputed province lying between the borders of Wiramzin and Wakkamzin."

Memory frowned.

"Do you have any sense of the world?" Kanstuhn asked.

"I know that Korvas lies to the east, because you have told me. Voran lies in that direction too."

Kanstuhn felt a chill that had nothing to do with the morning breeze. "I have never said a word of that land. No one speaks its name without reluctance. It is a dead place."

"Voran," Memory said again, slowly.

The word sounded too much like an incantation. "Any other places?" Kanstuhn asked quickly.

"Beresta," said Memory. "That is to the north. It belongs to the elves. Wiramzin. That is here. Gulsentia, the realm of the dwaves, lies south of Voran. Keteria still further east." He looked at Kanstuhn. "The home of the kauls."

"What is left of it," said Kanstuhn. "Do you know the extent of Wiramzin?"

"We are in the northeast corner of it. The lands extend far to the west, to the ocean, and down into the south."

83

THE SLEEP OF EMPIRES

"What of Wakkamzin? Or Puwirran?"

"I don't know those names. Or Appiran."

"Curious," said Kanstsuhn. "What about the other elvish realm, Deltia, north of Beresta?"

Memory shook his head. "I didn't know there were two."

"There is a pattern to your knowledge. It is a strange one. You know only the old names. The first names, from before the time when the human and elvish realms fractured."

"That was long ago?"

Kanstuhn laughed. "You may as well ask if mountains are old."

"I am going to bore you with my questions."

"Not at all. They remind me of a better time, of the life I had so long ago it must have belonged to someone else."

"What were you?"

"A scribe. Then I was taken by dwarf raiders and sold to humans. They made me into a gladiator, a specialty in Appiran."

"Why is that?" Memory asked.

"Wakkamzin and Wiramzin both lay claim to the province, but neither empire is strong enough to face the other in open war." Kanstuhn snorted. "Just look at Wiramzin. It can barely hold its parts together within its borders. The center is weak. These regions close to the border with Beresta are little more than clusters of fiefdoms. The powers in Korvas pay lip service, and nothing else, to the dictates from the imperial palace in Samustar. Wakkamzin is smaller, spread less thin, but also poorer in resources. The laws of neither realm are enforced in Appiran. There, the enslavement of the kauls has no restrictions. Nor do bloodsports."

"You must have been a good pupil," said Memory.

"So I have ever been, for my blessings and my griefs. The skills that made me valuable to my masters were also the key to my escape."

"Did you free yourself without bloodshed?"

"I most certainly did not. You might say that I instructed my masters."

Memory grinned. "I'm glad to hear it."

DAVID ANNANDALE

"I was making my way to Wiramzin, where at least my unchained existence is not illegal, when I found you."

"What was I doing?"

"Walking."

"Down a road?"

"Across a plain of sun-baked mud. You were wandering without direction, your path changing every few feet. I was traveling across the plain because the roads were too dangerous for me. You were doing so, as far as I could tell, for no reason at all. I thought at first that you were wounded. I needed an ally, so I approached you. Once I realized the nature of your condition, you responded well to me."

"Have I been a good ally?" Memory asked.

"You have been a good friend. I hope I have been so for you." He spoke with the possibility of a farewell at the back of his mind. Memory no longer needed him.

"I know you have been, in the same way I know how to wield my sword."

"Then I am glad."

They walked on, eyeing every bend in the road for its ambush possibilities.

"Have you thought about returning to Keteria?" said Memory.

"I have, and decided against it. I have been gone too many years, and it is too far. There is nothing for me there any longer."

"No family?"

"Killed in the raid that took me. The land is poor, and prey to the empires that use us, when they are not intent on exterminating us. No. I prefer to be the raider than the raided. I have lived as well as I could wish as a sell-sword. There is satisfaction in the choices I can make, and in seeing justice through blood."

"Then I look forward to remembering the justice we bring from now on." Memory held out his hand. He and Kanstuhn clasped forearms.

They heard someone coming up the road behind them, and turned around to see Latanna marching quickly to catch up.

85

THE SLEEP OF EMPIRES

"The protective bride," said Memory.

Latanna had spent the night at the farmhouse, a guest of the Hueslands, breaching tradition in order to act as another guarantor of Alisteyr's safety.

"Protective of more than her groom," said Kanstuhn. "She hopes to save her village."

"Do you think she can?" Memory watched her fixedly. "I would like to think so."

"I would like to think so too," said Kanstuhn. "Especially since we have been conscripted into her effort."

"Then we'll make sure she succeeds."

Kanstuhn heard no hint of mercenary considerations in his friend's voice. Then again, when had Memory ever had use for coin?

"I hope the morning after your victory has been a pleasant one," Kanstuhn said when Latanna reached them.

"A partial victory," Latanna corrected. "We're not married yet."

"Your groom's parents wanted to engage us to make sure he lives to see your wedding day. I told them you already had done so."

She nodded. "Thank you. They're not rich . . ."

"That doesn't matter," said Memory. "They are lodging and feeding us well."

You have a moral sense, my friend. I am glad of it. I seem to have mine still too.

"I know I'll wish that I could make your engagement here a permanent one," said Latanna. She held up a hand before Kanstuhn could protest. "I know. A wish doesn't make something possible. Anyway, I think the danger will diminish after the wedding."

"Why is that?"

"I'm hopeful my father will see the match does work to his advantage."

"What about Elgin Hawkesmoore?" Memory asked.

"That is what I wanted to talk to you about. I said last night that I had some other work for you."

DAVID ANNANDALE

"To do with cloudblossom," said Kanstuhn.

"Yes. I've discovered that is Elgin's real interest in Ghaunthook. There is a large plantation on the old Forgrym lands."

Kanstuhn's jaw tightened. He thought of his fellow slaves, and the addiction used to break them.

"Once Alisteyr and I are married, and the threat from my father diminishes, I want you to destroy that field," said Latanna.

"I would willingly pay for the privilege of seeing it burn," said Kanstuhn.

"Elgin will fight to protect his new source of wealth."

"I hope he does," said Memory.

"Then I hope so too," Latanna said, and smiled like a Forgrym.

The University of Korvas covered several blocks in the southeast of the city. It nestled close to the outer ramparts and surrounded itself with its own high wall. To the streets outside, it presented a blank face of gray stone, broken only by its iron gate on the north side. Garwynn had not been back to the gate since he had walked out of it for what he had thought was the last time more than a year ago. He approached it now with all the eagerness of a prisoner mounting the scaffold. The shame was so strong that he almost turned away.

Keep going. If you don't do this, things are only going to get worse.

He forced himself on and arrived at the sentinel's window, a small opening in the western gate tower.

The sentinel glowered at him. It was the same old man who had first admitted him to the university, and then seen him off when he had left. His name was Eggar, and he looked like he had been born old and disapproving.

"Garwynn Avennic," Eggar said, leaning his hooded head out of the window of his cramped chamber. "There can't be a good reason for you to be here." Behind the sentinel, rows of keys hung on the far wall. On a waist-high ledge to the left sat a record book, Eggar's ledger of the admitted and

87

THE SLEEP OF EMPIRES

the refused, open to a page scrawled in his crabbed, angular hand, every letter a shape of angry judgement.

Garwynn had hoped Eggar might not remember him after a year. He was dismayed, but not surprised, to find the sentinel's memory as iron-clad as ever. "I seek an audience with Magister Dunfeld," he said.

"Do you, now? Not asking for much, are you?"

"It's important I see her."

"I'm sure it is, for you. Not sure Magister Dunfeld would think so. Have my doubts, I do, *Master* Avennic. Have my doubts."

During his sleepless night, Garwynn had rehearsed and discarded a score of arguments to get him through the gates. There was no point in any of them. Eggar was unpersuadable. Anyone who did not have the proper authorization for admittance had no choice but to rely upon the whim of the sentinel. Garwynn knew this. So did Eggar.

"Please," Garwynn said, and left it at that.

Eggar scrutinized him. Garwynn thought he saw a slight upward twitch in the corner of the sentinel's mouth, as if he were gratified by Garwynn's acknowledgment of his power.

Finally, Eggar said, "Do you know what I'm going to do, *Master* Avennic? I'm going to convey your request to Magister Dunfeld."

"Thank you."

"Oh, I'm not going to do that because I'm doing you a favor. I'm doing it because I want to see the look on her face."

The sentinel withdrew into the gloom of his chamber, and then vanished through the low door on the right. Garwynn waited, no longer sure what he was hoping for. He had not really expected to get even this far. He had come because he had no choice. To be granted an audience or to be sent on his way felt like equally dark outcomes.

The day was cool and overcast, and it started to rain before Eggar returned. There was no shelter by the wall. Water trickled down Garwynn's hair and the back of his neck. By the time Eggar returned, the rain had become a downpour.

DAVID ANNANDALE

"She'll see you," Eggar said shortly. He wrote Garwynn's name in the ledger, then called out, "One in!"

Garwynn thanked him again, and moved to the gate. The guard opened the wicket gate next to the turret, and Garwynn entered the grounds.

The cobblestones of the quadrangle were slippery, and he cut across them carefully to avoid falling. The dark gray buildings of the university glowered over him, dark as the clouds, their leaded windows blank stares of indifference. Garwynn ducked into the south colonnade. Shaking the water from his clothes as best he could, he turned left and made his way to the corner staircase and took it to the fourth floor and the quarters of the senior magisters.

The vaulted hallway was somber, the weak daylight made even weaker by the grime on the windows. Veira Dunfeld's chamber was three down from the top of the steps. Garwynn stood in front of the iron-banded oak door, dripping onto the marble floor, trying to summon the courage to knock.

"Are you coming in?" said a voice inside. "I heard you on the stairs, so there's no point putting this off, is there?"

Garwynn swallowed hard and opened the door.

The magister's chamber was as he remembered it. Shelves, groaning with books, covered all four walls. Piles teetered on Veira's desk, and messy stacks of vellum left her with only a small space clear for current work. The tall back of the magister's chair made her seem smaller than she was, but also endowed her presence with an air of formidable rigidity.

Veira was in late middle age, her silver hair in a severe tonsure, her violet scholar's robes faded from use. Her skin had the texture and color of yellowing paper. She looked like an elder raptor, gaze sharp as ever. She stabbed a finger at the stool in front of her desk. "Sit," she said, the word a snap of dry kindling.

Garwynn sat. The low stool had him looking up at Veira, supplicant to judge. He had been in this position many times. Familiarity did not make the moment any easier.

THE SLEEP OF EMPIRES

"Right," said Veira. "Why are you here?"

"I need to ask you about magic."

Veira snorted. "You asked plenty when you were a student. You were even a promising one. Then you left."

"I couldn't afford to stay."

Another snort. "A lazy excuse. But you're not a student now. Our tutorials are done. What makes you think I would indulge your questions now?"

"Something's happened."

His tone must have conveyed the suggestion of import more than the vagueness of his words. Veira looked interested. "Go on," she said.

"You taught us that the exercise of real magic is extremely difficult," he began.

"It is."

"And it is difficult because the gods have withdrawn from us. They are not with us in the way they once were."

"Correct."

Garwynn twisted his hands together. He was approaching the point of no return. "Have you . . . Have you tried practicing it?"

Veira's eyes narrowed. "Of course not. My domain is the study and theory of magic."

Garwynn swallowed, his throat sore with tension. "I have been practicing it," he murmured.

"I don't think I heard you properly. It sounded like you said you've been practicing magic. Without your degree, that would be without temple or university authorization."

"I know. But I have been. I've been performing."

"*Performing*," Veira said, dripping contempt. "Stage magic, then."

"Yes. But with some real magic in the mix."

She stared at him, eyes as cold as a stone idol's, and waited for him to continue.

"The real magic *was* hard when I first prepared for my performances. But just recently, it's become easier. *Much* easier."

90

Veira's gaze didn't alter. "Show me," she said.

She doesn't believe me. "I don't know if I should. I can't always control—"

"Show me."

Garwynn nodded. He focused on the clear space of her desk. He whispered an incantation, the syllables coming so easily to him, it was as if the magic were reaching out to him now, no longer a seam to be tapped into, but a current whose strength would pull him in and drown him if he was not careful. He visualized a flower again, as he had during his performance, and as he had last night in his boarding house room. It was the most harmless thing he could think of to conjure.

A black rose sprang into being on Veira's desk, its petals glistening with dew. The magister jerked back, alarmed. The rose's long stem whipped back and forth, aggressive.

Garwynn had tried to conjure a red rose.

"That's enough," said Veira.

The blossom reacted to her voice. It tilted up as if looking at her. The outer petals curled inward. They began to look like teeth.

Garwynn spoke the words of banishment. The rose stood up taller, still facing Veira. He shouted the words, at the same time pulling himself back from the flow of the current. It took more effort than it had last night. With a mental yank that shot sparks of pain behind his eyes, he freed himself, and the rose vanished.

Droplets of dew remained behind.

Veira took a deep breath. She clutched the edge of her desk, her knuckles white. She let go, slowly, and folded her hands together, reassembling her calm. Garwynn had never seen her rattled, and that scared him almost as much as the flower that had defied him.

"I didn't want it to look like that," he said. "I didn't want it to behave like that. I can conjure things easily, but controlling them is becoming very hard."

"And you performed real magic," Veira said softly. "You performed it to an *audience.*"

THE SLEEP OF EMPIRES

"They can't be certain it was real." The rationalization sounded weak.

"The priesthoods will not be pleased with you," said Veira. "Not a one of them."

"Won't they be experiencing the same thing?" Garwynn asked hopefully.

Veira shook her head. She paused, appearing to wrestle with a decision. "You were taught that magic is rare and difficult. That is true. What is also true, but not emphasized, is that practitioners are rare too. Very rare."

"If it's becoming easier to use magic, then maybe practitioners are becoming more common too."

"The talent is there at birth. It can be nurtured. It cannot be created." Veira glanced over her shelves of books. "Unless all scholarship is wrong." She spoke as if she wasn't discounting that possibility. "And your suggestion presumes too much. You do not know what you are saying. I don't think you understand the profound implications of what you have just shown me."

"I don't know what they are, but I know enough to be afraid," said Garwynn. "That's why I've come to see you."

"Your visit is a curse," Veira muttered.

"What must I do?" Garwynn was pleading now.

Veira stood. "Stay here," she said. "Do not leave this chamber. Do not speak to anyone until I return. I will arrange accommodation for you at the university." She looked at him with something like pity. "You will have hard questions to answer in the days ahead," she said. "I hope you will have an appetite for them."

The hall of the Most Perfect Council covered the peak of Árkiriye's highest hill, near the center of the city. Eight slender towers of crystal surrounded a hemsiphere of marble one hundred feet high and two hundred feet in diameter. During the day, the towers appeared to be vertical slashes of sunlight. At night, the hundreds of lamps inside turned them into beacons, symbols in the dark of precision and grace. The marble of the dome was

DAVID ANNANDALE

polished to a mirror sheen that accentuated the light blazing from the towers.

Inside, the council hall itself occupied most of the dome. There was just enough space between the outer walls and the inner chamber for service halls and rooms, all of them invisible to the councilors, their presence felt only in the immediate ways the needs of the Most Perfect Council were fulfilled.

Twelve seats of gold and silver were arranged in a circle in the center of the hall. A sublime fresco covered the interior of the dome. It depicted the lands of Beresta outside Árkiriye. The reproduction was faithful to the last detail. Every year, surveyors and artists retouched the painting, correcting any elements that no longer reflected the reality. To sit in the hall was to see for leagues across the panorama of Beresta.

Skiriye stood inside the circle, surrounded by the Twelve of the Council. "I have come to you," she said, "because there is a flaw upon the face of Beresta. It is a flaw that I may correct, with the help of the Council."

"A flaw for which you are responsible," said Paketär ne Säle, the Councilor of the Army.

So word of the theft had reached the Twelve. Skiriye had guessed that it would have. *To conceal a flaw is to compound its crime.* The proverb was law in Beresta, so anyone who knew even a hint of what had happened in the library had been duty-bound to report it. The search she had commanded would have been more than enough to alert the Council.

"I must correct the misapprehension of the councilor," Skiriye said. "The flaw is one that lay hidden from me at the university."

"That is a fine evasion," said Motatsë ne Takär, the Councilor for Art. The twenty-year rotating headship of the Council was hers. For that period, she was the Immaculate, the supreme authority in Beresta. "That it is fine makes it no less of an evasion. You dishonor your post, Skiriye ne Sincatsë."

"I disagree. Yes, there has been a theft at the library. A book has been stolen. But not only was the book's nature concealed from me, so was the fact that it was even in our collections. I cannot protect what I do not know

THE SLEEP OF EMPIRES

exists. Even now, I cannot tell what has been stolen. How, then, will it be possible to recover it? Shall I be chasing air?" She paused just long enough for the silence of the Council to be felt. "Does any one of the Twelve know what has been stolen?" This pause was longer. "I thought not. The flaw we confront is a grievous one, but my hope is that it *can* be corrected. But we must know what we seek."

Now she let the silence linger. Significant looks passed between the members of the Most Perfect Council. A wordless debate circled Skiriye. She was not asked to leave, and she took that as a sign that she had carried the day. There was an imminent consensus, either for her or against her, and there had been no counter to her argument.

The Immaculate nodded, and rang the silver bell mounted on the left arm of her chair. A few moments later, an elf in the gold robes of the Most Perfect Council's service entered carrying a small ebony chest. Twelve locks, embossed in silver, held it closed. The servant presented the chest to Motatsë and withdrew. She, in turn, passed the chest to her right, to Kärwene ne Erkent, the Councilor for Commerce. From her robes, Kärwene produced a small, silver key on the end of a chain, and unlocked one of the latches. Then she passed the chest to her right. It went around the circle, each councilor opening one of the locks, until it returned to Motatsë, who used her key on the last. She opened the chest and removed the calf-bound ledger inside.

"The knowledge herein is kept from all of us for good reason," the Immaculate said. "We cannot encounter it without peril, and do so only because of the compelling possibility of a greater peril. Your argument and the fact of the theft show the existence of that possibility, First Librarian."

"Shall I withdraw?" Skiriye asked.

"No," said Motatsë. "You will, as you said you would, take part in the correction."

Motatsë opened the book, turning the pages of forbidden texts until she reached the one that corresponded to the missing catalog entry. She stiffened as she read. "The absent volume is *On the Calculations of the Void*," she said. "It is the work of a mathematician."

"An elf?" Skiriye asked, horrified, and reeling from the shock of the title. The word *void* echoed through her mind, a bell calling to all that was most forbidden, most repressed, most deliberately forgotten.

"No," said Motatsë. "No elf is guilty of so heretical a text. For that, at least, we may be grateful, and give thanks to Passomo. The author is human."

That was still bad enough.

"A practical treatise?" Kärwene asked, and Skiriye heard her own desperate hope reflected in the Councilor for Commerce's tone.

"A theoretical one," the Immaculate answered, her voice deadened with horror. She was no longer looking at the ledger. "A speculative one. And a religious one."

Skiriye's skin crawled. Even considering the idea of a work of theoretical mathematics was bad enough. That was the path to the greatest of all crimes against the gods, and the unraveling of all perfection. The treatise was of a kind she had believed had been eradicated centuries ago. The last wars against the humans had ended only when the humans had surrendered all their scholars of numbers to be executed, and had burned all their works. "You speak as if you know this text."

"I know what it is," said Motatsë. "That is more than enough. What is written here is not even its true title, merely a way of identifying the horror without committing the crime of writing its name. What has been stolen is the *Book of the Null.*"

Shock buzzed through Skiriye's frame. Numbing cold followed. The *Book of the Null* shouldn't exist at all. Its title alone was a foul curse, its memory refusing to be extinguished even though it lived only in the deepest recesses of unwanted thoughts, a thing whose only purpose was to be shunned. Skiriye did not know its contents. She did not need to. No one did. That they were a crime beyond naming was all anyone knew. "Why was this kept?" Skiriye asked. "Why wasn't it burned?"

THE SLEEP OF EMPIRES

Motatsë read in the ledger again, and she turned ashen. "It would not burn," she said.

Another silence fell over the hall, a stunned one, a fearful one. Skiriye had already heard far more than she wished to, and this detail made her regret her victory. For a moment she wished that she had suffered the worst of censures, and never learned what had been stolen.

"The book must be recovered," said Motatsë. "We must prevent the damage it would cause if the wrong eyes should see it."

"Or the wrong eyes understand it," Skiriye said. The thought she gave voice to felt like the cracking apart of the world.

CHAPTER 8

Latanna stayed at her father's for the five days leading up to the wedding. It was easier to keep track of him there. And Alisteyr wanted to be apart from her from now until the wedding, the desire another romantic impulse on his part. She agreed. She had no reason not to indulge him. She only wished she felt the romantic urge more strongly than the pragmatic one.

Elgin and his guards had left the house by the time she returned to it after speaking with Kanstuhn and Memory. They were still in Ghaunthook, and she saw them occasionally in the days that followed. She didn't know where they were staying. It wasn't at the inn. She suspected they had set up camp near their cloudblossom fields. Elgin looked like he was sleeping rough. Dirt did not bother him. Another pragmatist, then. That made him dangerous.

Marsen kept quiet during these days. He did not throw any barriers up against the marriage. He *did* spend a lot of time in his chapel to Tetriwu, and Latanna didn't think his prayers did Alisteyr any favors. There was nothing she could do about that. A kind of silent respect established itself between her and her father. Not so much a truce, more a reconfiguration of forces. The war would flare again, and she would have to be ready. She hoped she would be.

How long before he tries to make me a widow?

Not long. She would have to work fast to prove to him that the marriage was as advantageous to him as she had promised.

Three days before the wedding, she had the only discussion she would have with Marsen about the event. He had raised no objection to it being conducted on the village green. In the evening, he emerged from his chapel and came to find Latanna where she sat reading by the hearth in the main hall.

THE SLEEP OF EMPIRES

"What deity will you be invoking to bless your union?" he asked, stiffly, the word *union* sounding like a hair that had caught in his throat.

"It will not be Tetriwu," Latanna said. She and Alisteyr would not begin their marriage under the shadow of the god of war.

"It will not be Kamatris," Marsen countered.

Latanna shrugged. The adoptive father of humans, who embraced them after Passomo rejected his first creations for their imperfections, was the primary object of worship in Ghaunthook. The Hueslands attended his temple. She had not expected Kamatris to be any more acceptable to Marsen than Tetriwu was to her. For herself, she respected Kamatris only because she rejected her father and his beliefs. Her regard for the deity held little conviction, less faith, and even less love. And what little she had felt had withered to nothing in the last couple of days, though she wasn't sure why. "I see no need for a blessing at all," she said. "Let the mayor preside."

Marsen looked sly. "The marriage will be seen as illegitimate in some quarters."

"Only some," Latanna said. She had handed him a partial victory here, and created another vulnerability for her to guard against. She decided she could live with it. The decision felt more than pragmatic. It felt right. It gave her a sense of pride. Again, she didn't know why.

Marsen regarded her for a few moments, then gave her a curt nod, satisfied for the moment, and walked away.

Was that too easy? Or did I give away too much?

Later, in her bedroom, she held the tiara before going to sleep. She did so every night now. She ran her fingers over the convolutions, and it felt as if she were learning a new language. When she did this, the questions about whether she had ceded the advantage to Marsen disappeared. All her doubts did. The sense of pride grew stronger. The conviction that she had made the right choice became like iron.

On the day before the wedding, Memory walked around the village green, watching the preparations. This was the first rite he would remember. He

DAVID ANNANDALE

wanted to store every detail. He was also going to ensure it was successful, and its participants survived.

In the center of the green, a stage had been erected. The orange-and-white banner of the house of Forgrym and green-and-white one of Huesland flanked it, and someone had found the flag of Wiramzin to hoist in the center. It was an old flag, very worn, its crimson field cut by a diamond of gold faded to a deep red marked by watery yellow. Its neglected condition confirmed what Kanstuhn and Alisteyr had told Memory about the decayed human empires.

"The connections between the centers of power and the provinces are growing tenuous," Kanstuhn had said.

"Ghaunthook looks to the keep of Northope for its protection," Alisteyr added. "We feel a stronger loyalty to Lady Felgard than to the First Lord in Samustar. We are close to the border with Beresta, and the keeps that watch over it have grown independent. This region is really a collection of fiefdoms."

"A lack of unity that suits Beresta very well," said Kanstuhn.

But the flag of Wiramzin was there for the wedding, a ragged memory of past glories, and a gesture, perhaps, to the hope of better days, a symbol of the town's joy at the prospect of the end of a long and petty war.

Tables and benches surrounded the stage, and workers hired by the Hueslands were putting tents up to shelter the celebration. The weather was overcast, heavy with the fall chill and the promise of more rain.

The green was about twice as long as it was wide. On the north side, the town hall sat next to the temple to Kamatris. The mayor's residence was slightly larger than the other houses nearby, and smartly kept-up. The temple overshadowed it, and drew Memory's attention.

The only building in Ghaunthook made entirely of stone, the temple was also the village's largest structure. Six pillars surrounded its circular walls, with a door in each. They held up a low dome. The temple spoke of a time when the village had been more prosperous, and so more ambitious in its projects.

THE SLEEP OF EMPIRES

When Memory looked at the temple, he felt a stab of hostility, like resentment over an old wound. The sensation interested him. He wondered what root it sprang from. As his self took shape, he was finding things to like and to despise. The contempt he held for Elgin Hawkesmoore had been immediate and acute, and it was entirely explainable. He had no reason that he knew of to look at the temple as the home of an enemy. There was nothing about the village's priest of Kamatris that encouraged hate. Taver Derrun was a jovial figure. He stood outside the temple now, chatting with Hanby Bettring, the mayor and owner of the Laughing Chimera. They were looking on at the preparations with innocently smug approval.

The two men were near enough in appearance that they could almost have been brothers. They were both well-fed, and had the benign countenances of those sufficiently insulated from the hurt of the world that they could look upon it with a contented generosity. Both had lost most of their hair, and both moved slowly because they had rarely had to move quickly. Taver was about ten years older than Hanby, though they had both sailed through the onset of middle age without much of a struggle, and were ready to blend even further together as they faced the prospect of being actually venerable.

Taver, Latanna had told Memory, had no possessions of his own, but he ate very well thanks to the donations to the temple. Hanby was wealthy, at least by the standards of Ghaunthook. His ancestors had sold their land to the Hueslands and the Forgryms after the destruction of the enemies' original homes, and that windfall had provided full coffers for every generation that followed.

"Good afternoon," Taver said to Memory as he approached, while Hanby put on a practiced wide smile of greeting. The priest and the mayor had made a point of being polite to Memory and Kanstuhn since Latanna and Alisteyr had introduced them, along with giving the news that Marsen had agreed to the wedding. Memory could tell the two men were wary of the sell-swords. They were repulsed by Kanstuhn, and they were frightened of him. But they concealed their distress expertly. Memory suspected

100

DAVID ANNANDALE

they half-convinced themselves that they were pleased to see him. He gave them credit for the effort.

"Good afternoon," he said. He stopped beside them, and practiced dissembling his own feelings. He constructed a smile to cover the anger he felt at the temple. *Is this how you do it?*

He must have succeeded. There was no change in the contentment of the two men.

"Things are almost ready," said Hanby. "Going to be a fine thing tomorrow evening. A fine thing. A fine thing."

"You are without your friend today," said Taver.

"He's with Alisteyr." They were not letting their guard down, but Alisteyr was being cooperative, and having taken the measure of the Hawkesmoore party, Kanstuhn and Memory felt confident enough that they did not both need to be watching over the groom during the day. It would be useful, as well, for them to get a good sense of the setting for the wedding and its vulnerabilities before the event.

Taver nodded knowingly. Hanby looked up at the sky and smiled as if there were no clouds and he was basking in the sun. "Better days ahead, I like to think. Better days ahead. This is a good thing, this marriage. A good thing." He turned his smile on Memory. "You're bringing peace to the village. You'll have our thanks for that."

"Don't celebrate the peace before it happens," Taver chided gently.

"Of course, of course," said Hanby. "Don't want to be premature. But the prospect is there! It is, it is. And that's worth celebrating."

"I can't disagree," said Taver, smiling again.

"Now if only we could also erase the scourge of cloudblossom . . ." Hanby gave Memory a significant look.

"That is something Latanna Forgym has asked us for help with too," Memory said.

Hanby scanned the green anxiously, watching for addicts. "I do worry about the afflicted disrupting the wedding."

"They won't be a problem," said Memory.

101

THE SLEEP OF EMPIRES

"You aren't going to hurt any?" Taver asked. "They are to be pitied, not punished."

"We will not hurt them," Memory promised.

Hanby reached up to give Memory a clap on the shoulder. "Good man!" he exclaimed, then hesitated over the possible slight, and tried to recover as if he had never implied Memory's race. 'Good! Good! The news is better all the time."

"I saw you looking at our temple," Taver said, stepping in to rescue Hanby from further embarrassment. "Are you of the faithful to Kamatris?"

"No," said Memory, more sharply than he had intended. *Why am I angry?* "No," he said again, more gently this time. "I'm afraid not."

"What god do you follow?"

"None."

Both men looked taken aback. "You never have?" Taver asked.

"If I did, I cannot remember."

"Of course, of course," said Taver. It was his turn to be embarrassed now. "You must be very brave, to have no fear of the gods, though."

Memory shrugged. "Should I fear them?"

Again, Taver and Hanby looked shocked. "Well," Taver said, doing his best not to sound upset, "it is true that they are more distant from us than they once were. They have not forgotten us, though. We feel them still."

"I'm afraid I don't," said Memory.

"You feel ignored?" Taver asked, sounding solicitous now.

Memory thought about that. No, he didn't feel ignored. He felt something else, something greater and sharper, but he couldn't give it a name. It wasn't something he wanted to share with Taver, though, so he shrugged and said, "Perhaps."

The priest brightened, delighted to have made a diagnosis. "There are many who have felt as you do," he said. "Please take heart. The gods do not ignore us. Especially not Kamatris. Did he not embrace humans after they were rejected by the creator Passomo?"

DAVID ANNANDALE

"True," Memory said, noncommittal. On the one hand, Taver could have told him anything at all about any of the gods, and he would have had to agree, because he knew nothing about them. On the other hand, Taver's encomium of the adoptive father of humans made Memory want to grind his teeth. The anger that he could not explain was growing stronger, and he did not want to take it out on Taver. The priest was harmless. Memory had no ill-will toward him.

"If you would ever like to talk and learn more," Taver said, "it would be my pleasure. Who knows? We might discover you followed Kamatris all along, and have simply forgotten."

"We might," Memory said, forcing himself to be civil. He thanked Taver, said his polite goodbyes to the two men, and walked on.

His shoulders were tense with the urge to strike something. The need felt like desire for revenge.

On the evening of her wedding, Latanna felt more guilt than joy.

The rain had held off, though the clouds were a solid, heavy mass over the village. A light wind blew, just enough to be felt, but not so cold that it would make sitting outside an ordeal, and there was enough of a crowd on the green that collective body warmth would see to everyone's comfort. It was, she thought, as promising an evening as she could expect, for as happy a union as she could expect.

She hated herself for thinking that.

Latanna mounted the stage to stand with Alisteyr, and she faced the love in his eyes, and the transport in his face, and she thought, *What am I doing? How is this fair to either of us?*

She could still turn around. She could leave the stage and suffer through the consequences of what followed, if she thought that was the right thing to do.

I can't.

The thought of what that would do to Alisteyr was too awful. She could not bear that burden of guilt. Standing beside him, she looked out

103

THE SLEEP OF EMPIRES

across the green at the villagers, and she felt the hope they brought with them, the hope that tonight would begin the real healing in Ghaunthook, the healing that had never properly taken place after the injury the two houses had done to each other.

I've done this. I've given all of us hope.

She was right to include herself in that, she thought. She was not sacrificing herself or Alisteyr. She was giving herself hope too. The marriage was not a trap. Through it, she was escaping the prison her father would have done everything he could to throw her into.

I love him enough. We will be good together.

That would have to do. She thought perhaps it would.

The clopping of horses made Latanna look to the road on the far side of the green. She stiffened at the sight of Elgin Hawkesmoore and his men passing slowly by, giving the people the best of their contempt. Kanstuhn and Memory moved to the edge of the crowd. They faced the horsemen. Elgin kept going, but he looked across at Latanna. She met his gaze, felt its challenge, and stared back, making him a silent promise. If he hurt anyone in Ghaunthook, she would hurt him even more.

Elgin looked away.

The Hawkesmoore party moved on. On the other side of the street from the green, Latanna spotted her father. She had wondered whether he would make an appearance. No one in the village believed he was pleased by the wedding, and there had been no chance he would swallow his defeat and take part in the festivities. He stood with his arms crossed, his face grimly expressionless. He had come to cast a shadow.

Let him. He has still lost.

When the sound of the Hawkesmoore horses faded, the ceremony began.

After bowing to the people who had come to celebrate with them, Latanna and Alisteyr faced each other. They exchanged the objects that would be the symbol of the union. He gave her the ring she would place

DAVID ANNANDALE

on his hand. It had been his grandfather's, a gold band marked by the stylized "H" rune of the Huesland name. She handed him the tiara. It was a wrench to let it out of her possession even for the length of the ceremony. It was becoming more and more meaningful to her, even though she couldn't say what, exactly, it meant.

The ceremony broke with some of the traditions of Ghaunthook unions, but not radically. There had been others before where the mayor had officiated, when the couple had been followers of different gods. Alisteyr had also insisted that he and Latanna observe the practice of remaining separate from one another for five days. It would have been normal to exchange the ring and tiara at the start of that period, but Latanna had refused to let the relic out of her sight for that long. Alisteyr had not protested. He had it now, and would be placing it on her head very soon. That was something she had not done yet. She had held the tiara, but not worn it. The moment of its first donning had to be earned, and properly marked.

Also at Alisteyr's request, they had each written their own vows. That wasn't too unusual, either, and Hanby had accommodated them happily.

Hanby welcomed the couple and crowd. He spoke a few platitudes, ones so worn through overuse that Latanna couldn't keep her attention on them. She doubted anyone else was paying attention either. When he had invoked a sufficient aura of officialdom over the rite, Hanby turned to Alisteyr. "Will you speak your vows first?" he asked.

"I will," said Alisteyr, and Latanna held up the ring before him. "I invoke the names of all the gods. I name Passomo, the creator. I name Kamatris, father of spring and our adopter. I name Tetriwu and Parserin, warrior and trickster. I name Sánmaya of the laws, and Ártimára of love. I name Endelbis of the dwarves, and Gezeiras of the kauls."

Latanna was impressed. She had never heard Endelbis or Gezeiras called upon in Ghaunthook. The god of the dwarves was simply never mentioned, an irrelevance to humans. But the god of the kauls was an unmentionable. He was not truly feared, but the distaste most humans, elves, and dwarves

105

THE SLEEP OF EMPIRES

felt for the kauls extended to their deity. Speaking his name was an act of gratitude extended to Kanstuhn. Latanna wanted to embrace Alisteyr for the gesture.

"Let all the gods look down upon me from thrones of Dengennis," Alisteyr continued. "Let my vow reach up to the City Above the Stars. May the gods bless this ring as the symbol of that vow, and of my devotion to Latanna Forgrym."

"So witnessed," said Hanby.

"So witnessed," said the crowd.

Latanna placed the ring on his finger.

"The first knot is tied," said Hanby. He was trying to intone, but he sounded too cheerful to manage it. He turned to Latanna. "Will you speak your vows and tie the second?"

Beaming, Alisteyr lifted the tiara high. Latanna gazed at it. She had struggled with what she would say at this moment. She had stayed up most of the night, writing down one attempt after another and discarding them all. She had finally settled on something that she thought she could live with. Now, she could not remember those words. They were written by someone else, centuries ago. New words came to her as she looked at the tiara. She felt as though she could see past its jewels, through the gold, into the true heart of the tiara.

Alisteyr had invoked all the gods. It was suddenly the most important thing in the world for Latanna not to invoke any at all.

"Let the tiara be my symbol," she said, beginning with an echo of Alisteyr, and he smiled, delighted, apparently not realizing that she accepted its symbolism without declaring, or even knowing, what it represented. "Let this be my vow, heard by all. I swear to remain true to the symbol before me."

Alisteyr's smile faltered. That was not what he had been hoping to hear. Latanna was sorry for that, but she was glad of what she had said. It had been the truth. She had not compromised herself. She had meant every word.

106

DAVID ANNANDALE

Hanby hesitated, apparently thinking she might want to say more, and perhaps silently hinting to her that she should. When she did not, he said, "So witnessed."

"So witnessed," said the crowd.

Alisteyr placed the tiara on her head.

A flash of silver blotted out the world. Latanna's knees buckled and she fell, and fell, and fell. Pain ripped through her skull and down her frame. It exploded out of her fingertips, and it shredded the silver. The agonizing and agonized light peeled away at the edges and from the center. It flaked away, glinting ash, revealing the darkness behind, the absolute and merciless darkness. Latanna fell into a void eternal, vast, and holy.

As she dropped into nothing, embraced the nothing, and was embraced by it, she thought she heard a name.

Kanstuhn rubbed his eyes, dazzled by the flash that had exploded from the tiara. People shouted in alarm, and then they screamed when the ground trembled, thunder in the wake of lightning. Latanna collapsed, falling bonelessly to the floor of the stage. She landed hard enough that the tiara should have flown from her hair. Yet it remained where it was, and it had changed. The silver and gold sheen had vanished, swallowed by the profoundest black. Alisteyr kneeled over her, calling her name and trying to wake her. Latanna's stillness was heavy. It looked as if Alisteyr were trying to move a corpse.

"Curse Forgrym and his poisoned relics," Kanstuhn snarled. He started forward, expecting Memory to be at his side. Then he stopped and looked back at the big sell-sword.

Memory was holding his head, and bent almost double. Kanstuhn had never seen him hurt, not like this, not incapacitated.

"Memory?" Kanstuhn asked.

After a few moments, Memory dropped his hands and straightened. He looked stunned, though less by pain than by revelation. His eyes were wide.

107

THE SLEEP OF EMPIRES

"Vorykas," he whispered, the word a scraping of stone in deep night. "My name is Vorykas."

Kanstuhn stumbled back a step, frightened for the first time in living memory. In the syllables of his friend's name, he heard the rasp of the dead land, the dark land, the land of the world's nightmares.

Voran.

CHAPTER 9

The dream swept through the slumbering empires of Eloran that night, and they stirred uneasily.

The dream came as a nightmare to Alisteyr Huesland, and to Taver Derrun, and to Marsen Forgrym, and to Elgin Hawkesmoore, and to the other thrashing sleepers in Ghaunthook. Elgin was not alone in his family to wake, gasping. The nightmare shook the entire Hawkesmoore family in Korvas. Its vise closed around Garwynn Avennic too, and Magister Veira Dunfeld, and more than a few of the powerful and the religious in that city, especially those who had heard of Garwynn's magic.

The nightmare shook the sleep of Skiriye ne Sincatsë, among others in Beresta. North of that empire, in the rival elvish power of Deltia, there were many, mostly priests, who struggled in its grip. As in the lands of the elves, so in the lands of the humans in Wakkamzin, in Kamastia, in Gharabzin and Puwirran. So too with the dwarves in Gulsentia, and the kauls in Keteria.

The dream was the same for everyone, though its effect was not. For Kanstuhn in Ghaunthook, and for the other kauls in Keteria or in bondage elsewhere in Eloran, the dream was disturbing, but when they woke, they were not sure that it had been a nightmare.

Of all the dreamers, only Latanna Forgrym woke from visions of a wall of flame and the screaming of gods to feel invigorated, as if she were ready for war.

Vorykas, his reclaimed name still a burning sensation in his mind, did not dream at all. He did not sleep. He sat on the roof of the house, still as darkness, his meditations roiling with thunder.

Witárë ne Seritsi, Commander Divine of the Berestan army and priest of Passomo, was not asleep when the nightmare passed over Árkiriye. The

THE SLEEP OF EMPIRES

night was one of those that he passed in solitary devotion before the altar of the creator. His quarters were far simpler than those that were his right. He preferred the austerity of emptiness, where the lines of the fine pillars would carry his thoughts upward to the heavens. The quarters adjoined the Temple Supernal in the center of the city, and contained a smaller version of the altar in the temple, though magnificent in its own right. A diamond sphere four feet in diameter, suspended by prismatic filaments of elvish steel, its facets caught the light of the torches and cast them about the chamber. A cool breeze, captured by windows around the circular wall, blew through at the height of the sconces and agitated the flames, creating a sense of endless revolution of the light.

Witárë was sitting before the altar, cross-legged, his fingers steepled in the shape of the chamber's celestial vault, when the nightmare arrived. He jerked forward as if struck. Cold stabbed into his heart, the cold of dread and hate. It stopped his breath and held his body rigid, his arms shaking as, weakened by horror, they struggled to support him.

He forced himself to inhale and exhale again. Gradually, the cold drained away, as if a foul veil had caressed him and had now moved on.

Witárë stood up. He looked deeply into the glimmering of the altar.

"A war is coming, Supreme Father," he said. "I will be ready."

The messenger arrived for him from the Most Perfect Council at dawn.

After Kanstuhn woke from the dream, he could not get back to sleep. He wandered outside Latanna and Alisteyr's home, circling the house as his mind chased itself, revolving through the events of the wedding. At last, he climbed up to join Vorykas on the roof.

"Restless too?" Kanstuhn asked.

"Not tired," said Vorykas.

"You have recovered from the blow you suffered, whatever it was."

Vorykas nodded.

"Have memories returned?"

"No. I have questions for you, though."

Kanstuhn thought he might. "Yes?"

"Why does my name alarm you?"

Kanstuhn took a breath. So strange that his old self, his scholar self, should keep resurfacing. He could barely remember the Kanstuhn who had held that identity. That life had disappeared, drowned by blood, buried under layers of pain and violence. But the knowledge of that old identity remained. The old skills, the old instincts, they came back.

And his friend's name revived them with jolting force. The impossible had a way of doing that.

"Your name is made from a language and a place that are extinct." Kanstuhn paused, then corrected himself. "Extinct, but not without influence. Voran is dead, its language no longer spoken. But the traces of the reach it once had remain. They echo in the other languages of the world, especially in those realms closest to the dark plateau."

"Who were the people of Voran?"

"There were no people there. Only monsters. All the beings that haunt the imagination of the races. Or so the myths tell us."

"The myths? What of the histories?"

"They are one and the same." Kanstuhn gave Vorykas a speculative look. "You know the name of the land, but not its stories. Is that right?"

"Yes."

"Curious. Its name is spoken with reluctance by all. We have just said it aloud more times than, I am quite confident, anyone in Wiramzin has said it for generations. I would say this is true even in Korvas, where the watch against its awakening never flags."

"What killed it?"

"Its death is the last great story of myth. The March of the Gods brought an end to it."

"The March of the Gods?"

THE SLEEP OF EMPIRES

"The last and greatest war, the last action the gods took before they withdrew and magic drained from the world. The gods and all the races of Eloran marched together against Voran and its dark ruler."

"And who was this ruler?"

"A god of evil." Kanstuhn shrugged. "The myths never define the enemy much beyond that, and the fact that he betrayed and slew Xestun the Builder, the maker of the divine city of Dengennis. In vengeance, the alliance destroyed the enemy and laid waste to Voran. And so the world was saved forever."

Vorykas snorted.

"What?" Kanstuhn asked innocently. "You doubt the veracity of myth?"

"I know a lie when I hear it."

His vehemence took Kanstuhn aback. The kaul took no story at face value, but Vorykas hissed with anger.

"The story is remarkably consistent across cultures and faiths. I have yet to hear a significant variation. The gods and the armies responsible for the greatest heroism change from teller to teller, naturally. But the core is always the same."

"Self-serving lies," Vorykas hissed.

"For whose benefit?" Kanstuhn asked.

"The gods'," Vorykas said. He turned away, brooding.

Skiriye despised the concept and the reality of luck. The existence of chance defied the prescriptions of perfection. The random was, by definition, imperfect. She loathed those who called upon chance, because they should know better. What she hated most of all, though, was when she herself experienced the workings of luck, whether good or bad. To acknowledge luck was to seek to escape the blame of one's own flaws, or to denigrate the skill of accomplishment.

Even so, she knew that luck had played a part in what she would accomplish today. She had worked hard. Her attention to detail had been unflag-

DAVID ANNANDALE

ging. She had done everything in her power to have an answer that would help both her and the Most Perfect Council. They needed an answer, with so many days having passed since the theft. The urgency had grown more palpable at each successive meeting of the Council. Skiriye needed an answer in order to prove her worth.

She had one today, as she entered the chamber, and it was luck that had given it to her.

When she arrived, she saw that she was not the only guest of the Council today. The Commander Divine was present too, standing with his arms crossed behind the Councilor for the Army. Paketär had the authority to send out the forces of Beresta, but Witárë ne Seritsi led them in the field. His black hair swept back from a face calm as ice, yet seemingly carved by lightning.

The Councilor for the Army reported on the state of the search first. Paketär had sent hunting parties radiating outward from Árkiriye. "Some of our searchers have reached the western coast," he said. "Others are a few days from reaching the borders with Deltia and Wiramzin. There is as yet no sign of the thief or the book."

"Deltia." Kärwene shook her head. "I still think looking there is a waste of our resources. What would Deltia have to gain by this?"

"Our embarrassment, at the very least," said Paketär. "Which would appeal to their sense of decadence."

"Even at the cost of incurring such a risk?"

"We cannot rule out any possibility," said the Immaculate. "Any false assumption could lead to disaster. The Councilor for Commerce is correct. The risk is a considerable one. But Pilta ne Akwatse would have no trouble finding a rich reward for his theft there. More than almost anywhere else." Motatsë turned her attention to Skiriye. "But perhaps the First Librarian has more concrete guidance for us at last," she said pointedly.

"I do," said Skiriye. "The theft was paid for by humans."

"You sound sure," said Paketär.

"I am."

113

THE SLEEP OF EMPIRES

"You have found conclusive evidence?"

"I have followed lines of deduction through inference. But I am confident enough to say I have a specific target for our search."

"I'm glad to hear it," Paketär said, sounding far from convinced. "I'm also surprised that any human would dare, knowing the consequences."

"I agree," Skiriye told him. "That was my first consideration. Who would dare? My answer to that is that Pilta's sponsor is less likely to be based in one of the more stable human realms, such as Kamastia. They have too much to lose in another war, and they would know that is the risk they are running. Our attention should fall on those with less to lose, and where there is already much instability."

"Wiramzin," said Motatsë.

Skiriye bowed her head to the Immaculate. "Its chaos makes it a better breeding ground for recklessness. It also means the thief would have less far to travel."

"That any human would dare astonishes me," said Kärwene. "Do they not remember the last war?"

"Many humans would not," Skiriye reminded her. "The war happened beyond the memory of any humans now living. The fact that we had to fight this battle more than once is testament to their recklessness. It was not enough to exterminate that cult of Voran." The name squirmed in her mouth like maggots. "We had to return centuries later to destroy the mathematicians. Even that is the distant past for the humans now. It is not at all inconceivable that they are making dreadful errors again, without knowing their import at all."

"Wiramzin is still a vast area to consider," said Paketär.

"It is," Skiriye said. "I have been consulting the chronicles of the wars and the maps of Wiramzin. Wherever possible, I paid attention to the human names, though our records are not as complete and perfect in this regard as would be desirable." She paused. She was about to touch on the role luck had played. The entry that caught her eye was so crucial, yet it would have been so easy to overlook. "I suggest our focus should be Northope. There is a tower, part of the fortress' domain but some distance from it. I have found only one reference to its name, on a map captured during the last wars. The map itself is a relic, and fragmentary. It was grouped with other fragments, deemed unimportant because the information was duplicated on other, better-preserved documents." She realized she was revealing that luck had played a part in her discovery, but she wanted the Most Perfect Council to know how easily the information she found could have been overlooked completely. In fact, it *had* been overlooked until now, because if anyone else had seen that name on that torn map, it would not have been filed in the general archives of the library, open to the eyes of anyone who happened to look at it.

"And what is this name?" Witárë asked with sudden interest.

"The human name translates as 'Voidwatch.'"

The stricken silence that fell over the Council lasted for a long time.

Dusk fell with the caravan working its way through thickly forested hills. Two nights out from the border with Wiramzin, the firs and the menyë trees grew tall. They were old, packed closely together, and shouldered against each other in their slow struggle for supremacy to reach for the sun. The long, serpentine leaves of the menyë coiled and uncoiled with the rhythm of slow breaths, filling the woods with a pulsing susurrus. The red-brown glow of their trunks only deepened the shadows, turning them into an almost tactile black, and the caravan merchants had to light torches before sunset. Even then, the way forward was hard to see, sullen light and pooling darkness merging and parting over the ground like slicks of oil. The gloom whispered of emptiness, of being lost, and of things hidden and clawed.

The road sloped steeply downward and twisted around the banks of the hill. The caravan would have to stop soon, Pilta thought. The way forward was too much like having to cut a path through the night itself.

The woman with the book hadn't spoken to Pilta once in all the days of the journey. She had to know that he had seen through her disguise and

THE SLEEP OF EMPIRES

followed her, since his presence in the caravan would have been too huge a coincidence otherwise. He kept his distance from her during the journey from Árkiriye. The elves and the humans in the caravan did not mix any more than necessary, so staying away from her wasn't hard. He would have preferred to remain at the back of the line of pack horses and wagons, but it was not permissible for humans to be in the lead in Beresta. He kept to himself among the elves too. The merchants all knew each other from past voyages, and he was the only passenger. That made him the object of curious looks for the first few days, but he made sure his conversation was as dull as possible, and it wasn't long before the others left him alone.

Left him alone with his thoughts, most of which were variations on *What are you going to do?*

He had no idea.

As the second-last evening fell, the caravan reached a crossroad and split in two. The majority of the wagons turned southeast. That was the direction of Korvas, as far as Pilta had been able to guess. The smaller group went southwest. The woman was part that group, and there were no elves among them. Frightened by how much he stood out now, Pilta stayed with the smaller caravan.

You don't have to do this, he told himself even as he made the decision. *You could just head to Korvas.*

And do what? I'm not going to blend in, am I?

No, but the authorities in Árkiriye will be searching for the book. Wouldn't it be better not to be near it when they find it? Because they will.

I don't know that they will.

And sticking close to the book he had stolen gave him the semblance of a purpose, even though he still didn't know what that purpose was. He just felt that, at some point, in some way, he had to do something.

He had to believe that. Otherwise there was no purpose in anything at all.

He cursed the day he had agreed to steal the book. The money was meaningless. He hadn't thought beyond his immediate needs, his imme-

DAVID ANNANDALE

diate hunger. He hadn't thought beyond the act of the theft. Now the tangled consequences of his actions had caught him, and he was terrified.

An hour after the split, after much longer than Pilta had expected, the caravan stopped for the night. There were no clearings, and the merchants made camp in the middle of the road, bringing the wagons as close together as possible. They lit fires at both ends of the line and in the middle. The travelers gathered in three groups around the fires, standing near each other for company and warmth. Pilta stayed on the other side of the wagons, away from the others, but still at the edge of torchlight.

He kept staring into the breathing, shifting darkglow of the forest. The emptiness disturbed him. It had its own whisper. It made him think of the frost he had felt when he had touched the book.

A boot crunched on stone to his right. Pilta started, and saw the woman approaching him. She folded her arms and sighed. "So," she said. "What are you up to?"

Pilta shrugged helplessly. "I don't know," he admitted.

The woman nodded, apparently pleased by his answer. "Well, that's a start." Her stance relaxed slightly. "At least you didn't say that you just wanted to travel."

"I didn't," said Pilta. "I really, really didn't."

"But you followed me."

"Yes."

"That was a mistake."

"So was getting the book for you. I couldn't stay in Árkiriye. It wasn't safe. I can't go back."

"You're going to settle in human lands, then?"

Pilta winced at the absurdity of the words spoken aloud. "I can't go back," he said again, as if that were an answer.

"No, I don't suppose you can," said the woman. "By leaving, you made sure they know it was you who stole the book."

"They would have realized anyway."

"True."

117

THE SLEEP OF EMPIRES

"What is the book?" Pilta asked. "What's the harm in telling me now?"

"A lot," the woman said. "If I tell you, I'd be making your situation much, much worse than it is now."

Is that possible? He decided to believe her. "Can you tell me where we're heading, at least?"

"Northope," she said.

"Northope," he repeated. The name meant nothing to him. "And what do I call you?"

She thought for a moment. "Call me Arva."

"Thank you," he said. It was the first bit of real contact he'd had with another being since before the theft. Even if the name was a false one, it still felt like something valuable to hold. "I guess I'm going to Northope."

"To what end, the gods will decide, is that right?"

"I know I can't."

"It's good that you do. But do you really know what exile will mean for an elf?"

"I think I'm better off not knowing for now."

"You're sounding wiser by the moment," said Arva. "You'd better know this, though. You'll probably have to keep running."

"I know."

"I don't believe you. I don't think you thought about that until I said it."

Pilta shrugged again, nodded. "I don't really know anything at all," he said. "Not anymore."

Arva gave him a long, hard look. Then she smiled. It wasn't much of a smile. It was small and cold. It was still a smile. "That might just be the most sensible thing you've said to me. It might also be the best way for you to face what's coming."

The way she said that alarmed him. "What is coming?"

Her grin became broad. "I don't know either. Isn't that exciting? But things are going to change." She clapped him on the shoulder. "Thanks to you and me."

DAVID ANNANDALE

Pilta tried to smile back. He failed. Fear had numbed his lips, and they wouldn't obey.

The morning after the wedding, Elgin sat in Marsen's hall and drank as if he owned the house. He sat in Marsen's favorite chair, high-backed and close to the hearth. He sat sideways, swinging a leg over the arm. He drank Marsen's wine, downing it like it was water and not worth savoring.

Marsen leaned against the mantle, one foot on the hearth. He wasn't about to sit in a chair that might signal his capitulation to Elgin's claim.

"It's a shame the groom didn't fall ill instead." Elgin took another gulp of the wine, glanced into the cup with a mild frown, then drank again. "How is your daughter, by the way?" he asked as if inquiring about the weather.

"I'm still waiting to hear." No one had come to Forgrym Hall with news. Marsen wouldn't lower himself to knocking on the door of the house Latanna and Alisteyr had taken for themselves in the village. "She's strong. She's a Forgrym. She'll recover." If the worst had happened, that he would know. No one would have dared to keep word of Latanna's death from him. "Things can still happen to the groom," he added.

Elgin raised his eyebrows. "So soon?"

"I have no set date in mind. Perhaps you do."

"It will be difficult with those sell-swords about," Elgin said thoughtfully.

"Too difficult for you?" Marsen took some pleasure in seeing Elgin suddenly uncomfortable. He craved what an alliance with the Hawkesmoores would give him, but Latanna had been right about his subordinate position with them. It was good to see Elgin wobble on his self-erected pedestal of superiority.

"I don't know about too difficult," said Elgin, defensive. "It would be messy, though. You said you didn't want things messy."

True. With the entire village celebrating the marriage and what it represented, an obvious and bloody assassination could rebound against

THE SLEEP OF EMPIRES

Marsen, maybe to the point of making the Hawkesmoores lose all interest in him. "Depending on how long Latanna is ill, though, there might be some possibilities," he said. She would not be able to watch over Alisteyr. "The attentions of the sell-swords might be divided."

Elgin downed the last of his wine and held the cup out for more. "We'll watch and wait," he said.

"You won't be leaving soon, then," Marsen said, relieved.

"Not without what's mine."

Latanna and Alisteyr's small house sat at the end of the road that ran past the Laughing Chimera. The road stopped a hundred yards from the riverbank, and the house's modest hall looked out at the line of forest between it and the Ghaunt. The house was humble for the heirs to the Marsen and Huesland names. It was also something they could afford with the income granted happily by Alisteyr's parents, and reluctantly by Marsen.

Alisteyr had imagined many things about how his first morning in the house with Latanna would be. None of them had involved him sitting by himself in the hall while two sell-swords mounted guard outside.

None of them had involved what had happened to Latanna.

She had not woken since collapsing on the stage. She was breathing, at least, and Alisteyr had checked on her every hour since Kanstuhn and Vorykas had carried her here and placed her in the bedchamber. No one could wake her. Luva Stonebloom, the village wisewoman, had tended to her, but hadn't been able to do anything. Latanna was breathing comfortably, she was not feverish, and she did not seem to be ailing. She just wouldn't wake up.

And the blackened tiara would not come off her head.

Alisteyr sat at a table next to the hall window, tracing the rough grain of the wood with his finger. His eyes stung, and his head swam if he stood up too quickly. He knew he should eat and drink something, but he had no appetite, or the energy to fix himself something.

120

DAVID ANNANDALE

A numbing fog of worry and grief enveloped him. His mind kept replaying the battle in the crypt, as if with enough repetitions, the past would alter and he would walk away from the cursed tiara.

I was worried from the start. Why did I bring it back? Why did I give it to her? What have I let Marsen do to us?

He was still sitting there late in the morning, revolving his way through guilt and fear, when the bedroom door opened and Latanna emerged. She was still wearing her wedding gown. It had torn when she fell, and it reminded Alisteyr uncomfortably of Elisava Marsen. So did Latanna's appearance. She was pale, much paler than before the wedding. She seemed thinner, too, her cheekbones more prominent, as if her skull were closer to the surface.

Alisteyr jumped up and ran to her, arms out to support her. She waved him off. "I'm all right," she said. "I feel fine." Her eyes were bright, but Alisteyr couldn't decide if that was energy or fever he saw there. The green of her irises seemed darker than he remembered.

"You don't look well," Alisteyr said.

"Don't fuss over me, please. I know how I'm feeling." She looked down at herself. "I should change," she said.

Alisteyr looked at the tiara. "You should take that off too," he said, pointing. Maybe she would succeed where he hadn't.

Latanna raised her hand to her head. She touched the tiara gingerly. "I didn't know it was still there," she said.

"Do you remember what happened last night?"

She nodded, still fingering the tiara. "It feels different," she said.

"It looks like iron now. Only blacker."

"Huh." She rubbed its ridges. "Yes. It feels rougher." She didn't seem to be in any hurry to remove the relic.

"It hurt you, Latanna. You must take it off. Please."

"Very well." She sounded as if she were humoring him.

Latanna pulled on the tiara. It didn't budge. She pulled harder, and then harder yet, wincing. It didn't move at all, any more than if she had

121

THE SLEEP OF EMPIRES

tried to pull off her head. "I can't," she said. She didn't sound as worried as she should be.

"Do you want me to try?" Alisteyr asked.

"All right," she said, again as if she were humoring him. She bowed her head, giving him easy access to the tiara.

He reached out, hesitated for a moment, afraid of being struck by lightning, then took hold. It did feel like iron, and Alisteyr thought its shape had changed as well. It was larger than it had been, and there were protrusions along its crescent, like the buds of horns. The red jewel had vanished. Alisteyr pulled, gradually adding more force. "Tell me to stop if it starts to hurt," he said.

He was hauling on the tiara with almost all his strength before she said, "Stop."

Alisteyr let go and took a step back, his hand tingling unpleasantly.

Latanna touched the tiara again. "That felt strange," she said. "It didn't really hurt at all. I thought it would. I'm surprised you didn't pull my hair out."

"Your hair didn't move at all," Alisteyr said, his voice croaking a bit, just a little bit. "Like it isn't attached to your hair at all."

Latanna felt around the base of the tiara with both hands. She parted her hair, and for a moment Alisteyr saw the base against her scalp, and had the impression of it sinking down into the skin.

"It feels like it's part of my skull," Latanna said, confirming his horror. She gave the tiara one more tug, then dropped her hands. She still appeared more interested than afraid.

"This is . . ." Alisteyr began.

"Magic? Sorcery?"

"Of an evil kind." He had never witnessed anything sorcerous until going to the cemetery. He wished he never had. "We have to do something," he said helplessly.

"Well, we're not hacking it off with an axe."

DAVID ANNANDALE

"Someone must be able to help. Some other kind of magic, a blessing . . . I don't know!"

"I think this is a bit beyond what Taver Derrun can do."

"Then we should go to Korvas. Someone there could help."

"Who? Are you going to track down your friend Garwynn? See how far his magic studies have progressed?"

Alisteyr hadn't thought of Garwynn. "Maybe." Yes. Magic. They needed magic.

Latanna sighed. "I wasn't serious," she said. "He isn't even attending the university any longer, from what you said."

"He isn't," Alisteyr admitted. He felt a touch of guilt about how perfunctory his last few letters to Garwynn had been. He had felt sorry that his friend had had to abandon his studies, and had said so, but he had been so caught up in his own hopes and worries that he hadn't written more than the bare minimum. "Garwynn might still know something that might help."

"We're not going to Korvas," Latanna said, her tone final. "We have things we have to do here. And I feel fine."

"You have a cursed relic fused to your skull! You're not fine! You don't look well!"

"What I look like is not the point. I feel like I've slept for days, and I'm bursting with energy. We were going to help your parents on the farm, weren't we?"

"In a day or two," said Alisteyr. "And that was before you were sick."

"I'm not sick. I'm ready to work now." She turned to head back to the bedchamber.

"There's something else you should know," Alisteyr said, and told her about Vorykas. She listened, and was still for a long moment. She didn't say anything, then went into the chamber to get changed.

They met Vorykas on the way out of the house.

"I'm glad to see you well," he said. He gave the tiara a significant look.

123

THE SLEEP OF EMPIRES

Latanna smiled. "This is my new constant companion," she said. "I don't mind. At all, as it happens."

Vorykas nodded slowly.

"I hear you have your name now," said Latanna.

"I do."

Alisteyr envied the look of understanding they shared.

They are both mysteries now.

CHAPTER 10

Garwynn was awake when the knock came at the door of his lodgings. He had been awake since the dream, long before dawn, sitting by his smoke-grimed window, watching for the graying of the night. He could barely see the street one floor below, but he did see the glow of torchlight approach the boarding house door, just before the first hint of sunrise would touch the roofs of Korvas.

Each day since his meeting with Magister Dunfeld, he had woken with the expectation of a summons. She had told him she would find rooms for him at the university, but that had not happened yet, and each day he remained in his old lodgings, the prospect of the move to the university seemed more remote, and a less welcome invitation more likely. After the dream of this night, his expectation of a summons had become a certainty. It was almost a relief when he heard the knock on the street door, and then, a few moments later, the tramp of booted feet climbing the stairs to his room. Garwynn opened the door before his callers had the chance to hammer against it. In the hall were two temple guards of Sánmaya. Their long, black-and-violet robes covered their armor. They wore the golden masks of their faith. All the temple guards had the face of the goddess of laws. They were not individuals. They were Sánmaya's instruments, the human bodies through which she brought order to the world. That made them, in practice, the enforcers in Korvas.

Garwynn had guessed that these guards had come for him. His stomach still dropped in fear at the sight of them.

"Garwynn Avennic," said the guard on the left. The voice was a woman's. "You will come with us."

No explanation, just the statement of fact, its wording always the same. More powerful and frightening than a command, because it articulated a reality that could not be challenged.

125

THE SLEEP OF EMPIRES

Garwynn nodded. He was ready. He had donned a cloak as soon as he had woken, knowing he would be venturing out into the cold on this day. He closed the door to his quarters and headed down the stairs, one guard ahead of him, the other behind. Outside, they walked on either side of him. They did not warn him against trying to escape. There was no need. Everyone knew better than to run from a Sánmaya guard.

"I'm happy to do anything that will be asked of me," Garwynn said. He wanted the guards to know that he would cooperate. "This is why I came forward. I need guidance. I need to know the right thing to do."

The guards said nothing.

"Will you tell me something?" he asked. "Did either of you dream last night?"

Still no reply, though both guards looked at him, and the eyes behind the masks were cold.

They took him through streets that gradually woke with the coming of a gray day. An hour's walk brought them to the west end of the city, and the temple of Sánmaya. The city's prison stood next to the temple, a fact that Garwynn had always taken for granted, but saw with fresh, worried eyes today. The prison's dark, squat bulk seemed less intimidating than the imposing mass of the temple. The House of Law was a square-topped pyramid, its smooth, sloping sides seeming to plunge into the ground and take root, spreading the power of the goddess across the city. The goddess in marble stood on a plinth jutting out above the bronze doors of the entrance. She held a sword in her right hand. In her left was a star, its rays tipped with arrow points, striking out to all of Eloran.

The guards escorted Garwynn up the steps to the main entrance. There were two sentinels at the entrance. They pulled the doors, and Garwynn stepped inside.

The interior was dark. Only a single one of the huge lanterns hanging from the ceiling of the great prayer chamber had been lit, and its glow hardly touched the entrance hall. Garwynn saw only four shapes in front

126

DAVID ANNANDALE

of him, but he knew they were guards, and he knew now too that he had not been brought here to speak before a gathering of concerned scholars.

The guards he had arrived with pinned his arms behind his back and bound them. Another guard dropped a hood over his head and pulled it tight so the cloth pressed against his mouth and nose. He struggled for breath. Then they tied his legs together too, lifted him up, and carried him off to the left.

Garwynn lost all sense of distance and direction. The guards took him down a hall, and then through a door that opened and closed with the creak and boom of iron. Then there were stairs, and another door, and more halls, and more stairs. Caught in the smothering nightmare of the hood, he gasped and choked.

He knew where the descent would end, and the terror of that thought was greater than the claustrophobic terror of suffocation. The dungeon beneath the House of Law was a thing of rumors and whispers in Korvas. Everyone knew it existed. Everyone feared it. No one knew anything about it except to fear it. It was the place beyond prison, the hole that swallowed those who must disappear for the good of order.

Finally, after one more shriek and crash of doors, the guards shoved Garwynn onto a hard seat and removed the hood. He took in ragged gulps of air as he looked around. He was in a cell. A grate in the door ahead of him let in torchlight from the corridor beyond. Moisture trickled down walls of black, pitted stone. His seat was iron, marked with silver runes. The guards undid his arms and made him place them on the rests of the seat, then closed heavy clamps around his hands. He could no longer move his fingers. Then the guards shackled his legs.

A priest of Sánmaya oversaw the work. He wore no mask. White-haired, his face deeply lined by the years, he looked at Garwynn with an expression of mingled pity and anxiety.

"Why?" Garwynn pleaded. "I've done no harm. I will do whatever is asked of me."

127

THE SLEEP OF EMPIRES

"Harm," the priest said. "No one in these cells has ever meant to do harm, if I am to believe what they tell me. I hear many lies. Sometimes, though, I hear the truth, even before it is forced out of reluctant lips. I think you might be one of those few who is telling me the truth, or at least what you believe it to be." He shook his head slowly, sadly. "Harm," he said again. "You don't understand the word. You don't understand what it really means, and how it comes about. Intent is irrelevant, Garwynn Avennic. You have done harm already. Some would say you are doing more even now, simply by existing. They would, if allowed to have their way, put a stop to any chance of further harm from you right now. They may yet get their wish, but for the moment you are spared, because there are more, like myself, who think we must study what is happening more deeply before deciding on a course of action."

"What is happening?" said Garwynn. "What do I have to do with anything?"

"Magic is happening," the priest said. "Magic is happening with an ease and a power in a way that has never happened within the memory of our chronicles. And last night . . ." The priest paused, and watched him carefully.

"The dream," Garwynn said. There was no point in dissembling. He could not make things worse for himself. If he still had a chance, he thought, it would only come through perfect obedience and cooperation. He was too frightened to imagine saying anything except the full truth.

"The dream," the priest agreed.

"So I wasn't the only one."

"Far from it. You do not condemn yourself by that admission. You may, though, be condemned by your magic. I will not offer you hope where there is none. Do not expect to leave here. But be certain that whatever happens, your fate is governed by the law at its most absolute and rigorous."

"What is going to happen to me?"

"I cannot tell. No one can. Not yet. Until we know what must be done with you, you will remain here. You will be fed. You will be given water.

128

You will be prevented from casting spells. For this reason, your fingers are held immobile. And between your moments of food and drink, you will be prevented from speaking."

The priest nodded to someone behind Garwynn. Hands brought an iron framework down around his head. It was a bridle. Cold metal pressed into his mouth, holding his tongue down. Screws tightened the muzzle over his face. He choked, gargling inarticulate prayers. Saliva spilled over his lips and dribbled down his chin.

"Do not anger your jailers when they come to feed you," the priest warned. "Learn to savor your moments of relief, and hold your tongue. If you speak even once without permission, that will be the last time the bridle is removed."

Garwynn whimpered. He tried to beg the priest with his eyes.

The old man shook his head once more. "Accept the law," he said.

The priest and the guards left. They shut the door, sealing Garwynn away in the dark.

She grew worse in the evening. Latanna knew she had because of the way Alisteyr and Kanstuhn looked at her. She knew it because of the way her breath rattled. She knew it from looking at her hands. Her skin, now almost as pale as Kanstuhn's, had tightened around her bones, making her fingers seem too long and pointed. She had even less appetite than she had had in the morning, and she had barely eaten anything during the day.

She would not have known she had grown worse from the way Vorykas looked at her, though. He seemed curious, profoundly interested, as if what she was undergoing was as important to him as it was to her. He did not look worried.

She also would not have known she had grown worse if she had only paid attention to the way she felt. She was restless, energized. She had worked in the Huesland fields all day, and she was ready for more. Sleep was for other people. She needed her next task.

THE SLEEP OF EMPIRES

The next task, though, was one she would have to leave for others. It required skills she did not have.

Not yet, said a voice she knew as hers, but that she didn't fully understand.

"How many cloudblossom addicts did you see in the fields today?" Latanna asked the other three. They were sitting in the house's tiny hall. The room felt even smaller with Vorykas' hulking shape inside.

"Four, I think," said Alisteyr. Kanstuhn nodded in agreement.

Latanna had counted the same. The drug did not have a full hold on them yet. They were able to work, though slowly and clumsily. They kept looking into the middle distance, their expressions going slack and vague, as the hallucinations they longed for teased with the phantoms of the reality more cloudblossom would create for them.

"There were six," Vorykas corrected. "The other two are in much earlier stages. They can still hide their symptoms. They still believe they aren't addicted."

The others looked at him in surprise.

"How can you know that?" Alisteyr asked. "You don't know those people. You don't know what they're like normally. How do you even know all the symptoms? You didn't know your own name before yesterday."

Vorykas shrugged, not offended. "I know," he said simply. "I could tell they were believing in lies." His eyes narrowed, their anger directed outside the house.

"There were more in the village today too," said Kanstuhn.

"I don't want to wait any longer," Latanna said. "It's only going to get worse, with such a huge supply so close." She looked at Kanstuhn. "How soon would you and Vorykas be ready to attack the plantation?"

"Tonight," the kaul said simply.

"Good," said Latanna.

"I must ask if this is wise," said Kanstuhn.

"Good," said Alisteyr. "Because it isn't. Latanna is not well. She's more vulnerable than ever to anything her father or Elgin might try."

130

His protectiveness made her bristle. "I don't think either of them is planning to stage a raid on this house the day after the wedding. That would be stupid, and the one thing I'll grant them is that they're not stupid. I am not weak. You might think so, Alisteyr, but I'm not. I've never felt better." She realized the protestation sounded feeble with the loud, crackling gurgles her lungs were making. "I'm more than capable of looking after myself." She almost said *both of us*, and felt that to be the truth. She didn't, out of respect for Alisteyr.

"I agree," Vorykas said. He nodded once, as if putting an end to all doubts.

Kanstuhn eyed him. "You are gifted with more and more certainties. They give me pause."

"I understand. I would like to know how I come by them too."

"How can you agree with her?" Alisteyr protested. "Look at her!"

"I see what you see. But I'm also listening to what she is saying, and I believe her."

"Thank you," said Latanna. To Kanstuhn she said, "If you can destroy that plantation tonight, then please do."

"Very well." Kanstuhn rose, and Vorykas followed him out of the house.

Alisteyr looked stricken.

"Stop worrying," Latanna told him.

"How can you ask that of me? You know there's something wrong. We have to *do* something to save you."

"We've been through this already."

Alisteyr stared at her in open disbelief. "We're not talking about whether we should wear blue or red tomorrow. That thing . . ." He pointed at the tiara. "That thing is killing you."

"No," she said. "I don't think so."

"You don't think so? You look feverish. You're thinner than you were this morning. Each breath you take sounds like it could be your last. Somehow, we have to remove the tiara."

THE SLEEP OF EMPIRES

"*No.*" Her vehemence made him recoil. She gathered her thoughts, fingering the points on the tiara. "I'm not deluded," she said. "I know this is doing something to me. I feel it every moment. I do, Alisteyr. I really do. I know that what it's doing is serious."

"Then why . . . ?"

"Because I want to know what is going to happen."

She hadn't thought Alisteyr could look even more disbelieving. "Even if it kills you?" he sputtered.

"It won't."

"I think it will."

Latanna put a hand on his wrist. "What's happening to me is important. I don't know anything other than that, and I'm at peace with that. I'm excited about what is happening. I know that you can't be." She looked down at her fingers, and found herself thinking of talons. "I understand completely why you can't be. But I'm asking you to accept my decision."

She squeezed his arm in reassurance.

He winced in pain.

Vorykas and Kanstuhn approached the ruins of Forgrym Castle with two flasks of oil and a bundle of unlit torches. That was enough for a good night's work.

They stayed in the shelter of the woods near the base of the east side of the rise leading up to the ruins. Invisible in the night, they eyed the walls.

"Young Hawkesmoore has been busy," Kanstuhn whispered. "There have been repairs."

"The walls look solid," said Vorykas. Latanna had told them of the gaps she had seen. They were gone. Torches had been mounted at regular intervals along the parapets, illuminating the defenses, revealing the new patches of stonework. The castle shell would not withstand a siege by an attacking host, but it would hold off most raiding parties. "And Hawkesmoore has reinforcements," Vorykas added. There were far more men on the wall than

132

had been accompanying Elgin the night of the confrontation at Forgrym Hall.

"The talent of the roads," Kanstuhn said. "We met some of their kind when we arrived in Ghaunthook. Elgin has purchased their loyalty and their labor of blood. I wonder if he has purchased discipline for them as well."

"Let's find out," said Vorykas.

"The riches inside those walls are great, and will command steep resistance to what we intend. They will seek to interrupt us. I think it will be necessary to kill everyone there."

"That's their decision. I won't regret their choices. They will."

"Your anger," said Kanstuhn.

"What about it?"

"You do not know any of the people we are about to fight. You know little about anything other than what you have been told. But you are speaking more like a zealot than a sell-sword."

"You don't know them, either," said Vorykas.

"No. My acceptance of the need for a massacre has been won through long experience. You have none."

"I know enough to judge."

"So it seems. But how?"

"Does it matter? We're here to burn cloudblossom."

"Indulge me for a moment. Your eagerness to destroy the plant is interesting. Do you remember our encounters with its victims? We have seen many in our travels."

"I don't remember any before Ghaunthook." Vorykas paused. "No. Wait." He raised his hands. His fingers closed slightly, muscle memory recalling acts of mercy. "I don't remember them," he said, "but my body remembers what I had to do."

"The past keeps reaching for you, then, a little at a time."

"The reason for my anger lies there too. I need to destroy illusions, and the flowers of lies."

"Then we have come to the right place."

THE SLEEP OF EMPIRES

They moved on through the trees, heading north, where the slope of the hill was less steep and the forest drew closest to the wall. They watched for gaps in the stonework, and between the sentinels. They saw none. Elgin was spending his gold to preserve the prospect of making much more.

They stopped again at the northwest corner. The tower that had once stood here had collapsed, creating a slope of rubble outside the wall.

"An easy, fast climb," said Vorykas.

Kanstuhn took up his bow. "An easy target too." He drew an arrow from his quiver and took aim at the sentry. "When you're ready."

Vorykas charged out of the forest cover, sword drawn. As he started his uphill sprint, he had a moment to wonder how many times, over how many years, he had fought and killed. He didn't know, and he didn't know how he came by his skills. How had he developed and retained them while having no memories? It didn't matter. His body knew. His instincts knew. In two steps, he discarded his doubts and questions, and became a vector of death.

The sentry spotted him right away. The man started, surprised. Before he could shout, Kanstuhn's arrow pierced his throat. He pitched forward, off the wall and onto the rubble of the tower. His fall made noise. Vorykas didn't care. He and Kanstuhn had the first kill, and the advantage in the battle. The enemy just didn't know it.

Vorykas hit the slope of fallen stone. He raced up it, leaping between jutting points, almost flying, his footing sure. He grinned.

Other guards had seen the fall of the sentry, and the cry went up. Vorykas reached the top of the wall, and the first of the other guards was only a few yards away, coming south along the western wall.

Vorykas ran to meet him. In the corner of his eye, he saw two other sentries rushing along the north wall, just a bit further away. They thought they had him cornered.

Kanstuhn's arrows took them down. Vorykas heard the *thunk* of the impacts and the cut-off screams of pain at the same time as he and the other sentry collided. The man tried to run Vorykas through as they closed.

134

DAVID ANNANDALE

Vorykas batted the man's arm away with one hand, knocking the sword from his grip, and brought his own blade in from the side. A single blow decapitated the guard. Vorykas ran past the toppling body and through a wash of blood without breaking his stride. Two other hirelings had been charging toward him, but now they hesitated.

They're frightened. Good. They should be.

They could also wait for his attentions. He jumped to his left, off the wall, and landed in the cloudblossom. The white flowers shone like bone in the torchlight. The blooms nodded away from him in a wide circle, as though the lies they embodied recognized the threat he presented.

He carried the oil flasks over his shoulder. Their bulk had not slowed him. He had barely felt it. He took one now, opened it, and splashed the oil on all sides.

An arrow thudded into the ground next to him.

Vorykas took flints from his belt, knelt and struck them. Sparks flew, and the oil ignited. He grinned again, feeling the sudden wind of flame against his face.

More shouts from the walls. There was a brief volley of arrows, but the fire dazzled the guards and their shots went wide. Then Kanstuhn dropped two more on the north wall. Half the guards ran to try to stop his attacks. They shot arrows into the dark of the woods, fighting shadows. The others grouped together on the western wall, preparing for a massed attack.

Vorykas counted another fifteen hirelings altogether.

He pulled torches from the bundle on his back, lit them, and threw them further into the field, spreading the fire. Then he opened the other flask and threw it too. It trailed oil, and flames chased it, catching it as it landed and setting off a small but satisfying explosion.

Cloudblossom ash and smoke rose over the field. The poison in the air wasn't concentrated enough to be dangerous, but when he breathed, Vorykas felt a tickle at the back of his mind, lies prying, searching for a crack, a way in, and failing.

THE SLEEP OF EMPIRES

The men on the wall shouted at him and at each other. One of them was Dawun, Elgin's big man of arms. He seemed to be in command, or at least was trying to maintain it. He pointed at Vorykas, ordering an attack, but the others were reluctant to descend into the growing fire, as if they thought the cloudblossom would catch them if they did.

Vorykas solved the dilemma for them. He leapt through the flames and rushed the wall. He felt the intense heat on his skin as something at a distance, information about sensations, but he did not feel pain.

Something hit him hard in the back of the neck. It hurt only for a moment, and then receded from his consciousness. It did not slow him, and so was unimportant.

The hirelings reared back as he jumped up to the parapet. They outnumbered him eight to one, but they reacted as if they were the ones who were cornered.

"I don't see your employer," Vorykas said to Dawun. He took a slow, threatening step toward the guards, then another. "Run away, has he?"

At the head of the guards, Dawun advanced, his face taut. "He has other things to do."

Vorykas snorted. "I don't doubt it. Such an important man. I guess this field doesn't matter to him after all? Why are any of you here, then?"

"You are arrogant scum," said Dawun, reaching for bravado.

"Not really," said Vorykas. "I'm just better at what I'm hired to do than you are." The taunt was close to a lie. He would be here whether Latanna paid him or not. He didn't care about gold. He cared about turning the field into a waste of cinders.

Dawun came at him, roaring, flanked by two other guards. Next to Dawun, they were poorly armored, and their swords were crude. Dawun had been armed by Hawkesmoore riches. He had lived well by working for Elgin. He was a man used to being feared, and who liked it. Tonight was a new experience for him, one he did not like at all.

Vorykas' blade was long and broad. Anyone else would have wielded it with two hands. He could make it flash like a rapier, and coupled with

136

DAVID ANNANDALE

his size, the reach of his steel was much greater than that of the men coming for him. He began his attack with a diagonal slash down from the right. He cut through the first man's left arm and chest, then into Dawun's gut. He angled up, back through the other hireling's chest, and then flashed back down again. In a single, unbroken movement, he carved a figure-eight in the air and in flesh.

The men on either side of Dawun staggered away, clutching their wounds. Dawun fell to his knees, his life pouring out of the rip in his torso. He tried to gasp something, but all he managed was a wheeze of hatred and fear. Vorykas ran past him, leaving him to his death, and closed with the other hirelings.

They ran from him.

He ran faster. He became their end. He became *the* end. His perception narrowed until the purity of annihilation defined his being. This was not a struggle, not a clash of arms. His sword was not a weapon. It was the manifestation of his will, and his will was the destruction of existence. He was no longer aware of his movements. Something deeper, more primal and more powerful than instinct possessed him. For the guards, reality bent and broke at his coming. They saw him, and then there was only darkness, and he tasted their terror of the ending.

When he had finished, he stood motionless for a few moments, purposeless in the absence of enemies. It took Kanstuhn's voice to bring him back to himself.

"I said, do you need help?"

Vorykas blinked. Kanstuhn was at his side, his eyes wide with concern. "No," he said. "They're all dead." He looked back. Bodies lay in pieces behind him, a trail of absolute death.

"I mean with your injury."

"My injury?"

Kanstuhn's look of concern deepened. "The arrow."

"Where?"

"In your neck."

THE SLEEP OF EMPIRES

Vorykas frowned. He remembered the impact, and an echo of something like pain. He reached back, and felt the shaft sticking out from the base of his neck. He pulled it free with an irritated jerk and tossed it away. "I'm all right," he said.

"You should be bleeding."

Implications sank in. "You mean I should be dead," Vorykas said.

Kanstuhn said nothing.

"Has this happened before?"

"You have always been resistant to injury," said Kanstuhn. "Resistant to a point that has made me wonder. But you have also always been skilled at *evading* injury. I believed your survival was due to skill and luck." He grimaced. "At least, I told myself that was what I believed."

"And now?"

"Now we have still more questions, don't we?"

"And no way to answer them."

The flames had spread across the entire field. They filled the interior of the ruins and rose higher, licking the tops of the ruined towers. The oils in the flowers burned more ferociously than Vorykas had imagined, but he welcomed the blaze. He and Kanstuhn tossed the pieces of bodies into the cloudblossom pyre. The sundered flesh vanished into the anger of the flames.

The glow accompanied Vorykas and Kanstuhn all the way back to the village. They were almost at the outskirts of Ghaunthook when they heard, coming from the ruins, the sharp, thunderous cracks of the earth splitting open.

CHAPTER 11

The roar in the earth jolted Marsen from his bed. He jumped up, on his feet before he was awake, heart pounding with the need to run or fight. A dim, dark orange light pulsed against his window. He stumbled over to it and looked to the north. Something burned in the night, beyond the other side of the village, uphill from the river.

Marsen's jaw dropped. Only one thing could be on fire in that direction, a direction in which he looked with the pain of damaged family pride every night.

May Tetriwu crush you, you bastards. May Tetriwu crush your skulls beneath his iron heel. May your blood anoint his soles.

Tetriwu curse you, Latanna. You don't know what you've done.

She had to be behind this.

Marsen turned away from the window. He sat in a high-backed chair beside the bed. He clasped his hands and beat a slow, steady rhythm against his chin, thinking. Elgin had changed his mind about lingering in Ghaunthook and watching for an opportunity to kill Alisteyr. He had grown bored with the plan almost as soon as he had articulated it. He had business in Korvas he wanted to attend to, and had left the previous afternoon.

"We'll settle things when I get back," had been his parting command to Marsen. "Sort out what needs to be done."

What needs to be done now? How bad is this? The cloudblossom is gone.

It could be worse. If Elgin had stayed, he might be dead. If the plantation was on fire, then none of the Hawkesmoore men left to guard it were around to stop the destruction. At least Marsen wasn't facing the prospect of the entire Hawkesmoore clan descending on him, looking for blood.

Could be worse, but not by much. Elgin will be back within a month. What do we tell him?

THE SLEEP OF EMPIRES

When do we tell him?

Marsen hauled on the bell pull beside the chair. While he waited for a servant to arrive, he lit a lantern and sat at the writing table in front of the window. He wrote quickly, and kept the message short. He only needed a sentence to convey what had happened. Embellishment would serve no purpose. The only thing Elgin would register would be the destruction of the cloudblossom.

The bedroom door opened. The sentry on night duty entered.

"Take this," Marsen said before the man could speak. He held out the letter. "Ride the Korvas Road with all speed. Do not stop until you catch up with Elgin Hawkesmoore. And then do not stop until you return to me with his answer."

"As you command." The guard pocketed the letter and withdrew.

The glow of the burn pulled Marsen's unwilling gaze back to the window. His hands tightened into angry fists. *Latanna, what did you think would happen? I can guess. You thought Elgin would lose all interest in Ghaunthook if you destroyed his main reason for being here. You thought this would mean no more Hawkesmoore presence here and in your life.*

Spear of Tetriwu, after all this, you really are a fool.

Latanna thought she could read Elgin. She thought he was governed by gain.

You've given him a new interest in Ghaunthook. Revenge.

Marsen looked to the days ahead. Elgin would be coming back for blood. There was no point, at least for now, in trying to imagine a way Marsen could still forge an alliance with the Hawkesmoores. That would be for later. For now, he had to ensure his own survival. He had to see to it that Elgin's vengeance didn't fall on him. The message was the first step, informing Elgin immediately. *I am not trying to hide anything from you. I'm as angry as you are.*

I'm also frightened of your anger. As I should be.

And I have anger too, that people should be afraid of. They haven't been.

140

DAVID ANNANDALE

Time to change that.

It astonished him that Latanna would challenge him so directly. *Doesn't she know I'll retaliate? Or is she not concerned?* Both possibilities enraged him. He had kept his word and let the marriage to the Huesland whelp go forward. He had never planned to let it last, but he had thought he would give Latanna at least until Elgin's return to enjoy her victory. A month had seemed long enough for her guard to be down, and the sell-swords to be on their way.

Marsen glared at the dirty light of the fire. He couldn't wait until Elgin's return. He would have to present Elgin with Alisteyr's death as an accomplished fact.

Give it a few days. Stay quiet. Do nothing to attract Latanna's attention. Maybe the sell-swords will leave.

If they don't?

Then he would throw all the strength he still had into one final attack to end the war with the Hueslands.

I have the men to take those sell-swords by surprise. If they and Alisteyr die, then I've won. It won't matter if the Hueslands try to hit back. Anger in Ghaunthook won't matter. I'll have the Hawkesmoores with me.

He had to believe the dice would roll in his favor. He had no choice but to throw them.

Midmorning, Vorykas and Kanstuhn returned to the castle's hill with Latanna and Alisteyr. The fire had burned itself out. A pall of black smoke lingered over the land, reluctant to end its reign.

Latanna was thinner still, her skin tighter and more sallow. The horns of the tiara had grown longer. That was how Vorykas saw them. They were horns, five of them, radiating out from Latanna's forehead.

Vorykas and the others stopped just beyond the forest, with the bare crown of the castle's hill before them.

The ruins were gone.

THE SLEEP OF EMPIRES

After a few moments of silence, Latanna said, "I didn't expect you to be *this* thorough."

"Neither did we," said Vorykas, as surprised as she was.

"How?" said Alisteyr. He sounded almost upset. "How did you do this? *What* did you do?"

"We burned the cloudblossom," Kanstuhn said.

"And . . . ? What else?"

"That was all."

"What did you use?"

"Two oil flasks and some torches," Vorykas told Alisteyr.

Alisteyr gaped. "Is cloudblossom so combustible that it could do this?"

"It is not," said Kanstuhn.

Vorykas started up the hill. The others followed.

"Wasn't the peak higher than this?" Latanna asked.

"It was," said Vorykas. "Look, even the foundations are gone."

They reached the new crest and, perching on broken rock, peered down into a crater.

"A fire could not have done this," said Alisteyr.

"No natural one," Kanstuhn agreed.

"But it was a natural one you set."

"That we set, yes," said Kanstuhn. "Somehow, it became something else. Does it not seem to you, as it does to me, that without knowing it, we called, and something answered?"

The crater was at least fifty feet deep. The shell of Castle Forgrym had crumbled into it, and it had burned. The stones and bricks of the walls were scorched black, and reduced to a scattering.

"Can stone become ash?" Vorykas mused.

"I have been wondering that too," said Kanstuhn. "There is too little rubble."

"And what *is* that?" Alisteyr demanded, his gaze fixed on the structure that had been buried beneath the foundations of Castle Forgrym.

142

DAVID ANNANDALE

A temple sat at the bottom of the crater. A ring of granite pillars, half-embedded in the rock wall, surrounded a granite dais. The splintered, burned remains of the castle rested on it like the bones of devoured prey.

"We have seen this design before," said Kanstuhn.

Vorykas nodded. "You recognize it, don't you?" he said to Alisteyr.

Alisteyr grimaced. "Yes," he said, sounding reluctant and worried.

The dais was constructed of two perfect semicircles of stone, positioned a few inches apart, creating a diagonal line of absence between them. The gap should have been filled with earth, Vorykas thought, but it was empty, as if the symbol had such strength that once it emerged into light, it would permit nothing to mar its meaning.

What is your meaning?

The need to know burned through his blood. Something spoke to him, called to him with mysterious urgency. All the religious symbols he had seen since he had started forming memories again had inspired only anger in him. This site did not anger him, but he felt no desire to worship, either. The pull was different.

Understanding hovered out of reach.

Latanna touched the darkness where the tiara's jewel had been. "The same design," she said.

Alisteyr looked stricken. "I didn't know you'd seen it in the jewel."

"The altar, the jewel, and here," said Kanstuhn. "Buried, defaced, hidden." The scholar in him had resurfaced once more, fascinated by the relic below. "What has been done is more than an act of forbidding. It is an act of forgetting, one accomplished with rigor and determination, and taking generations. What that temple represents has been erased completely."

"Not completely," said Vorykas. "It is emerging from its grave."

He scrambled down into the crater, Latanna right behind him. Alisteyr called after her, fruitlessly begging her to stop. Kanstuhn stayed with him, keeping guard.

Most of the descent wasn't difficult. The last fifteen feet, though, were sheer. Vorykas lowered himself over a lip of the drop and let himself fall.

143

THE SLEEP OF EMPIRES

He landed, looked up to catch Latanna, but she had already leapt a few yards away. Her recklessness alarmed him, and she landed hard. He moved forward to help, expecting her to be hurt. But she sprang to her feet, nothing broken. She turned around slowly, her eyes wide, drinking in the sight of the black pillars and the black dais. She crouched and ran her hands over the smooth surface of the dais. She held them motionless over the gap between the semicircles. When she looked up at Vorykas, her eyes shone feverishly. She looked even sicker than she had a few minutes before. At the same time, she radiated waves of ferocious energy.

"This is a sacred place," she said. "Can you feel it?" She moved to the center of the dais, and stood astride the gap.

"No," said Vorykas.

"Nothing?"

"I feel something. Not the sacred." Would he know the sacred if he did experience it? Possibly not. *This isn't it, though. I really don't think it is.* Nothing called on him to worship, to kneel before a greater force. The idea repulsed him as much as it had before the temple to Kamatris.

"What, then?" Latanna asked.

He thought about it. "I'm not sure. A sense of belonging, perhaps." *Homecoming?* He shook his head. The idea was dangerous. He could not afford to trust its lure while his past still hid from him.

Up above, Alisteyr kept calling to Latanna, real pain and fear in his voice.

"Your husband is distressed," Vorykas said.

"Yes," Latanna said, the word holding a developing sadness. "We should go."

They headed back up, and Vorykas noted Latanna's stamina, at odds with her appearance and the rattling of her breath. Alisteyr rushed forward to help Latanna up over the lip of the crater. The way she took his hand made Vorykas think she accepted his help more out of kindness than need. And once she was up, Alisteyr let go quickly. He looked ashamed, but his hand twitched as if he had touched something unpleasant.

DAVID ANNANDALE

Latanna kept looking down at the temple, reluctant to leave. "We don't know anything about this," she said. "Or this." She touched the tiara. "That isn't good enough."

"Gods be praised," said Alisteyr. "You finally understand."

"No," she said. "You're the one who doesn't understand. I want to know what is happening. I want to know what it means. I still don't want to stop it."

Alisteyr rubbed his forehead in distress.

"Will you help me?" Latanna asked him.

He nodded unhappily.

She looked at Vorykas.

"I need to know as much as you do," he said. With those words, he articulated a purpose. The first that truly belonged to him. He relished the promise of meaning.

"There is another issue we must address," said Kanstuhn. "Elgin Hawkesmoore was not here last night, nor was most of his escort. He is still a threat to you."

"He's going to retaliate," Alisteyr said gloomily. He gave Latanna a look that told Vorykas how hard Alisteyr had pleaded with his bride not to provoke Elgin or Marsen.

"If he's still in Ghaunthook, he would be at my father's," said Latanna.

"I was there just before dawn," said Vorykas. "I saw no sign of them."

"Then he's probably on his way to Korvas. That's where the Hawkes-moores have their seat."

"Where does that leave us?" said Alisteyr.

"We can sit and wait for his return, and get ready for what he might attempt." She turned to Kanstuhn. "Or I could ask you to pursue him, if you are willing."

"We are," Vorykas said, before the kaul could answer.

"Yes," said Kanstuhn more cautiously. "There are risks in that course of action."

"There are risks in either one," said Latanna.

145

THE SLEEP OF EMPIRES

"How far do you want to take this?" Alisteyr asked. When Latanna didn't answer right away, he pushed harder. "Do you understand how far this might go?"

"I do," she said. "I think last night was a blessing. I think the risk is less if Elgin isn't killed in Ghaunthook."

There was another pause. It was the first time Vorykas had heard Latanna speak so directly about assassinating Elgin. The target last night had been the cloudblossom. That Elgin and his men would be casualties of the raid had been an unspoken assumption, not something she had called for.

"By the gods," said Alisteyr. "You sound like your father."

Latanna's matter-of-fact discussion of violence seemed at odds with what she had stood for in the days leading to the marriage, though Vorykas thought that this appearance was misleading. Latanna did not sound angry or bloodthirsty. She spoke calmly, pragmatically. She accepted death as the inevitable result of the struggle against Marsen and what he wanted for her and for Ghaunthook.

"Elgin has suffered two losses," Latanna said to Alisteyr. "He would never accept either one. Or am I wrong?"

Alisteyr shook his head.

"He's going to kill you if he isn't killed first. I was wrong to hope he would die last night." She gave Vorykas and Kanstuhn an apologetic look. "I shouldn't have asked you to destroy the cloudblossom without knowing where he was. I was too eager to see it gone. We were lucky. He mustn't die anywhere near Ghaunthook," she repeated.

"Because his family mustn't look this way," said Kanstuhn.

"Exactly."

"Then we will wait until Korvas. A man of his character will have his share of enemies there. And his family would be unlikely to believe anyone in this village could reach that far."

Latanna nodded. "Another thing," she said, and looked uncomfortable. "Before you agree to too much."

146

DAVID ANNANDALE

Vorykas headed her off. "You're worried about payment."

"Yes. A journey to Korvas goes far beyond what we have asked of you thus far."

"I won't speak for Kanstuhn," Vorykas said, "but I would be following Elgin whether I was being paid or not." He glanced at Kanstuhn, who motioned for him to continue. "I do not know who I am." He looked at the humans and the kaul, then at the gray of his skin. "I do not know *what* I am. I'm uncertain about what beliefs I might have, except for a few. I do not like illusions and lies, because I feel as if I had been buried by them. Cloudblossom is the material being of lies. Elgin Hawkesmoore exploits the misery and the death caused by his harvest of lies. I am going to stop him."

"You have found your name," said Kanstuhn. "Now you are finding your cause."

The Keraps River marked the boundary between Beresta and Wiramzin. Guard towers on either side watched the crossings on the roads, and there were few of them. There was trade between the elves and humans, but it was limited. At least, the official trade was. There was coin to be made in the exchanges that the Most Perfect Council resolutely ignored. The border was a long one, and though the Keraps was wide and deep, there were ways to cross it.

The caravan arrived at the Northope crossing in the early morning. The dawn was cold, and mist rose from the water, obscuring the far bank. Nothing indicated the existence of the crossing except heavy ropes hanging from two trunks at the river's edge, fifteen feet apart.

Pilta watched the leader of the caravan wave a torch back and forth three times. Another torch, barely more than a spark in the fog, answered from the other side. A few moments later, the ropes slowly rose from the water, straightening out as they were tightened on the Wiramzin bank. After another few minutes, the ferry appeared, a dim bulk in the gray limbo at first, then becoming clearer. Two men pulled at the ropes, bringing the

147

THE SLEEP OF EMPIRES

wooden platform over the river to the shore. It was big enough for two wagons to fit on it at a time.

"This is going to take a while," Pilta said to Arva.

"Are you in a hurry?" she asked.

He shook his head. "Just wondering. Do these merchants have to go through this process every time?"

"If they don't want to deal with elvish guards at the border, yes."

"Only the elvish guards?"

"We aren't far from Northope. If you think there's anyone there who doesn't know about this ferry, then you really are a fool."

It took two hours to get the caravan across to the south side of the Keraps. There, past the ferry's dock, a path wound through the forest, up a gradual slope. Here the gloom of the woods did not pulse. Menyë trees did not grow outside of elven boundaries, and Pilta greeted their absence with more relief than loss. The caravan arrived at a ridge, and the ground levelled off. Around midmorning, the forest came to an end, and the caravan arrived at the farmlands of Northope.

The wagons were on a road again, heading east through fields in late harvest toward the outer wall of the town, about a league distant. The town was ringed, on the east, south, and west, by a rugged upthrust of granite that leaned out north over a bend in the river. Northope Castle, hard and forbidding, crowned the rock. From this distance, it looked to Pilta as if had been extruded from the stone. It had none of the grace of the fortifications of Árkiriye. It was brutish, a weight of architecture so crushing it seemed to demand war to justify its existence.

South of the city, beyond the fields, another, larger road ran past the thick forest skirt of a high plateau. Barren, broken slopes climbed to a jagged top. The plateau made Pilta think of something that had been smashed, a mountain ruined by the blow of a monstrous hammer.

Arva had purchased a cloak from one of the merchants a few days back and given it to Pilta. It covered his clothes well enough, camouflaging their elven weave. As the caravan drew closer to the city walls, he tried to sink

DAVID ANNANDALE

deeper into the hood. He was short for an elf, no taller than any of the merchants in the caravan. His features, though, would stand out.

"Stay close to me," Arva said.

"That was my intention."

Above the walls waved banners of green and red, at their center the black icon of a single tower. The iron gates of the outer wall opened to the caravan, and they passed through into the city. It was the first time Pilta had seen how humans lived, and he wondered how they could see the crude, thick walls of their buildings every day and not go slowly mad. The ornamentation, or what passed for it, only made things worse. The engravings were the work of children with broken fingers.

He kept his observations to himself.

The caravan traveled down the main street of the town, past cramped stone houses with steeply gabled roofs. The road curved left and right, sometimes sharply, and Pilta could never see more than a hundred yards ahead. The houses leaned in, making him feel claustrophobic, and the glowering fortress came in and out of sight. Finally, the street arrived at the market square, and Pilta breathed more easily to find himself in open space.

Arva didn't let him linger. She took him by the arm and set off away from the square, through a maze of narrow streets and alleys. When they arrived at the base of the castle rock, it seemed to come at them with the suddenness of an ambush.

Three sides of the rock were sheer. Only the southern face was accessible, and this meant taking a steep trail that switchbacked sharply.

"You couldn't ask for a better defensible position," Pilta remarked as they began the climb. "You almost don't need fortifications when you have this rock."

"It's called the Prow," Arva said.

"I can see why." It jutted over the river like a warship cresting a wave.

"And the fortifications *are* necessary," Arva continued. "Beresta has made certain of that."

149

THE SLEEP OF EMPIRES

Pilta didn't reply. Arva was too young to remember the last war between elves and humans. For that matter, so was Pilta, though he was much older, in mortal terms, than she was. Yet Arva spoke with the anger of someone who had fought in the conflict. The memories of humans were passed from generation to generation, polished and sharpened, heirlooms made more jagged with every passing decade.

Pilta looked up at the heights of the Prow. He met the cold gaze of the gate towers. *Tread carefully. Behave as you would in the presence of the First Librarian.* He would be facing the same kind of merciless scrutiny.

It was a long climb, and Pilta felt it in his legs. He pitied the attacking force that would try this ascent in armor. When he and Arva finally set foot on the top of the Prow, the portcullis of Northope Castle clanked heavily upward.

"We're expected?" Pilta asked.

"I am," said Arva. "Pull your hood back. This is not the time to try to conceal yourself."

Pilta obeyed. He felt horribly exposed. His cheeks tingled with anxiety.

The walls of the castle were massive, the round towers monolithic in their presence. When he followed Arva through the portcullis and into the barbican, Pilta struggled with the simultaneous sense of being devoured and crushed. The curtain wall was even more colossal. His earlier disdain for human architecture now seemed like the disdain of an insect for the hand about to destroy it. He knew, rationally, that the fortifications of Beresta were as strong as this, and stronger, while conveying the airy elegance of a spider's web. What he knew and what he felt, though, were two different and opposing things.

He kept his head down as Arva took him across the outer ward, and through another wall to the inner ward. Voices called to one another, pointing him out. He tried not to listen, and focused only on the steps ahead, along the cobbled surface to the high keep that rose before him like a judge of stone. Its rounded walls resembled a cluster of towers grouped

150

DAVID ANNANDALE

together. A single, much larger tower thrust up from the center of the keep, the greatest of the sentinels keeping watch over Northope.

Guards in plate armor flanked the doors to the keep. One of them nodded at Arva and opened the door, a monster of heavy oak banded in iron.

The interior of the keep was as comfortless as the exterior. Tapestries hung on the walls, and banners from the vaulted ceilings. They did nothing to make the halls seem less bare. Arva marched through the keep with purpose, ignored by servants and guards. Pilta followed her, relieved when, going up a narrow spiral staircase, he no longer felt the looks of the humans on him.

At length, they came out onto the keep's northern battlements. A woman, alone, stood at the parapet, leaning forward with her hands on the crenellations. Over her armor she wore a cloak of a violet so deep it was almost black.

"Have your companion wait there," she said, without looking back.

Pilta stopped where he was. He rooted himself to the spot. Arva walked over to the woman. They spoke briefly. Arva opened her pouch she carried and presented the book Pilta had stolen. The woman nodded, satisfied.

Arva signaled to Pilta, and the woman turned around. He approached with, he hoped, the proper show of deference.

"Lady Ossia Felgard," Arva said. "This is Pilta ne Akwatse."

Pilta bowed.

The ruler of Northope had been weathered by the years into hard lines. She wore her gray hair short, and eyes were careful, taking much in and giving nothing away. "You have traveled further than you ever intended, I think," she said to Pilta.

"I have, Lady Ossia."

Still holding the book, Arva said, "Shall I . . . ?"

"At once," said Ossia.

Arva bowed and left, marching quickly.

151

THE SLEEP OF EMPIRES

The wind blew over the battlements, strong and cold. Pilta resisted shivering while Ossia gave him a long look.

"Well," she said. "What are we going to do with you?"

"I would very much like to know that too, my lady."

Ossia cracked a tight smile. "Not so overawed that your sense of humor has departed you," she said. "At a guess, you did not ingratiate yourself with your betters in Árkiriye."

"I did not," Pilta admitted.

"What is it that you hope for?"

"I wish I knew," he said with feeling. He had given up hoping for anything beyond surviving to see the next day.

"Do you regret stealing the book?" Ossia asked.

Do not lie to her. She'll know. "For what that theft has done to my life, I do. I did not think about the consequences. Only the gold. And that is useless to me now."

"So it is not guilt that causes your regret."

"No."

"You are not an elf of conviction."

"If I were, I would not have stolen the book in the first place."

Ossia's quick, dry smile appeared and disappeared again. "And so it is a simple act of selfishness that has brought war to Northope."

"War?" Pilta asked, his voice small.

The quick smile came and went again. "Yes, war, though you can't have known, and it was my decision to bring on that consequence. You don't imagine Beresta will ignore the loss of this book? Its armies are searching for it even now, and sooner or later, they will know it came here. One way or another they will know. And so we must now prepare for the war that I have invited."

"I see." He did only partially, and wished himself a thousand leagues away from here.

"For the present," Ossia said, "I can offer you the protection of Northope. I think I might even be able to find something useful for you to do."

152

"Thank you, my lady," said Pilta. He started to bow.

Ossia held up a finger, stopping him. "I'm not done. For the protection to hold, and for me to be sure that *I* do not regret this decision, you will not be permitted to leave the castle."

"I won't want to," Pilta said. The thought of stepping outside this sanctuary terrified him.

But he also felt the prison he had created for himself close in. Despite the wind and the open air, he found it difficult to breathe.

CHAPTER 12

She was dying.

Latanna knew that now. She knew that when the sun went down, her strength would go with it.

"You were right," she said to Alisteyr. He sat at her bedside, his eyes red, his face almost as pale as hers.

No, not almost. Not even close. Even in the dim light thrown by the flames in the bedchamber's small hearth, the contrast between her skin and his was stark. He was merely pale with grief. Her flesh was white like teeth, so white she thought it might shine in the night.

"I'm sorry I didn't listen," she said. Even now, she couldn't be sure that she *was* sorry. But she owed him the apology, sincere or not.

She had been burning with energy all day. Though she knew what she looked like, though she knew that she gave every sign of withering to nothing, her strength had still been undiminished. She had felt driven, needing to work, to push herself, to do more and more and more.

And then this night fell, and so did she. She lay in her bed, and she could feel her body die. Her limbs were so heavy, it seemed they should sink through the bed and into the earth. Her skin was tight parchment over her bones, on the verge of tearing and flaking away. Each breath sounded like drowning. And the tiara's horns had grown longer.

Everything Alisteyr had feared had come true. The tiara was killing her. Latanna knew she would not see the dawn.

The thought did not frighten her. Though she could barely move, her mind burned incandescent with the excitement of possibilities. Out of kindness for Alisteyr, she worked to keep the tremor of delight from her voice. If this was death, it was exhilarating.

"I'm sorry," she said again. "I'm sorry for the marriage I've given you." A genuine apology this time. She felt sorry for Alisteyr, and for what he

154

DAVID ANNANDALE

was going through. She had never wanted to hurt him. "I know this is a nightmare for you." She managed to raise her right hand a few inches. She could almost see the bones beneath her skin.

"A nightmare for *me?*" Alisteyr said, his voice breaking.

With an effort, she pulled her lips back in what she meant to be a reassuring smile. It did not have the desired effect. She saw Alisteyr suppress a recoil, but his eyes widened in shock. *I am a grotesque. I wonder if I remind him of what he saw beneath the cemetery.*

"A nightmare for you," she said. "Don't worry about me. There's no pain."

Alisteyr rose, poked at the fire to encourage the flames, and sat down again. "I should have done more."

"No. There's nothing you could have done. I put the tiara on because I wanted to. Everything since the wedding has been my choice. And even if we had set out for Korvas, we wouldn't have reached it by now. I'd rather the end be here than on the road. I'm comfortable here."

Alisteyr shook his head, rejecting comfort, shouldering guilt. "What can I do?"

"You can go and rest. You must. I'm all right. I've been sleeping like the dead every night since the wedding. I'm ready to sleep again."

"But . . ."

"Go. Please. Be good to yourself." She closed her eyes as if she were falling asleep.

That, though, was a lie.

Alisteyr sat in front of the hearth in the hall, trying to draw warmth from it, if not comfort. He kept looking at the bedchamber door. He wanted to go back inside. He also had to respect Latanna's wishes.

The fire snapped, loud in the silence of the house. With Vorykas and Kanstuhn gone, the emptiness chilled him. They couldn't help Latanna either, but at least he wouldn't be alone in his helplessness. But they were on their way to Korvas, off to start or end a war. They were also

155

THE SLEEP OF EMPIRES

going to carry out an errand on Alisteyr's behalf, one that no longer mattered.

He had taken Kanstuhn aside just before they left.

"I have a friend in Korvas," he said. "His name is Garwynn Avennic. He used to be a student at the university. Find him, please. Tell him what is happening to Latanna. He might know someone who could help."

"We will seek him out," Kanstuhn had promised.

The request was a wild grasp at straws. Alisteyr didn't really expect anything to come of it. He had to try something, though. But when he had spoken to Kanstuhn, he had still been thinking that Latanna had time. He hadn't expected her to die tonight.

Now he did.

He didn't believe she was asleep. He had watched the wasting sleep of the previous nights. He had watched her body devouring itself a bit at a time, with the rhythm of stentorian breathing. Tonight, Latanna's eyes were too wide, too ferocious, as if she could see death approaching. She wanted to face it on her own. He bowed to her wishes.

It shamed him that he felt a sliver of relief that he would not have to witness her encounter with death. He was scared of what he might see. He was terrified he would see her excitement.

Something scratched at the outside door. Alisteyr turned around on his stool. The scratching came again, the sound of a dog asking to come in.

"Hello?" Alisteyr called, feeling foolish.

Another scratch, a tap, then another scratch. It could have been the branches of a tree, except there were none near the house, and the night was still.

Frowning, Alisteyr stood up. He crossed the small hall to the door. Through the window beside it, the darkness was too deep for him to see anything. He leaned an ear against the door, listening.

Scratch. Tap. Tap. Scratch. Scratch.

156

He swallowed, his throat suddenly parched.

It's probably nothing.

"Probably" isn't a certainty.

He wished Kanstuhn and Vorykas were here.

It isn't Elgin. He would just burn the house down.

Alisteyr took his sword down from where it hung over the mantle. He went back to the door, knuckles whitening as he clutched the blade.

Scratch. Tap. Tap.

He began to pull the door open slowly.

A heavy weight slammed into the door, threw it wide and knocked him back. He tripped over the stool and fell on his back. Marsen Forgrym's hired sword, Seck, strode into the house, a dagger in each hand. He grinned his bisected grin.

"Oh, you're an easy one and that's the truth."

Alisteyr scrabbled back. He started to bring up his sword. Seck kicked his wrist, sending the weapon clattering across the room. He stomped his boot down on Alisteyr's arm, pinning it, and leaned down, holding one of the daggers to his throat. Alisteyr stopped moving.

"That it?" Seck asked. "No more fight in you?" He pricked Alisteyr's skin just below his left eye with the other dagger. "An easy one and no fun at all, and this after the trouble you've caused. Doesn't seem fair to my master. Really isn't fair to me."

Alisteyr said nothing. The dagger points sank a little deeper into his flesh.

"Tell you what," said Seck. "I'm going to earn my pay by taking a bit of time. Having a bit of fun. I'll tell the master you put up a struggle. How does that suit? Make you sound a bit better than you are. Like that?" Seck paused. "'Course, taking longer means it's going to hurt more too." He shrugged. "Can't have it both ways."

The door of the bedroom flew open, and Latanna hurled herself across the room with a shriek that froze Alisteyr's blood. She slammed into Seck, wrapping her arms and legs around him. Seck fell back, struggling for

THE SLEEP OF EMPIRES

balance. He brought the daggers up on instinct. But the moment he had them angled to plunge into Latanna's flanks, he hesitated.

He's here to kill me. Not her. He's not allowed to kill her.

The thoughts flashed through Alisteyr's mind as he forced himself to his feet. There was hope. If he could stop Seck before Latanna killed herself . . .

Stop him how?

Two bodies flailed as he picked up the sword. He raised it, but did nothing. He couldn't attack without hurting Latanna. "Stop!" he shouted, and he was pleading to both of them. If Latanna released Seck, and Alisteyr had a clear path, he knew what would happen. Seck would kill him.

Latanna dropped her head forward, gouging Seck's face with the horns of the tiara. He yelled, and then yelled again when she sank her teeth into his throat. His left hand spasmed and dropped its dagger. His right no longer hesitated. He drove the dagger into Latanna's side. She grunted and jerked her head back violently. She pulled away a flap of flesh and muscle.

In the midst of his horror, Alisteyr wondered where she came by the strength.

Seck's blood jetted across the room. Latanna released him and dropped to the ground in a crouch, the dagger sticking out of her left ribs. Her breathing, beyond ragged, sounded like an announcement of the end.

Seck clutched at his neck. He stumbled in circles, spraying blood across the walls and windows. It struck Alisteyr across the chest, and he stared at the red, unmoving, the sword useless in his numb hands.

Seck dropped to his knees. He stared at Latanna. Alisteyr saw a man burning with hatred and disbelief that he should be dying because of her. He gurgled something, and blood poured from his mouth. Then he fell and was still, the pumping of blood losing force. The pool spread gently across the floor, then stopped.

The silence of the night crept into the house again. Tendrils of fog drifted slowly past the door.

"Latanna," Alisteyr said. He dropped the sword and took a step forward.

DAVID ANNANDALE

She turned around slowly, and he stopped. He couldn't go any closer. Her eyes were black pools. They had seen death, and taken it in. Her skin was almost translucent, and Alisteyr could see the outline of her bones beneath. Seck's blood dripped down her chin and onto her white nightgown. The wound in her side ran freely, soaking the linen.

Alisteyr reached out, staring at the dagger. He tried to bring himself to step forward, to help her, but she frightened him too much. "Latanna," he said again. "You're wounded . . ."

What a stupid thing to say. *How is she still standing?*

She looked down at her side. She took the hilt with her right hand, her movements slow, as if caught in a dream. She pulled the dagger out and looked at the wet blade. She did not wince or stagger. The fact of the blade had no more importance than clothing that needed adjusting. "It's not that I'm wounded," she said, her voice cracked and rough as her breathing. "It's that I'm dying."

"Let me get you back into bed," Alisteyr said, though he still didn't move.

"No." She looked at him with what he thought was sadness, but it was hard to tell through the gathering pall of death. "I'm sorry, Alisteyr. I keep saying that, but it's true. I'm sorry. I have to go."

"What? No. You can't go anywhere. You have to lie down. You have to—"

She cut him off. "I have to make sure you're safe. I have to stop my father." The anger with which she said *father* jolted Alisteyr.

Is anger the only thing keeping you alive?

He did not think it was love for him.

Still holding the dagger, she ran out of the house, into the darkness.

The shock of her flight jolted Alisteyr out of his immobility. He tripped over Seck's corpse, and then he was out, chasing after Latanna through the night. She had a good lead, and she moved fast, too fast, a wraith in the dark. When she reached the edge of the village, she turned off the road and cut through the forest.

159

THE SLEEP OF EMPIRES

Alisteyr tripped over roots. Branches whipped his face as he tried to keep up. Moonlight fell through the trees in broken shards, and he could barely see his way forward. Latanna, a flickering shaft of white, a figure spun from the glow of moon and fog, sped between the trunks. Alisteyr chased a dream, and he felt her slipping from his grasp forever.

"Latanna!" he called. "Stop!"

The wraith vanished again, and he ran straight into a tree. He fell, ears ringing, nose pouring blood. He cried out to her again, and his voice was lost in the darkness.

Marsen heard the doors of the mansion open. He rose from his seat and began to cross the great hall, expecting Seck to enter with news of Alisteyr Huesland's death. Instead, he heard a struggle. Bodies crashed against wall and floor. Furniture overturned. Grunts of effort became a repeated thumping that ended in wet cracks.

Marsen froze in place, held motionless by confusion. If Latanna's sellswords were still in Ghaunthook, he would know what was happening. But they weren't, and if that was the noise of Alisteyr forcing his way into Forgrym Hall, then nothing made sense any longer.

Silence now. He should call for more of his guards. He should defend himself. There was a shield and sword mounted above the mantle. He should take them.

He couldn't move.

The door opened. Latanna entered, a dagger in one hand, a mace in the other. Blood dripped from the blade. Blood and matted hair clung to the head of the mace. Blood coated Latanna's chin and soaked her night clothes. She was skeletal, her eyes dark and glittering. The iron horns of the tiara jutted from her hair.

Horror and fear had been foreign to Marsen for years. He was the one to be feared. He was the one with the plans. He was the one with the destiny.

He had never loved Latanna. He had never thought of her as anything other than a possession, as something of value only as long as she remained

160

DAVID ANNANDALE

useful. Now she frightened him. She must have killed Seck, and that was impossible. She had never had any training for combat. He had made sure of that.

He didn't understand how she had killed the entrance guard.

He didn't understand how she was still walking. She looked like she had died hours before.

"You promised," she hissed, advancing on him. Her voice was rough, a sword being drawn from its scabbard. "You promised you wouldn't harm Alisteyr."

Marsen backed up slowly, his thoughts on the weapons on the wall. "We had an agreement," he said. "I agreed not to hurt him if you didn't harm my interests. You broke your word first."

"Maybe I did," said Latanna. Her frame quivered, as if the force inside was about to break her apart. "Did you ever have any intention of keeping yours?"

Marsen felt the fire hot at his back. He was almost at the hearth. "Probably not," he said.

"We deserve each other," said Latanna. "I'm a Forgrym after all, in spite of my best efforts."

"What do you think you're going to do?" Marsen asked.

"Kill you."

"You think you can?"

"Seck would say yes. If he could."

"That is impressive." Marsen tensed, readying himself. "I have no idea how you managed that."

"Neither do I." She tapped the tiara with the dagger's blade. It rang, its resonance too long. "There's a lot I don't understand. I hope I will, though it seems I have to die first." She took another step toward Marsen. "But not before you."

Marsen whirled, snatched the shield and sword from the wall, and in a fluid movement turned back to Latanna to block her lunge. She smashed the mace against the shield, and the force of the blow jolted down his arm.

161

THE SLEEP OF EMPIRES

She was strong, too strong. That was not his dying daughter who had struck the shield. He felt as if a horse had kicked him.

Grunting in pain, he thrust back with the shield, forcing her arm up, and stabbed with the sword. The blade went home, slicing through her gut. It ground against her spine and came out her back.

She dropped her weapons.

Marsen jerked the blade up with anger born of revulsion. He glared into the rictus of Latanna's face. "You should know better," he snarled.

"But I do," she said, and she grabbed his head with her hands and squeezed.

Marsen gasped, pain shooting through his skull. A vise tightened around his temples. He stabbed her again, and again, and black blood gushed from her mouth. She only squeezed harder, and her thumbs moved over his eyes.

Marsen screamed. In the last moment before the pain exploded, before his skull fractured, and before his daughter gouged out his eyes, he screamed with a new purity of emotion, a purity of terror in the face of the thing she had become.

Alisteyr found Latanna on the porch of Forgrym Hall. She had crawled that far, and no further. The door stood open, and a thick trail of blood led from her body down the corridor. One of Marsen's sell-swords lay halfway down, his head smashed to pulp.

Latanna's night dress was soaked black with her blood. Alisteyr thought she was dead when he leaned over her, but then her hand moved. He fell to his knees and clutched the cold talon.

"Take me home," she wheezed. "I don't want to die here."

He couldn't carry her that far, he thought. He wasn't strong enough.

Then be strong enough.

"I'm scared I'll hurt you," he whispered.

"You can't."

162

He put his arms under her, and blood gushed from her wounds. He lifted. She weighed so little. She had nothing left but bones and a thin sheath of skin.

The burden of her lightness almost broke him.

He carried her down the road from Forgrym Hall, and back through the village. In the deep night, Ghaunthook slept. Even so, Alisteyr thought he felt, from behind the shutters, the eyes of the villagers on him and his blood-soaked bride. When he passed the temple of Kamatris, Taver Derrun emerged and came to help. And when they drew near the Laughing Chimera, Hanby Bettring joined them. Neither the priest nor the mayor said anything to Alisteyr. They didn't ask what had happened, because there was only one person anyone could imagine being responsible for her wounds. Their faces showed Alisteyr their sorrow, and that was the closest thing to comfort he could have. Their grief was for Latanna and for him. It was also for the hope the marriage had brought to Ghaunthook.

The house was as he had left it, door open, Seck's body in the middle of the floor. Without a word, Taver and Hanby went past Alisteyr, picked up the corpse, and carried it out.

"We can stay and help," Taver said.

"No," Latanna answered, startling them all. Her breath had been so irregular, and so weak, that Alisteyr had thought he had already heard her last words. "Let us be alone," she said, with a voice of sand against glass.

Hanby hesitated. "Do you need protection? We can round up some people to help."

"My father is dead," said Latanna, rallying for a moment with the strength of ice.

Relief, and then guilt for feeling relief, washed over the faces of Hanby and Taver.

"Oh," said Hanby. "I'm . . . I mean I . . ." he struggled.

"There's nothing left to protect," said Alisteyr. He left the two men and carried Latanna into the bed chamber.

THE SLEEP OF EMPIRES

He put her down, and her blood spread over the sheets. He kneeled beside her, holding her hand. His throat was too sore with pain to speak.

Latanna drew a long, wretched breath. "I'm not afraid," she said. "I'm not afraid at all."

She drew lips back in a grin that made Alisteyr drop her hand and jerk away from the bed.

Then she stopped breathing.

Alisteyr stayed beside her for most of the night, feeling her hand grow colder, seeing her skin turn yellow. Finally, emotional and physical exhaustion drove him from the side of the death bed. He staggered into the hall and slumped into his chair before the hearth. The fire had burned itself out, but he didn't have the energy to light a new one.

He stared at nothing. He felt nothing. He finally had the comfort he had longed for earlier, the comfort of the numbness that came in the wake of grief's heaviest blows. He wanted to stay here, in the nothing. Here there was an end to all hopes and fears and loss, an end to the need to act. Perhaps even, if he stayed here long enough, an end to the need to draw breath.

He hadn't moved when morning crept into Ghaunthook. The fog had grown thicker and the view from his window was of still more nothing, a gray-white expanse with the vanishing hints of trees in its depths. The morning brought no relief. Only the promise of endless nothing.

A hand clasped Alisteyr's shoulder. He screamed.

"I'm hungry," said Latanna.

CHAPTER 13

When Kanstuhn woke, he knew instinctively that it was just a few minutes before dawn. He was curled up against the base of a tree trunk. Vorykas sat next to him, still awake, staring into a distance beyond the gloom.

Kanstuhn and Vorykas had chosen a spot a hundred yards off the Korvas road, in the forest that hugged the base of the plateau. They had ridden hard since leaving Ghaunthook, and had stopped a short distance from Northope. They had tied the horses the Hueslands had provided them to the next tree over, and then Kanstuhn had slept, leaving Vorykas to take the first watch.

But now the night was over.

"Why didn't you wake me?" Kanstuhn asked, sitting up.

"You need to sleep. I don't."

Kanstuhn rubbed fatigue from his eyes. "What do you mean?"

"What I said. I don't sleep. I haven't, at least, since the cemetery. Did I before?"

"I don't know," Kanstuhn admitted. "I could never tell, and I couldn't ask you. I would sleep when I had to, and I always had to first."

"I'm glad I didn't wander off."

"You seemed content to be my guard. But I did not sleep well at first. Be certain of that."

He stood up and stretched. Vorykas rose, fluid as water.

"How do you pass the night?" Kanstuhn asked.

"In thought. In stillness. The stillness feels like home. I seem to pass out of existence, though I'm aware of everything. Acutely so." He paused. "Something happened in Ghaunthook during the night."

Kanstuhn's breath caught. He didn't question Vorykas' certainty. He had to accept it, just as he had accepted Vorykas' skill in dealing death even when he had had to be told what to do, moment by moment in every

165

THE SLEEP OF EMPIRES

other circumstance. *How do you know?* would be the most pointless of questions. "What has happened?" he asked. "Something bad?"

Vorykas frowned, concentrating. "Something important," he said, sounding frustrated about being cryptic.

"Do we need to return there?"

"No," Vorykas said after a moment. "It has happened. It is past. Going back would make no difference. I think we should continue."

Kanstuhn nodded, uneasy all the same. They ate quickly, then readied the horses and walked them back to the road. Once there, they mounted and rode off. The Korvas Road passed Northope an hour later, the city a dark glower rising over the misty fields.

Vorykas' attention was on the plateau. Kanstuhn saw him look repeatedly up at its peak. "What is up there?" Vorykas finally asked.

"Nothing, to my knowledge," said Kanstuhn.

"Nothing," Vorykas repeated, his intonation giving the word a resonance that Kanstuhn felt without understanding. He drew his horse to stop and stared up.

"What do you see?" said Kanstuhn.

"Nothing," Vorykas whispered, but Kanstuhn wasn't sure it was in answer to his question.

Vorykas stared at the plateau for a long time before he shook himself, and they rode on.

The quarters Lady Ossia Felgard gave to Pilta were small, but not uncomfortable. Human linen was rough by elven standards, but he had known coarser too. The room was on the sixth floor of the keep, in its southeastern corner. He slept the first night in Northope Castle grateful to be off the road, and not looking over his shoulder.

He slept *most* of the night.

His window faced south, toward the plateau. The rise drew his curiosity, though he didn't know why. He looked at it as darkness fell, until its mass vanished into the night. He looked for it again when he woke before dawn, and saw the huge shape gradually emerge once more with the slow return of light.

Something else returned too. Pilta saw the torches of a small group of riders crossing the fields from the direction of the plateau. He was too far away to make out any details. From the configuration of the torches, though, it seemed that the riders carrying the lights were surrounding one without.

An escort, then.

For Lady Ossia Felgard, perhaps?

Why would she go to the plateau?

I don't need to know.

He didn't. He really didn't. He was lucky to have found safe harbor, at least for now. No reason to jeopardize his situation.

Only his curiosity wouldn't leave him alone.

You will not be permitted to leave the castle, Ossia had said.

I don't want to, he had told her. That had been true, then. Something, chance or a quirk of instinct, had held him back from saying, *I won't want to.*

I might even find something useful for you to do. Ossia had said that, too. As the morning drew on, Pilta waited in his chamber to be summoned or to be directed. Neither happened. An hour after sunrise, he opened the door cautiously, half-surprised to find it wasn't locked. He was at the end of a corridor, and a guard was posted at the entrance to the spiral staircase on his right. When the guard looked at him, Pilta felt as self-conscious as he had been in the streets of Northope. The guard showed little interest. "If you're hungry," he said, "you can get something from the kitchens." He nodded at the stairs.

Pilta thanked him. He went down, and met with the same indifference from the other people whose paths he crossed. They knew who he was, it seemed, and that was enough for them. They had their duties to attend to. He caught a number of surreptitious glances, enough to know some people, at least, considered him to be a subject of interest, but no one said anything directly to him. In the kitchens, a cook gave him hard, dark bread

THE SLEEP OF EMPIRES

and some mutton. After he had eaten, still without any sense of what was expected of him, he wandered the castle to get his bearings. He made a point of sticking to the center of the corridors, of being seen to be visible. But he noted the shadows where he saw them.

He might need them yet.

In the middle of the afternoon, he ventured into the inner ward. He lingered there for a while, watching Ossia's troops train. He spotted Arva crossing from the outer ward, and he caught up to her as she reached the door to the keep. She wore an officer's uniform now.

"You're still alive, not in irons, and I haven't heard of anything stolen," said Arva. "You're doing well, so far."

"Well enough," said Pilta. "But I don't know what I *should* be doing."

"You at a loose end is a dangerous thing. Is that what you're saying?"

"No, not at all," Pilta said hurriedly, alarmed by her perception.

Arva gave him a tight smile. "If you think Lady Felgard has forgotten you, you're wrong. She has to weigh your use against your risk. She has to know how far she should trust you."

"That's fair."

"You'll know her decision soon enough."

"And in the meantime?"

"Don't make her regret giving you sanctuary."

Pilta nodded. "I can do that much," he said.

He didn't think he lied. He didn't realize he had until much later, when evening fell, and he was back in his chamber, thinking about Ossia, and the plateau. He didn't know that it was her he'd seen returning last night. And if it was her, he didn't know that she had been up to the plateau.

But his gut told him he was right, and he wondered.

He wondered, too, what Arva had done with the book.

And he wondered what he was going to do.

Can I stay here? Is this where I'm going to live?

Too early to ask himself that question. He'd only been here a day. The question forced itself on him all the same. It wouldn't leave him alone.

168

DAVID ANNANDALE

Pilta kept watch at his window late into the night. The sky was clear this time. The moon outlined the broken, jagged outline of the plateau, and cast a dim, silver wash over the city and its fields. Pilta had a partial view of the inner ward, enough for him to see the gate to the outer ward, and he kept track of the movements below him, waiting for something he wasn't sure he'd recognize.

What are you hoping for?

I have no idea. I don't know enough.

There's a cure for that, isn't there?

Yes. It's called knowing more.

What if nothing happens tonight?

Then he would keep his head down, observe nothing that wasn't meant for him, and do exactly as he was told.

In other words, do what Arva wants you to do now. You owe her that much.

All true. But the instinct that had made him follow her through the streets of Árkiriye gnawed at him again. He had already destroyed his life once by stealing the book. There wasn't much worse he could do now.

Ossia and her escort left shortly before midnight. Pilta knew it was her. He would have spotted her armor and her stance from further away than this. He watched her and four guards ride out through the gate to the outer ward, and then he left his chamber.

He made use of the shadows he had learned during the day. There were more of them now, and he slipped into them easily. In Árkiriye, he had become adept enough to escape the sight of most of his fellow elves. Evading the gaze of humans was almost too simple. Almost. He remained alert and moved carefully. He refused to doom himself through overconfidence.

There was a guard at the stairs when he opened his door, and he nodded to the man, walking casually and slightly heavily, as if clumsy with sleep. Once he was alone in the staircase, he hurried to the ground floor of the castle. There, the shadows embraced him and guided him from the keep. In the kitchens, he slipped out behind a pair of servants hauling out refuse. At the gates, he did the same. Though it was late, the business of the castle

THE SLEEP OF EMPIRES

continued without pause, and, with his hood up, he became an ignored part of the groups of servants passing in and out of the gates as they carried out their duties.

He left the castle and traveled quickly down the rock and into Northope. His sense of direction had always been strong, and the maze of alleys became his path of shadows. Crossing the city in the day, he had been exposed, intensely vulnerable even though he had been under Arva's protection. Tonight, he felt almost serene. What he was doing was madness. If he was discovered, then he would have thrown away his last chance at even a remote possibility of being safe. But he felt like he danced invisible to the dull eyes of the humans. He could go where he pleased in their city, and they would never know. He had stolen a forbidden text from the University of Árkiriye. If he could do that, then moving undetected in a human city was barely a challenge.

He knew he shouldn't be overconfident.

Don't be reckless.

Too late. I already am.

He sped down the cobblestones, unseen as wind. On either side, the dark façades leaned in toward each other, the rooms behind their shutters dark. They saw nothing but the night.

He moved so quickly that he caught up to Ossia and her escort as they drew near the outer wall. Now, he had to be careful, and he was. He couldn't pretend to be a member of this party. He hung back, staying in the darkness just beyond the torchlight, where eyes, dazzled by the flames, would see only the deepest black. He stayed close to the walls, and moved silently, the echoes of hooves on stone an aural shadow to hide in.

The lady of Northope left the city, and Pilta followed. When the portcullis slammed shut behind him, and no arrow pierced his back, he smiled with the first real triumph he had felt in weeks.

Pilta held back, letting the party pull ahead of him, and then hurried forward again as the horses picked up speed. The road that Ossia took across the fields was a narrow one, barely more than a ribbon of beaten earth. Pilta

170

DAVID ANNANDALE

thought it did not see much use. The party had to ride single-file, and it was easy for him, ducking down, to remain hidden by the bales of hay on either side.

He followed over the fields, across the Korvas Road, and through the woods. When the path climbed the plateau, he slowed down again, feeling more exposed on the cliff face. The road became steep, almost too steep for the horses. It was so roughly cut from the cliff that it seemed to be a natural formation, a fracture in the stone that, by chance, granted access to the top.

The treacherous footing forced Pilta to slow down even more, until he lost sight of the torches. Breaks in the path, some more than a foot wide, waited for him, gaping to plunge him into the darkness. The moonlight showed him the way, but it also cast deep shadows, and they were not his allies any longer. They were traps, offering concealment when what they concealed was death. Rock formations sharp as talons jutted over the path, spreading more darkness.

Pilta was exhausted when he arrived at the top of the plateau. There, he found no relief. The ground was uneven and jagged, gullies spreading like veins through broken glass. Boulders were scattered across the plateau in heaped mounds and precarious towers. In between them, the torches of the horse party wove in and out like fireflies, still heading south.

Pilta scrambled over the plateau. He had to be a lizard now, sure of his footing on rock and leaping over the gaps. Without a torch of his own, he had trouble keeping to the road as it twisted through the rubble and around the crevasses. After what seemed like hours of painful progress, the ground sloped down, gradually at first, and then precipitously. Pilta climbed to the top of a wide boulder and paused, looking at the moon-bathed wound of the plateau. It looked as if Tetriwu himself had struck the plateau with an axe. The ground dropped sharply into a gorge that ran as far as Pilta could see to the east and west. Past the lip, the cliffs were sheer. In the night, the blackness of the gorge promised a bottomless abyss. The mouth of the gorge looked hungry, and Pilta felt, in his bones and in his blood,

171

THE SLEEP OF EMPIRES

that it would look as deep and dark and ravenous when the sun was at its height.

He could make out the road again. He had wandered several hundred yards to the right of its path. It snaked down to the edge of the drop, and ended at a tower perched over the abyss.

The structure was ancient. It looked much older than anything in Northope. The disturbing thought came to Pilta that it was older than the spires of Árkiriye. He didn't like the idea of a human construction outlasting elvish ones.

Is it a human tower?

The more he looked at it, the less certain he became. The millennia had gnawed it, roughening the lines of its round walls, but it was so solid, it defied the millennia to come. In the moonlight, Pilta couldn't make out any stonework, as if the tower had been carved from a single pillar of rock. It seemed one with the plateau, a sentinel that had come into being with the blow that had carved out the gorge. The only things to break the expanse of the tower's blank, forbidding face were the iron door at its base, where Ossia's escort waited, and a single window that looked out over the gorge. Pilta could just make out the glow from a lantern, a dull red leak from the tower, an eye staring blankly out over the darkness of the chasm.

Cold spread through Pilta's blood. It was the same cold he had felt when he had touched the book. He knew where Arva had brought it. The book belonged here, with the stone watcher, and the abyss it guarded.

He should never have stolen it.

The cold gripped him harder, strong as fear, unshakeable as the dread of fate.

CHAPTER 14

Alisteyr leapt out of the chair and backed up against the wall. His limbs trembled, flash-freezing numb with terror and disbelief. After his scream, his breath turned into a hitching moan. He stared at Latanna, willing himself to wake, willing the world to right itself, willing the horrors to end.

Latanna looked at him with understanding and sympathy, and that made things worse. If she had come at him, instead of keeping her distance, that might almost have been better. If she had become a monster, if she had turned into the thing that he had seen beneath the cemetery, then he would, at least, have been able to understand what was happening.

Latanna had dressed, and showed no sign of having been wounded. No blood seeped through her green tunic. She seemed to have recovered completely. No longer gaunt, she was as beautiful as she had been before Alisteyr had placed the tiara on her head. She was as beautiful as she had been in his last glorious moments of happiness during the wedding ceremony. No, he corrected himself. She was even more beautiful. She had the perfected beauty that was hers in his dreams and in his memories.

Her beauty made his flesh crawl. The death beneath her flesh reached out for him. It raked his heart, and his throat closed in revulsion. Her beauty was a sheen, and though it hid the appearance of the grinning skull beneath the skin, it was the thinnest and falsest of masks, its lie making the power of the skull even stronger.

Her crown of horns had grown resplendent in its blackness and the viciousness of its points. The sight of it drew blood from Alisteyr's soul.

He had heard it said that kauls were despised because to look at them was to be reminded of death. Alisteyr distrusted the reasoning because it had been used so often to justify the enslavement and persecution of the race. But he also recognized the truth of the saying. He had fought back

173

THE SLEEP OF EMPIRES

his own unease when he had met Kanstuhn, ashamed of his prejudice but unable to suppress it entirely. The disgust the kauls inspired was nothing compared to what he felt now. He drew back from Latanna as from a rotting corpse.

"You were dead," he croaked. She was worse than a kaul. She didn't remind him of death. She *was* death.

Latanna looked thoughtful. "Was I dead?" she said. "Maybe so." She spoke as if the idea were fascinating instead of terrible. Her voice was her own, but there had been a change. It carried more weight. It had become a melody filtered through the grave.

"Are you alive now?" Alisteyr feared the question and the answer he might receive.

"I don't know," said Latanna. She held her arms out and examined her hands. "I feel alive. Does that mean I am?"

"You said you were hungry." The idea made him tremble.

"I am."

"Let me get you something." He edged away from her, hurried to their kitchen, and cut her a thick slice of bread. He went back, handed her the bread, and took a quick step out of her reach.

Latanna looked at the bread. She dropped it to the table and shook her head. "No," she said. "I'm hungry for something else."

"What then?" Alisteyr asked. He drew further away.

"Something else," she said again, frowning as she tried to think of a better answer. Then she turned and headed for the front door.

"Where are you going?" said Alisteyr.

"I don't know," Latanna answered. She paused. "But I'm going to find out."

She closed the door behind her, leaving Alisteyr alone with his terrors.

Latanna walked though Ghaunthook. She hadn't decided consciously to stroll past the green and the temple. She had not thought of the effect of displaying her resurrected self. She didn't even think of herself that way.

DAVID ANNANDALE

She had become something new, something she couldn't give a name to, but she was not a ghost, not a ghoul.

In the fog of questions and self-discovery, she hadn't considered how others might see her. She had only registered Alisteyr's fear as distant information, something to be examined more closely when time permitted.

The truth sank in as she arrived in the center of Ghaunthook. People fled when they saw her. Doors and shutters slammed closed at her passing. The village that she loved emptied, and she walked alone under the sun of a morning turned brittle with terror.

Terror that she caused.

It's more than terror, she thought. The look on Alisteyr's face hit home, the look of disgust as well as fear.

She stopped in front of the temple to Kamatris. Taver had stepped out of the door closest to the green. He and Latanna were the only ones outside. He seemed to be wrestling with his emotions. Horror and revulsion, she knew. Probably duty and the urge to run as well.

Duty won out. He approached her with the most wan smile she had ever seen.

I suppose that's as welcoming as anyone is going to look at me today.

"Latanna," Taver said. He stopped several feet away, as if to come any closer would be fatal. "I thought it beyond my hopes to see you again."

To his credit, he did not sound as if he were lying. He felt wonder, too, which was more than she could say for Alisteyr.

"And what do you make of me?" Latanna asked.

Taver seemed thrown by her directness. He took a breath as if for courage, and then plunged ahead. "I don't know," he said. "Not yet. To have healed so quickly, and from such serious wounds . . ." He spoke as if hoping she would confirm what he had said.

"Does rising from the dead count as healing?" she asked dryly. She refused to go along with any pretense.

Taver's smile grew even weaker. "You died?"

"Yes."

175

THE SLEEP OF EMPIRES

"You're sure? You might have just seemed—"

She cut him off. "I was dead. This morning, I'm not."

Taver made a heroic effort. Latanna saw a man who desperately wanted to feel wonder. "Truly, this is the work of the gods," he said. Because he had to. He did not sound convincing.

"Is it?" Latanna touched the crown embedded in her skull. The horns seemed longer yet, curved, and vicious.

"Or of something else." The words seemed surprised out of Taver. He frowned and shook his head. "What am I saying? It can't be anything else."

"There are other forces." She genuinely wanted to know what Taver thought. He might know something that would explain what she was to herself. "Remember what Alisteyr found in the Forgrym vaults." She touched a horn again, pressing against the sharp point with her finger.

"I haven't forgotten," said Taver. "But everything comes from the gods. Even that."

"How?"

"A creature of Gezeiras perhaps," said Taver. Few humans worshipped the god of the underworld. He stood as a figure of blame for ordeals, and for the things that humans wished did not exist. They believed the creation of the kauls was his doing.

"Is that what I am?" Latanna asked.

"I don't know," said Taver. "It could be argued that you have been rejected by the underworld."

"It certainly could."

Taver ignored her sarcasm. "Will you . . ." he began, stopped, then tried again. "Would you . . . Would you come to the temple?"

"Why?"

"To be anointed anew."

"What do you mean?"

"You were anointed as a child?"

"I would have been, yes, but my father was a follower of Tetriwu."

176

DAVID ANNANDALE

"Then all the more reason to come with me. If this is a second life you have, let it be under the protection of Kamatris."

The gods have always been strangers to me. That is not going to change now. Only at the moment of Latanna's vows during the wedding, when the crown had been placed on her head, had she felt a rush that she would have called faith, even if she couldn't name its object. She still couldn't, though she sensed its existence somewhere beyond the horizon of her and Taver's knowledge. The thought of now bending the knee to Kamatris revolted her.

"No," she said.

Taver continued as if she had not spoken. "And once you have been anointed, we could more easily . . . uh . . ."

"Examine me?" Latanna asked. "Determine what I am?"

"Well . . . Yes . . ."

Latanna glared at Taver, who took another step back. His smile collapsed completely.

"I don't want your blessing," Latanna told him. "I don't need your help, and I *won't* submit to the questioning of you or your god."

"Kamatris is your god as well as—"

Latanna held up a hand, silencing Taver. "That's enough."

"I'm sorry," he said. "But you must have questions, just as everyone else in the village does."

"Questions. That's a polite way of describing how they feel about me right now. And of course I have questions. But I know I won't find the answers in your temple."

She walked away across the green, and he did not follow.

Where to now?

Out of the village, at least for the moment. She frightened everyone, so she would spare them the sight of her until that terror passed.

Will it?

She put the question away. Others were more urgent. The hunger was growing more intense. It did not pain her, but it weighed, more and more

THE SLEEP OF EMPIRES

insistently, on her awareness. She felt strong, but also empty. Something in her needed feeding, and she didn't know what to give it.

Because she couldn't think of anywhere else to go, she made her way back to Forgrym Hall. She stopped while still at a distance from the house. Other than the open door, her home looked normal. She felt as though its façade should declare that a massacre had taken place inside. The blood should have flooded the grounds.

She kept walking, and the first blood she saw, dry and dark now, was her own. It covered the porch.

She went inside. She walked through the rooms, looking at the corpses she had made.

How did I do that?

She wished Vorykas was here. Even though he wouldn't have answers for her, it would be a comfort to speak with someone who had the same questions.

She entered the great hall last. She stood over her father, looking at the holes she had made where his eyes used to be. She examined how she felt. Was there grief? Sorrow? Guilt?

No. At least, not for killing Marsen. That had been simple justice.

Simple? That's a lie. She had taken too much satisfaction from the act for it to be only about justice.

The hunger thrummed. What she had done here last night was linked to it.

What, though? Had she fed? If so, on what? She looked more closely at Marsen. Apart from the fatal injuries, the body was intact.

Not that kind of feeding, then.

She looked around the hall, at the space that she had grown up in, the space that had now become strange with the presence of death. The hall of the Forgryms, with all the layers of history and generations. But also, and more particularly, the hall of Marsen. Everything she saw was an expression of her father's pride, whether the objects had been his acquisitions or not. Most were not. The decline of the Forgrym fortunes had meant selling,

178

DAVID ANNANDALE

rather than amassing, valuables. But enough remained, here and in the rest of the house, to stroke Marsen's vanity. He was dead, but the house still belonged to him.

Latanna imagined burning the house down. One last act to destroy the Forgrym legacy forever. The idea tempted her. She gave it serious consideration for a full minute.

She looked down at the floor, at the rug stained with her blood and Marsen's. The sword that had killed her lay next to her father. She picked it up. It felt good in her hand, well balanced, a work of fine craft. It had hung on the wall for as long as she could remember. She doubted her father had ever taken it down, except to kill her.

She swung it through the air a few times, enjoying its motion, enjoying the feel of her muscles knowing what to do with the weapon. They had not known this before.

The hunger throbbed, and she began to guess at its shape.

"This is mine now," she told the corpse. "My blood washed it, not yours."

Latanna put the sword down and went in search of a scabbard.

She would not burn the house, she decided. She would purge it of her father's taint, and make it hers.

Later, wearing the sword now, she wandered through the halls and rooms again, still hungry, but planning now, the hours slipping away as she worked out how she would reshape the nature of the house.

Alisteyr stepped into the cool interior of the temple to Kamatris. Concentric rings of benches surrounded the circular, marble pulpit. The fresco of the shallow dome, faded but still clear enough, depicted Kamatris as a bearded father, his face in the center, his arms reaching out to embrace a human race abandoned by its dissatisfied creator. Eight great rays of light extended from the dome, coming down the plain white walls to encompass each entrance to the temple. Kamatris welcomed all humans. Everyone who passed through the doorway received the blessing of his light.

THE SLEEP OF EMPIRES

Alisteyr needed that blessing more than ever. He wished he had felt it more strongly as he crossed the threshold. He wished he had felt it at all.

Taver was kneeling inside the pulpit when Alisteyr entered, eyes shut tight in prayer. Alisteyr walked up an aisle until he reached the middle ring of pews, then cleared his throat. Taver finished his prayer and stood up. He came over to Alisteyr, hands out in greeting, eyes grave and troubled.

"I was hoping you would come to see me," said Taver. He invited Alisteyr to sit with him on a pew.

"And I'm hoping you have some advice for me."

Taver made a slight grimace. "To be quite honest, I'm not sure that I do. But maybe, together, and with Kamatris' help, we can find wisdom."

"Have you seen Latanna?" Alisteyr asked.

"I have."

"What has happened? What is she? Is she cursed? Because this doesn't seem like a blessing." He groaned and buried his face in his hands. "If I had left that tiara where it was . . ."

Taver put a hand on his shoulder. "Slow down," he said. "Let's try some other questions first. Shall we?"

Alisteyr nodded. Taver's calm tone comforted him.

"All right. Firstly, did Latanna really die last night? It makes a difference whether she just healed dramatically or rose from the dead. She thinks she died, but is her perception true?"

The piercing look Taver gave him made Alisteyr hesitate.

"Think carefully," Taver urged. "Either possibility is alarming, but one is much more troubling."

"If I were to say that she didn't die . . ." Alisteyr said carefully.

"That would be the correct answer," said Taver. "The one that gives us hope and time."

"Time?"

"Time during which I do not have to report what has happened."

"Report? To whom?"

"To the district High Priests. At the very least."

"What would happen to her?"

"That hasn't already?" Taver sighed. "I don't know. There is so much here that I don't understand. But Latanna has always been someone who worked for the good of our village. I don't want to do anything to add to your sorrow and hers, if I can avoid it."

"She might still be that person." It horrified Alisteyr that he couldn't bring himself to state that she *was*.

"I hope she is too."

"And if," said Alisteyr, "I say that she did die . . ."

"Is that what you are saying?"

"No, I'm just asking what if I said that. What if she lay there, dead, through the night. Then, this morning, she woke me." He shuddered. "What then?"

A shadow fell across Taver's features. "Then I will have to seek counsel from those who are wiser and more powerful than I am."

Alisteyr said nothing. He looked up at the image of Kamatris. He found no inspiration, and no comfort. The silence in the temple pressed in, as cold as his future. "What do we do?" he finally cried. The words of his pain bounced around the temple.

Taver took his time before he answered. "Where is she now?"

"I don't know."

"Try not to let her out of your sight," said Taver. "Watch her closely. Tell me what you see. We have to know more than we do now before we act." He gave what Alisteyr supposed was meant to be a reassuring smile. "After all, she only . . . awoke a little while ago. Who knows. Maybe in a couple of days, our worries will seem silly."

The concern in Taver's eyes showed that he knew how unconvincing he sounded.

Watch her closely.
But I can't.

THE SLEEP OF EMPIRES

There were places Alisteyr could look for her. He could go to Forgrym Hall. Latanna might be there. It would be a logical place to start.

He didn't go. He couldn't make himself go to a place where he might see Latanna. He couldn't face that prospect. Not yet.

So he pretended to himself that he had looked, and that when his gaze darted nervously around the village, that meant he was trying to find her, instead of being terrified that he would.

He went back to the Huesland farm, but he did not speak to his parents. They would have heard what had happened. He didn't want to face them or their fears either. So he worked in the fields with the farmhands, trying to numb his senses with the exhaustion of labor.

As the day ended, he went home. Latanna had not returned. The thought of being there, alone, when she did became intolerable. The fall of night drove him out the door again. He hurried to the Laughing Chimera, desperate for company, even if no one there would speak to him.

They did, though.

His friends and his neighbors shared his grief and his fear, and because *he* shared *theirs*, they welcomed him. Peitur Cherum, the butcher, brought him a tankard and made him sit at a crowded corner table. People hugged him and patted his back. Peitur made sure he had several good swallows of ale before he replied to any of the commiserations.

"A hard day," said Peitur, shaking his heavy, shaggy head emphatically. "A hard day after a hard night, and hard times to come. You don't deserve it. Just isn't right."

"Thank you," Alisteyr said to Peitur and to the others. "I wish . . ." He stopped. "I don't know what I wish."

Genna, Peitur's wife, placed her hand on his. "We wish you better days," she said, and gave his hand a reassuring squeeze. He had played with her and Peitur as a child, and it meant a lot to feel that continuity of friendship in this moment.

"If Latanna . . ." Genna began, and then it was her turn to stop.

182

DAVID ANNANDALE

If Latanna what? he thought. *Dies again? Bursts into flame? Goes away?* What was the right wish? At least no one, for the moment, said anything about Latanna that he should, as her husband, speak against. Because he wouldn't be able to.

He was well into his second tankard, and wondering just how long he could avoid going home, when the door to the tavern opened. Conversation died as if beheaded.

Latanna stood in the doorway. She strode through the stricken silence to the center of the room.

Alisteyr's breath caught. She did not look as she had before. Night had transformed her. In the daylight, she had been beautiful, uncannily so, and he had been horribly conscious of the skull beneath her flesh. Now, the skull was visible. Wherever her clothing exposed what should have been flesh, Alisteyr saw only bone.

She had become a skeleton, like Elisava Forgrym, and also unlike her. No whirling dance of madness possessed her. Latanna stood still and composed as the patrons of the Laughing Chimera stared at her. And where before, Alisteyr had looked at beauty and felt horror, now he looked at death and it compelled him as much as it frightened him. Latanna was sublime, commanding, powerful. He could not look away. Nor did he wish to.

Though her flesh had vanished, her long black hair was still there, framing the skull. She wore riding breeches, boots, and leather armor, and had a sword at her waist. She had donned a black cloak as well, and had the hood thrown back. She stood with arms akimbo, and she turned around slowly, taking in the entire tavern with the black gaze of her empty eye sockets.

"You see me as I am," she said. Latanna's voice, as Alisteyr had always known it, as he had heard it this morning, as strong as it had ever been, and perhaps even stronger. It rang with confidence and power. Though she had no visible lips, the jaws of her skull opened and closed as she spoke. "You see *what* I am," she continued. "But do you *know* what I am? No, and

THE SLEEP OF EMPIRES

I don't either. But let me tell you a few things I do know, because I don't intend to hide anything from you. Last night, my father tried to have Alisteyr killed. I stopped him. We fought to the death, and I won. Now I will erase his memory and his shadow from Ghaunthook. I am reclaiming Forgrym Hall, and things will not be as they were before. I will need servants, and I will pay well, and treat everyone who chooses to work for me with kindness. I swear it.

"And this is something else I know: you don't have to be frightened of me. I will never do anything to hurt this village. You have my oath on that too."

The Laughing Chimera hummed with the energy of fear and excitement. Latanna's presence filled the entire space. If she had asked, Alisteyr would have followed her into war. So, he knew, would everyone else in the tavern.

Latanna told Alisteyr that she would be staying at the hall, and that he should join her there when and if he decided he could. She didn't wait for his answer. She left the tavern, heeding the call of the night.

She wasn't tired. She felt as if last night had been the last time she would ever sleep.

Of course it was. Because you're dead.

No. I'm not.

You're not alive though. You exist, but you're not alive.

No, that felt wrong too. But the question paled before the insistence of the hunger. It would not be denied any longer. She walked quickly out of the village, bursting with energy, and soon she was running. Her cloak billowed out behind her, and she wanted to fly.

She ran, chasing the night, following the hunger, seeking its shape through her thoughts. She thought about the experience of killing her father and the sell-swords. Had there been a sense of feeding then? Yes, there had been. One that she had not fully realized at the time, and one that seemed to her now embryonic, a prologue to the need she now experienced.

184

DAVID ANNANDALE

But something had happened. After each sell-sword fell, it became easier to kill the next. Not because her resistance to murder dropped. She had attacked Seck with no hesitation, and his death brought her satisfaction, not guilt. No, she had become better at killing each time.

She had become something else. When she had killed last night, the transformation had only been partial. Her feeding not what it would be now.

Now.

She grinned at the dark. She knew how to feed the hunger. She knew what she was doing.

She was hunting.

Latanna made for the Korvas road, looking for prey. Though the cloud-blossom field was gone, the addictions would not fade as easily, nor would the crimes of its traffic. The road was dangerous at night for lone travelers. Gangs roamed it, looking for the desperate, the foolhardy, and the unlucky.

Sure-footed, the night as clear to her vision as the day, she raced down the road, prepared to sprint as far as Northope if she had to. About a mile from Ghaunthook, she saw the flicker of a campfire to the right, a hundred yards ahead. Someone was not afraid of being seen. They might just be innocent travelers, then, though it seemed unlikely that they would stop for the night so close to the shelter of Ghaunthook.

Latanna slowed to a walk and pulled her hood up. She drew the cloak around herself, concealing her armor and sword. She walked down the middle of the road, nice and visible bait.

Four men sat around the campfire. They were not merchants. They wore leather armor almost as scarred as their faces. Blood-spatter tattoos covered their cheeks, a droplet for each victim. They passed a wineskin between them as they watched Latanna go by.

"What's your hurry?" one of them called out. He was the biggest of the four, and had a beard that straggled down from his cheeks like tangled vines.

The other three brayed laughter, overcome by their leader's wit.

185

THE SLEEP OF EMPIRES

Latanna stopped. She turned to face the highwaymen, her face concealed within her hood, her hands hidden in her cloak. "What hurry?" she asked.

The laughter came to a halt. She had not behaved according to the rules of their hunt. Rules had been broken, and they gave her puzzled frowns. They weren't wary. Not yet. They couldn't imagine they had reason to be of a lone woman.

"Get over here," the leader said.

"All right," she said, and walked toward them.

The four stood, very confused.

"You shouldn't be out there," said one. He was bald, and had a very broken nose.

Latanna stopped a few feet away from them. "No," she said. "You're wrong. This is where I belong. *You* are the ones who shouldn't be here." She pulled back her hood.

The men gasped. Three took a step back. The leader held his ground, but, like the others, froze for a moment before he reached for his sword.

Latanna leapt at him, hands outstretched. Her fingernails had become claws, and she plunged them into the highwayman's neck. Her fingers sank into flesh as if they were daggers, and blood gushed out over her hands and arms. It coated her, and sank into her, absorbed by her being.

The man staggered back, pulling her with him. He choked, more blood spurting from his mouth. He sank to his knees, and she held him up, taking his blood, taking his essence, feasting.

Feeding the hunger, fueling her transformation.

The being of the highwayman flowed through her, his life and self becoming hers. Memories flicked by, an accumulation of violence that she sifted and discarded in an instant. She kept knowledge, and she kept skills. They were the meat her hunger had sought, and she consumed them hungrily.

Pain lanced into her side. The bald man had stabbed her, puncturing phantom organs. Latanna hissed. She kept her left hand embedded in the

186

DAVID ANNANDALE

leader, and the flow of his blood instantly soothed the pain in her gut. With her right she drew her sword and fought the bald man off. She fought with the skills she had half-consumed the night before, when she had not yet achieved the metamorphosis that would come with death, and she fought with all the skill of the man who, dying, still bled into her hands. She parried the bald man's blows, countered those of the other man who joined the attack, and thrust the body of the leader up and at the fourth, knocking him down.

She batted away another strike and thrust her blade home through the chest of the bald man. She spun, keeping him skewered, and sank her claws up into the armpit of his comrade. The blood of two men washed over and into her, and she took what had been theirs. They screamed as they died, feeling the theft of their lives and identities.

The fourth man shrugged off the body of their leader and stabbed her in the back. The blood of his fellows replenished her faster than he could wound her. When she did not flinch, he turned and ran.

She caught up before he had gone five yards, leaping on his back and slashing his throat open with a single swipe. He fell, and then she had the luxury to move from body to body, absorbing the vintages, learning and growing, reveling in the feast.

CHAPTER 15

Vorykas and Kanstuhn arrived at Korvas a week after leaving Northope behind. Toward the end of the second day, they saw a body lying by the side of the road. The dead man's throat had been cut. He wore Forgrym livery.

"What does this mean?" Vorykas wondered. He and Kanstuhn dismounted to examine the corpse. "A victim of highwaymen?"

"Always a possibility," said Kanstuhn. "But what would a servant of Marsen's be doing out here?"

"A messenger? Delivering communications back and forth between Marsen and the Hawkesmoores?"

"I think so. The question is why is he dead?"

"And why is he out here at all, with Elgin having been with Marsen so recently?"

After a moment, Kanstuhn said, "Because of the news we created."

"The cloudblossom field," Vorykas said, understanding now.

Kanstuhn clucked his tongue. "Elgin must have been in a hurry to get back to Korvas. This man could not ride fast enough to catch up until now, much too late for Elgin to turn back. The bearer of tidings both bad and late. An unfortunate combination."

"And so his reward."

They remounted.

"I think," said Kanstuhn as they rode on, "that we will find the Hawkesmoores in a foul mood."

"I doubt we'll improve it," said Vorykas. "But we have another task first."

As they traveled, he kept looking into the distance. He could not see the walls of Korvas yet, but he could see what rose beyond the city.

Voran. The immense plateau, big as an empire, that held a continent's collective fears. The dead land that had given him his name. Its looming cliffs, thousands of feet high and mercilessly sheer, were black as terror.

DAVID ANNANDALE

Vorykas had hoped that his first sight of the plateau would have opened a floodgate of answers. It did not. The cliffs pulled at him, but told him nothing.

When he and Kanstuhn arrived at Korvas, late in the afternoon, they stabled their horses inside the city walls, then made for the lodging of Garwynn Avennic. Alisteyr had told them where they could find the former student. Kanstuhn had been in Korvas before, and knew his way through the tangle of streets at its center. Vorykas thought they might have searched for weeks otherwise.

The boarding house was a cramped, narrow building, looking as if it were trying to tuck in its shoulders, squeezed hard between the other houses on the block. Its façade was grimy, its windows opaque. The hunched woman who answered the door to their knock looked as squeezed as her house. Her wrinkled face eyed them suspiciously. "What?" she asked. "No room for you," she said to Kanstuhn.

There were kauls about in the city, but almost all the ones Vorykas had seen wore collars of service. A free kaul would not find much welcome in Korvas. Nor would Vorykas, not clearly belonging to any identifiable race, and keeping company with an unregulated kaul.

"We aren't seeking rooms, dear lady," Kanstuhn said, his unctuous manner stopping a hair's breadth short of irony. "We are hoping to speak with a friend, Garwynn Avennic."

The woman recoiled. "Get away," she said. "Go on! You're not wanted here."

"Isn't he here?"

"No!" the woman snarled. "He's gone! He won't be here again."

"Gone where?" Kanstuhn asked, his voice becoming smoother and calmer as the woman became angrier.

"Gone to Sánmaya, gone to the House of Law. Now go! *Go!*" She slammed the door.

Vorykas and Kanstuhn moved off.

"The House of Law?" Vorykas asked.

THE SLEEP OF EMPIRES

Kanstuhn looked grim. "The temple to Sánmaya. Few who are taken there ever leave. The stories are that what happens to you there takes a long time. I believe the stories."

"Then we have to get him out of there."

Kanstuhn grunted. "Easier said than done."

"Show me."

Kanstuhn led him west, back out of the cramped web of streets, and onto the wider roads that ran past the prison and the temple. They walked past the front of the House of Law. Vorykas took in the grand entrance and the guards. He paid attention to the sides of the building with no entrances, the fortress-like walls sloping up, the windows looking down in judgement at the city.

He saw some possibilities. He weighed options and risks, mindful that he and Kanstuhn had two purposes in Korvas. This had become the more important of the two, or at least reason made it so. Something was happening to Latanna, and Alisteyr hoped Garwynn could help her.

She doesn't need help.

Vorykas had no evidence for his conviction. He had only the conviction itself. But he and Kanstuhn had promised they would seek this help, and he would be true to his word.

And there was the fact of the House of Law itself. With every passing second, his hatred for the building and what it represented grew. The hostility felt like the one he had experienced for the temple to Kamatris in Ghaunthook, but deeper, stronger, as if in proportion to the size and power of the temple here.

"House of Law," he muttered. He strode away from the building, forcing Kanstuhn to increase his pace to keep up. "What law? Whose law?" He growled. "We're getting Garwynn out," he said to the kaul.

"A tall order," said Kanstuhn.

"There's a way."

"How are you even going to find out where in the temple he is being held?"

190

DAVID ANNANDALE

"By asking," Vorykas said.

"You're joking."

"Not really. No."

"All right." Kanstuhn shook his head in disbelief. "And when do you propose to free him?"

"Tonight."

They found lodgings in a squalid house not far from the city prison. Here, the passages of Korvas no longer pretended to be streets. They were muddy paths between shacks, rough houses divided into too many rooms, and the makeshift shelters of the homeless. The air stank of human waste and desperation. Vorykas and Kanstuhn made their way past a drunken brawl to get to the door of the boarding house, a two-story hovel built of wood and resentment. The room barely had room for a bed of rags and a wobbly stool. It stank of urine and sweat.

It would do. They had no belongings they did not carry with them, so they would not have to leave anything behind to get stolen. Kanstuhn rested while Vorykas watched over him and thought through what he had to do. Shortly after midnight, they headed out again. Vorykas bought some rags from a beggar and wrapped the stinking cloth around his face to serve as a mask. Insects squirmed in its folds.

Vorykas brought them to a shadowed doorway opposite the House of Law. There, Kanstuhn would be hidden from the guards, but have a view of the entrance and the west side of the temple.

"You still haven't told me your plan," said Kanstuhn.

"Because there isn't much of one. You wait for me here, and I'll go in."

"Alone?" Kanstuhn objected. "We've never fought apart."

Vorykas rested a hand on the kaul's shoulder. "No, we haven't. But we can, now, and that makes us even stronger."

"Me standing here and doing nothing doesn't feel like taking part in the fight."

191

THE SLEEP OF EMPIRES

"You can't go in there," Vorykas said gently. "I will be seen, sooner or later. Masked, I pass for human. No one will know who I am, and we will be free to go after the Hawkesmoores."

Kanstuhn nodded unhappily. "But a kaul invading the House of Law would be remembered."

"Yes." Kanstuhn's size and frame would give him away as a kaul, even if he wore a disguise. So would the smallest patch of visible flesh. Vorykas' gray skin might be mistaken for dirt. "And together, we are a pair that people remark."

"All right," said Kanstuhn. "I'll wait."

"Good." Vorykas grinned. "If I'm not back by dawn, feel free to ask the guards for news of me."

Vorykas moved across the street, to the shadows that lay between the House of Law and the eastern wall of the prison. The ground here was covered in heaps of broken brick and jagged stone. It was not a passageway. Anyone trying to navigate it would risk breaking a leg during the day. At night, with no lanterns, the stones became invisible traps.

Not for Vorykas. The darkness welcomed him as its lord. He hopped up from stone to stone with a spider's skill until he reached the middle of the temple's wall. This far in, he was hidden from the streets that ran by the House of Law to its north and south.

Vorykas looked up at the thirty-foot height of the prison wall. A sentry passed along its rampart, bearing a torch, head turned to look inside the prison courtyard. The man had no concern about what happened outside the wall. No one would be trying to get in.

Vorykas wouldn't either. He was happy to use this space that passed beneath the notice of guards and priests.

Light shone from a window twenty feet up the pyramid of the House of Law. Vorykas would start there. He didn't want a deserted room. He needed someone to interrogate.

Vorykas pressed his hands flat against the wall. He felt the texture of the façade. The temple had been constructed of massive, carved granite

192

DAVID ANNANDALE

slabs. The joins were minute, almost imperceptible. They offered nothing for hands and feet to grip.

Vorykas was glad Kanstuhn hadn't asked him how he planned to get inside. *I'm going to climb*, he would have answered.

How? Kanstuhn would have wanted to know.

And he would have had no answer, other than the certainty that he could, and would.

Nothing for a handhold, and the nothing embraced him, because it was his. He did not know why. He felt the ownership, and he used it. He grasped hold of absence and began to climb. He went up quickly, still the spider, scaling the wall as smoothly as he had moved over the stones. He reached out for the nothing between the stones and pulled himself higher and higher, a shadow moving across darkness, inseparable, unseen.

He arrived at the window. He peered in cautiously. A robed priest of Sánmaya sat at a desk, poring over a thick book. Hands together beneath his chin, index fingers steepled under his nose, he read with a frown of pious concern. A lantern on the desk and a chandelier cast flickering light over a study lined with shelves, and a floor covered with richly woven rugs.

A space of meditation and tranquility, Vorykas thought, his lip curling. A space for the morally superior to ponder what should happen to the wretches in the dungeons below, and to take satisfaction from their own sanctity.

In his anger, he sensed a deeper hypocrisy too, one that went far beyond, and far above, the human priest. Like so many other things, its true nature hovered beyond Vorykas' grasp, a truth as mysterious as it was absolute.

I will know, he promised himself. He would cross the horizon that hemmed in his memories, and know what lay beyond.

For tonight, he would satisfy himself with crossing the threshold of this temple.

He moved to the right and climbed a bit higher, bringing himself beside the window, his feet level with the sill. Then he kicked, smashing the glass, and threw himself in. He landed on his feet and marched over to

THE SLEEP OF EMPIRES

the terrified priest before the man could react. He grabbed the priest by the front of his robes and hauled him into the air. "Garwynn Avennic," he snarled.

The incomprehension in the priest's eyes told Vorykas that this man had no idea who Garwynn was.

"I . . ." the priest began.

"Be quiet."

Vorykas tore long strips from the man's robes, then bound and gagged him. "Contemplate your laws," he instructed, and left the study.

He paused when he stepped into the hallway, listening for sounds of alarm. He heard none. The corridor was deserted. If anyone else on this floor had heard the noise of breaking glass, they did not think it concerned them. Merely someone dropping something. This high off the ground, how could it be otherwise?

Vorykas moved down the corridor, walking silently on polished marble of a deep shade of violet. He tried the bronze handles of each oak door he passed. Most were locked, the stillness of emptiness behind them. But some opened when he pushed, and he found other priests studying deep into the night.

He questioned them, and when they did not know who Garwynn was either, he left them as he had the first.

He tried every door in the hall, then reached its landing.

Up or down? he wondered.

Up, he decided. The higher he went, he reasoned, the greater the privilege and the authority he would find.

He found no one at all on the next floor, or the one above it. On the third, there were a couple of occupied studies. As he had expected, they were larger and more opulent than the ones before. But as rich as their decor became, with jeweled ink pots on the desks and real gold threaded into the tapestries, a strict order governed them. The layout of objects was as rectilinear as the architecture of the room. Nothing existed in these studies that did not follow the dictates of some law, be it geometrical or aesthetic.

194

DAVID ANNANDALE

Brass plaques on the doors bore the names of the occupants of the studies, suggesting a permanence of place that clerics below had not quite earned.

The first priest reacted to Garwynn's name with the same incomprehension as the others. But the second, Sanctor Jareth, did not look puzzled. His eyes widened in still greater fear, as if he perceived a purpose in Vorykas' presence deeper than Vorykas knew.

He put his hand around the priest's throat. He didn't squeeze. He just held the man in place with pressure, and with the threat of murder. "Where is he?"

Jareth surprised him. He had managed to conceal a diamond-hilted dagger in the huge sleeves of his robe, and with a desperate lunge, he stabbed up through Vorykas' lower jaw. The blade punctured his tongue and palate. Pain flashed, then faded.

Irritated, Vorykas slapped Jareth's hand away, then jerked the dagger out and tossed it to the floor. Blood filled his mouth. He swallowed quickly, and the bleeding stopped almost as quickly as the pain.

As with the arrow during the cloudblossom raid, then. *Have I always been like this? What am I?*

He would find no answers here. He pushed the questions aside.

"Do not try that again," Vorykas warned. His tongue felt thick in his mouth, but only briefly. "I'm not as angry with you yet as I might be."

Jareth's arms fell, his body going limp with horror.

Vorykas hauled him one-handed out of the chair. "You're going to take me to Garwynn Avennic," he said. "And you're going to take me there quietly. Because I don't believe there are any grand staircases that descend to the dungeon. That would disrupt the ordered flow and beauty of your temple. So you will have a hidden way." The hypocrisy of this temple demanded it. "We're going to take that path, and if you try to deceive me, what will happen to you will be as slow as it will be painful."

The hours and the days had become meaningless for Garwynn. He existed in an endless continuity of agony, one whose interruptions were so brief,

THE SLEEP OF EMPIRES

they became half-remembered dreams as soon as they ended. The guards unshackled him from the chair twice a day, when they brought his meals. They allowed him a few minutes to walk around the cell and void his bowels in a bucket. The whole time, he had to be careful to keep his hands visible and his fingers as immobile as possible. When he ate, he had to be just as cautious and deliberate in his motions, never making an unnecessary movement, or he would be back in the chair in an instant, his hands buried once more in the iron bonds.

Between meals, and through the night, he sat, trapped, his cramped muscles screaming for relief, his saliva dribbling around the bridle and down his chin. He couldn't swallow. He felt as if he were perpetually choking. After the first hour of wearing the bridle, he had thrown up, and a lot of the vomit had gone back down his throat, burning him and drowning him.

He had been careful to fight back the nausea and panic since then. That struggle gave him something to do.

The gloom in his cell never changed. He sensed the days passing only through the rhythm of the meals. Priests came and interrogated him for hours during the first couple of days. He gave the same answers again and again, because they were the only ones he had. Nothing he said satisfied his inquisitors.

A few of the sanctors told him their names. Jareth was the first, the one who had spoken to him when he arrived, and who was present at all the interrogations. Sometimes, he spoke to Garwynn in a tone close to pity, and that, more than anything, destroyed Garwynn's hope of ever leaving the House of Law. The pity implied Jareth knew that Garwynn had nothing to tell them, and that didn't matter. There would be no help or mercy for him.

After the first day or so, the interrogations became shorter, less frequent, and then stopped altogether. Once in a while, now, a small group of sanctors would come to his cell, look at him, and murmur to each other, their conversation too quiet for Garwynn to make out. Otherwise, he sat alone in the eternal gloom of the cell.

196

DAVID ANNANDALE

He wondered why they didn't have him executed. He no longer appeared to be of any use or interest to them. He had become a thing stored away, out of sight and out of mind, but not killed just in case they wanted him for something else, someday, in some vague future.

He wondered how long it would be before they forgot him completely. On that day, the meals would not come, and he would be left to die of starvation and thirst.

Sometimes, his back arching in agony, his breath quickening in incipient panic around the bridle, he hoped the day would come soon.

In calmer moments, he went around and around with the question of what had happened to him. Had Magister Dunfeld arranged his incarceration?

He didn't think so. He didn't think she would have lied to him. He believed she really had planned to bring him into the fold of the university, where she could keep a sharp eye on him.

But then the dream happened. And she would have had to speak to higher authorities. His story would have traveled through ranks and channels until it reached the ears of the sanctors.

Garwynn thought this must have been what had happened. The logic satisfied him.

What difference does it make?

None.

There would be no comfort for him. The last hope left to him was that death would not be too painful.

The sounds of a struggle broke the monotony of his suffering. Someone new, he thought, being brought to the dungeons. Someone who might add to the chorus of moans that rang, a desultory melody, from the cells. Someone who thought they could break the iron grip of the temple guards.

The noises continued, grew closer and louder, and he realized he was wrong. People were fighting. Metal clashed against metal, guards yelled and guards *screamed*. Bodies thudded against the wall and floor.

THE SLEEP OF EMPIRES

Why are the guards screaming? How can that be?

The impossibility of the event frightened him.

Boot heels clattered. People ran toward the fight. More yelling, more screaming, and in the midst, an old man sobbing.

What is happening? What is happening?

The fighting stopped. Someone moaned in pain, a person in the corridor, not in a cell. Then quiet, except for the weeping. Booted feet walked to Garwynn's door, then stopped. He held his breath.

Keys rattled in the lock. The door opened, and a huge, masked figure strode inside, dragging Sanctor Jareth with him. He tossed the priest into a corner of the cell. Jareth curled up into a quaking, whining ball.

Garwynn didn't know if the figure was a man. He seemed too big. He unlatched the bridle and removed it from Garwynn's head, then opened the shackles that held his arms.

"Garwynn Avennic?" the warrior asked.

Garwynn nodded. He coughed and cleared his throat, trying to get his voice working.

"Come with me." The warrior helped him out of the chair, and halfcarried him to the hall, then closed and locked the cell door behind them, leaving Jareth to his fears.

Garwynn stared, wide-eyed, at the hall. The bodies of guards littered its length, their armor dented and broken, masks torn asunder, swords bent. Blood pooled across the floor, glinting in the torchlight.

Garwynn looked at the towering figure beside him. "Who are you?" he croaked.

"My name is Vorykas." A grunt of a laugh. "That's as much as I know."

He started down the hall, unlocking one cell after another.

Garwynn followed close behind. "Did you kill all those guards?"

"I did. They tried to kill me. And they are keeping people here for perceived crimes against religion." Vorykas snorted in disgust. "I do not recognize the reality of such crimes."

198

DAVID ANNANDALE

Where prisoners were chained or otherwise bound, Vorykas entered the cell and freed them. Hesitantly at first, unsure of the miracle that had come to them, the prisoners stumbled out of their cells and into the corridor. They gathered around Vorykas, who led them down other corridors, to open other cells. Before long, there were close to a hundred of them, crowding around him.

And a few more dead guards.

When he had emptied the last of the cells, Vorykas spoke to the prisoners. "I will lead you out of the House of Law," he said. "What you do after that is up to you, though I would suggest leaving Korvas."

No one seemed inclined to argue the point.

As they headed for the exit to the dungeon, Garwynn finally had the chance to ask, "Why have you rescued me?"

"You are needed in Ghaunthook. Alisteyr Huesland sent me to find you. Latanna Forgrym, his wife, is ailing." Vorykas frowned, uncertain. "Or she seemed to be," he said, more to himself than to Garwynn.

Alisteyr calling for him. Alisteyr married. To Latanna. The news came in faster than Garwynn could process. He could not take it all in, and all that it meant to him. Except the fact that Alisteyr needed him back. That was the most important thing. That put strength back in his limbs.

"Why does Alisteyr think I can help, though?"

"Sorcery is involved. Or something like it." Vorykas raised his voice. "Is there anyone here who will be heading east, perhaps as far as Northope?"

Quite a few called out that they were. One woman said that she had family in Northope, and would be making her way there.

"Good," said Vorykas. "I know you will stick together." He looked at Garwynn. "Go with them."

They arrived at the foot of the stairs leading up to the dungeon door. "Follow me quickly," Vorykas told the prisoners. "But don't get too close. Give me room to fight. There will be more guards."

"Where are we going?" a woman asked.

199

THE SLEEP OF EMPIRES

"Out the front door," said Vorykas.

He went up the stairs, sword drawn, a figure dense with night. Garwynn ran to keep a few paces behind. His body ached with the effort, but hope energized him. So did the need to see what Vorykas would do.

The warrior unlocked the dungeon door and hurtled down the corridor beyond it. It turned sharply, ended at another door, and Vorykas slammed through it and into the grand entrance hall of the House of Law.

Violet marble gleamed in the light of scores of torches mounted on spiral pillars. They rose twenty feet to a triangular vault, a pyramid within a pyramid. On the walls, runes of inlaid silver proclaimed the sacred laws of Sánmaya. The words blurred as Garwynn ran, and it seemed to him the silver had turned fluid and ran down the walls, a wash of glittering slime, the words losing meaning. They had become empty for him.

A dozen sentinels rushed to meet Vorykas. He charged them even faster. They faltered, slightly but perceptibly, unprepared for anyone who did not tremble at the sight of them. Garwynn shouted, and so did the other prisoners. To see these guards afraid, that was a grand miracle in and of itself.

Vorykas tore into them like judgement. Their armor did nothing against his blows. His blade found every chink, every weak spot. He countered their strikes as if they were children, yanked off their helmets, and cut off their heads.

The sight of those guards dying, falling like leaves before the unknown avenger, stunned Garwynn. It was like seeing the death of a god, and he had to force himself to keep running, force himself not to stop and stare at the sight that could not possibly be real.

Behind him, people stumbled. They, too, struggled with the awe of seeing the hands of Sánmaya shattered.

The battle was quick and brutal. It passed in a blur of violence and blood, and Garwynn had trouble understanding everything he witnessed. He would have sworn that he saw a guard's blade strike Vorykas in the back. He even thought he saw a sword stick there, impaling him, before he reached back and yanked it out.

That couldn't be right. He'd imagined that.

But when the last of the guards lay dead, and he came up closer behind Vorykas, he saw rents in the leather armor.

Vorykas hurled the outside doors open. The guards on the wide porch turned in shock, and died before they could bring their spears to bear. They sprawled on the steps, guts spread out beneath them, the shafts of their weapons broken.

Vorykas and the prisoners ran out of the House of Law and into the street. A kaul emerged from a doorway and gestured to them, then led the way to an alley that opened off the boulevard, promising more darkness and shelter.

Garwynn paused for a moment at the entrance to the alley with a number of his fellows. He knew they had to keep moving. What had happened this night would convulse the city, and the greater force of Sánmaya's guards would spread out across Korvas, searching for escapees and anyone else on whom to vent their wrath. But he needed a last glimpse of the figure who had harrowed the dungeons of the House of Law.

Vorykas had stopped at the edge of the pavement to look back at the temple. The way he stood, motionless as granite, fists closed, terrified Garwynn. He seemed to be staring at the House of Law as if he could smash it down with the back of his hand.

Then and there, Garwynn believed that he could.

CHAPTER 16

"This won't make it easy to get around in Korvas," said Kanstuhn as the last of the prisoners disappeared down the alley.

"Should I have left them all in the dungeon?" Vorykas asked.

They moved down the alley too, staying deep in the shadows. The hue and cry from the temple would not be long in coming, Vorykas thought. He knew they should try to be as far as possible from the House of Law before that happened, but part of him wanted to be in earshot of the uproar.

He wanted to hear what a wounded cult sounded like. *How do you like it to be on the receiving end of terror?*

"What do you want to do next?" Kanstuhn asked. "Free everyone in the prison?"

"I know we can't do that," Vorykas said. "But the choice in the House of Law was easy. I had the opportunity. I took it. And you didn't answer my question. Would you have done otherwise?"

"Of course I would not have," Kanstuhn said, irritated. "I was just pointing out the consequences. They will be real."

"And we will deal with them."

"You do sound pleased with yourself."

"I guess I am," Vorykas admitted.

"You don't like the gods, do you?"

"I despise them." Vorykas surprised himself with the speed and vehemence of his answer.

"I wonder why," said Kanstuhn.

"So do I."

They reached the end of the alley and paused in its darkness.

"Well," said Kanstuhn, "that's our first duty complete, and on a rather grander scale than I had imagined. What now?"

202

DAVID ANNANDALE

"Let's go have a look at Hawkesmoore Hall," Vorykas said. "I'd like to see how they expect to keep us out."

The Hawkesmoores' great house squatted in the north-central region of Korvas. The district, the wealthiest in the city, lay a short walk away from the warren of streets where Garwynn Avennic had found his dismal lodgings. No physical barrier separated the regions. The wide expanse of Lenders Lane, running east and west, marked the geographical boundary between the two. Money changers, bankers, and jewelers' shops lined the northern side of the street. On the south side, taverns and pawnbrokers served the crowded, desperate inhabitants of the city's center.

Officers of the Korvas Watch roamed the handsome, clean streets that ran past the walled-off mansions of the wealthy and powerful.

"I can't imagine the Watch is much needed here," said Vorykas.

He and Kanstuhn watched a patrol go by from the dark passage between the outside walls of two courtyards.

"Oh, but it is," said Kanstuhn. "Its officers are not here to do anything except, by their presence, ensure that nothing happens. They're here to keep the vermin off the streets. You know, the rest of the city."

"Bad luck to them," Vorykas muttered.

When the patrol had passed, he and Kanstuhn emerged from the passage and padded through the sleeping streets. Few of the homes here fronted onto the roads. Almost all hid behind walls, preserving their secrets, protecting their inhabitants from the contagion of the unwashed.

Vorykas followed Kanstuhn's lead, and the kaul found Hawkesmoore Hall easily enough. Learning its location had been simple. Everyone, it seemed, knew of the Hawkesmoores, and knew where they lived. Kanstuhn had asked one of the prisoners as she ran by, and she had told him. It seemed the Hall was as prominent a landmark on the mental map of Korvassians as the House of Law. The Hawkesmoores were that intimidating. From what Kanstuhn had said about the woman's reaction to his question, people made sure to know where the Hall was so they could avoid it.

203

THE SLEEP OF EMPIRES

If they are this powerful, why care about Ghaunthook? How much more influence could they want?

Vorykas told himself not to be naive. *Power creates envy in its wielders. Power hungers for power.*

Hawkesmoore Hall's defenses were the most fortress-like in the district. The wall around the grounds rose over fifteen feet. The only glimpse of the house itself from street level came through the bars of the forbidding gate on the south side. Guards in Hawkesmoore livery stood watch on either side of the gate. The house itself was a brooding mass of black.

Vorykas and Kanstuhn surveyed what they could from a distance, then withdrew. They found a square, abandoned for the night, unlit by street lanterns, and stood beneath the oak in its center to consider what they had seen.

"It's different from the others," said Kanstuhn.

Vorykas nodded. "No light at all."

At least a few windows glowed with the light of candles or hearths in every other hall before whose gate they had passed. Nothing at all showed from the windows of Hawkesmoore Hall. Not even the courtyard had a lit torch. The wall enclosed only darkness.

"As if it were deserted," said Kanstuhn.

"Do you think it is?"

The kaul made a helpless gesture. "If it is, where are they? Elgin and his men were on their way here. If they went elsewhere, where?"

"And why?" Vorykas added.

"*That* is what I find most worrying."

"And if they are there, what are they doing in the dark?"

"I find that speculation unwelcome as well," said Kanstuhn.

Vorykas sighed. "We need to get inside."

"We will, yes, but without rushing," Kanstuhn cautioned.

"Agreed." Vorykas had taken the House of Law by surprise. The temple guards of Sánmaya had had no reason to believe anyone would dare do what

204

DAVID ANNANDALE

he had done. But Elgin knew to be wary of him. More than that, the Hawkesmoores had enemies, and expected them.

"I saw you climb the face of the House of Law," said Kanstuhn. "Can you climb the Hawkesmoores' wall, too?"

"I don't know," Vorykas admitted. "The House of Law has that slope." Tackling it had felt natural. "A vertical one . . ." He shook his head. "I don't know," he repeated.

"You may have to try."

"That's true." He thought about the sense of grasping nothing, and holding on to it, and how in that way he had rushed up the wall. On a vertical surface, there would be even more of an absence. Wouldn't that mean he *could* scale it?

Does this even make sense? Is this any kind of reasoning?

The frustration of not knowing.

Who am I? What am I?

Maybe he could climb the wall. But how? If he believed strongly enough that he could? He didn't feel that kind of faith at the moment.

There were other ways in. He and Kanstuhn would find them.

They returned to their lodgings. Vorykas sat up and thought while Kanstuhn caught a few hours' sleep. He considered possible approaches to the Hall. He asked himself if he believed they would get in and out without being seen.

Do we even want to? We're here to topple the Hawkesmoores. We haven't come to be thieves. We're here to lay siege.

Ideal strategy did not involve going in without knowing what they might encounter. Reality might not give them a choice.

He could see a way in. He would wait until the following night, though. He would see what he and Kanstuhn could learn during the day first.

An hour before dawn, Vorykas heard someone pick the lock of the door to the room. He raised an eyebrow, curious. The faint glow of a candle flickered under the door.

205

THE SLEEP OF EMPIRES

He tapped Kanstuhn on the shoulder. The kaul woke, instantly alert.

Vorykas pointed at the door. Kanstuhn shook his head in disbelief. Whoever was breaking in either hadn't seen them, or else felt very confident about slitting the throats of two sleeping targets.

Vorykas remained where he was in the chair next to the bed, beneath the paneless window. Kanstuhn, dagger drawn, moved to the wall next to the door.

The lock clicked. The door eased open, revealing two men, both carrying short swords, one holding a candle. They took a step into the room, then stopped when they saw Vorykas was awake.

"Good morning," Vorykas said, and gave them a flippant wave.

Kanstuhn whipped around the door frame and stabbed his knife into the thigh of the man with the candle. He cried out and fell, knocking his comrade forward. Still sitting, Vorykas reached out, grabbed the belt of the man as he stumbled, and swung him against the wall, cracking his forehead hard. The man dropped his sword and clutched his head, knees buckling. Vorykas gave him another yank and hurled him to the floor.

Kanstuhn kicked the other man down, then kneeled on his back and pressed the tip of the dagger against his throat.

"Stay," Vorykas instructed the pair. He picked up the fallen candle and set it on the windowsill. The light wavered violently in the noxious breeze that wafted in.

The men cursed under their breaths, but did not move.

Vorykas examined their captives. They both had the same crude spider tattoo across their bald domes. Gang markings, he assumed. Not a gang of great importance, though, to judge by how filthy their clothes were. And they were not hunting in promising territory.

"Tell us," said Kanstuhn. "Why were you so incredibly stupid as to open that door?"

"Thought you were asleep," said the man with the bleeding leg.

206

DAVID ANNANDALE

"Clearly," said Kanstuhn. "Did you choose us on your own initiative, or was this someone else's silly idea?"

"Looked like you might have gold," said the man at Vorykas' feet.

Kanstuhn sighed. "You are not very good at what you do, are you?"

"What's your gang?" Vorykas asked his victim. "And don't bother to say they'll make us pay for this. They won't."

"Sons of the Spider."

"I suppose I should have guessed a name like that from your tattoo." Vorykas looked more closely at the men's markings. "Those are fresh," he said. "New inductees, are we?"

Kanstuhn clucked his tongue. "Your bosses will not be pleased at all. How does it fare for Sons who embarrass the Spider?"

The men started breathing faster.

"I see," said Vorykas. He opened the pouch on his belt and pulled out a few coins. He jingled them in his palm. They didn't add up to much in the rest of Korvas, but in this district, they were more than worth killing over. They would be a believable haul from what these two unfortunates had been planning to do. "There is a way," he said, "for you to leave this room alive, and richer too."

They looked up at Vorykas with disbelieving hope. "How?" the nearest one asked.

"Tell us a few things. For instance, the Sons of the Spider pay tribute, don't they?" When the men nodded, he asked, "To whom?"

The thieves looked as if Vorykas had asked the name of the city.

"The Hawkesmoores," they replied in unison. They continued to stare at Vorykas, unable to believe he would be willing to pay for such obvious information.

"Everyone does," said Kanstuhn's prisoner.

"Everyone," the other repeated.

"They have no rivals?" Vorykas asked.

Snorts. "Some have tried to be," said the first.

207

THE SLEEP OF EMPIRES

"Didn't live long," said the second.

Vorykas and Kanstuhn questioned them a bit longer, then, to the astonishment of the men, gave them their coins and sent them on their way.

"Come up with a good excuse for that leg," Kanstuhn admonished.

The men gave them a lingering look of confused gratitude, and then clattered down the narrow staircase of the house.

"Have you been to Korvas before?" Vorykas asked Kanstuhn.

"Once, and briefly. It was not a friendly place for me."

"Does what they say sound right to you?"

"It does. I didn't know who the Hawkesmoores were then, but I did get the impression of a . . . regulated . . . underworld."

"To hear them talk," said Vorykas, "the Hawkesmoores run Korvas."

"Who is to say they don't? At least as much as the House of Law permits them to."

"Not a natural alliance, I would have thought."

"I'm not talking about an alliance," said Kanstuhn. "More a kind of toleration. If the Hawkesmoores keep theft and murder within tolerable limits, and in tolerable areas, then Sánmaya's faithful will see that as a kind of law."

"Order instead of justice," Vorykas muttered to himself.

Kanstuhn overheard. "It seems that is something you have had to learn anew."

"Not really," Vorykas said, thoughtful. "That was disgust you heard, but not surprise. For some reason, I feel like I have known this truth for longer than you have."

"I doubt that," Kanstuhn said sharply. "A kaul is born with that knowledge."

"I know you are," said Vorykas. "I would never suggest otherwise. What I meant is that somehow this knowledge is still older than that. I can't explain why." He pressed his fingers against his temple, as if their pressure would pin down the half-thoughts and shards of truth that careened through this mind like leaves in foaming rapids. Then he stood up, shaking off the

208

DAVID ANNANDALE

mood. "Never mind," he said. "Just another thing for my collection of puzzles."

They waited until full light, then headed out and found a rag-seller two lanes over from the lodging house. They acquired some loose clothes to drape over themselves, poor enough to make them look like laborers, but not so ragged as to mark them as beggars. They bought a couple of sacks, too, and enough of the rag-seller's stock to fill them up. Now they had burdens to carry.

Once they left the slum, they threw the sacks over their shoulders and walked with a heavy, stolid trudge, eyes fixed on the pavement in front of them. They had become bored, tired workers. Whoever saw them, in whatever district, would see two figures weighed down with the banal purpose of their errand. They could not walk into the Hawkesmoores' district looking like mercenaries. As laborers on an errand, they could pass unnoticed.

As they made their way through the crowded streets, they saw the effects of Vorykas' actions in the House of Law. The temple guards had come out in force. They were everywhere, the grim faces of their helmets now images of anger. They stopped people at random. Vorykas heard the sharp tones of interrogation when they passed within earshot, and he saw some people being dragged away.

He fought to contain the snarl building in his throat. His breath came out as a rattling hiss.

Kanstuhn glanced at him. "Did you think you had emptied the cells of the House of Law forever?" he asked without dropping his expression of bored drudgery.

"No." Vorykas sighed. "But it would have been nice to have had that illusion for at least a day." He saw another pair of guards up ahead, shouldering arrogantly through the bustling market street. He lowered his eyes before his look turned into a glare. "I should have razed the temple to the ground."

"The way you say that, I believe you will yet," said Kanstuhn.

THE SLEEP OF EMPIRES

The crowds here were so thick, progress was slow. Vorykas and Kanstuhn couldn't move at more than a shuffle without pushing hard like the guards. So they moved back and forth, pausing when they had to, advancing through the masses of people as if through a tide of molasses. Ahead, the guards drew closer, marching in a straight line down the center of the road. They moved through the crowd like the prow of a ship parting waves.

"If they stop us?" said Kanstuhn.

"They don't take us," said Vorykas.

"Agreed."

A fight would complicate matters. Capture would be worse.

They tried to move off to one side, out of the way of the guards, but the currents of the crowd kept pushing them back toward the center. Vorykas hunched over lower under his sack, reducing his height.

The guards appeared before them. Vorykas and Kanstuhn used the fear of the crowd. They lowered their heads and turned sideways, pressing back with everyone else. They stopped moving, waiting for Sánmaya's sentinels to pass. The stall owners fell silent, the chorus of hawked wares going still around Vorykas.

He held his breath. His hands twitched. He half-wished the guards would turn on him, and he would teach them the lesson he had taught their fellows.

But that would not lessen the anxiety of the people around him. It would only frighten them more.

The guards passed him, ignoring him, and the bubble of fear that surrounded them moved on.

"I appreciate your restraint," Kanstuhn said as they started walking again.

"It wasn't the time or place."

For the rest of their journey, they managed to avoid another close encounter with the temple guards. They entered the Hawkesmoores' district without being challenged. There were others like them on the streets

DAVID ANNANDALE

here, burdened with the missions given to them by the residents. The rich of Korvas were on the streets too, carried about in carriages or mounted on expensively bred horses. Some were on foot, out in their finery, walking with the confidence of those who own the streets. Vorykas and Kanstuhn bowed low and moved well out of their way.

We know our place, Vorykas thought. *You do not see us, because we are beneath notice.*

They arrived at Hawkesmoore Hall, and walked around its perimeter wall slowly, studying it from the corner of their eyes.

"Solid defenses," said Kanstuhn.

"They don't want anyone getting inside," Vorykas agreed.

"If they have taken and held the throne of the Korvas underworld, then they have to keep the unwelcome out."

"And show that they can do it."

Two new guards kept watch outside the gate. Otherwise, the house seemed as quiet and dead as during the night.

"Not even a servant in the courtyard," Vorykas said once they had completed their circuit and moved off, heading back for the greater anonymity of the more crowded streets.

"We had a view through the gates for only a few moments," Kanstuhn reminded him. "Someone could easily have been there seconds before or after we passed by."

"Do you really think so?"

After a short pause, Kanstuhn said, "No. It feels deserted." He held up a warning finger. "That doesn't mean it is, though."

"We've done what we can from the outside," said Vorykas. "And that isn't much. We're going inside tonight."

Kanstuhn sucked air in through his teeth. "I don't like the idea of launching our campaign against an enemy so hidden from us. You don't think this is how their rivals have failed?"

"It probably is. But do you see a choice?"

"There's always the choice to walk away."

211

THE SLEEP OF EMPIRES

"Are you testing me?"

"Just reminding you of our options."

"Except that isn't an option."

"No," said Kanstuhn. "We gave our word." He nodded to himself. "And there's the cloudblossom and everything else that they pollute."

"Did we engage in righteous wars before I could remember things?" Vorykas asked.

"We didn't have that luxury. But we didn't engage in injustice, either. I swear it. We were not thugs for hire."

"I didn't think we were, but I'm glad to hear you say it." Vorykas smiled. "How do you like fighting for a cause?"

Kanstuhn grinned back. "It makes a change."

In the deepest pit of the night, the streets nearest Hawkesmoore Hall were deserted. No one had any reason to pass near the gate, not when to do so would invite the scrutiny of the family within.

If, Vorykas thought, *the family is even there.*

He appreciated the caution of the other residents of the district. It made his work easier.

He and Kanstuhn sprinted toward the gate from opposite corners of the wall. The guards, surprised by the extreme unlikelihood of an attack, reacted sluggishly. They brought their spears to bear, but they did not shout a warning.

Kanstuhn slid under the reach of the spear and stabbed upward with his sword, catching the guard in the throat. Vorykas grabbed the other guard's spear with both hands. He yanked it from the man's hands, spun it around, and plunged it into his chest.

The sounds of the attack were barely a ripple in the silence.

Kanstuhn took a set of keys from his guard's belt. The largest one fit the lock on the gate.

"I'm still not convinced this is much of a plan," he whispered.

"I never called this a plan," said Vorykas. "It's an approach."

212

DAVID ANNANDALE

The gate clanked. Kanstuhn gave it a push, and it swung slowly open, grinding in the quiet of the night. Kanstuhn stopped. A gap of a foot was wide enough for them both.

The kaul entered the courtyard. Vorykas followed. They paused, waiting for the sound of the gate to bring more guards out.

When no one appeared, they crossed the courtyard. Moonlight frosted the gables of the house and washed over the paving stones. The house surrounded them on three sides. Stables had been built into the wing on the left, and kennels almost as large on the right. Both were empty.

"The animals are not at home, then," said Vorykas.

"Both kinds?"

"It looks that way." *But why?*

"The front door?" Kanstuhn asked, sounding doubtful.

"You have the keys, so why not?"

"I can think of a few reasons."

"If this is a trap, and they know we're here, it doesn't matter if we go in the door or the top window."

The kaul shrugged. Swords drawn, they approached the front door. While Kanstuhn tried the keys, Vorykas eyed the chapel that grew out of the house's east side like an angular, eight-sided tumor. The god of war's iron spire, the crossed axe, spear, and sword surrounded by a crown of blades, stabbed up into the sky, its mass and edges limned by the moon. Hate built in Vorykas' chest. In his mind, he saw the temple falling in ruins and flame.

"Got it," said Kanstuhn.

Vorykas snapped out of his reverie. He cursed himself. He should have been watching for guards.

Kanstuhn opened the door into blackness beyond. Moonlight shone wanly through the windows of the entrance hall.

"Can you see?" Vorykas asked.

"Not as well as you, I wager, but well enough." The kauls' facility to move about in darkness was further proof, for the other races, of their debased nature.

THE SLEEP OF EMPIRES

But for Vorykas, the shadows might as well be day. They were home. They hid him when he wished, but they kept no secrets from him.

If the kauls are debased, then whatever I am is worse yet.

The idea of being even more accursed in the eyes of the powers he despised pleased him.

They crossed the hall and stopped at the foot of the grand staircase. It led up to a gallery whose balcony looked down on three sides into the hall. Paintings hung on the walls of the entrance hall, huge portraits of men rich in finery, power, and cruelty. Vorykas could see them quite well in the dimness, and noted the unmistakable Hawkesmoore features. Elgin would fit in very well with his ancestors, if his portrait did not already hang elsewhere in the house.

Vorykas and Kanstuhn listened, and the quiet was deeper and thicker in the house than outside, as if they had found the wellspring of silence.

Vorykas took a look through the door on the left. He saw a large reception room. Huge cloth sheets covered the furniture, creating vague, somnolent humps.

"There's no one here," he said. "The guards were watching an empty house."

"So where have they gone?" Kanstuhn said, then added, "It would be a good idea to learn that before you burn the place down. If that's what you have in mind."

"Don't tempt me."

They went up the stairs, looking for a room that would show them something more than absence. They found empty bedrooms, with more shrouded furniture and mattresses turned on their sides. To the right of the steps, a library took up most of the northeast corner of the second floor. Its shelves held many books, too many to sort through in the time they would have before the bodies of the guards were discovered. On the north wall, between the windows, hung a painting of a fortress. A squat, circular keep, surrounded by a massive curtain wall, rose from the thick forest on a hill. Kanstuhn stopped before it, his head cocked.

214

DAVID ANNANDALE

"What is it?" Vorykas asked.

"That tower looks familiar. Doesn't it?"

"Yes," Vorykas said after looking more carefully at the painting. "Where have we seen it before?"

Kanstuhn remembered first. "On the road to Korvas," he said. "When we still had a day's ride ahead of us. We saw it from a distance, a few miles north of the road."

"Do you know the place?"

Kanstuhn shook his head. "But I wonder if that is where everyone has gone."

"The question remains why."

In the far corner of the library, recessed beneath a shelf, they found a small iron door. None of the keys fit its lock.

"For the family only," said Kanstuhn.

"Can you pick the lock?"

"Pride requires me to say yes."

Kanstuhn knelt and produced his tools from the pouch at his belt. Vorykas stood to one side and waited. He listened to the house, and confirmed its emptiness. The only sounds were the faint metallic clicks as Kanstuhn probed the lock.

The lock resisted. It took several minutes, but at last Kanstuhn grunted in satisfaction, and the lock surrendered.

The door opened onto a stone staircase heading down. They took it, and it descended far below the ground floor of the Hall. The staircase took them to a large chamber in the foundations of the house. Here they encountered illumination. Long strips of smooth bark, glowing reddish brown, lined the ceiling.

"Menyë bark," said Kanstuhn. "I don't understand. I've never heard of it being exported from Beresta. The elves are very possessive of the light tree."

A line of granite pillars surrounded an octagonal pool in the center of the floor. Manacles hung from each of the pillars, and gutters ran from their

215

THE SLEEP OF EMPIRES

bases to the pool, which held a thick, black, coagulated liquid. The stench of blood assaulted Vorykas' senses. It filled the air, cloying and sharp and pungent. Dark stains ran down the pillars.

"What is this place?" Vorykas said. He didn't ask because he needed an answer. He asked because horror forced the words from him.

"Sacrifice and cruelty," Kanstuhn whispered.

A grid of chains covered the pool. An altar to Tetriwu dominated the wall next to the staircase. At the other end of the chamber were a long table and behind it a throne, both of marble. The back of the chair had been sculpted to resemble flames.

Documents covered the surface of the table.

"Some things we should see over there," Vorykas said, and stepped forward.

The stone under his feet sank into the floor. He heard the sudden running of machinery. An iron door slid across the entrance to the stairs and slammed shut. The grid of chains pulled back from the pool, disappearing inside its walls. The crusted surface of the blood stirred.

"So we aren't alone," Vorykas said. He took the lead, advancing on the pool.

The beast erupted from the blood with a buzzing, gargling howl. Its fifteen-foot-long, segmented body had a dozen chitinous legs, all ending in pincers. A sheaf of chitin projected over its head, narrowing into a vicious point. Mandibles thicker than Vorykas' arms opened and closed so fast their movement blurred, their clacking turning into a teeth-loosening vibration. It launched itself at Vorykas and slammed into him. The mass hurled him back and to the ground. The beast landed on him. Three pairs of legs held him down. Three others began tearing through his armor and flesh. The monster dug into his body, pincers grabbing for muscle and organs, and for the first time since memory had returned to him, he experienced the truth of agony. The beast sliced into him, and his body repaired itself, but the creature slashed faster and deeper than he could heal. Pain roared

DAVID ANNANDALE

through his frame, a fire on his nerves. His blood gushed out, spreading out like a tide on the floor.

The beast had his arms pinned. He couldn't raise his sword. He felt himself weaken as the monster cut him into pieces. Kanstuhn stabbed at it, dancing out of the reach of its other legs, then coming in to strike again. The monster lashed out at him, swinging its hindquarters back and forth, its rear legs snapping in anger. Kanstuhn jabbed his sword through the armor, and green ichor spewed out, but the monster kept hold of Vorykas, and would not be distracted. It had its prey, and was intent on feeding.

Mandibles closed around his neck, ready to decapitate. Vorykas lurched up against them, smashing his forehead against the beast's, just below the sword point of its armor. He hit it between the eyes, and it jerked back, the gurgling howl coming again from its throat. Kanstuhn attacked again, with a two-handed swing against the leg that pinned Vorykas' right arm. He shattered the armor and broke the leg. It snapped at a sharp angle, and the pincer opened.

The monster screamed and stabbed downward with its head. It speared Vorykas through the shoulder. A new pain joined the tapestry of agony. His arm went loose. It felt a hundred leagues from the rest of him, his commands arriving at the muscles only in distant echoes. He could no longer feel his hand grip his sword. He willed the arm up, willed it to stab the monster, and far, far away, an arm moved. It carried a sword. The arm thrust the sword into the monster's left eye.

The beast shrieked, the sound of a thousand cats drowning. It reared up, away from Vorykas. He rose with it, and felt as if he were leaving half his body behind. He did not think of his wounds and of what was falling from his gaping sides. He rammed the sword home, skewering the brain.

The shrieking stopped. The monster quivered down its length, and then collapsed. It lay still, ichor oozing out to mingle with Vorykas' blood.

217

THE SLEEP OF EMPIRES

Vorykas slumped down, soaked in sweat and gore. Different shades of pain fought through his frame. He bled, and he healed. He stared dully at a chunk of flesh, the size of his hand, on the floor a few feet from him. It broke down as he watched, turning from meat to jelly, from jelly to slime, from slime to water, and from water to nothing. When it vanished, so did the hole in his right flank.

Gradually, the pain diminished. His body put itself back together again. The pieces it had lost disappeared from the floor as they knitted themselves back into place.

Kanstuhn knelt beside him. "Are you all right?" he asked, in clear disbelief that it was even possible to ask that question and get an answer.

"I will be," said Vorykas. It hurt to talk. It hurt to breathe. But the pain was receding, gradually, a reluctantly ebbing tide. He winced. "A useful lesson." He paused, waiting for the pain to flow out a bit more. "A warning to be careful."

Kanstuhn looked thoughtful. "I wonder what would have happened if it had cut your head off."

"You keep wondering." He thought he might be able to stand soon. "I'd rather not find out." He turned his eyes to the corpse of the beast. "What *is* that?"

"A corprollax, I think."

"You've encountered one before?"

"No. I've read about them. It too is from the elvish lands. From the swamps of Beresta. The elves used them in the last war, if what I read is true."

"Did the Hawkesmoores capture one?"

"I doubt it. The last war was too long ago. I don't think a corprollax is immortal."

"Then how do they come to have one?"

"The same way they have menyë bark."

Vorykas stared at Kanstuhn. "Trade with the elves?"

218

DAVID ANNANDALE

"I can't see how else they could have such a guardian."

Vorykas leaned forward to pull his sword out of the corprollax's eye. He planted the tip on the floor, and used the sword to lever himself to his feet. His joints were floppy, but he no longer felt like his mind had to shout to his limbs at a distance. "Is trade with Beresta something that happens in Wiramzin?" he asked.

"In a limited way, yes. But not at a scale that would involve such treasures of the elves winding up here. Wiramzin has nothing the elves want that badly."

"Maybe not Wiramzin, but the Hawkesmoores must."

Vorykas tried walking. The motion felt like something new he had no practice in, but he managed. He and Kanstuhn moved down the length of the chamber, past the bloody pillars, to the table and the throne. The material on the table appeared to be letters.

"A strange place to work," Vorykas said.

"Not for Roylence, Lord Hawkesmoore," said Kanstuhn. He pointed at the throne. "The seat of majesty, from which to issue commands, and to observe the suffering of those under his power."

They sorted through the letters. They were almost all unremarkable. Abject apologies from debtors, with assurances the gold would be paid the next day. Receipts from tradespeople. The mundane correspondence of a powerful man. Only one stood out.

"Listen to this," Vorykas said. "From another son, Barrat. 'Father, the dispositions at Glasta Keep are excellent. Also, our partners in this venture have once again reassured me that our claim will be uncontested. I'm inclined to believe them, if not actively to trust them. They don't care about Felgard one way or the other. Their interest doesn't seem to go much beyond Skaitaias.'" He looked at Kanstuhn. "Skaitaias?" he said.

"No idea," said Kanstuhn. "But Glasta Keep . . . Felgard . . ."

"Glasta Keep is the fortress in the painting, yes. Who or what is Felgard?"

219

THE SLEEP OF EMPIRES

"Lady Ossia Felgard of Northope," said Kanstuhn grimly. "And this talk of a claim and partners. They are going to attack Northope."

Vorykas looked at the glowing bark, and at the dead corprollax. "In an alliance with elves," he said.

He had never seen the kaul look so stricken. "This is not a criminal enterprise. This is war."

CHAPTER 17

By the time they were within striking distance of Northope, Garwynn's travel companions numbered only five. They had been more than twenty when they struck out from Korvas. By ones and twos, they left the group as they arrived at their home villages. Each refugee that arrived at safe harbor then gave what coin they could to help the travelers. In this way, the shrinking group had enough to pay for food, and sometimes lodging, at the inns along the Korvas Road.

The travelers shied away from the sound of horses, getting off the road and hiding in trees, where such shelter existed, whenever they heard what they imagined to be a patrol riding out from the city. On the second day, the sound of horses galloping at full speed had Garwynn hyperventilating with terror. From the brush where he crouched, he saw Vorykas and Kanstuhn pass by, not temple guards.

For the most part, the other people Garwynn and his companions encountered were merchants or itinerant laborers. Now and then, warriors overtook them, sell-swords by their looks. They worried Garwynn almost as much as the thought of guards. His traveling party, unarmed and on foot, would be easy prey.

The sell-swords seemed to have other things on their minds, though. They rode fast, with purpose.

Something's going on.

He wondered what, and fretted, but he had no answers at all until he and the last five came within a day's journey of Northope. With the setting sun a glare of broken red through the forest ahead, a barricade blocked the road. Constructed of logs armed with iron spikes, high and solid, it would have taken some time to construct, and would take even longer to remove. The only way past it was on the right-hand side. There, soldiers guarded an open bit of road just wide enough for a cart to pass. Tents on either side

THE SLEEP OF EMPIRES

of the road suggested the soldiers would be here for some time. At least they weren't sell-swords, Garwynn thought. They bore the red and green of Northope.

They interrogated every traveler on the road, and a long line had developed, stretching back hundreds of yards. When Garwynn's party arrived, the soldiers began by demanding names.

Does the House of Law's arm reach this far? No, this can't be about us. We aren't that important, and there's no love lost between Korvas and Northope.

Garwynn's turn came last. The guard, an imposing woman a head taller and much broader than he, asked where he had come from.

"Korvas," he said. "Like my friends."

"What is your business in these parts?"

"I'm going home to Ghaunthook."

"You're from there originally?"

"That's right." He hoped the truth would cast him in a good light.

The guard waved to a comrade near one of the tents. He started over to their group. "Right," the woman said. "Consider yourselves enlisted in the defense of Northope and its dependent villages."

Garwynn blinked. "But I have to go to Ghaunthook," he protested, even as he realized the futility of his words. "There are people who need me there."

"You're needed here," the soldier said. "Anyway, if the people you want to see in Ghaunthook can hold a spear, they'll be in Northope soon enough."

There were no barricades on the eastern roads yet when Vorykas and Kanstuhn rode to Northope. As they approached the city, they could see the signs of mobilization, but none to suggest its sentinels looked for a threat in the direction of Korvas.

The guards looked at them with the appropriate degree of caution when they arrived at the gate, though. Vorykas approved of that.

"State your business," one of them said, sounding like there would be no sort of business that would convince him to let them pass.

DAVID ANNANDALE

"We must speak with the Lady Ossia Felgard," said Kanstuhn.

Both guards looked surprised, and an officer passing behind them stopped to listen.

The first guard recovered first, and snorted. "You have ambitions. I'll give you that. Now be on your way."

"She will want to hear what we have to say," said Vorykas. He spoke past the guards and to the officer. She seemed more curious than dismissive. "She will want to hear that the Hawkesmoores are allied with Beresta, and are preparing to march on Northope."

"That's enough," said the guard.

"Wait," said the officer. "Let them in."

"But Captain Arva," the second guard protested. "A kaul? And a . . . I mean, we don't even know *what* he is."

"That's why you're going to let them in," said Arva. "The responsibility is mine."

Begrudgingly, they opened the small, iron door next to the gate.

Once inside, and heading through the streets escorted by Arva and two other soldiers, Kanstuhn said, "I am curious as to why you agreed so quickly to our request."

"Because you are an unusual sight," said Arva. "And because I do not know what your friend is."

"An argument that is unusual in its turn," said Kanstuhn.

"I have had to do unusual things lately. I think I have become attuned to the importance of the anomaly."

Pilta had never seen a town move onto war footing before. It terrified him. The last war between the elvish empires and the humans had taken place long before his birth. Intellectually, he had always known that the soldiers and weapons he saw in the streets of Árkiriye were a visible sign of Beresta's might, a force of violence awaiting only the order to be unleashed. Emotionally, he had taken them in as background, as part of the ornamentation of the city.

223

THE SLEEP OF EMPIRES

He could not look at the soldiers of Northope in that way. They had become the dominant presence inside the city walls, and their numbers swelled with new recruits every day. Urgency colored every action in the castle, as if even the cobble-sweepers worked to the rhythm of a war drum. When he ventured into the streets of the city, he found the same atmosphere. It seemed to him that everyone moved more quickly, and was possessed with a grimmer purpose than before. This morning, he had seen an old woman close the shutters on her window. She performed the mundane act as if blocking enemy arrows.

He felt more and more self-conscious. He did not like to be seen, even when he knew it was best that he be visible. He didn't know the nature of the storm heading for Northope. He felt, though, from Arva's guarded manner when he saw her, that it had something to do with him.

How can that be? Skiriye ne Sincatsë can't have sent an army after me.

Not after you, fool. After the book.

Really? War over a book? It can't be that important.

No, the coming war had to be caused by human politics, of which he knew nothing. It was sheer arrogance to think that he, even indirectly, could be the subject of the conflict.

So he told himself. Yet he could not shake the feeling of Skiriye's grasp reaching across the leagues to grasp his neck.

Lady Ossia had spoken with him on three occasions since his arrival. Her questions had struck him as careful, designed to elicit information from him in such a way that he could not guess what she really wanted to know and why. She asked him about his life, inside and outside the university. She had probed him about his reasons for taking the gold and agreeing to steal the book. She did not ask him about military dispositions, or the specifics of anything he read in the library.

She gave him duties in her own library, updating its catalogue. That gave him something to do and kept him out of the way and out of sight, much to his relief. The Lady's book collection was large, he supposed, by

224

DAVID ANNANDALE

human standards, though insignificant beside the library of Árkiriye. The books were also nothing that would have raised concern in that library. They gave him a picture of Ossia as a reader of wide-ranging curiosity, and with a deeper interest in histories and exegeses. If she had more books like the one he had stolen for her, they weren't here.

He didn't suppose they would be, of course. She had put him where he could do no harm. That's what he would have done. In her place, he would not have trusted an elf who stole from his own kind.

With war coming, the best thing he could do was work quietly in the library and behave. No more secret outings like when he had followed Ossia to that tower.

When have you ever done the best thing? his curiosity wanted to know.

What is in that tower? it also asked. *Why is that place so important?*

His fear told him to stay away. He didn't have nightmares about the tower any longer, as he had for the first few nights after seeing it. But the memory still lingered, hard and sharp. He should not go there.

But the book had gone there, to a dark place. That was his fault. The mad fantasy of somehow righting the wrong he had committed had come to him the morning after his first nightmare. He could not shake it, and it fused itself with his curiosity. The fantasy and curiosity grew stronger than his caution, and the fear about the consequences of his theft gradually became stronger than his fear of what might be in the tower.

For two days, he watched the flow in and out of Northope's gates. The traffic was heavy, with the usual arrival and departure of merchant caravans augmented by the influx of recruits, and the coming and going of patrols. At dusk, the guards closed the gate and barred it shut. They would not reopen it until after daybreak. Anyone arriving during the night had to identity themselves to the watch, and then wait out the hours of darkness for admission.

The plan presented itself as foolproof, at least as far as his curiosity was concerned. It worried his caution, which imagined all sorts of things going wrong, and advised him to stay put.

225

THE SLEEP OF EMPIRES

If I had listened to you, he told his caution, *we would never have come here at all.*

Precisely.

But I want to know. I want to try to fix things. This will work.

He had never been one to listen to his caution.

The guards at the gate were much more concerned with those entering the city than those leaving it. Getting out would be easy. He just had to lose himself inside a departing caravan. Getting back in would be harder. Depending on how long he was outside the walls, he might have to spend the night in the woods on the hills. Then he would have to mingle again with another caravan. Tricky, but not impossible.

I'm going to do this.

He had no illusions of being redeemed and welcomed back to Beresta. But he did not want Passomo to damn him. He feared that as a real possibility. He had done something far worse than steal a valuable book. He had given a dangerous book to something dark.

A small train of wagons and carts set off in late afternoon. Its first stop would be Kakintun, only a few hours west, an easy march before nightfall. Pilta flitted through the crowded streets until he came up behind the last wagon in the staging area just inside the outer wall. The wagon inched its way forward, the process of leaving slowed down by the arrival of another caravan.

Smaller and slighter than any of the adult humans in the vicinity, beneath their notice as they concentrated on their tasks, or on getting to where their tasks awaited them, he slipped under the wagon, past its rear axle, and took hold of its underside. He hauled himself up, becoming a ship's barnacle.

He held tight and listened to the wagon's slow progress. He heard the voices of the merchants bidding goodbye to the guards, and then the wagon's movement shifted from a stop-and-start, snail-like pace to a steady advance, the frame jouncing as the wheels rolled over bumps in the road. He stayed

226

DAVID ANNANDALE

where he was, refusing to be shaken off, for several more minutes. He had to wait until the caravan was out of the wall sentries' sights.

The ground began to rise, the air became cooler as the caravan entered the forest's shadow, and the road curved.

Now, Pilta thought, and let himself drop. He stayed motionless, under the center of the wagon, until its rear wheels had safely passed, and then he rolled up into a crouch and ran silently into the woods. He started back in the direction of Northope, and up the plateau toward its riven surface, the gorge, and the tower.

Dusk had fallen when he set eyes on the tower again. The gathering evening felt cooler than it should have, as if the gorge drained the sunlight from the sky and sent up darkness in its stead. Pilta hesitated when the tower came into sight. As before, a glow of red extended from the window that looked out over the gorge. There were no other windows that he could see, none that looked back over the plateau. The road to the iron door had no shelter, but if no one could look this way, he would not be seen.

A strange defense, he thought. Why did the tower's vigilance appear aimed in the direction from which it could not be approached?

Maybe there were apertures he could not see. Or other ways of observing that he could not imagine.

You're here. Do what you came to do. Waiting isn't going to make things better or easier.

Pilta hurried down the road before he could change his mind. The tower grew larger in his sight, and he could still see no sign of stonework in its form, more dead than bone, as natural in its shape as if it had grown. Even the entranceway, as he drew near, looked as if it had flowed into being.

He examined the door, and wondered now if it really was a door. It appeared to be a single slab of iron, rounded at the top. There was no handle, no lock, and no features, as if it were not really iron, but a substance carved from the darkness in the gorge.

227

THE SLEEP OF EMPIRES

He placed his hand against it, and it swung open, a mouth gaping in a silent yawn.

Pilta made himself go inside before he could hesitate again. He found a staircase, as natural and untouched by mason's hand as the exterior of the tower. It circled up, lit at regular intervals by torches. Even though their sconces seemed as spontaneously created as everything else about the tower, they were reassuringly ordinary, and they gave him the courage to climb the stairs.

He traveled up, round and round, and almost immediately lost all sense of progress. He didn't know how high he had come. The stairs no longer had a beginning, and they would never end.

But they did end. Pilta slowed down as the light grew stronger from above. The red, so sinister seen from outside, now seemed more familiar, less threatening, tinged with the warmth of the hearth. He took a few more steps, then paused, listening.

Someone stirred above him. Robes rustled. A page turned.

Pilta touched his belt. He had secreted a kitchen knife under his tunic. What did he think he was going to do with it? What, really, was his plan?

He didn't have one. He had made himself come here, because he had to try something, hoping inspiration would strike.

It did not. He rocked back and forth, too scared to climb, too scared to go back down.

"Come on up," said a voice, rough with age but not unfriendly. "It's thanks to you I have the book. Don't you want to know what it is?"

Pilta took the stairs through the last twist and arrived in a circular, vaulted chamber that took up the entire peak of the tower. A large fireplace blazed away on Pilta's left, and lanterns hung around the periphery of the room provided cheerful illumination. A bed nestled against the wall opposite the entrance. To the right, a chair and desk sat next to the window.

Something happened to the light near the window. It turned darker, becoming blood-red, as if stained by the darkness of the gorge, or by the single book that lay on the desk.

DAVID ANNANDALE

An old man stood with one hand on the back of the chair. He wore a simple black robe, frayed at the cuffs and hem. His white hair and beard were unkempt, looking cut by a distracted hand. He had kind yet serious eyes.

He waved Pilta in. "I'm sorry that I have only the one chair, but please, join me. Come in. Come in."

Pilta took a couple of cautious steps forward. He thought of the knife in his tunic. This man presented no danger. Pilta could kill him. It wouldn't be hard.

Except for the act itself. He had never committed any kind of violence. He wouldn't be able to now, either.

"You must be Pilta ne Akwatse," the man said, his elvish pronunciation excellent.

Pilta nodded. "Who are you?"

"My name is Skaitaias Kenneye. I am a mathematician."

Pilta frowned. He knew that scholars of numbers existed in Beresta, but they were very rare, and their study was regarded as a minor hobby, separate from their actual field of endeavor. "Is that a common human profession?"

"No," Skaitaias said sadly. "I have never met another. I hope I am not the only one in Wiramzin, but I might be."

"And the book was for you?"

"That's right."

Pilta eyed the book on the desk. "It's a book about numbers?" How could that be dangerous?

"It is, yes, at least partly. It is about numbers, and about the gods."

Was that all? He came closer, reassured by Skaitaias' manner and frailty. He remembered the chill he had felt when he touched the book. There had to be more to it than numbers and stories. "I don't understand," he said. "Why is it forbidden?"

"Because it is the *Book of the Null*. It is about the number zero."

"Zero?" He did not know that number.

"The number of nothing. The number of the void."

229

THE SLEEP OF EMPIRES

Pilta snorted. "There is no such thing."

Skaitaias smiled as if Pilta had said something amusing. "How right and wrong you are. Yes, there is no such thing. Because there is no *thing* there. Only absence. And yet here is a book about the absence, a book suppressed and destroyed across all of Eloran, feared by the elves, whose memories go back so much further than humans'. Feared, too, I venture to say, by the gods."

"That's just nonsense," said Pilta, aware that he sounded defensive, and anxious to be proven right.

"If it's nonsense, then it can hardly be dangerous, can it?" said Skaitaias. He picked up the book, flipped through the first few pages, then held it up for Pilta to see. "This is the void." On the page was a rune in the form of two halves of a circle, separated by a diagonal space. "It has disappeared from all our languages, but traces of it, and what it means, still remain."

"Where?"

"Right here," Skaitaias said. "You're standing in one. This tower is the Voidwatch." He closed the book.

Pilta twitched. He checked to make sure the walls had not begun to close in around him.

"Did you not want to know?" Skaitaias asked gently. "I thought that was why you came here."

"I want to understand," said Pilta, and that was true, he really did, even though he feared what he would learn. "Why is this number so dangerous?" It just sounded useless to him. What was the point of being able to count nothing?

"Because it is destructive. It creates chaos in numerical systems. It is destruction, and yet creation is impossible without it, because it lies at the center of all things. Before there was a beginning, before there were the gods, there was Nothing."

That sounded like blasphemy to Pilta. The gods were eternal. *There is nothing before them*, he thought, and then realized the meaning that lurked in those words. His mouth went dry.

230

DAVID ANNANDALE

"Is that what the book says?" he asked.

"Some of what it says. There are tales of the gods, too. Tales of betrayal, though I am still working to learn its precise nature. The translation is laborious."

"It's written in elvish?"

"No. Most of it is an ancient form of the language of Wiramzin, though there are some passages, prayers, I think, that are in a much older tongue."

"Which one?"

"Voranian."

Now Pilta could not swallow. His skin prickled with cold terror. The darkness from the gorge pressed in at the window, licking inside, a night serpent's tongue. "That can't be," he said. Nothing could come from the dead land.

Nothing will come from the dead land, he thought crazily. *Already, Nothing crawls this way.*

"Why not?" said Skaitaias. He caressed the spine of the book. "Voran was not always dead."

"But the gods killed it."

"Yes, they did, but there had to be something to kill, no? And the dead leave traces. Most of the traces of Voran have been killed, too, but not all of them. The land itself remains, and so do other echoes of what was." He put the book down gently, with reverence, on the desk. "The tales in here are another such trace. A very important one. They are tales of truth, Pilta ne Akwatse, a truth to make the gods tremble."

Pilta took a step back, as if to distance himself from such open heresy.

"Lady Ossia has had enough of the lies upon which everything we know is built. She, like me, needs to know what it is that the lies conceal."

"How does she know they are lies?" Pilta objected. "Just because you don't like something, that doesn't mean it isn't so."

"She knows, as I do, because a piece of the truth is here. It always has been. Though we did not know until the plateau split and the Voidwatch revealed its purpose."

231

THE SLEEP OF EMPIRES

"I don't understand."

"Let me show you." Skaitaias moved to the window and gestured for Pilta to join him. "Don't be afraid," he said when Pilta didn't move. "No harm will come to you."

What about to my soul? Pilta wanted to ask. But his curiosity moved his feet for him, and he advanced to Skaitaias' side.

He looked out the window.

And he had to grip the sill hard to keep from falling out.

The red light plunged like a cataract into the gorge, a curve of illumination vanishing into the abyss. The cliff walls vanished into the dark too. Pilta had no way to tell how deep the gorge went, or where its bottom might be.

There is no bottom.

Born of the vertigo that held him in its claws, the thought struck him like a dagger, and like the truth, and he clutched the sill even harder. If he fell, he would fall forever, because there was no floor to the gorge. At the center of its darkness was only nothing, *nothing*, the void in absolute form, the void he could not imagine because the imagination could not grasp the primordial absence that came before all things, and would take them all in the end. For the void, the beginning and the end were the trivial markers of the insignificant interlude that was existence.

The void called to him, eager for his return. He began to lose his balance as a sensation made of awe and fear and fascination and, strangely, guilt swept through him. He felt as if his feet were about to rise from the floor, and then he would fall with the light.

A hand clutched his arm, steadying him.

"Careful," said Skaitaias.

The grip and the voice gave Pilta the strength to break the spell. He hurled himself back from the window, tearing free of the void's insinuating whisper. He fell over, and crawled backward, toward the stairs. He could barely move his limbs. He didn't know if he would ever stand

232

DAVID ANNANDALE

again. A black spot of *nothing* hovered in his mind's eye, branded there for all time.

"You see," said Skaitaias. "That is the mystery we seek to solve. And the book you gave us is the key."

Pilta staggered to his feet and stumbled down the stairs. The knife fell from his tunic and clattered on stone. He left it behind. He was too weak to attack, and too frightened to do anything but flee.

What have I done? What have I done?

CHAPTER 18

It took Alisteyr more than two weeks before he found the courage to move into Forgrym Hall. Latanna left him alone, allowing him to make up his mind with no pressure from her. He appreciated and regretted her consideration. Sometimes, when he was alone in their house, he felt her absence, or at least the absence of the person she had been. Then he grieved for their stillborn marriage, and cursed himself for his cowardice in not going to her.

But when he saw her during the day, even from a distance, her grave-shrouded beauty made him hide. At night, he stayed inside, knowing that he would run to her if he saw her as he had in the Laughing Chimera. The next morning, it had been frightening to think of the urge he had felt to follow her. He didn't trust himself not to succumb.

If he was going to join her in Forgrym Hall, he would make that decision during the day.

He went to the temple every day to pray, and to speak with Taver Derrun. The priest urged him, gently but insistently, to move to the Hall.

"No one else can be as close to her as you," Taver said.

Alisteyr shuddered.

"You're the only one who will have the chance to see what needs to be seen."

"How will I know?"

"You'll know. Trust in the guidance of the gods."

At last, in the middle of the day, after he had managed to go almost a week without even catching a glimpse of Latanna, he decided he had the courage to trust in that guidance. He shamed himself out the door of the house that would now never be the home he had dreamed of, and set off for Forgrym Hall.

234

DAVID ANNANDALE

When the Hall came into sight, his heart quailed when he saw the door open, and Latanna waiting for him on the porch. How long had she been there? From how far away had she seen him approach?

Conscious that he had slowed down, he forced himself to keep moving. He had made the decision. He would not go back on it.

The stories he had wanted to emulate came back to him, his old impulses remembered and tasting sour. He had gone on a quest and won the hand of the princess, and the fulfilment of his wishes had turned them to ashes. Now he felt as if he were confronting another monster, and the thought made him want to weep tears of self-hatred.

Latanna smiled, her expression friendly but cool. She looked radiant in the sunshine, and maggots squirmed in Alisteyr's gut.

"It's good to see you," she said.

Her tone, too, was friendly. Alisteyr did not hear love in it. Had she ever loved him? He had never even asked himself the question. He had been so caught up in the narrative conjured by his love for her.

It's good to see you too. He couldn't bring himself to say the words. "I thought I should come," he said instead.

Her smile became amused. "You've always believed in duty, haven't you?"

He couldn't tell if she was mocking him or not. "I suppose so," he answered.

"Come in, then." She stood aside and gestured for him to enter the house. "Welcome to your home, if that's what you want it to be."

That sounded like a promise not to block his escape. He felt relieved, and then guilty for the relief.

He felt more relief when he found that he was not alone with Latanna. Servants bustled about, engaged in the ongoing transformation of the house. From his small acquaintance with what the Hall had been like under Marsen's rule, he could see that Latanna had been busy. All traces of the Forgrym coat of arms had vanished, along with icons and symbols of

235

THE SLEEP OF EMPIRES

the worship of Tetriwu. No other god had taken his place. Alisteyr hadn't expected such a miracle, but he did look around in the faint hope of something reassuring he could pass on to Taver. The house seemed brighter and warmer, but when Alisteyr looked at Latanna, that light and warmth felt like an act, a gesture made for the comfort of those who worked in the house, and of no real interest to the woman who owned it.

The weapons on the walls remained, though. And there had been additions. Over the hearth in the great hall, a line of swords, daggers, axes, and maces had appeared, standing vertically side by side. Even with his untrained eye, Alisteyr knew they were undistinguished weapons. Some of the blades were rusted, others pitted. None had been forged with the care of Marsen's collection. None were clean, and most had blood stains.

They looked, Alisteyr thought, like trophies.

"How do you like the new Hall?" Latanna asked.

"It's a much more welcoming place," he said. He didn't ask about the weapons. He would if and when he thought he had the courage to hear the answer.

Latanna chuckled. "It could hardly be less welcoming than before, could it? But good, I'm glad it feels that way to you. I refuse to have this house be a place of fear for Ghaunthook any longer."

She took him to the second floor, and to a bedroom midway down the hall. The walls had been repainted a fresh white, and the sheets on the bed looked new.

"This used to be my bedroom," Latanna said. "I thought it might be yours now."

Yours. Not ours.

Did she want him to object? Did she want him to say no, he had come to the house to be with her, and he wanted them to sleep in the same bed?

He couldn't. The idea made his flesh crawl.

"Where will you be?" he asked.

236

DAVID ANNANDALE

Her answer took a moment, as if she had to remember what people did at night. "I've taken my father's chamber." She pointed to the end of the hall.

Not right next door, then. That's good.

"But I don't sleep," she added.

"Not at all?"

"Do the dead sleep?"

"Yes," Alisteyr said, grasping at a straw that would prove Latanna was still, in some form, alive. "They only sleep. They don't move about and talk."

"What would that make me, then, alive?" It felt like she was pushing him.

"I don't know," he said.

She raised an eyebrow. "An honest answer."

But not a brave one, he thought.

That evening, in the dining hall, they sat at opposite ends of the long table. Alisteyr ate, the food tasting like dust. Latanna had no plate before her. She drank from her wine goblet, and she spoke about her further plans for the house, anodyne conversation filler that waited for him to say something of more consequence.

He finally made himself rise to the challenge. "You don't eat anymore?"

"When the mood strikes me. The same with drink. I can still enjoy the taste. I just don't need it."

"You don't need any sustenance?"

"I wouldn't say that. Just not in the usual sense."

She didn't seem inclined to elaborate, and he didn't push the matter.

When the sun set, her transformation came. Alisteyr didn't see the change happen. They had finished dinner, and she left him in the great hall for a few moments, and when she returned, the woman had vanished, and the skeleton had taken her place. As before, he could not take his eyes from her. Trivial conversation was impossible now, and she seemed to feel the same.

237

THE SLEEP OF EMPIRES

"I imagine you'll want to retire," she said.

"Yes, I think I will." It was early yet, but the emotional strain had exhausted him.

She did not invite him to her bedchamber. She stayed in the great hall and let him go. If she had asked him to come with her, to finally consummate their marriage, he knew he would have gone, and once he was out of her presence, his blood ran cold.

What would he have felt when he touched her? Invisible flesh?

Bone?

He ran upstairs, shut and locked the door to his room, and sat on the bed, trembling.

He had fallen into a legend, but the wrong kind, and it had trapped him.

He lay awake for a long time, waiting to hear the creak of her tread in the hall. It never came. He lay there, eyes open, rocked back and forth by currents of hope and dread and eagerness and terror, before emotional and physical exhaustion at last forced him to sleep.

He had the same experience for the next several nights. During the day, he divided his time between helping with the refashioning of the Hall, and working in the Huesland fields. He didn't try to avoid Latanna, but he didn't seek her out, either. When they met, they kept their conversation mundane. In the evening, when he ate and she did not except to sample the taste of the food, he had the chance to probe.

"You can ask me whatever you want," she said. It didn't seem to matter to her whether he was curious or not.

"I don't know where to begin," he admitted.

She shrugged, and left the matter in his hands.

Each night, he listened. If she came up the stairs or used the master bedroom, she did so after he slept, and went back down before he woke.

But she didn't sleep, she had told him. He wondered what she did with her nights. The question became more fearful the longer it went unanswered. On the fifth night, he decided to find out.

DAVID ANNANDALE

He had to know what kind of story he had fallen into. He had to know if he kept house with a monster.

His bedroom looked out at the front of the house. He put out the candles and sat in complete darkness at the window, invisible to the outside. He watched. An hour went by, and then another. On the verge of giving up for the night, he saw light spill out from the opening of the outside door.

Latanna strode out on the drive. A cloak concealed her, but it had to be her. Alisteyr stood, left the room, hurried down the stairs, and went out the front door. The drive glowed a blurry gray in the moonlight. Latanna had almost pulled out of sight, a moving shadow in the night.

Alisteyr followed, hurrying as much as he could while keeping quiet. He winced at the sound of gravel beneath his heels, and he was relieved when Latanna turned off the drive and onto a dirt trail.

It headed off, deeper into the night, away from Ghaunthook.

Alisteyr's relief gave way to frustration when the path entered forest, and began to twist and turn. He had to slow down to avoid walking into trees. He could no longer see Latanna. He had to hope that she had not taken some other path he had missed. He also hoped he wouldn't round a bend and find her waiting for him.

He walked through the woods for more than an hour, with the path climbing steadily. It finally came out from the trees, running along a steep slope that led down to the Korvas Road.

A body lay sprawled across the path, a man in rough leathers. Someone had put out both his eyes.

Midway down the slope, another man struggled with Latanna. He was doing all the struggling. She seemed to parry his sword blows more out of casual interest than need. Then, as if growing bored, she stepped forward suddenly and cut off his sword arm at the elbow. He screamed and fell to his knees. She sheathed her blade and grabbed his head with her skeletal fingers.

The ends of her fingers pierced his flesh. He struggled in her grip, then sagged, turning into a bag of bones and meat.

THE SLEEP OF EMPIRES

Alisteyr's legs turned weak. They would no longer support him, and he sat down hard on the path.

Latanna looked up at him. Then she turned back to her victim. When she was done, she tossed the corpse aside and came back up the hill.

She put her hand out to Alisteyr. He scrabbled back.

Latanna put her arm down. "You have questions now, I think," she said.

"What . . . What did I just see?"

"Me feeding. That's the kind of nourishment I need now."

"Blood?" He wondered why he didn't see gore on the skull's teeth.

"Not exactly. I take what they were. Their memories, their dreams, their skills. Most of it I throw away." She tapped her forehead with a skeletal finger, just below the crown of horns, and there was no click of bone against bone. "I don't want things to get too crowded in here," she said. She paused, with the teeth of her skull slightly parted, and Alisteyr heard a smile in her tone. "The skills, I keep. They accumulate. These days, not by much each time, but there's always something."

Alisteyr looked at the bodies. "Who were they?"

"Thieves. Highwaymen. I don't attack anyone who doesn't attack me first, Alisteyr. You don't have to be afraid of me. I don't feed on the innocent."

Maybe not now, he thought. *What about later? How big a supply of thieves does the Korvas Road have?*

"You do this every night?" he asked.

"I hunt every night. I often don't find any prey."

"Does that weaken you?"

"No. It frustrates me. No worse than that. I know why you want to know, and let me tell you again that you don't have to worry. My appetites don't control me." She held out her hand again. "Let me help you up. Please."

He feared her, but her presence compelled him, too, and he could not refuse any longer. He took her hand.

He had wondered if he would feel bone or flesh if he touched her. He felt both at once and neither. When he tried to focus on the sensation of his flesh against bone, he felt warmth and softness instead. When he focused

240

DAVID ANNANDALE

on that, her touch became cold and dry and fleshless. A hand of life and death and the uncertainty between held his.

She pulled him to his feet, and then let go.

The skull cocked to one side. The dark eye sockets regarded him, and he felt the gaze of her absent eyes. "You need your freedom," she said.

"I'm not . . ." he stammered. "I mean I'm not sure . . . I don't know . . ."

"Yes, you do," she said gently. "You'll never be happy or at ease with me. Go home. To your parents' house, or to the one that would have been ours. Whatever home is for you. You'll know. But it isn't Forgrym Hall. I think that's clear to both of us."

"I made a vow to you," he began.

"Oh, Alisteyr," she said, and to hear such pity from a skeleton nearly broke him. "You hold fast to your illusions, don't you?"

"They're not illusions. They're principles. We both took vows to each other. We're wed. We can't just throw that away." But he wanted to be free. He really did. He wanted out of this story.

"You're wrong," Latanna said. "You know you are. We aren't wed. Our marriage is a lie. You did make your vows to me, but I didn't make mine to you. I made them to this." She touched the crown. "I pledged myself to something else that night."

"Pledged yourself to what?"

"I don't know. Not yet. But I did, and so you're free."

She had made the argument along the terms of his principles, he realized with gratitude. He could accept it with a clear conscience. He felt the chains of the frightening story fall away from him.

"You'll always have my friendship," Latanna said. "If you want it."

"Thank you." The words were so inadequate, but deeply meant.

They faced each other for a few moments in silence, marking the dissolution of the marriage. Later, Alisteyr might properly mourn the end of his long-held dream. For now, he felt only relief. He could put some distance between himself and the nightmare, though it would remain present for him every time he saw or thought about what Latanna had become.

241

THE SLEEP OF EMPIRES

"What will you do now?" she asked.

"I'll leave in the morning," he said. He could have fled to the Huesland farm that instant. But the charisma of the creature held him, and he imagined that by staying at Forgrym Hall for the rest of the night, he would be performing an act of grace and courage.

Freed of one story that had trapped him, he looked for another.

"And then?" said Latanna.

"I don't know. I might go back to the farm." He could see no point in staying at the house in the village. It represented nothing except the marriage that had never been.

"And then?" Latanna pushed. "Will you denounce me? Will you tell Taver Derrun what you saw tonight?"

So she knew. Or perhaps she had only guessed.

"He doesn't wish you ill," Alisteyr said. "He's just frightened."

"Frightened people often make poor decisions."

"What does that mean?" It sounded like a threat.

"Nothing. Just an observation."

"You aren't going to harm him, are you?"

The skeleton's shoulders rose and fell as if she had sighed. "How many times do I have to say that I don't hurt the innocent? Don't you listen, or don't you believe?"

"I'm sorry. I'm trying to do both. But you understand that others are going to have even more difficulty. Like Taver."

"I know."

"If he decides that *he* has to denounce you, what then?"

"I'm not worried about what might happen to me. What I don't want is temple forces rampaging through Ghaunthook. So what you say to him matters."

"I don't know what would convince him not to worry," Alisteyr said unhappily.

"Then that is your quest." After he nodded, Latanna said, "You should go. Get some sleep."

242

DAVID ANNANDALE

He left her, glad to be going back alone. When he arrived at the Hall, he fell into his bed, but sleep eluded him for another hour, and then came only fitfully, broken by dreams of twitching bodies.

When he woke, late in the morning, he looked out the window and saw Latanna outside, holding a scroll. She waved at him to come down.

"What is that?" he asked when he joined her.

"Commands from Lady Ossia Felgard. The town crier has been busy in the village." Latanna's beautiful, ghastly eyes shone eagerly, as if the solution to many problems had just arrived. "Northope is calling to its vassal towns. Everyone fit to fight is conscripted. It's war, Alisteyr."

The idea did not thrill him as it had in his daydreams. "Against whom?"

Latanna unrolled the scroll to show him. She shook her head in disbelief. "Against the Hawkesmoores and the elves."

CHAPTER 19

On the day the army made camp not far from the banks of the Keraps River, a delegation of humans arrived to take part in the war council. Skiriye ne Sincatsë watched them arrive, and thought, *I have made this happen.* Commander Divine Witárë gave the orders to the soldiers, but he did so in the service of her plan, the one she had presented to the Most Perfect Council.

I have made this happen.

The idea gave her mixed feelings.

She believed in the plan. The book had to be recovered, and the danger of the Voidwatch destroyed. But the Council did not want a mission to achieve that goal leading to a wider war. Wiramzin remained the weak, disorganized buffer between the elvish empires and the human ones. A conflict that engulfed Wiramzin would draw the other, stronger human powers in.

But a human force participating in the attack on Northope would make a difference. If they were seen as the principal aggressor, if the battle appeared as a struggle between regional rivals, then the involvement of the elves might not unduly disturb the peace, or what passed for it. If a fortress changed hands, but the hands remained human, there would be no cause for a clash of empires.

It had been easy to find human pawns needed for the war. They were already in place. Beresta kept watch over the political convulsions of Wiramzin, ready to intervene, subtly or otherwise, if it should show signs of unification behind a single leader. The elves knew who would have to be played against whom to keep the collection of feudal regions divided against itself. Decades earlier, the Hawkesmoores had responded eagerly to the overtures from Beresta. They had no loyalty except to themselves, and were happy to grow strong with the elves as patrons. Their greed, given free rein, became insatiable. The Hawkesmoores wanted more overt power than they

244

DAVID ANNANDALE

had in Korvas. They ruled Glasta Keep, a minor holding, but had the strength and the ambition for more. For all their influence in Korvas, they could not claim themselves as lords of the city, nor conquer it by force. They could, though, hope to make Northope theirs, if they had help. And with Northope as their new center of power, they would have a region of influence covering a long stretch of Wiramzin east of Korvas.

Now the Council had offered them the help they needed.

It was a good plan. Skiriye believed in it enough that she requested leave from the Most Perfect Council to take part in the campaign. She knew that she would have been ordered to go if she had not made the request. The loss of the book was her responsibility. She could salvage her honor and her position only if she played an active role in its recovery.

And if the plan went wrong . . .

No. It will not.

She would not give in to the fears of what that would mean.

Even so, she felt the weight of the responsibility. She had made this happen. Because of her, armed humans had crossed into Beresta, and had come to be welcomed in an elvish war camp.

This is your doing.

A thousand infantry and three hundred cavalry, under the Commander Divine's guidance, had marched from Árkiriye. The army came purposefully, swift and pointed as a dagger, to cut Northope's throat. Only the crossing of the Keraps remained before the dagger would strike home.

The encampment took up many acres of the woods to either side of the road. To any but elvish eyes, it was invisible from the road, and even a passing elf, one who did not already know of the army's presence, would be unlikely to notice anything. The material of the tents blended with bark and leaf, a mirror of their surroundings. Many of the troops took up stations of rest and watch in the trees. They looked north, toward the Keraps, alert for what might come from that direction, expected or not. Some had the task of looking back the way the army had come. No one expected treachery, but no one would let it catch them by surprise, either.

245

THE SLEEP OF EMPIRES

No one would permit the imperfection of the unguarded flank.

The horses were kept several hundred yards away from the road, not far from the command tent. Pitched in a large clearing, it was octagonal, and fifty feet across. Its front entrance, covered by a wide awning, stood open, awaiting the arrival of the delegation. Inside, Witárë and his officers pored over terrain maps laid out over a large table. Skiriye stood outside, a few feet to one side of the entrance. She wanted to be the first in the inner circle of command to see the humans she had summoned.

Inner circle of command. Was that true? Witárë had taken care not to suggest otherwise. Yet Skiriye had no illusions. Though she had been invited to attend the planning sessions each evening, she had not been asked to contribute her own thoughts. She did not offer them, preferring to avoid the possibility of rejection.

She heard the humans coming long before she saw them. They moved through the woods as if they were cutting them down. Even their horses sounded heavier than they should have, plodding with excessive weight.

This is what I have brought to the soil of Beresta.

A man and a woman in haughty middle-age rode at the head of the human party. Roylence, Lord Hawkesmoore, Skiriye presumed, and his wife, the Lady Aldora. Roylence had narrow features, made narrower yet by the projection of a sharp, pointed white beard. He had no moustache. He had the face of a man who had attacked the world with hammer and chisel, forcing it into the image of his desires. Aldora, blonde and pale, had gray eyes that looked out in judgement from behind narrowed lids.

Behind them rode two men, one a few years younger than the other, both clearly brothers, blond like their mother, their facial hair an imitation of their father's. It took Skiriye a moment to remember the names of the two eldest sons. She had read them in one of the dispatches.

Ah, I have it. Barrat and Delen.

A third son rode behind them. He looked sullen, a man recently disappointed by life.

Elgin.

246

DAVID ANNANDALE

Good. She knew who they were. She doubted they knew the names of any of the elves. No doubt, in their arrogance, they thought that an unnecessary effort.

An escort of twenty men-at-arms accompanied the nobles. They looked hardened, Skiriye thought, reshaped and scarred by battle. Those physical signs would, in an elf, be signs of imperfection, of persistent failure in battle. But for humans, she understood that these were the marks of survivors, of warriors who had come through the fire of war, and were ready to return to it. If that was so, then the men and women who accompanied the Hawkesmoores would be useful on the battlefield.

The Hawkesmoores dismounted. Flanked by his officers, the Commander Divine, resplendent in his silver and blue armor of light elven plate, came out of the tent. Witárë ne Seritsi stood a handwidth higher than Elgin, the tallest of the humans.

In the barbaric tongue of Wiramzin, humans and elves greeted each other with wariness, gestures of respect stiff and minimal. Skiriye felt her gorge rise with contempt and loathing as she stepped forward to join the group. The look in Aldora's eyes showed the humans felt the same as she did.

We hate each other. But our value to each other is, for now, greater than our hate. A very great value indeed.

Witárë walked back into the tent, leaving it to the Hawkesmoores to follow. Inside, the walls of the tent created the illusion of being outside as completely as their exteriors blended in with the forest. Witárë strode to the round table in the center. It took up half the diameter of the space. The maps showed the approaches to the banks of the Keraps in exquisite detail. Skiriye noted with satisfaction that Roylence could not conceal his awe at the way the tent seemed to vanish, and at the meticulous reconstruction of the land on the maps. He pulled off a glove and stretched out a hand as if he expected to feel dirt and leaves on the parchment.

"This is impressive," he admitted.

"We know what we can observe from this side of the Keraps," Witárë said. "Beyond that, though, our information is less detailed. We do not

247

THE SLEEP OF EMPIRES

know all the streets of Northope. We do not know much at all about the interior of its keep. The further south the map goes, the less we know. This is particularly true of the Voidwatch."

Delen shook his head. "This looks pretty complete to me."

His mother shot him a venomous look at his rush to compliment, and he shut his lips tight.

"We know what we could gather during the last war," said Witárë. "If you have more to add, though . . ."

"About the layout of Northope, yes," said Roylence. "Not about the plateau, though. We've never had a reason to go up there. Not worth catching Felgard's eye in doing so."

"That is disappointing." Witárë kept his tone neutral, as if any insult to be read into his words were purely the result of a misunderstanding on his listener's part.

Roylence stiffened. "There are realities," he said. "They come with limitations."

"Of course, of course. You do bring us news, though, I think? Yes?"

Roylence nodded, looking uncomfortable. "Northope is mobilizing."

"They know you're coming?" Skiriye put in. She wasn't surprised, and she shouldn't even be dismayed. Given the noise this party made traveling, the Hawkesmoore army could probably be heard in Árkiriye. Of course, Northope had received word of the Hawkesmoore advance.

"Not just us," Aldora said coldly. "They are making ready for you, too."

"They've cut all the ferry lines across the Keraps," said Barrat.

"Someone must have warned them," said Roylence. "Someone who knew about our alliance."

Witárë pursed his lips but said nothing. Skiriye also did not comment on Roylence's grasp of the obvious.

If she had been in her domain of the library, though, things would have been different. She would have seen Roylence punished for the futility and fatuity of his remark, and for the failure it represented.

248

DAVID ANNANDALE

The failure would have a cost. She and Witárë had hoped that the elves would have the chance to take the keep by surprise, while Ossia Felgard's attention was focused on the Hawkesmoores. But now she knew who was coming, and from where, and was preparing. The hope of a nearly instant victory had evaporated.

"We don't know who warned them, or how they knew to do so," Roylence went on.

"You have a traitor in your ranks," said Witárë.

"Apparently." The lord did not sound offended. Treachery among humans, it seemed, was common as rain. "We are looking for who that might be, but . . ." He shrugged. "They are likely safe in Northope by now."

"I wouldn't call them safe," said Aldora.

"Only for now," Roylence added.

Witárë looked at the map. "The loss of the ferries is more symbolic than significant."

"They would still have been useful," said Roylence.

"In a limited way. We were always going to be dependent on your barges."

There were no bridges across the Keraps. None had been rebuilt after they had all been burned in the last war. Though having to trust humans on any front went against elvish instinct and policy, in order for the infantry to make good time, they had to rely on the Hawkesmoore promise to have barges ready to transport the army across the river. The elves had brought some light, easily transportable craft with them, which Witárë had planned to use in a night assault on Northope, part of the plan they now had to discard.

"More damaging," Witárë continued, "is the loss of the element of surprise."

"We still have the barges," Barrat spoke up, sounding defensive. "We'll get you across quickly."

"How quickly?" Skiriye asked him, unable to keep quiet in the face of idiocy. "In a single crossing?"

249

THE SLEEP OF EMPIRES

"No, of course not." Barrat's face darkened as he realized the humiliating backtracking he would have to do. "But within a day."

"A day," Skiriye repeated, tone murderously neutral.

"Where are the barges?" Witárë asked.

"Two leagues west of here," said Roylence.

Witárë pursed his lips. His success at reining in his temper reminded Skiriye of the need to do the same with hers. They could not lose this alliance, no matter how incompetent the humans were.

"I see," Witárë said with deliberate calm.

"Any closer," said Roylence, "and the risk of sabotage from Northope would be too great."

"Very well. Then we shall make for your embarkation point."

"I know the situation isn't ideal," said Roylence. "I would prefer not to attack from a single direction, either. But our combined forces are much larger than Northope's. We'll hit them hard, and the siege will be brief."

"What do you mean by one direction?" Skiriye asked. "We have two targets."

"Yes, I know," Roylence said quickly. "Nothing has changed about that. I meant on our initial approach."

"Is Northope defending the Voidwatch?" Witárë asked.

"Yes. Our spies can't get close enough to get a precise sense of Felgard's dispositions, but we know that they are attempting to protect both it and the town."

"I can't understand why they're doing that," said Delen. "Splitting up their strength is madness. They might as well surrender now. If there's someone or something in the Voidwatch that's so precious to them, why not bring it to Northope?"

"There may be aspects of the Voidwatch that cannot be moved," said Skiriye.

Elgin spoke for the first time. "What aspects?" His eyes gleamed with sudden, covetous interest.

"Nothing of use to you," said Witárë.

250

DAVID ANNANDALE

"I think we should be the judge of that."

"No," Witárë said, calm yet absolute. "It is for us to destroy. Those are the terms of our alliance, and they are unalterable."

"I don't see . . ." Elgin began, but Roylence shut him up.

"Be quiet. You are ignorant in these matters, and so you have nothing to say. Especially when you've proven yourself incompetent in matters you should know everything about."

Elgin's face reddened with humiliated anger. He said nothing.

"You have the siege engines as discussed?" Witárë said to Roylence.

"We do. This will still be a brief campaign. We'll have to hit harder, but we can do it. We trap the defenders in Northope and wear them down, and take out the contingent at the Voidwatch."

Witárë nodded. "The principle remains sound. When one falls, so does the other."

Yes, the principle is good, Skiriye thought. It distressed her that it had to depend so heavily on the proven imperfection of the humans.

251

CHAPTER 20

In the austere throne room of Castle Northope, Lady Ossia Felgard waited for a villager to arrive. Pillars flanked the throne, holding the high, bare vault of the ceiling. On the walls, warring figures on tapestries, dim shadows in the torchlight, seemed to move with the flickers of the flames. The sun had almost set, its rays reaching through the leaded glass of the windows to bathe the hall in blood.

Ossia's commanders stood at the bottom of the throne's dais. Vorykas, the deepest shadow, leaned against one of the pillars to Ossia's left. Next to him, like a diminutive echo of death, Kanstuhn watched the throne room door.

A week earlier, Lady Ossia Felgard would have dismissed the idea, if anyone had been eccentric enough to propose it, that she would invite anyone from Ghaunthook to attend one of her inner circle's briefing sessions for the defense of Northope. The village owed fealty to Northope, and had sent its conscripts. They were not trained soldiers, though. There were almost none of those to come from the farming villages. The communities could provide bodies to swell a sortie, to add to the defense of the walls, and to help hold back an attack on the gates.

They did not provide skilled warriors, let alone commanders.

But the rumor that rushed ahead of the Ghaunthook contingent had caught her attention. The rumor of a figure inspiring fear and devotion in equal measure among the villagers. The whispers made her curious, but it was Vorykas whose advice tipped the balance.

"I think you should meet with her," he said.

"You know her?"

"I might. I can only think of one person this might be, though I don't know how it *can* be her."

DAVID ANNANDALE

Vorykas' words carried weight with Ossia, which was something she still hadn't fully adjusted to. Only a short time ago, she had never heard of him. She still did not know what Vorykas was. Neither, when she brought the warrior to see him, did Skaitaias. But the mathematician agreed with her that the mystery of his being was important.

When his news was confirmed by Ossia's patrols, he became someone she listened to carefully.

When he and Kanstuhn brought back the heads of Hawkesmoore spies several nights running, he and the kaul became invaluable.

So when he suggested she should meet with this leader from Ghaunthook, she agreed to do so.

The Ghaunthook conscripts arrived at the approach of dusk. Ossia heard raised voices outside the doors to her throne room, shouts that might have been wonder or alarm. She started to move her right hand from the armrest of the throne to the pommel of her sword. Then she saw that Vorykas had not shifted from his relaxed stance. He gave no indication of anticipating a threat.

Two officers of Ossia's personal guard opened the doors, and the leader from Ghaunthook entered. The last, dying ray of sun fell on the features of a woman whose beauty made Ossia recoil as from the embrace of a serpent. A night-dark crown sat on her head. At least, Ossia told herself it was a crown. It emerged from her long, flowing black hair like a tangle of twisting horns. Her face, when it had been human, would have been attractive, but now all flaws had died, leaving a perfection of alabaster skin and crimson lips that filled Ossia's imagination with visions of maggots and blood.

She glanced at Vorykas and Kanstuhn, gauging their reactions. They recognized the woman, she saw. They looked at her with intense curiosity, but none of Ossia's horror. The stricken faces of her commanders reassured her that her reaction was the common one.

The woman crossed the hall. In the time it took her to reach the foot of the throne's dais, the sun's final glimmer had vanished. Ossia

253

THE SLEEP OF EMPIRES

stared as the woman transformed, dead beauty giving way to the majesty of death. She regarded the armored skeleton with genuine awe. If the woman had demanded the throne, in that moment Ossia would have surrendered it to her. But instead, the skeleton took a knee and lowered her head.

"I have come," she said, "to give you my oath that I will defend you and Northope."

Ossia found her voice. "You have my thanks," she said. "What is your name?"

Vorykas spoke up. "This is Latanna Forgrym," he said. "Kanstuhn and I knew her in Ghaunthook." He grinned. "Though when we last saw her, she was looking very unwell."

Latanna stood and faced Vorykas. They seemed to Ossia to be a disturbing kind of matched pair. One a creature who should have inspired terror instead of admiration. The other a gray being whose features were an indecipherable blend of all the races of the world, while, at a deeper, uncanny level, belonging to none of them.

"We were worried about you," said Vorykas.

"It turns out you didn't have to be."

"So I see. Alisteyr asked us to send a friend of his to help you. I imagine he's been added to the roster of recruits here by now."

"There would have been nothing for him to do if he had reached Ghaunthook," Latanna said. After a moment she added, "Though Alisteyr might well have wanted him to try."

"Is Alisteyr here too?"

"Yes."

Ossia thought Vorykas wanted to ask more, but he restrained himself.

Latanna turned back to Ossia, waiting to be dismissed.

Ossia rose from her throne. "Come with me," she said to her commanders. With a nod she included Vorykas and Kanstuhn. And with a lack of hesitation that surprised her, she said "You as well," to Latanna.

254

DAVID ANNANDALE

The small group followed her through the door at the rear of the throne room to a smaller chamber. Here she had battle maps of Northope, its environs, and the Voidwatch laid out on a table.

She did ask herself why she had decided to trust Latanna, a creature whose nature she did not understand, and whom she had never met before. She asked herself only for the formality of having done so. She knew the answer. It amounted to far more than Latanna's overwhelming presence. She had brought Vorykas into her inner circle after a very brief acquaintance as well. Roder Hearthkin, the head of her army, had misgivings, and she understood them. But he did not fully know what was at stake, and so he could not appreciate the full impact of the sudden arrival of these two beings.

They are here for a reason, even if they don't know it themselves. This is fate, not coincidence.

She could not afford to turn away from this gift.

It had not come from the gods. Of that, she was certain, for reasons known only to herself and Skaitaias. And that gave her confidence in her decision.

The old mathematician had come down from the Voidwatch. He sat in a corner, in a chair pulled back from the table, and nodded in greeting to the arrivals. Roder and the other officers looked puzzled to see him. Vorykas and Kanstuhn appeared interested.

Latanna looked at him, but there was no expression possible in the skull to give her thoughts away.

Skaitaias drew himself up at the sight of Latanna and Vorykas. *Yes, they mean something, don't they?* Ossia thought. *The two of them together.* Latanna appeared to be a welcome surprise, to judge by Skaitaias' reaction. Ossia's hopes rose.

I don't know how they were brought here against the will of the gods, but I know they must have been.

She had never felt more committed to her cause of truth. And now she and Skaitaias would reveal the truth to others. Even Roder only knew a

THE SLEEP OF EMPIRES

part of what was happening. The scale of the gathering events made her dizzy. She hoped she would be worthy of them.

With a gesture, Ossia invited her company to stand about the periphery of the round table. She took up a position closest to the map of Northope. "Some of you," she began, nodding to Roder, "know the broad lines of my intentions to confront the coming siege. I will expand on them now. This is the hour for questions and answers. Please speak as freely as I intend to do.

"To begin with, the essential disposition of our forces will be as follows. The conscripts, lacking experience, will remain inside the city walls to take part in their defense. The protection of the Voidwatch cannot be left to those who have never picked up a sword in their lives. The soldiers of Northope, then, will be split evenly between the city and the tower.

"The trebuchets have fixed positions. But I want a line of mangonels at the top of the plateau. The terrain, I hope, will play its own role in holding back attackers.

"Finally, there are the harrying tactics. I have soldiers who are trained to worry the enemy's flanks." She looked at Vorykas. "I believe this is your specialty too."

He and Kanstuhn nodded.

"And mine," said Latanna.

"Thank you," Ossia said, again finding herself grateful that Latanna hadn't suggested she take command of the city's defenses.

"I have to ask why you are dividing your forces in this way," said Vorykas. "I understand the desire to hold on to ancestral land, but is the Voidwatch worth the sacrifice? This is a huge risk you're taking. We don't know how big the elvish contingent is going to be, but the fact remains that Northope is up against two armies, not one."

"The protection of the Voidwatch is at least as vital as that of Northope," Ossia said.

Roder's subordinate officers looked shocked, but he nodded slowly. She had told him just enough for him to have an idea of what was at stake.

256

"The Voidwatch and what it contains are why the elves are coming," Ossia continued. "They have no interest in furthering the political ambitions of the Hawkesmoores. They are allies of convenience. The Hawkesmoores want Northope for themselves. We've known that for a long time. They don't care about the Voidwatch. I doubt they'd given it the most passing thought prior to this campaign. The elves want only the Voidwatch, and its contents."

"That's twice you've mentioned the contents," said Latanna. "May I ask what those are?"

"You may," said Ossia. "Especially because I believe your arrival is in some way connected with their presence. They are this man, Skaitaias Kenneye." She pointed to the mathematician. "And a book stolen from the elves."

"The elves are waging war over a book?" Kanstuhn asked in disbelief.

"For this book, yes."

"I have to ask my question again," said Vorykas. "Can't this man and the book be protected more easily in Northope than in the Voidwatch?"

For the first time, Skaitaias spoke. "I could be, yes." He stood and approached the table. "But I am not important."

"That is far from true," said Ossia.

"Then I am the least important element. My location does not matter. But the book's does. It is linked to the Voidwatch. As I have been deciphering it, and hearing the voice from its pages, I have sensed a stirring below the tower. An awakening has begun. That is what the elves fear, and since they are on the march, that means they know of the Voidwatch, and its nature. It is no longer enough for them to recapture the book. They must destroy the Voidwatch utterly, and put to the sword everyone who knows its significance."

"Which means," said Ossia, "for them to be certain, everyone in Northope must die."

"A massacre over a book," Kanstuhn said softly.

THE SLEEP OF EMPIRES

"This is not the first time the elves have taken such extreme measures. Humans have as well, for the same reasons. These are the rare occasions that they have acted with a common purpose, if not necessarily in concert. The dwarves have, too."

"And the kauls?" Kanstuhn asked.

"Rarely. Most often, they were the victims of the slaughters, though so were large numbers of humans."

"Never the elves or the dwarves?"

"No, never," said Skaitaias.

"How surprising," Vorykas said dryly.

"The reasons why the killings did or did not happen go beyond the prejudice against the kauls," Skaitaias said. "That prejudice is, I would say, a symptom of the reason for the massacres."

"This is all to do with the gods, isn't it?" said Vorykas, his eyes shadowed with anger.

"More than you can imagine," said Ossia.

Skaitaias nodded vigorously. "The elves and the dwarves did not turn on each other because their faiths are monolithic. The elves serve only Passomo, the dwarves only Endelbis. Humans are divided in their worship. That creates the possibilities of schism, and of the forbidden. As for the kauls . . ."

"We have no god, and no protection," said Kanstuhn.

"Isn't Gezeiras your patron?" Ossia asked.

"That is one of your beliefs. We are not his creation, and we do not have his protection."

"Once, you did have a protector," said Skaitaias.

Kanstuhn stared. Uncomprehending silence fell across the chamber.

Now we come to it, Ossia thought. *Now is the time for truth.*

"What god?" Kanstuhn finally asked.

"The god betrayed and slain by the others. The god of the void." Skaitaias produced a piece of parchment from his robes and laid it on the table. On it was a symbol, a circle broken diagonally into two halves.

258

DAVID ANNANDALE

Vorykas and Kanstuhn's eyes widened. The effect was noticeable even in Latanna, who stiffened at the sight.

"You've seen this before," said Ossia.

"Yes," said Vorykas. "More than once. As a ruin, too, of what looked like a temple."

"It would have been," Skaitaias said.

"How long ago? One of the other representations we saw was in the remains of a farmhouse that was *beneath* a cemetery."

"Another age." Skaitaias looked dreamy. "One not so much forgotten as expunged from history. But despite the efforts of the elves, traces remain, in ruins, in a book, and in their immortal memories."

"What is the symbol?" Kanstuhn asked.

"The symbol of absence. It is the null number, and it is the mark of the void god."

"I've never heard of this god," said Latanna.

"Oh, but you have, just under a different designation. The god of evil. The lord of Voran. I deduced that there must have been a god of the void, because my study of mathematics led me to understand that there had to be a null number. The rules forbade it, but at the same time they required it for their own being. Everything comes from the void, and everything returns to it. The void precedes all being. The god of the void precedes all the other gods, and is their creator. The stolen book is the revelation of zero, and the revelation is the story of creation and betrayal."

"Betrayal *by* the gods," said Latanna.

"Yes. The legends that form the foundations of the world's beliefs are lies. The gods were the betrayers, not the betrayed."

"The void god did not slay Xestun?"

"Oh, yes, but only because Xestun attacked first. The second to be created after Passomo, Xestun built Dengennis, and declared its wonders eternal. The void god warned him against the delusion and reminded him that what had come from the void still had the void at its heart. It had not always existed. It could thus return to the only true eternal, and

259

THE SLEEP OF EMPIRES

become nothing once more. Enraged, Xestun sought to preserve his city forever by killing the void. He failed, but the other gods took the wrong lesson.

"They did not accept their mortality. They could not abide that they, and everything they created, owed their existence to the void. They could not tolerate the constant reminder that existence could end, and they with it. So they decided to follow Xestun's example. They bided their time, and then all of them, without exception, took part in the betrayal. They took their creator by surprise. I imagine a subterfuge, a broken trust." Skaitaias shrugged. "The book itself does not say. However they went about it, they attacked. The void cannot be destroyed, but they rendered the god into untold fragments, and directed their own followers to annihilate all trace of the void god's worship."

"Did this god have a name?" Vorykas asked.

"That, too, was erased, if there ever was one. The *Book of the Null* does not record a name."

"The erasure was impressively accomplished, if that book and rare, buried ruins are all that remain." Vorykas shook his head. "To purge the world's memory so completely . . ."

"Remember that this took the efforts of the entire pantheon," said Skaitaias. "And of the elves, the dwarves, and the humans. Was it very close to complete? In many senses, yes. But there is a greater trace that remained."

"Voran," said Latanna.

"The land of our nightmares," said Skaitaias. "The object of fear that the sentinels of Korvas still watch, though it has been dead ever since the shattering of its ruler."

"That was the void god's home?" said Vorykas. "A god walked on Eloran?"

"If the *Book of the Null* speaks truly, and on this point the myths agree with it, then many did, in that other age. They withdrew from the world after their crime. It diminished them in ways they had not foreseen. And the age of great wonders passed."

"But why does all this matter so much to the elves now?" Vorykas insisted. "Why make war over a record of history that, however shameful, is ancient?"

"The void god was shattered, but not destroyed, remember."

"You mean the god could return?"

"I don't know. But the elves fear that possibility. Why else march to war? Especially now that the book has come here, and I have read a great deal of it, and passed on to you what I know, and so the truth spreads."

"You still haven't explained why the Voidwatch must be protected," Vorykas said.

"Because it is precisely what it is called. In the gorge below the tower is a fragment of the true void."

Kanstuhn frowned in frustration. "I can't grasp what that is supposed to mean."

"Neither could I," said Ossia. "But I have always needed to know, ever since my mother first told me what has been the legacy and secret of the Felgards. We have always been sentinels over the thing in the gorge."

"Has anyone gone down into the gorge?" Latanna asked. "Has anyone touched the void?"

"No one who has ever returned," said Ossia. "It has been my life's work to learn the true nature of that darkness. I feel that work is almost done. Or at least its first great task."

"You have taken a huge risk," said Latanna.

"You are obviously no stranger to risks taken for greater truths."

"No, I'm not."

"Then you'll understand."

The skull nodded.

"Northope has always stood on its own. During the last war with the elves, it received no help from Korvas. Northope has fought for Wiramzin, but Wiramzin never thinks of Northope. We are a people of no gods.

THE SLEEP OF EMPIRES

Some of us abandoned them. Others were abandoned by them. We owe them nothing. Most especially, we do not owe them allegiance."

"Does your population know what you have found?" Vorykas asked softly.

"No. Not yet. But they know what I stand for. They know that my first allegiance is to the truth."

"And the people of Ghaunthook, and the other village conscripts? Do they know why they have to fight? Do they know what has brought them to war? Do they know why they might die?"

"Would they be better off with Hawkesmoores on the throne of Northope?" Ossia fired back, stung.

Vorykas looked at her levelly, but said nothing. He knew she had no better answer.

Ossia looked away. He was right, and she would have to live with the consequences of what happened to the people she had commanded to defend Northope. Everyone in the city would be shouldering the responsibility of her decisions.

This is my doing. Not theirs.

They had not chosen to steal the *Book of the Null*. The people of the city had willingly cut themselves off from the gods, but that was not the same thing as inviting their wrath.

"The Hawkesmoores would have come sooner or later," Roder said, defending his Lady.

"With elves?" said Vorykas.

"Maybe not, but this way, we can see them coming," said Latanna. "We're going to break them," she said to Vorykas.

He nodded, clearly as intent on that goal as Latanna. Ossia wondered about their past history with the Hawkesmoores. She knew the youngest son had been seen in Ghaunthook. If that had been preparatory to an attempt to take control of the village, and establish another outpost on Northope's opposite flank, nothing had materialized.

262

DAVID ANNANDALE

"Now or later, a moment such as this had to come," Skaitaias put in. "The lies of the gods could not live forever."

"They may yet if this goes badly," said Vorykas.

"No. One day, the lies will end, even if the elves win this battle."

"They won't," said Latanna.

Her words, a promise and a cold statement of fact, made Vorykas smile.

"No, they won't," he agreed. He put out his hand, and she took it, gray flesh and white bone meeting in a warrior's grasp that made Ossia's heart soar.

Vorykas grinned again. "I have so much to ask you."

"I think many of your questions will be the same ones I am asking myself." She touched the tip of one of the crown's horns, the gesture as unconscious a habit as brushing back hair.

"Forgive me," said Skaitaias. "Will you tell me, have you always been as we see you?"

"No," said Latanna. "I was . . . normal . . . until recently." She said *normal* as if she had acquired a distaste for the word, and was still seeking to understand what she had been, and what she had become.

"And do you know what caused your . . . your change?"

"This crown." She touched the horn again. "Or the tiara it once was. After I put it on, I could not take it off, and that's when things began."

"The tiara," said Vorykas, wary understanding spreading across his face. "It was in a chamber with the symbol of the void god. In its initial form, it also had a jewel with that symbol."

Ossia's eyes widened. She locked gazes for a moment with Skaitaias, who seemed on the verge of cutting a caper.

"We were right!" he exclaimed. "We were right! Your presence here has nothing to do with chance. You are meant to be here. The void is stirring. The lies will fall." He came to Ossia and took both of her hands in his. "My Lady, have no doubts. This *is* the moment. This *is* where the end of the lie begins."

263

CHAPTER 21

They locked Pilta in his quarters after his meeting with Skaitaias. He wasn't surprised. He would have done the same. And though he was quite sure he had returned to the keep without being seen, he had also been certain that Skaitaias would tell Lady Felgard about the encounter.

She came to see him with the guards who would become his jailers. She said nothing. She just looked at him, her gaze steady, studying, her expression unreadable. Pilta held himself still, all the old feelings rising as if he were back before Skiriye ne Sincatsë again. He braced himself for punishment. He wondered if he had bought himself execution, and cursed his foolishness and his curiosity. But Ossia Felgard turned and left, still without saying a word. A guard closed the door behind her, and Pilta heard the lock turn.

Nothing worse happened in the days that followed. No one came to haul him away in chains. Meals were brought to him. They were simple, but he could not complain about malnourishment. His quarters were comfortable. He could not leave, and that was the extent of his punishment.

He had one visitor. Arva came to see him on the second day. The look she gave him, part disappointed, part pitying, and part amused, made him wither inside.

"You just can't help yourself, can you?" she said.

He grimaced. "If I could, I suppose I wouldn't be here in the first place."

"True, and Skaitaias wouldn't have the book. So that works out well for us, if not for you."

"What's going to happen to me?"

Arva shrugged. "For now, nothing. After things are over, I can't say. If we're unlucky, Lady Felgard might have the decision made for her."

"After what things are over?"

264

DAVID ANNANDALE

Arva cocked her head. "You haven't heard? I thought ferreting out secrets was your calling. And this isn't even a secret. The War of the Book is going to happen."

"The elves are coming?" His stomach twisted with terror, and with a demented kind of hope.

"Allied with humans. Did you ever imagine you'd be the cause of that?"

Pilta found he couldn't swallow. When he tried to speak, his voice croaked out of a throat suddenly dry as stone. "What should I . . ."

"Do?" Arva finished. "That's what I'm here to tell you. Nothing. Do nothing. You've done what you were paid to do, and you've done things here that show you can't be trusted. Don't make it worse. Don't risk making yourself look like a danger. Unless you're tired of living. In which case, there's always the window. We're high enough that you can make it quick."

Pilta shuddered. "I'm not tired of living."

"Then behave. Be quiet. Be still. Don't give Lady Felgard, or me, or anyone else in Northope, any reason to think about you. Do you think you can manage that?"

Pilta nodded. Arva nodded back, harder, as if driving the point home. "Good," she said. "I don't actually want to see you beheaded, you know."

She left. For the rest of that day, and for the three nights and two days that followed, Pilta did as Arva had told him. He kept still. He was very, very quiet. And he listened at the door to the sounds of footsteps, quiet exchanges, the rattling of the lock as it was checked, and the barely audible shifting of feet that marked the presence of guards. He spent the nights learning the patterns outside his prison. He discovered that there was not always one present. The needs of Northope, as war approached, pulled them to more important duties. The guards came at regular intervals, checked the lock, and then stayed for a while.

By the third night, Pilta felt he had the pattern down. He could reasonably count, he thought, on the better part of an hour between spot checks on the door.

265

THE SLEEP OF EMPIRES

The fourth night, during one of the periods no guard stood outside the doors, Pilta made himself acquainted with the lock. He still had the tools that had given him access to the secrets of the Library of Árkiriye. He had scattered and hidden them around the room, working them into cracks in the masonry and woodwork of the sill, turning them into unnoticeable features that belonged in the room. He had done so without any plan of mischief. He had just wanted to keep the means of an open door and flight by his side.

Opening the lock was quick work. He found the human ironwork crude, almost insultingly simple. What took a bit longer, and was the first real risk he ran since Arva had spoken to him, was learning how to lock himself up again. He couldn't take the chance of the door being found open.

He practiced unlocking and locking the door, then did nothing the following night, waiting to see if his efforts had disturbed the pattern.

They had not.

And so the next night, he left his room for the first time. He did so every night afterward, ranging a bit farther each time, flitting from shadow to shadow in the dark halls of the keep. He set about learning what the castle kept hidden. He had no plan in mind. He worked hard not to think about anything beyond the next day. The instinct to explore and to find secrets was too hard to ignore. So he gave it free rein.

His window looked out toward the east. The morning came when, standing at the casement, he saw the war arrive. The banners of the Hawkesmoores waved with the colors of Beresta. The fields beyond the walls of Northope filled with soldiers.

Pilta saw his future shrink down to the point of collision between his past and his present.

The leather armor Alisteyr had been given felt heavy and awkward. He didn't know how to move with it on. In his fantasies of heroism, he had imagined himself in full plate, sprinting across the battlefield, leaping over

266

DAVID ANNANDALE

fallen foes. But now, just wearing this cuirass made him hot and sweaty. He could not imagine running.

He met Latanna at the foot of the east face of the city's outer wall. Other recruiters, from Ghaunthook and elsewhere, as well as from Northope itself, were climbing up the stairs to the ramparts. Drums beat on the wall, and in the fields beyond, competing rhythms united in the promise of bloodshed, the promise drawing closer and closer as the day went on.

"I'm frightened," Alisteyr confessed.

"That's good," said Latanna, beautiful but terrifying as war in the daylight. "Listen to your fear and be cautious." She didn't look afraid at all. She looked eager to be out in the field. Of course she did. Alisteyr wondered if she had any reason to be afraid of anything now. Could she die a second time?

"I don't want to be a coward, either."

"You won't be." She smiled, crimson lips pulling back over perfect white teeth, and Alisteyr had to suppress a shudder. "You've faced a lot already, including me."

Alisteyr lifted the bow in his right hand. The quiver of arrows felt like a premonition of doom on his back. "I've never used a bow before."

"There will be a lot of targets out there. It will be hard to miss."

"Is that supposed to be reassuring?"

"Just do what your commanders say," Latanna told him. "Launch your arrows when they tell you, and stay under cover when you can."

He would have liked her to add *and you'll be fine.* But she didn't make that promise.

No promises in war.

A hand patted his shoulder, and he turned to find Kanstuhn had joined them. The kaul had a bow slung over a shoulder. "I'll guide you too."

"You're staying?"

Kanstuhn nodded. "Vorykas and Latanna need to go out and be reckless. He can afford to be. I think she can too. I'm like you—I still have to be careful if I want to see the next dawn. And I would like to."

267

THE SLEEP OF EMPIRES

"There you go," said Latanna. "Follow his lead. He knows what he's doing."

"And I don't." Alisteyr grimaced. "I really don't. I don't know what I'm fighting for."

"You're fighting against the Hawkesmoores. As you were in Ghaunthook."

"But why are they here? With elves? I knew what I was fighting for in the village." *At least, I thought I did.* "But why is this war happening?" He gave Latanna a hard look. "Do you know?"

"I know something," she said. "I don't think anyone knows all of it. But this does seem to be part of what happened to me in Ghaunthook. We are fighting on the right side, Alisteyr."

"Is the fight worth dying for?"

"Is anything?"

"I think you know the answer to that better than I do."

"Maybe I do," said Latanna. She looked off into the distance for a moment. "I have no regrets. None for what has happened to me, or for the choices I've made. And I don't regret being here. What happens here now is important. Very important."

"Will you tell me what I'm fighting for?"

"Lady Felgard says that we are fighting for a truth that the gods would destroy, and I believe her."

"Fighting against the gods," Alisteyr whispered.

"Is that a grand enough purpose?" Latanna asked. "Does that feel legendary?"

"It does," he said, his voice sounding dead in his ears. There would be no escape, then, from the punishment for having wanted to live a heroic life. The reality of legends was bloody and terrifying. It had him in its maw, and it would never let him go until his death.

That might not be long in coming.

"Fight well," Latanna said. "And stay alive." She left, heading off to enter the nightmares of the enemy.

268

DAVID ANNANDALE

Numb, sweating with terror, Alisteyr followed Kanstuhn up the stairs to the top of the wall. Once there, he found a lot of familiar faces mixed in with Northope troops.

"Is this Gaunthook's section of the wall?" he asked.

"In a sense," said Kanstuhn. "People fight harder when they are surrounded by comrades they know."

"Alisteyr!" a voice called.

He turned, and almost fell into Garwynn's sudden embrace.

Alisteyr hugged him back. "They found you!"

"They rescued me," said Garwynn. He took a step back and gave a look of gratitude to Kanstuhn.

The kaul shrugged. "A poor rescue," he said. "One that brought you to a war."

"Better this than the House of Law's prison."

Alisteyr tapped the end of his bow against Garwynn's. "Have you used one of these before?"

Garwynn shook his head. "Never." He looked pale. "I don't know if I could kill someone even if I had the skill."

"You will," said Kanstuhn. "You will because you'll have to. And I'll guide you. Now come to the ramparts."

Alisteyr entered a blur of time, one punctuated by the shouted commands of Captain Arva. He had gone through what training there was time for the day before. He knew to stand and crouch behind a crenellation. He knew the orders to expect, and Arva took him and the other recruits through their paces again and again as the foe appeared in the distance.

Then it was time to stop and wait and watch.

The Hawkesmoores and elvish armies seemed small at first, a stain emerging from a distant wooded rise. Alisteyr felt a short period of hope as they spilled out into the fields between the plateau and the river. There couldn't be enough of them to fill the space, he thought. There could certainly be no question of their being able to breach the walls of Northope.

269

THE SLEEP OF EMPIRES

They couldn't possibly encircle it well enough even to pretend to lay siege to the city.

But as the soldiers and the drums drew nearer, they acquired strength. They ceased to be an abstraction. They became a reality, a mass of armed individuals fused together with a single purpose.

They kept coming, far more than Alisteyr had thought at first. The illusion of distance had betrayed him. He finally realized the strength of the Hawkesmoores. The family might not have the power to challenge all the other powers in Korvas, but they were the strongest individual House. They had come with all their might, gathered not just from Korvas but from a score of vassal keeps and villages. Alisteyr looked out at the flags, so many fluttering like ragged afterthoughts beneath the great banner of the Hawkesmoores, and thought about how close Ghaunthook had come to being another of their number.

The elves were fewer, but that did not mean they were few. Crouched behind the crenellation, peering out to the side of the stonework just enough to see the encroaching threat, he gazed at the precision of the elves' march, and at the exquisite shine of their armor, which seemed to glow with reflected sunlight even under the overcast sky. He thought about the stories about the last war between humans and elves, and of the hills of corpses, all of them humans cut down with the cold elegance of perfection.

He thought about the harm just one elf might do on the ramparts.

We'll be slaughtered.

And so his next thoughts became *Keep them down. Keep them down. Keep them off the walls.*

He saw the long siege ladders carried by the Hawkesmoore troops, and, a bit further back, the wheeled mangonels followed by the carts carrying their stone projectiles. From within the woods, barely audible over the marching feet, the rhythmic clatter of sword against shield, and the pounding of the drums, came the sounds of a different, much more rapid sort of hammering. Something was being built.

DAVID ANNANDALE

"I wish . . ." said Garwynn, on Alisteyr's right.

"What's that?" Alisteyr asked.

"Nothing. I was thinking about magic." He pulled his lips back in a sick, frightened smile. "If I could wave them all away . . ."

"I wish you could too."

"We can do this," said Kanstuhn, the firmness of his tone rebuking their fears.

"They have many more skilled warriors than we do," Alisteyr said.

"They do, but we will have sheer numbers on our side, and that matters. And we're about to cut them down a little." The kaul grinned darkly.

"And they us," said Garwynn. He held his bow as if he thought it might bite him.

"We are shooting down," said Kanstuhn. "That gives us an advantage. We can hit a bit further than they can, and we will. Get ready. The enemy is almost in range."

"Where do I aim?" Alisteyr spoke too quickly, panic bubbling up from his chest.

"You don't have to," Kanstuhn told him. "You are part of a hail of arrows. It isn't the individual hailstone that matters. It's the storm it is part of." He gave Alisteyr a steadying look.

Alisteyr started breathing again.

"Now get ready," Kanstuhn repeated.

Alisteyr took an arrow from his quiver and nocked it. A moment later, the captain shouted, "Archers at the ready!"

Kanstuhn had his bow and arrow prepared as well. He was behind shelter, but edged around, looking at the enemy with a quiet concentration that told Alisteyr that the kaul had very definite targets in mind. His arrows would not be just another part of the general hail.

How much closer? Alisteyr thought. He could picture the forward lines sprinting forward suddenly with the ladders, the enemy swarming up the walls and over the ramparts, blades hacking down the defenders, his throat

THE SLEEP OF EMPIRES

sliced wide, his blood gushing warmly down his torso and arms while he choked and choked and choked into darkness, and—

"Now!" Arva shouted.

Alisteyr obeyed, his body racing ahead of his mind and his fear. He and Garwynn jerked up above the crenellations, part of a unified line of archers. They were all one. They were him, and he was an extension of the archers to his left and right, a great and unbreakable wall. In this first heartbeat, his fear vanished.

He let fly his arrow. It arced into the sky with hundreds more, and in this second heartbeat, as he witnessed, for the first time, the awful beauty of the art of war, exhilaration filled his chest. He was invincible. He was immortal. His hand laid waste to the foe, because there, and there, and there, as the arrows descended, a black rain, warriors fell. Some writhed, clutching at their wounds. Some were stilled in the instant. Death struck the front lines of the army.

I did this.

Then the next heartbeat.

"Cover!"

The urgency of the cry broke through the thrill of adrenaline. Again, Alisteyr's body reacted ahead of his brain. He dropped behind the stonework, and before his heart beat once more, arrows flashed over his head, silver and ferocious as lightning.

Some archers did not get down as quickly as Alisteyr. A woman to his right fell back, a haft projecting from her throat. She made no sound, her mouth and eyes wide with terminal surprise. The man next to Garwynn spun around, an arrow in his shoulder. He screamed in pain, and then another shot caught him through the back and silenced him. Death brushed its fingers over the ramparts, and its reality banished Alisteyr's exhilaration.

Before the fear could seize him again and root him to his shelter, the commands came to rise and shoot once more, and he did, faster this time,

DAVID ANNANDALE

up and down again without waiting to see the result. Answering arrows from humans and elves slashed over his head, smacked against the battlements, and clattered down on either side of him.

"You're doing well," Kanstuhn said. "Both of you. More of that. Keep going fast. Never hesitate."

The kaul ducked sideways, between crenellations, fired his arrow and sprang back. He moved in a blur, too fast for anyone to target him, risking only the vagaries of luck. He struck with a different rhythm than the shouted orders of the captain. Random, unpredictable, he also fired with intent.

"Who are you killing?" Alisteyr asked, catching his breath behind the stonework again a few minutes later.

"Elves," said Kanstuhn. "When I can see them." He darted out, fired, and withdrew again.

Alisteyr saw the battlefield in fragments, a quick view in the moment of letting his arrow fly, seen so briefly that it was only once he crouched behind shelter that he could process the sight. The armies were still drawing closer, the nearest of the siege ladders less than a hundred yards from the wall, their mangonels, hauled by horses and soldiers, grinding just as close.

We aren't stopping them.

The thought was absurd, and he knew it. The first battle had barely begun. The siege might go on for days, weeks, months. Northope could not hope to win in the first few minutes. It couldn't fall that quickly either.

A shadow passed over him. He looked up. A huge chunk of stone flew by, arcing beyond the wall. An entire volley of stone, a greater and more terrible hail, descended on the foe. The trebuchets had launched their missiles. Massive engines constructed on recessed platforms along the wall, powered by thirty-ton counterweights, they hurled projectiles across the entire depth of the besiegers' formation. Stones weighing two and three and five hundred pounds smashed into flesh.

273

THE SLEEP OF EMPIRES

When Alisteyr rose to shoot, he paused for a second, risking everything to see the moment of impact. His soul drank in the devastation of flesh the boulders created. The stones crushed soldiers, shattering armor and turning bodies to pulp. They gouged scars into the ground, rolling over limbs. A ladder exploded into fragments from the impact. Warriors shouted and tried to scatter, but they had no protection from the fists of Northope that battered and crushed them.

Alisteyr took shelter. He grinned, hearing the screams of the injured and dying below. He willed the artillery teams to reload the engines and launch again. He wished for an endless torrent of rock from the sky, hammering down until the fields were gone and in their place were mountains with roots of blood.

"Rise! Loose!"

Alisteyr obeyed, and as he let fly, he saw stones in the air again, but heading his way.

The enemy mangonels had responded.

"Cover!" Arva shouted with greater urgency.

He dropped down and hugged the stone. He grimaced, as if bracing himself for the pain of a direct hit.

The mangonel missiles were smaller than the trebuchet stones, no more than the size of skulls. They hit hard enough. The wall stood up to their battering, though Alisteyr felt the vibrations of the impact, and pictured cracks appearing and spreading under sustained assault. A stone smacked into an archer too slow to get under cover and jellied his skull. Another hit a soldier like a battering ram and sent her flying off the wall. Others landed inside Northope. Lady Felgard had ordered anyone not engaged in the fighting to stay inside and seek shelter, and the missiles cracked loudly in the empty streets. Some impacts did damage, shattering wood and glass. From broken windows came the cries of the frightened and the injured, a cloud of war's agony spreading out to embrace the city.

"Now the war is in earnest," said Kanstuhn, his face set and grim. He fired again.

274

"What can we do?" Garwynn begged.

And then the commands to *rise, loose, cover* came once more, and Alisteyr obeyed, the movements coming on instinct now, devoid of meaning beyond the need to strike.

"We fight," Kanstuhn said simply.

CHAPTER 22

Latanna and Vorykas circled the flanks of the attacking armies. They moved through the woods at the base of the plateau, sticking to the edge of the cliff face. They flew through the brush at a run, their sprint untiring across the steep slope of the land. They watched for enemy scouts. High above, a line of archers at the edge of the plateau waited for the war to come to them. The foe was out of range of arrows, but the mangonels had joined the fray, adding their stones to the siege engine fire coming from the town.

"Kanstuhn says you don't sleep," Latanna said. They were still some distance from their goal, the ridge where the enemy had stationed their engines of war.

"I don't," said Vorykas. "I gather you don't, either."

"No. Do you breathe?"

"Yes. I'm never winded, though. And you?"

"I breathe out of habit, and when I speak. But I think I'm losing the habit."

They reached a clearing that gave them a view of Northope's walls and they paused to look. The first of the ladders were about to be raised.

"We have to stop that," said Latanna.

"We will," Vorykas said. "In the way that causes the greatest disruption." He adjusted the shoulder straps of the load he carried on his back.

Latanna nodded, and they moved on.

"Do you know what you are?" Vorykas asked.

"No. Not really. I wish I did."

"It is frustrating," said Vorykas. "You'll get used to it. You won't ever like not knowing, but you'll manage."

Even while running with her sword drawn, her eyes scanning for foes, and almost everyone she knew facing death, she felt a blessing of relief to

DAVID ANNANDALE

speak to someone who understood what it meant to become a stranger to herself.

"I like what I am," Latanna said. "At least, I think so. I like what I can do. I like that that I'm no longer at the mercy of a lot of things, and of a lot of people now."

Vorykas grinned. "I can't imagine Elgin Hawkesmoore would be keen on pursuing your hand in marriage now."

"I think you're right."

"More fool he."

Latanna discovered that she could no longer blush. But her skin tingled with the phantom memory of the sensation.

"I am still adjusting to being a predator. I wonder if I've always been or not."

"What matters is who we make our prey," Vorykas said, and the *we* of fellowship gave her joy. "Can you die?"

"You mean again? I don't know. I don't even know what happens if I'm injured."

"Assuming you can be."

"I guess I'll find out. I do know that I don't want one of those boulders coming down on me."

"Neither do I. On either of us."

They heard movement through the woods at the same time. They crouched motionless next to a tree, screened by brush, and waited. A few moments later, three men in Hawkesmoore livery appeared. They moved cautiously up the slope. They were looking, Latanna thought, for a way past the defenses on the plateau. She wondered if any of the other Northope scouts had run into their enemy counterparts yet. Lady Felgard had sent some out the night before. They would be further out than she and Vorykas. But they didn't have the means or the permission to hit where they liked, as hard as they liked.

She and Vorykas waited until they were sure there were no other scouts in the group. They sprang out from cover when the men were still fifty

277

THE SLEEP OF EMPIRES

feet away and rushed down the slope. Latanna leapt over bushes and roots with an agility formed from the fusion of a score of collective memories and skills. The way she used to move, the limitations of her old body, were memories still fresh enough to keep the sense of her new, evolving abilities novel. It sometimes felt as if she watched her body from afar, not recognizing the being that claimed to be her.

Close by, Vorykas streaked through the brush as if it were air. His skills came from somewhere else, a place even he didn't know. Latanna had a moment to wonder what that would be like, not to know what had shaped one's identity.

We are mysteries to ourselves. We share that.

The Hawkesmoore men lunged to meet them. They only died faster. Vorykas hit one with so much momentum that his sword stroke decapitated the soldier. Latanna speared the other up through the armpit, where his armor was weakest, pinning him. The man gasped and dropped his sword. She sank her fingers into his cheek and fed. The third tried to run. Vorykas caught him, threw him to the ground, and cut his throat.

The forest was thick here, and they could no longer see how far they were from the rear of the enemy armies.

"What do you think?" Latanna asked. "Is this close enough?"

"Let's say that it is."

They took off at full speed, no longer worrying about stealth. It would do the enemy good to hear them. It would be good for Hawkesmoore and elf to wonder, and perhaps to begin to fear.

They came out of the trees near the base of the ridge, and Latanna had her first close look at the foe.

She felt she had come to the shore of a sea of warriors. From here, near the rear of their formations, it looked like an endless tide rushing toward Northope, weapons drawn.

This was very different from her nights of hunting. On those, she knew that she would overwhelm her targets. They had never had the strength to

278

DAVID ANNANDALE

outnumber her. Now she faced strength in a mass, and there were elves here, beings she had never tested herself against.

She touched her fingers to the horn tips of the crown. *I'm ready.*

She nodded at Vorykas, and they attacked as they had planned, a thin dagger blade stabbing the enemy from behind. The first soldiers fell without knowing what had come upon them. The next ones turned to fight, and died just as swiftly.

Latanna ran abreast with Vorykas, sticking close, and they fought as a single entity, a four-armed creature of blades. They took turns blocking attacks while the other struck, slicing a deep wound into the Hawkesmoore army. Latanna sliced and blocked, jabbed and blocked, and whenever she blocked, Vorykas slashed, and they ran through showers of blood. Panic spread outward from the crimson horror they had become. Disorder spread through the ranks, alarm turning to fear and then panic.

Latanna didn't pause to feed. She didn't have time.

There would be time later, if they survived this strike.

They kept up the momentum of the charge. No pause, no quarter, no chance for the troops closest to them to recover or think. From further off, Latanna heard the shouts of officers trying to regain order and mount a counterattack. They made some headway, hurling troops back against the ones who were fleeing, and a few attacks arrived to Latanna's flanks and rear. She couldn't block every blade, and nor could Vorykas. Not all his wounds bled, but the deeper ones did, and they added to the dripping coating on his armor.

Blades cut her too. She felt the iron part her flesh, but she felt no pain, and no blood poured from the wounds.

She didn't feel weaker, at least for the moment, and so she ignored what could not be helped and kept going.

Their dagger-stab took them to one of the mangonels. After the initial volley of stones, the Hawkesmoore troops had turned to flaming matter, dousing their projectiles in oil and setting them alight before launching.

279

THE SLEEP OF EMPIRES

Beneath the overcast gloom of the late afternoon, red comets soared over the walls of Northope. Smoke rose from the city in thin curtains, growing darker and thicker.

The Hawkesmoores made it easy for Latanna and Vorykas. They already had fires burning. Latanna cut down the soldiers operating the mangonel while Vorykas took one of the oil flasks from his pack. He spread oil over the siege engine, hurled a torch onto it, and hacked through its ropes. Timbers and rope burned. Troops fell back from the rising flames.

Vorykas hurled himself at the stumbling soldiers, slashing with wide, double-handed strokes. He became a scythe, opening bellies and strewing the ground with steaming blood and organs. He roared, and cries of fear answered him. For a few seconds longer, the retreat accelerated.

Latanna shot across the space Vorykas had created, building up speed and momentum to plunge into the ranks beyond. Vorykas joined her, and they fought their way back toward the wooded slopes of the plateau.

The enemy pressed harder this time. The initial shock of their attack had worn off, and the officers had quelled the disorder. Latanna felt no fatigue, but she found it harder to fend off the blows. They came so fast now, from all sides. More and more of them got through. Her skin moved in strange ways where the swords had struck home. Vorykas bled from a dozen wounds. They healed quickly, but the enemy opened new ones just as fast, and he had become a specter soaked in gore.

For the first time in her second life, Latanna felt real danger. She could be overwhelmed. A mass of soldiers could bring her down and make certain she did not rise again.

Her awareness tunneled to the blades around her, and to the next block, the next slash, the next cut, and the next piece of blood-sodden earth where she would place her foot. The thunder of metal against metal and the howling rage of a thousand throats filled her ears. The walls of struggling humanity tried to crush her, stab her down, and trample her.

Do not fall. Do not fall. Do not fall.

If she did, she knew she wouldn't rise again.

DAVID ANNANDALE

Vorykas lunged forward, a battering ram, ignoring the swords that dug into his armor, and the one that cut open his throat. He choked and swore, and smashed through the last few ranks. The way open, he and Latanna sprinted into the woods. They ran uphill at a speed the humans could not follow.

They lost their few pursuers within a few minutes.

They found a cleft in the cliff face large enough for them to hide in. They rested there, or did what Latanna understood as rest for the thing she had become. Vorykas stopped bleeding. His flesh knit itself closed. Scars lined his face briefly, then disappeared.

Latanna shifted, feeling the tears in her skin and muscle, and the nicks on her bones. They didn't hurt, but they didn't go away. Her hunger, though, had grown to an acute, obsessive need. She had to feed. It took an effort to think about anything else.

"How was that?" she said, trying to distract herself.

"A good start," said Vorykas. "I looked back at the end. The fire had taken well, and the first siege ladders have been knocked back down from the ramparts."

"We've given them something to think about, then."

"How are you doing?"

"I have to feed." A tremor of hunger swept through her. "Badly."

"Can you wait until nightfall?"

"I think so." It would be difficult. But if she could hold on, she would have the opportunity to take individual prey. She could not do that in a pitched battle. Small, targeted attacks would also give her and Vorykas the chance to spread fear and uncertainty. "What do you have in mind?"

"I think we should try our hand on the elvish side of the army."

"Yes," she said, controlling the tremors. "I think so too."

That night, she killed her first elves, and learned what it sounded like when they screamed.

281

CHAPTER 23

During the days, and for much of the nights, Pilta sat at the window and looked east, reading the progress of the battle through the signs he could see and hear. The walls of Northope stood firm, though he knew many of their defenders had fallen. On the first day, he had seen flaming projectiles come over the walls and start fires in the city. That barrage had eased before the coming of dawn. Something had happened to the enemy's siege engines.

But that didn't stop the fires. In the days that followed, elvish arrows carried flame into Northope. At night, the walls and the streets flickered with the burn spots in the darkness flaring dark and angry until they were put out.

Fires dotted the slopes leading up to the cliff face of the plateau as well. Pilta thought those were more likely to have been set by the defenders. True or not, if there had been an attempt to storm the plateau, it had failed. The line of mangonels on its summit remained intact.

The city held fast against the attackers. It bled, but it held. The siege looked like a stalemate. Pilta had never seen war. He knew, though, that he could not trust his impressions. He guessed that a siege could appear to have nothing significant happening for a long time. When it ended, it would end suddenly. Especially if the city fell.

And the city would fall. He couldn't imagine any other outcome. The elves had come all this way because of the book. No one in Northope could understand the determination that represented. They couldn't understand what it meant. The elves would never leave until they had achieved what they had come to do.

Wouldn't they? Was there some way that the humans of Northope could prevail?

282

DAVID ANNANDALE

Would knowing that help him with his decision?

He spent two nights wrestling with the choice. If he did nothing, and the armies stormed Northope, he knew what would happen to him, and he doubted the end would be mercifully quick.

But what if Lady Felgard's forces won? All he had to do was nothing, and he would survive this war.

There was a way, though, that he could take the guesswork out of the situation. He could determine the outcome, if he had the courage.

The thought of what he had to do terrified him. It could go wrong in so many ways, almost all of them fatal.

On the third night, he faced the truth. He wasn't hesitating between two choices. He was working up the nerve to do what had already been decided for him.

Skaitaias had forced his hand. Skaitaias had told him the truth of the book. Through his theft, Pilta had betrayed Passomo. Every heartbeat that passed without atonement compounded his sin.

Do this, he told himself. *You must. No matter what happens to you.*

He had never deliberately acted for a cause larger than himself before. He had done so unknowingly, when he stole the book. His selfishness and ignorance had placed him among the damned. He knew better now. Tonight, he would break the habit of a lifetime and do the right thing, with no thought for himself.

That isn't true either. I don't want to die.

But maybe, just maybe, the righteous path could also save his physical being as well as his soul.

Pilta turned away from the window and moved to the door. He put his ear against it, listening for movement. Silence. The guards' presence outside his chamber had become very spotty since the siege had begun. The lock rattled once every few hours, but no one seemed to stand sentinel anymore. As long as he locked the door again when he left and stayed hidden, he had the entire night to move about.

THE SLEEP OF EMPIRES

He picked the lock, opened the door, checked the hall, and then fastened his false prison closed again. He moved quickly and silently through the corridors in a castle that felt empty. He could hear the clank and clatter of activity elsewhere, but it seemed very far away, down below in the great halls. The upper reaches of the keep were, if not deserted, much more sparsely populated than they had been, the war drawing everyone who could be spared to the front lines.

He had no difficulty keeping out of sight. He traveled so easily, the keep felt like it belonged to him. When he reached the throne room, now with a purpose he hadn't had before, he imagined himself arriving as a conqueror.

That wasn't too far from the truth, was it?

No torches burned. The great hall lay in shadow. Moonlight filtered through glass, cold and gray. Pilta moved to the wall directly behind the throne, to the secret he had found two days before the siege had begun.

He reached up, running his fingers along the seams of the stonework, looking for the latch. It wasn't easy. He had found it the first time only because he had discovered other, less well-hidden passages elsewhere, signs that the keep had been constructed with the need for secret escape in mind. He told himself that the throne room must have an emergency way out, one close to the throne itself.

He found the latch. A piece of iron disguised as mortar sank into the wall. A mechanism released, and a section of the stonework, the size of a small door, swung out. It made surprisingly little noise, and left a gap just wide enough for a human to squeeze through.

Pilta brushed the dust from his hands. He wondered again if anyone else in the castle knew this secret. He supposed Lady Felgard did, unless the knowledge of the passageway had somehow been forgotten between generations. It had clearly not been used for a long time, to judge by the dust on the wall. Perhaps there had never been a reason to use it. He didn't know when and if Northope had last fallen to enemies within or without.

284

DAVID ANNANDALE

No matter. It would fall now, if, as he expected, this passage led outside the city walls.

He hadn't ventured into the tunnel when he found it, but he had carefully examined the door and discovered that it could only be opened from the throne room side.

Unless it never properly closed at all.

He drove one of his picks into the lock at the top of the door, jamming the latch open. Then he stepped into the tunnel beyond and pulled the door closed. He strained, fingertips barely gripping the edge of stone, to pull it as flush as possible.

Now he had two doors he couldn't afford to have someone notice. He had raised the stakes of his gamble. But no one had ever looked in on him during the night, and there was no reason for anyone to check on this door.

No reason other than bad luck.

Pilta wanted to tell himself he was due for some good fortune. He feared the presumption of even articulating that thought. But he had lost everything he had known because of his foolishness. Tonight was different. Tonight, he sought atonement. Tonight, he was acting for Beresta, and for the gods.

With the door closed, he could see nothing. He reached out in the darkness, felt around, and his hand landed on a rope. It ran along the wall, passing through iron rungs, a guide for the fleeing ruler who had not had time to take up a torch.

Pilta started down the hall, stepping carefully, alert for a change in the angle of the rope. The change came, warning him of stairs. He took them as fast as he dared in the pitch blackness. The passageway curled around itself, descending through the keep.

The route felt long, longer, he hoped, than it really was. The stairs ended, then started again. The passage curved, went straight, took sharp angles, and looped through variations again and again. Pilta lost all sense of orientation. He had become a mouse working its way through a zigzagging

285

THE SLEEP OF EMPIRES

fault in the stone of the keep. Finally, the descent and the twisting stopped, and the passage ran straight and level for a long way. The air had become cooler, and more humid. It smelled earthy.

A faint breeze touched Pilta's face, and then, like the blessing of the gods, there came a graying of the darkness. Little by little, moonlight washed into the tunnel. Pilta no longer needed to hold the rope. He hurried down the last dozen yards and out into the night.

The tunnel had taken him well beyond the outer walls of Northope, and to the bank of the Keraps. A steep, high bank hid him from the city. A few feet away, hidden in weeds, a dock and a rowboat waited.

He could escape. He didn't need to do anything more that frightened him. He could take the boat that had waited, unneeded, through the generations of Felgards in Northope, and head off down the river, away from the siege, away from anywhere he might be known.

No. Do the right thing.

He turned away from the temptation of the boat, and worked his way east along the bank, toward the sounds of the siege.

The battle had gone on without cease by day and night since the beginning. The Hawkesmoores and the elves had not given Northope a single hour of respite. Elves needed much less sleep than humans, and so the attackers remained fresh, wearing down the defenders.

Yet they could not breach the walls. And perhaps, with the city holding firm, that was why no force had tried the plateau yet. They would be exposed on the slopes to assault from above and below.

I'm going to change all of that.

Pilta repeated the assurance to himself over and over, and with greater urgency the closer he came to the front lines. His heart pounded. What if a sentry killed him on sight? He didn't even know how to call out, how to signal his presence, how to ask to be taken to someone in command and be listened to.

He didn't even know when he should turn and climb.

286

DAVID ANNANDALE

He paused, looking up into the night, and the gloom of trees lining the top of the bank. He would be level with the armies now, he thought. Maybe this was good enough.

Dark figures emerged from the brush on either side of him. They seized his arms before he could run.

"What does this mean?" one voice asked, speaking elvish. "One of us, in ragged attire, skulking in the dark?"

"It means we've found him," said the other. "We've found the traitor."

"Please," said Pilta. "Please take me to—"

"To Skiriye ne Sincatsë?" said the first. "Have no fear, little thief. That's exactly where we're taking you."

Oh, no.

The First Librarian? Here? He hadn't imagined that possibility, not even in his nightmares.

Why is she here?

She has come to punish you. She has come a very long way. She will not be merciful.

He opened his mouth to beg to be taken to anyone else, even to be killed where he stood. There would be no point in pleading, though. And he would do his cause no favors. He said nothing, and let himself be led up the bank, through the trees, and down past the ranks of elves firing flaming arrows at the city. Some distance away, a huge siege tower ground slowly toward the walls. Humans on its upper platform fired more flaming arrows at the defenders.

Concentric rings of warriors surrounded the command tent. The level of alertness surprised Pilta. How much of a threat could the forces of Northope be this far from the wall? The soldiers looked as if they expected a massive counterattack at any moment.

Guards parted at the entrance, and Pilta's captors marched him into the tent.

287

THE SLEEP OF EMPIRES

There were officers present, and the commander, his radiant armor almost as stern and magnificent as his face. An older human was present, lordly in bearing and arms, though the metal work of his breastplate and the embroidery of his cloak were crude next to elvish craft.

Skiriye stood next to the round table. She cut a figure more terrible than ever by being dressed for battle. Her eyes widened at the sight of Pilta, and she gave him a look of the purest hatred.

She took a menacing step before him. She had traded in her usual cane for a heavier, more lethal one. "Commander Divine Witárë ne Seritsi," she said, her tone formal as a death sentence, "behold the singular cause of this war, Pilta ne Akwatse."

Witárë gazed down his nose at Pilta, as if he were contemplating a squashed grub. "Where did you find him?" he asked the captors.

"On the riverbank. Heading this way."

Witárë shook his head. "Is it pure stupidity that has brought us to this day? I ask because only a fool would betray his empire, flee it, then stumble back toward those who have come to punish his actions."

"I have come to atone." Pilta's words emerged a desperate, whispered croak.

"What is that?" said Skiriye. "My ears must have deceived me. I thought I heard you use the word *atone*. There is only one kind of offering the gods will accept from you. It is a burnt one."

"Take him away," Witárë ordered, his lip curling in disgust.

"I know a way in!" Pilta blurted.

Witárë held up a hand, halting the guards as they started to pull him from the tent. "A way in?"

"A passage that runs from the river to the throne room."

Skiriye snorted. "A lie. The only perfection he has ever shown is in his lies, Commander Divine."

"Come with me," Pilta pleaded, feeling his life teeter on a sword point. "I'll show you. I'll take you to the heart of the keep."

"To the heart of an ambush, he means."

288

DAVID ANNANDALE

Witárë studied him carefully. "That would be in keeping with your actions, to be sure."

"May Passomo blast me where I stand if I am lying." Pilta fought to hold back tears of frustration and fear. How could he make them believe when they had every reason to doubt him?

"Passomo has turned his back on you, as you have on him," Skiriye said. "He is deaf to your words. As are we."

"Your trap will not be sprung," said Witárë.

"But why would I do something that would be certain to get me killed?" Pilta asked, trying one more time. "How could I expect you to fall into such a trap and expect to survive myself? Why would I come anywhere near you at all?"

Skiriye and Witárë shared an uncertain glance.

"You know him better," said the Commander Divine.

"He is a fool, but one governed by selfishness," she said. "Nothing in his behavior tonight is in keeping with his past. It makes no sense."

Witárë stroked his chin, pensive. "So great a deviation gives me pause. Perhaps you were wrong, First Librarian. Perhaps, unlikely as it seems to me as well, Passomo has not abandoned him. Perhaps the hand of our Father guides him without his knowledge."

"To let him live another moment is to risk much. As I have learned."

"As have we all. I wonder, though. I wonder if the gods have opened the way for us. There have been . . . forces . . . arrayed against us and our divine purpose. This may be the counter to that evil."

Witárë's vague reference to forces made Pilta feel queasy. Whatever they were, had he unleashed them too by getting the *Book of the Null* to Northope? Were they the reason for the massive number of guards outside the tent? He felt the tally of his sins grow still larger.

"I know what the book is now," he said. "I didn't before. I just thought it was . . ." he shook his head in shame.

"You just thought it was worth gold," Skiriye said, her words etched in the acid of contempt.

289

THE SLEEP OF EMPIRES

Pilta nodded, his face burning. "I know better. The book must be stopped." There had to be a better way of phrasing what he feared. He didn't have time to think of it. He had to make them believe he meant what he said. If not for his own sake, for that of Beresta, and of the world, and of the gods.

In the end, to his astonishment, Skiriye decided to put his sincerity to the test before Witárë did. "With your leave, Commander Divine, I will take a squad with the prisoner to see if this passage exists. I will send back word if it does."

"Agreed," said Witárë. He looked at Pilta. "If what you say is true, you will have given us victory this night."

"That's why I came."

Witárë gave him a thin smile. "A true step toward atonement."

Pilta lowered his head. "Thank you, Commander Divine."

The guards took him outside. They waited with him, a few yards from the tent, while Skiriye and her squad prepared to head out. When they were ready, Witárë emerged from the tent to watch them leave, the human lord a step behind.

Skiriye crossed her arms and bowed. "Passomo guide us all," she said.

"Passomo guide us," Witárë echoed.

"The Voidwatch . . ." she began.

Witárë nodded. "If you succeed, then you open the way to that too."

"The mist . . . ?" said the human.

"If this is the moment," said Witárë, irritated by the interruption. "We have only enough for one assault. It must be the one that counts." He turned back to Skiriye. "I believe this is the time. I feel Passomo's hand. The Voidwatch will fall."

"Then my only regret will be not to be present for the end of the threat," said Skiriye.

They parted. At the head of a group of twenty warriors, Skiriye marched over to where Pilta was held.

"Release him," she said.

290

DAVID ANNANDALE

The strong hands let go of his arms. He made sure to stand very still. His muscles ached from being gripped so long.

"I would shackle you," said Skiriye, "if I did not want to avoid the clanking of your chains."

"I will not try to flee."

"I almost wish you would. I need very little excuse to kill you."

"I understand."

"Do you? I have my doubts. Your understanding has always been deficient."

"It has," he said with feeling. She couldn't imagine how utterly he agreed with her.

"Show us the way, then," said Skiriye. "Prove to me that you speak truly for once."

They moved off, off the fields, into the trees, and back down to the path along the riverbank. The party marched in single file, Pilta at the lead, Skiriye close behind him. Pilta kept his pace even, careful not to give the slightest hint of wanting to break into a run.

The journey back took less time than the outward one, but it seemed longer. Pilta felt the presence of Skiriye at his back like an unsheathed blade.

If I'd known she was here . . .

He stopped the thought.

You'd have done the same thing, because it must be done. It is the only right course of action.

It would be comforting to believe that of himself. It would make him feel heroic.

They arrived at the dock, and Pilta found the entrance to the tunnel. This time, there were torches, and he could see the rough-hewn stonework of the passageway. It looked ancient, as if the rest of the castle had grown up around it.

The elves moved in silence, blades at the ready. Pilta hurried faster, urged by the impatience at his back. He wished they were already at the

THE SLEEP OF EMPIRES

throne room door. He prayed to Passomo that nothing had happened, that no one had come by to lock the door.

Down the passage, up the flights of stairs, back and forth through the switchbacks and the spirals, he took the squad deeper and higher into the keep. Almost there, he told himself. Almost there, and Skiriye would know he had been telling the truth.

He would give Beresta its victory. He would prove he could atone. Perhaps, in time, he might even earn forgiveness, at least from the gods.

When he finally walked the final stretch of hall, he saw the very slight unevenness where the door met the wall, and he knew the way lay open. "There," he said softly, and pointed. "That's the door. On the other side is the throne room."

Skiriye put a hand on Pilta's shoulder, her grip like iron. She pushed him to the side, and her warriors flowed past him. The lead listened at the door, then nodded to the others.

"Good," said Skiriye. "Send word."

Two elves ran back down the hall, heading off to bring reinforcements.

The lead warrior pushed the door open, and the elves began their invasion of Northope.

Skiriye's grip did not slacken. She held Pilta in place, making him face forward.

"You see?" he began.

"Yes, you spoke the truth." No warmth in her voice. He hadn't expected there would be. But the anger had not diminished at all. "I, too, spoke truly."

The blade shoved through his back and out his chest. Silver pain filled his body.

"This is the only offering the gods will accept from you."

She pulled out the sword. The silver pain exploded, and then fell into the last darkness.

CHAPTER 24

The siege tower burned brightly, flames raging up from the base. They engulfed its timbers, their anger and oil pushing them higher and higher until the tower became a torch. Hawkesmoore soldiers hurled themselves from the top, fleeing the flames to die when they hit the ground. Others, caught inside the shutters, burned like rats in a chimney.

Vorykas hacked at the axle of the rear wheels while Latanna kept the soldiers at bay. She moved faster, and with greater skill, than she had the night before. Each night she improved her art. The feast she had made of elves strengthened her even as it spread fear through the ranks of the enemy. They had not been able to strike deep enough into the elvish army for her to sink her claws into any officers, but her prey served her well, Vorykas thought, against humans.

He snapped through the axle. The wheels came off, and the platform slumped backward. Weakened by the fire, the tower jolted, wavered, and then collapsed, a great column of timber and flame roaring down on the soldiers behind.

Vorykas sidestepped the fall with Latanna and cut down retreating Hawkesmoore troops. Burning wreckage spread across the field, forcing the enemy back, creating a gap near the front gate.

The fall of the tower was the signal. The gate opened. Riding out at the head of a mounted force, Ossia Felgard led Northope's first sortie against the attackers.

Vorykas and Latanna turned back from pursuing the enemy to join the head of the charge. They flanked Ossia, helping forge the way forward for as she drove into the foe, spear out, the tip impaling skulls and chests.

The Northope cavalry rode in a wedge. It hammered the Hawkesmoores, splitting the ranks wider and forcing them back.

293

THE SLEEP OF EMPIRES

"For Northope and the Voidwatch!" Ossia cried. "Defy the gods and ride for freedom!"

Defy the gods, Vorykas thought. He wiped blood from his face and blocked a blow so violently he broke the man's wrists. "Defy them," he growled, and cut the soldier's arm off. *Yes. Tear them from the sky. And ride, but not too far. This isn't victory yet.*

The sortie should be a probe, a quick stab to weaken the enemy a bit more, and then pull back to the strong point. Ossia rode in fury, as if she would trample all Hawkesmoore troops and elves beneath her horse's hooves in a single run. The momentum of anger and justice would doom her if she went much further, and the regrouping armies cut off the retreat. To the north, where the elves held the field, the hail of flaming arrows dropped to almost nothing.

Why have they stopped? They can't be retreating. They have no reason to.

Ugly premonition squeezed his chest. Somehow, Ossia had chosen the wrong moment to charge.

Fifty yards, a hundred, a hundred and fifty, two hundred.

Enough. He did not command here. He had no right to direct the conduct of the war. But he could see what would happen, and if Ossia were on the wall and not caught up in the frenzy of retribution, she would too.

"Lady Felgard!" Vorykas called. He chopped the legs out from under a solider who lunged forward to grab the reins.

Screams and the sounds of battle from the rear cut him off. They brought Ossia up short. The charge faltered as everyone looked back.

New fires had broken out in Northope. Smoke billowed out of the windows of the keep itself. The sight of the impregnable fortress alight had spread panic in the streets of the city. The enemy had found a way in. Before long, the foe would be on the walls, and then Northope would fall.

If it hasn't already.

And then, to the north, a sudden fog spread up from the base of the plateau. It glowed in the night, a sick orange streaked with angry red and flashes of green. Its tendrils reached up toward the peak of the plateau, a writhing promise of death.

One front had become three. The disaster revealed itself to Vorykas in moments, and the helpless need to be in multiple places at once showed him how wrong everything had suddenly gone. Then he saw the shift in the battlefield as if from a great height, as if he were a god looking down on the trivial, expendable pieces of a game. The retreat of the Hawkesmoores had been a feint to draw Ossia further from the city. Ossia's troops were caught in a pincer, with enemies on both sides of the city wall. The defenders of the Voidwatch were isolated. No reinforcements could reach them. With the city on the edge of destruction, the elves had a free hand to assault the plateau.

That mist was the work of elves. It had to be. Even as it crawled up the cliff, a pulsing foulness, it shimmered with beauty. Care had gone into its crafting. Art had been yoked to poison.

"Go!" Ossia shouted, her cry raw with anger, grief, and desperation. "You and Latanna, go! You can get through that horror. I know you can! Save the Voidwatch! If Northope falls, the truth must not die with it. Save us from the gods and their lies!"

She wheeled her horse around, and charged back into the regrouping enemy, back toward her city and its agony.

"Don't concern yourself with what's behind us," Kanstuhn ordered. "Keep shooting at the foe below."

When the fires began in the keep, and the sounds of battle reached the streets, distress rippled along the ramparts. The steady, relentless hail of arrows faltered. The rhythm of *rise, loose, cover* had become automatic for Alisteyr. Even during his brief shifts away from the wall, when he had the chance to eat and sleep for a few hours, he launched arrows in his dreams.

The eruption within the city broke the discipline on the ramparts. The soldiers, trained, kept to their posts. The recruits began to panic. It took Kanstuhn's voice to hold Alisteyr in place. Garwynn obeyed too.

THE SLEEP OF EMPIRES

"Rise!" Captain Arva's voice was hoarse and stressed, but the shout came all the same, as if disaster was not unfolding at her back. *"Loose! Cover!"*

Alisteyr did, and he saw the need to keep the arrows flying. The siege tower had fallen, but the Hawkesmoores were moving forward, more of their ladders already at the wall. Alisteyr caught a brief glimpse of the cavalry riding hard back to the gate, a reversal that hurt his heart as much as the ride out had giving him hope.

When he crouched, he couldn't help himself.

"Don't look back," Kanstuhn repeated. "What happens there is nothing we can affect. Not yet."

Alisteyr looked back anyway. High up on the Prow, black smoke billowed from the unreachable keep. Along the switchback of the approach up the castle rock, elves and Northope guards fought. The elves cut through the guards as though they were barely worth the effort. How long before they reached the city streets, and then the wall?

Minutes, Alisteyr thought. Minutes that would feel like seconds.

"What's going to happen?" Garwynn asked.

Rise. Loose. Cover.

"We're going to keep the Hawkesmoores off the wall as long as we can," said Kanstuhn. "And Lady Felgard will take the fight to the elves in the streets."

"And then?"

Kanstuhn fired quickly, three times. He killed men hoisting a ladder, and it fell back.

"We don't know, and it doesn't matter," he said. "We fight as we must."

Alisteyr swallowed. He glanced at Garwynn. "If you could find your magic," he said, "now would be the time."

They ran through the fog, sprinting uphill to catch up with the force of elves. The mist crawled over Vorykas' flesh, slick as oil, yet digging in like a million biting insects. It reached under his armor. In moments, blood soaked his face, his arms, his torso. It ran down his legs and pooled inside

296

DAVID ANNANDALE

his boots. When he breathed, filament needles sliced into his throat and lungs, and he coughed up wads of gory phlegm. The mist pierced his eyes, and though he healed and healed and healed, his vision smeared with pain and blood.

He kept running and did not slow, racing up through the spasming cloud that grew thicker and more abrasive closer to the top of the plateau. Beside him, Latanna flew through the cloud, her bare skull untouched by signs of blood.

"Are you all right?" she asked.

He nodded, spat blood. "It can't quite hurt me fast enough," he said. "Do you know what this is?"

"It's in some of the memories I ate. It's a mortal killer. Harmless to elves."

"And to the resurrected, it seems."

"But to you?"

He spat again. His mouth kept filling with blood. "A great irritant."

They reached the top of the plateau. They tore past the line of abandoned mangonels. The corpses of Northope soldiers littered the ground. They lay twisted in their final throes of agony, their flesh torn and melted, their eyes punctured. Their bones protruded, white and smeared with red, from the broken sacks of their bodies.

The mist thinned out after the first dozen yards, dissipating across the expanse of the plateau. Ahead, the elves had surrounded the tower. As Vorykas and Latanna pounded down the path, the elves broke through the door. A number of them went up, while most of the force remained on the path, turning to block access to the Voidwatch. They launched a volley of arrows.

Vorykas ducked and weaved. Latanna, faster now than he was, knocked arrows from the air with her sword. They both took hits, but not enough to slow them down.

On the right, the gorge yawned, filled with a darkness so thick, Vorykas imagined he could swim in it. The dark seemed to ripple with strength,

297

THE SLEEP OF EMPIRES

with the absolute end to all questions. It tugged at the edge of his vision, like a promise, like a lure.

He pulled away, kept his focus on survival. He and Latanna ran the gauntlet of the arrows and hit the elves like a spear point. He used his mass and speed, smashing into the warriors. He broke bones and shields, and Latanna came in lower, slashing open bellies, blocking attacks as fast as they came, fighting with the accumulated skills of consumed mortals and immortals. They crashed through the defense and into the Void-watch.

They didn't slow. The narrow space of the stairs would work in their favor, at least for the moment. Until they reached an open space, they could not be overwhelmed by numbers.

Vorykas took the lead, loping up the stairs three at a time. His flesh had sealed itself again. His lungs felt strong, and his vision had cleared.

But even though he could no longer see the gorge, the darkness clawed at the edge of his consciousness, scrabbling for a grip.

He burst into the chamber at the top of the stairs, and stopped dead. So did Latanna. The scene held them back.

There were six elves present, all of them in the raiment of the elite. One of them had Skaitaias pinned against the far wall, his deceptively elegant rapier held at the mathematician's throat. It had pricked the flesh just under the chin, and a thin trickle of blood ran down the old man's neck. The leader, marked out by armor even richer in minutely worked engravings than the others, stood in the center of the chamber, sword in one hand, dagger in the other. The rest of the troops flanked him. They blocked the way to Skaitaias. Their stance seemed relaxed, but Vorykas read the ability to leap in any direction.

These ones are dangerous, he thought. He saw no arrogance or foolish assurance in their eyes. They regarded him with a cool, cautious, measuring awareness. *They know how to fight.*

Two humans had accompanied the elves. Roylence and Elgin Hawkes-moore hovered at the rear, staying out of the way. Masks hung at their sword

298

belts. Their silver-threaded material looked suppler than calfskin. They had, Vorykas guessed, seen the two men safely through the mist.

"So you are what has been troubling us," the leader of the elves said. He regarded Vorykas and Latanna as if they were serpents caught under his boot. "An obscene mongrel, and one of the void's grotesques."

Latanna stiffened. If the elf meant to imply that he knew more about what she was than she did, the bolt had struck home. She hit back. She cocked her skull to one side, as if considering the curious being in front of her. "And you," she said, "appear to have decided, for some reason, that you should be very pleased with what you are."

The elf's lips twitched slightly, the only sign of suppressed displeasure. "I am Witárë ne Seritsi, Commander Divine," he said. "Destroyer of the Voidwatch, and all the vermin I find therein."

"How nice for you," said Vorykas. He thought about throwing a dagger at the elf holding Skaitaias prisoner. No, he decided. He knew how quickly ordinary elf soldiers could move.

Booted feet tramped up the stairs. Witárë held up a finger, staying the advance of the troops, keeping the space uncluttered with excess bodies.

"Speaking of vermin," said Latanna. "I see some Hawkesmoore varieties. Hello, Elgin. Did you still want my hand in marriage?"

Elgin jerked back, bumping into the wall behind him, eyes wide. His father hissed at him, and he straightened, trying to look menacing instead of frightened.

Witárë sniffed. "Come and be destroyed, then, when you choose. I have other matters to attend to." He glanced over his shoulder. "So, heretic. You see. There is no rescue for you. Where is the book?"

Skaitaias said nothing. The elf's blade poked a bit harder, and his blood ran more freely.

"Where is the book?" Witárë repeated, facing forward. "You have no choice."

"You are mistaken," said Skaitaias. "You would not want me to lean forward and impale myself. Then you would never find the book."

299

THE SLEEP OF EMPIRES

Witárë smiled tightly. "*Never* is a word you have no right to utter, mathematician. Your understanding of time is too weak. We have come to destroy this tower. The only thing your decision affects is how quickly we will go about it. If we have to demolish it one stone at a time, then so be it." He shrugged. "Now where is the book?"

"The elves are going to kill you, too," Latanna said to Elgin. "You shouldn't have come here."

"We came to see the victory here," said Roylence. "We don't want to know what it means."

"We don't?" Elgin asked, genuinely confused.

"Be *quiet!*" Roylence rounded on him. "I should not have let you accompany me. Do not shame me further."

"Do you want to know what the book is about?" Latanna asked. "I can tell you."

"*No!*" Roylence yelled. He jerked forward, sword raised, instinct urging him to silence the threat.

Startled, the elf holding Skaitaias looked away for a moment.

Vorykas threw a knife. It impaled the elf's right hand, and he dropped the sword. Skaitaias slumped down and to the side.

Vorykas and Latanna attacked. Witárë and his escorts stepped forward to meet them, their movements as unhurried as if they had already rehearsed and memorized every step of the coming dance.

Vorykas closed with Witárë. He brought his sword down with a two-handed slash, counting on his greater strength and mass to break through the block the elf would have to attempt. The block came, but turned into a feint. Witárë moved into a dodge, his body flowing with the ease of water. Vorykas overshot, his momentum carrying him to the space of an absent foe. He hit the stone floor with his sword. Sparks flew, and the elvish blade, viper-quick and venom-strong, stabbed through his armor as if it were paper, plunging deep into his side. Witárë struck twice before Vorykas could turn. Pain spread through his midsection, a liquid fire.

DAVID ANNANDALE

He swept wide as he came at Witárë again. He forced another elf back who had come to aid her commander. Witárë appeared unconcerned. He regarded Vorykas with a mixture of mild curiosity and spiritual disgust. He invited attacks, then sidestepped them as if they were beneath his notice, and thrust viciously home.

Vorykas healed, yet the wounds came faster and deeper. Agony ripped through his veins and muscles. He felt as if Witárë were cutting the strings that animated his body one at a time. He lost coordination. His attacks became clumsier, even easier for Witárë to avoid.

He had fought and killed elves during the first nights of the siege. They were quicker and more agile than the humans he was used to fighting, but they had not presented a real challenge. This elf was different. His skills surpassed the common run of his troops as a mountain towers over a foothill. Centuries and millennia had honed his craft to perfection.

At the edge of his awareness, Vorykas saw Latanna fighting hard, outnumbered but holding her own. She had elvish speed and an accumulation of skills and memories, but she had not fed on officers. They had her surrounded, a siege in miniature. Chips of bone hit the ground, mixing with elf blood.

The Hawkesmoores stayed at the rear, watching, content to let the war be won without risk.

Witárë shifted to more direct attacks. His limbs loose and sluggish, Vorykas backed away, forced onto the defensive. For every thrust and lunge that he parried, two more got through, weakening and slowing him further.

Witárë drove him back. The elf fought with one arm loose at his side, his walk casual, a swordsman engaged in a minor exercise.

The windowsill dug into Vorykas' waist. Emptiness whispered eagerness.

Witárë snorted, bored. "You are not worth the trouble you have caused. You are no challenge."

THE SLEEP OF EMPIRES

In a blur, he held his sword with two hands. The overhead slash came. Vorykas tried to block it, but it descended at an angle he had not foreseen. The blade cut his right arm off at the elbow.

"You are nothing," said Witárë.

The shock of the pain and explosion of blood dizzied Vorykas. He lost his balance and tipped over backward.

He felt the unseen maw of the gorge open to receive him.

"Nothing at all," said Witárë.

As Vorykas fell, it seemed to him that he had always known he would.

CHAPTER 25

They were so fast. When Garwynn first saw the smoke coming from the keep, and Kanstuhn kept his and Alisteyr's focus on defending the wall as if the disaster was not upon them, he made himself believe that the invaders could be turned back or that they would have to fight long and hard to reach the wall and put an end to Northope.

He had been wrong. The elves went through Lady Felgard's troops like water roaring through a steep stream bed. The narrow streets and sharp turns of the city, which would have worked in Northope's favor against a human enemy, played instead to the elves' advantage. With no space for the greater numbers of the defenders to be brought to bear, all that mattered was skill and speed.

And now the elves had arrived at the base of the wall.

Garwynn let fly another arrow below, and then sounds of battle from the other side of the wall froze him in uncertainty. He shared a panicked look with Alisteyr, who trembled, his eyes darting back and forth.

Kanstuhn hissed in anger. "Curse this race," he said. "Curse their arrogance and their skill." He fired two more arrows below, and then rushed to the rear edge of the wall.

The Northope officers tried to marshal a dual defense. They ordered the fighters closest to the main gates to defend the rear. Garwynn and Alisteyr obeyed. Garwynn's body had gone numb. He moved with the certainty that he ran to his death.

He hadn't taken three steps when the first elves appeared on the wall, and the slaughter began. The elves spread out along the ramparts, cutting down guards and recruits alike with contemptuous ease.

Garwynn dropped his bow and pulled out his sword. He looked at the blade, at this clumsy tool in his ignorant hands, and knew he could do nothing.

THE SLEEP OF EMPIRES

Kanstuhn attacked an elf the moment the enemy reached the battlements, and held his own. He used his smaller, slighter frame to evade the elf's blows, though the elf blocked all of his strikes.

Alisteyr howled, less with defiance than with despair, and rushed forward.

No. I won't let you end your saga in futility!

Garwynn sprinted at his side, and an elf turned to meet them.

Maybe two of us, the two of us, maybe.

The elf gave them a crooked grin and raised his sword.

So fast.

Garwynn and Alisteyr reacted together, with instinctive terror. They brought up their swords in an accidental cross of defense that blocked the descent of the elf's blade. The force of the blow knocked Garwynn's weapon from his hand. He and Alisteyr stumbled and fell.

The elf shook his head in disgust and stepped forward to finish them off.

Garwynn raised his hands to ward off death, and sent all his will and need for something, something, *anything* to happen, for the power that ran now and then through his veins with perversity and alien whim to help him now, now, *now*.

Now!

Desultory sparks danced in mockery over his palms.

Vorykas fell. He shouted defiance at the coming impact. He roared at his failure, at the battle he had lost, and the cost his failure would mean for those he cared about.

He thought about Latanna, and shouted even louder.

Then the dark swallowed him, and the tower vanished from his sight.

The end now, then, he thought. A few moments more of the air streaming past.

Only he no longer felt the wind of his plunge.

304

DAVID ANNANDALE

He felt only dark, complete and utter and eternal unto itself with the total purity of untainted void. It took him. It entered him.

It had waited so long.

And he knew not to fight.

At its touch, recognition flowered.

It is mine.

No, no, more than that.

Recognition, understanding, *remembering.*

IT IS ME.

The sky shook.

Not the wall, not the ground. The sky itself. The tremor yanked Garwynn's attention from the elf, his mind flailing with the inability to comprehend what his eyes were telling it.

The elf paused in his attack, and looked up. His jaw gaped in shock.

And when the screams from the sky began, the fire leapt from Garwynn's open palms, and turned the elf into a writhing torch.

They heard the screams in Ghaunthook. They heard them in Korvas. They heard them everywhere in Wiramzin.

And across Beresta, and in the northern elvish empire of Deltia.

The screams poured from the shaking sky in the south, over the majestic human cities of Kamastia, and to the east, inside the hollowed-out hills of Gulsentia, the dwarves clapped their hands over their ears and fell to their knees.

Still further to the east, in impoverished Keteria, across the land blighted by an endless age of conquests and exploitation, the kauls kneeled too, and looked up, and wondered what would make the gods of their tormentors wail in terror.

And in Korvas, in the watchtowers that looked east where uncountable generations of complacent guards had known only boredom, a cry of panic went up.

THE SLEEP OF EMPIRES

"The flames! The flames!"

The bell sounded, the bell that had not rung in the remembered history of Korvas, the bell that spread panic across the city with the news of what the guards had seen, what all who looked east toward the towering plateau of Voran could see, as could every settlement within sight of the vast, dead land.

A wall of flame, five thousand feet high, erupted from the base of the vertical cliffs. The great belt of flame surrounded all of the dark plateau.

Voran had awoken.

With tremor and howl and fire, the sleep of empires shattered into a million nightmares.

Latanna kept her feet when the gods screamed. She felt awe, but no terror. She felt an even greater sense of expectation. So did Skaitaias. While the elves and the Hawkesmoores staggered and fell, she and Skaitaias turned to the window, and witnessed the moment in which the Voidwatch fulfilled its purpose.

They saw Vorykas return.

He floated up, draped in night, and entered the chamber. Tendrils of darkness fluttered behind him, like torn banners in a wind. His face had changed. Latanna still recognized him, but where before his gray skin and blend of features had given him the aura of resembling every race in Eloran, now he truly resembled none. His face had become a mask that barely concealed the void that preceded and determined and followed all being.

Nothing concealed the void of his right arm. From the elbow to the fingers was the shape of a limb, carved from the black of true absence.

Vorykas stood quietly until the sky screams faded. In the silence that came after, he said, "I remember."

Latanna had never heard so deep and consequential a rage carried by two simple words.

Witárë recovered first among the elves. He staggered to his feet. "Weiakasask," he hissed. "Betrayer of Passomo!"

306

DAVID ANNANDALE

Vorykas reached out with his right arm. The black void stretched out and seized Witárë. It lifted the elf into the air. "That is not my name. And that is not my crime. Your god and your liars gave me that name. Mine, the one I chose, has always been Vorykas, though *my* betrayers tried to stamp it out."

Witárë struggled in the blackness. He choked. His flesh began to run in rivulets.

"No more lies," said Vorykas, and the void devoured Witárë.

Some of the elves tried to attack him. Some of them tried to flee. It didn't matter. The arm spread out, a physical shadow, and took them. It covered them, ended their screams, and withdrew, leaving emptiness where they had been.

He only took the feet of two of them. They fell, agonized, close to Latanna.

"You're hurt," he said, anger giving way to concern.

She nodded. She had lost several ribs and her left hand in the fight. The fractures in her legs made it difficult to stand.

"Will they help?" Vorykas nodded at the two elves.

"Oh, yes," she said. "And be useful, too." She finally had the chance to feast on the elite warriors of Beresta.

They fed her well, in memories and skills, and when she rose from their husks, she felt better than renewed. She moved toward Vorykas. As if he had been waiting for that signal from her, he stepped her way as well. He touched the tip of her horned crown with his dark fingers, the gesture as tender as his anger with Witárë had been savage.

Latanna felt the touch of the void through the crown. With mounting joy, she began to understand what she had sworn herself to on the night of her marriage. She touched Vorykas' face with wonder, sensing now the mask.

She was about to take his void hand, but he stopped her.

"Please wait."

"Is it dangerous for me?"

307

THE SLEEP OF EMPIRES

"I don't know yet. I remember, but not everything yet. I've only regained the first fragment of my self."

"Fragment?"

"The other gods could not kill me, but they did shatter and scatter me. I'm not whole. I don't know everything I should."

"Can you be whole again?"

"I will be." The words rang with the deep anger of an abyss, and the face barely contained the roiling of the void behind it.

"I will be with you on that day," said Latanna. She touched his face again, and then kissed him, skull touching mask, death meeting a membrane over emptiness.

"I could not ask for a greater gift," said Vorykas.

He turned and pointed at the Hawkesmoores. "What about them?" he asked. "Are they useful?"

The two men had backed all the way up against the wall, looking as if they would press themselves through the stones if they could. The blood had drained from their faces, along with all remnants of their arrogance. Only fear remained. Roylence had his sword out, but no longer seemed to know how to use it. Elgin had dropped his. He had his hands up over his mouth and hyperventilated loudly.

Latanna advanced toward them. She shook her head at Elgin. "You have nothing I need," she said. "And I really don't want to taste your memories."

The blackness flowed out of Vorykas' arms toward the youngest Hawkesmoore.

Latanna faced Roylence. "You, though. I bet you're just full of schemes worth knowing."

Roylence lunged with his sword. Latanna sidestepped the strike and sank her fingers into his throat.

Alisteyr scrambled away from the explosion of fire. The elf screamed, and then the screams burned away, and the thing of flames staggered, arms

308

spinning from within the core of fire. The elf flipped over the parapet and fell among the Hawkesmoore troops.

"Garwynn?" Alisteyr asked.

Garwynn looked at his hands. They flickered with little flames running over them in streams. Garwynn smiled. *Smiled.* "I can make this happen," he said, his voice quivering with delighted awe. "I can control the flame." He shook his head. "I can *do* this!"

"How . . ." Alisteyr began, but then Garwynn sent a ball of fire streaking over the spot where he crouched. It hit another elf in the chest, setting him alight, and the impact knocked him flying. Garwynn turned and unleashed more flames, and then again, and then again, burning more and more of the enemy, forcing the elves back, giving the Northope troops in this region of the wall the chance to turn the tide.

Alisteyr struggled to his feet and picked up his sword. For the moment, there was no enemy near him. The battle raged just out of his useless reach. He existed in a bubble of calm, one where he could observe and think.

That scream. The shaking of the sky. How can anyone still fight? Why hasn't everything changed?

He moved to the parapet, sheathed his sword, and picked up his discarded bow. He nocked an arrow, because he could do nothing else, and so he understood why the armies fought, and why they fought with ferocious desperation.

Things have ended. Things are beginning. We're fighting to say that we matter, that we have meaning, because what if we don't?

Kanstuhn showed none of the desperation. He fought with a savage joy, as if he had tapped into the same magic as Garwynn. As the war shifted and the world spun out of control, he leapt at the disoriented elves with a renewed energy, his sword stabbing like the fangs of a feral wolf. He shot Alisteyr a ferocious, bloody grin, then jumped onto the crenellations to hack at the soldiers climbing up a ladder to die.

Alisteyr shot at the foe below, and tried not to think.

THE SLEEP OF EMPIRES

Movement on the slope of the plateau drew his attention. He looked, and his hand stayed. He stared, new fear seizing him. A darkness so great it made the night seem like noon descended the plateau. Narrow, sinuous, profound, it headed for the plains of Northope, leaving stillness in its wake.

A small thing, from this distance, yet huge as a wound in reality itself. Alisteyr trembled, frozen by the thought that this moving wound had shaken the sky and made the gods scream.

Skiriye had let her troops race on ahead of her, down through the keep and into the streets of Northope. With her imperfect leg, she could not match their speed. She gave them their orders and set them loose. They did not need her leading from the front. The humans of Northope had no chance of standing up to the attack. They had lost.

She took her time descending the keep. It was hers now, after all. She passed through the throne room, thought how it would never be used by the Felgards again, and then sought out a window that looked south and east. From high in the keep, she would see the full vista of the triumph.

Then the sky shook, and the wails forced her into a horrified crouch. When she looked again, the sliver of void descended the slope, coiling and uncoiling with the strength of the unholy. No one pursued it. The top of the plateau was still as death.

The moving darkness confronted her with failure, a failure whose scale she could not grasp without hurling herself from the tower in despair. She wished she could kill Pilta again, and more slowly, and she wished too that he still lived, so he could see what he had wrought.

She owned the failure too, because he had stolen the book on her watch, and now . . .

Now . . .

She could not let herself think it. She could not face it.

Skiriye turned from the window and ran, fleeing for the tunnels that would take her away from this place, fleeing from the coming future and the nightmare she had not stopped.

310

DAVID ANNANDALE

* * *

Vorykas arrived at the battlefield. Latanna rushed ahead of him, death triumphant and majestic. He followed, his arm the blackness that comes after death. He sent out the void. He sent out himself. He became a narrow stream, a whip, a serpent of ending. What he touched vanished at his will. There was pain in the vanishing. The shrieks that came with it, though short, keened the great notes of rarified despair. He lashed into the Hawkesmoore army, carving it apart like a long-awaited feast.

He felt a tug at his consciousness. On the ramparts, masses of fire flew left and right.

Sorcery, he thought. *Magic.*

And he thought: *That too is me.* The magic came from nothing, and he was nothing. His partial reconstruction made the impossible possible.

So much more to do.

The recovery of this fragment of himself made him all the more aware of what he had lost, and what remained missing.

So much more to find.

Kanstuhn appeared on the ramparts. In triumph, the kaul seemed bigger than the dying elves not far from him. Vorykas saluted, and Kanstuhn answered with a wave.

So much to tell you, my old friend, my savior.

Vorykas flexed the dark absence, and the long coil of his arm swallowed a dozen soldiers.

For now, though, this would do.

He would scour Northope of Hawkesmoores and elves, and that would be a fine beginning.

CHAPTER 26

Late in the afternoon, they stopped on the western shore of the Athar River. The current ran hard and deep, black water foaming gray. Dark steam rolled in thick clouds. On the other side, only a few hundred yards away now, the flame barrier of Voran roared, volcanic curtains shifting back and forth in a dance of fury. Had he been human, Vorykas' flesh would have blistered from the heat. Latanna, her unnatural dead beauty untouched by the intensity, looked up at the barrier, eyes shining with eagerness.

"Come with us," Vorykas said to Kanstuhn. He had to try once more. He used his void limb to create a shadow around Kanstuhn, shielding him from the heat. "After all the road we've traveled, we should be together for this moment."

"But this isn't the end of the road, is it?" said Kanstuhn.

"No," said Vorykas.

"We're all just at the beginning. Lady Felgard at the start of her crusade. Garwynn and who knows how many like him coming into the first true manifestations of their abilities." Kanstuhn smiled. "All of Eloran facing the first days of its awakening."

"Me still learning what I have become," said Latanna.

"Exactly." He looked steadily at Vorykas. "All of this because you have taken the first steps of your . . . reclamation of your being."

"Why did you hesitate?" Vorykas asked.

"He almost said *vengeance*," Latanna guessed.

"Did you?"

"Should I have?" Kanstuhn asked.

Now Vorykas hesitated. The monstrous flames roared their welcome, calling for his commands. "I'm not sure yet."

"The other gods are. We heard them. They are terrified and will act. You are at war."

DAVID ANNANDALE

"Yes, I am." Driven by a memory of betrayal and crime ages old, anger warmed his blood. Most of his body was still a prison of flesh. Only his right forearm was truly him, an incomplete echo of the unlimited strength of nothingness.

It was enough to begin with. Through it, he knew who he was. He knew what had been done to him. He would find the rest of his scattered self, and he would bring the edifice of divine lies down in ruin.

"So you see," said Kanstuhn. "All just a start."

"All the more reason for you to be with us."

"I was there for the true beginnings in Ghaunthook and at Northope. I will join you later." The kaul gave the flame barrier a look of longing. "I want to see the wonders. But there will be time for that."

Vorykas sighed. "After Korvas, then."

"Yes. After Korvas, at the very least. The crusade will need its spies and saboteurs."

"And you said Alisteyr will be there."

"Yes. He has hopes for the university."

"I don't think he wants his sagas anymore," Latanna said sadly. "They haven't been kind to him. Maybe he'll be happier buried in scholarship."

"For now," said Kanstuhn. "No one will be able to stay hidden when the gods go to war."

"Then he'll need a friend," said Latanna.

"I'll do what I can."

"Thank you."

Vorykas held out his left hand, and Kanstuhn took it. "I owe you more than can be repaid," he said.

"I am alive to see the twilight of empires," said Kanstuhn. "No small gift."

He left them, and they swam across the river, submerging often and for a long time, but neither needed to breathe. They emerged from the water only a few yards from the edge of the flames.

313

THE SLEEP OF EMPIRES

"These are yours," said Latanna, her voice soft, yet sounding clearly in Vorykas' ears over the thunder of the fire.

"Mine," Vorykas murmured.

He walked forward. The flames parted for him. He reached out with his void arm, and fire coiled around the darkness.

The awakening land welcomed home the nightmare.

The End of Book One

Acknowledgments

The gestation period of this novel has been the longest of any I have ever written, what with its earliest stirrings in my imagination dating back to the 70s. Given this, a full accounting of the debts I owe is shamefully beyond the reach of my memory. And so, I begin with apologies to all whom I should have mentioned here and have forgotten to do so.

Huge thanks to my agent, Robert Lecker, for all the years of support and encouragement, and for having found this long-held dream of mine a home. And thank you to everyone at Start Publishing for giving it that home. I am particularly grateful to my editor, Rene Sears, for her belief in the book, and for her unerring guidance. Many thanks also to Ashley Calvano for the stunning cover, and to Meghan Kilduff whose eagle-eyed copyediting has saved my present self from the errors of my past self.

I really cannot overstate how much I owe to Michael Kaan. The forms that Voranian and elvish languages take here owe everything to his linguistic expertise, and his suggestions and explanations involving Baltic Prussian and Tocharian. It's a cliché to say that anything that works in this department is due to him, and anything that doesn't is my fault, but I have rarely felt this truth so viscerally. Our writing sessions also did a great deal to keep me on track.

And on the subject of writing sessions, not to mention general mutual encouragement, advice, and friendship, thanks are also due to Stephen D. Sullivan.

Over the course of writing *The Sleep of Empires*, I had the opportunity to put family and friends through a tabletop RPG conversion of the narrative. This was huge fun for me, and the brainstorms it triggered fed back into the creative process. For having gone through this adventure with me, I have to thank Veronica Young, Devon Kinley, Robert Baxter, Bill Kerr, Dale Krawchuk, William O'Donnell, and Kelly Stifora.

315

ACKNOWLEDGMENTS

And then there is my family. I am, and always will be, beyond honored and humbled to have been shown by Kelan and Veronica Young what a privilege it is to be a stepfather. And to my wife, Margaux Watt, who was there for me in every way (including taking part in the games) during the writing of the project, who is and has always been there for me in more ways than I can count or articulate, all my deepest love and profound gratitude.

And finally, thank you, gentle reader, for having come with me this far. That you have done so makes this all worthwhile.

About the Author

David Annandale is the author of forty books of fantasy, science fiction, and horror. He has written *Horus Heresy*, *Warhammer 40,000*, and *Age of Sigmar* fiction for Black Library. For Aconyte Books, he has written novels set in the *Arkham Horror* and *Legend of the Five Rings* universes, along with a trilogy of Doctor Doom novels. He is also the author of the horror novel *Gethsemane Hall* and the Jen Blaylock thriller series. When he is not creating and/or destroying worlds, he teaches university courses on English literature, film, comics, and video games.